THE TRUTH HURTS

Other Titles by Hanes Segler:

Spoils of the Desert
Patriot
The Paradise Key
Always Unfaithful
A Lie Told Often Becomes the Truth

THE TRUTH HURTS

HANES SEGLER

THE TRUTH HURTS

iUniverse books may be ordered through booksellers or by contacting:

iUniverse
1663 Liberty Drive
Bloomington, IN 47403
www.iuniverse.com
1-800-Authors (1-800-288-4677)

ISBN: 978-1-5320-3590-6 (sc)
ISBN: 978-1-5320-3589-0 (e)

Library of Congress Control Number: 2017916797

Print information available on the last page.

iUniverse rev. date: 12/27/2017

My thanks to the Mueller Family — Mike, Amanda, and their darling girls, Sarah and Anna—who supported me with their friendship and company during the process of writing The Truth Hurts.

CHAPTER 1

You mean hide the stuff inside the, uh...*body*?"

"Yep. Cash going down and contraband coming back."

"Jeez, Carlton, that's sick! How the hell did you dream up something like that?"

Carlton Westerfield shrugged and leaned back in the uncomfortable wooden chair facing Faustino Perez's scarred desk. "There were rumors that it happened in Vietnam, but I don't know. It sounded pretty far-fetched to me at the time, but we believed it anyway. We were kids, Tino. I was only eighteen, nineteen years old, trying to keep my head down, put in my thirteen months and get back to Texas alive and in one piece. I helped put a bunch of guys into body bags for their return trip, and I didn't want to go home that way. But I didn't check any bodies to see if they'd been gutted and stuffed with heroin. We just tagged 'em, bagged 'em, and put them on the plane."

Faustino Perez sighed and rubbed his face. He leaned forward in his chair and put his elbows up on his desk, his chin in his hands. "*Body bags!* Damn, I don't ever want body bag duty again." After a pause, he added, "Guess I should be glad you learned that job skill in the Army. We couldn't have done it without your help that day."

Carlton frowned and grunted in agreement. "Thank God it wasn't my full-time job, then or now. But I got plenty of OJT, more than I wanted. Vietnam *and* South Texas."

Both men fell silent as they recalled the aftermath of a firefight with a helicopter carrying three or four marksmen shooting fully automatic M-16s into three vehicles—not on the Ho Chi Minh Trail, but traveling in convoy toward Laredo, Texas. Tino had been driving one of the vehicles. Taking fire from above while speeding down IH-35, four of his employees had died and three others were injured. Carlton had been summoned to a cheap motel in the tiny town of Encinal where he, Tino, and the survivors managed to get the dead men into large trash bags for concealment during the gruesome trip back to San Antonio.

The bloody incident had taken place a few months before and, like most traumatic events, the memory's clarity ebbed and flowed depending on the mood during the moment of recall. Nearly all experiences—even really bad ones—fade away with time, only to resurface with shocking starkness under the right circumstances. Right now, the massacre was vivid in the men's minds, no doubt a result of the current discussion of Tino's business tactics. It had been on a trial run employing another tactic that the shooting had occurred. The result of that day had been far-reaching—no, *life-changing*—for an entire community. It also provided yet another milestone in a chain of events that had altered Carlton's quiet, solitary life forever.

The purpose of the convoy toward Laredo hadn't been to pick up cheap Mexican pottery and art work for Tino's vast flea market operation on the south side of San Antonio, although that happened regularly. Along with pottery and lawn art, the large outdoor market on Highway 16 had dozens of stalls selling everything from televisions to tampons, velvet paintings to vestry garments, cell phones to cellulite cream. The vendors, all Mexican-Americans, rented the stalls from Tino, bought most of their merchandise from him, and looked to him as they would have looked to their *patrón* under the *ejido* system a hundred years earlier in Mexico.

No, the ill-fated trip wasn't a pottery run; its purpose had been to pick up another popular Mexican import handled by Tino Perez; namely, cocaine, in return for that all-time favorite American export product, currency. Carlton had been the one to suggest that Tino use the fixed assets of another of his sideline businesses, an independent ambulance service, to deliver money and pick up the contraband. He had seen ambulances being manufactured and noticed that the driveshafts in Ford vans were unusually large—and hollow. What better way to allay suspicion than to use an ambulance carrying elderly patients between San Antonio and the border city of Laredo? Even the most hardened Border Patrol agent might hesitate to pull ailing Uncle Pablo's stretcher out into the South Texas heat while lawmen swarmed over the ambulance looking for contraband. That was the theory, anyway. And since Tino owned an ambulance service, plus a big auto repair facility that did driveshaft work, why not use the hollow driveshafts for carrying cash to Laredo and drugs back into San Antonio?

Tino had wanted to try it for dual purposes. First, the ongoing cat-and-mouse game between smugglers and the Drug Enforcement Agency demanded that traffickers constantly refine their tactics to avoid discovery of contraband. Faustino Perez needed a method to haul the cocaine undetected back to San Antonio and disburse it to street vendors in return for enormous profits, and the driveshaft trick seemed a good one to try. Second, Tino had long suspected an information leak in his operation, and he wanted to use the trial run to expose the traitor by dropping subtle hints about the ploy and seeing what happened.

On the fateful day, Tino ordered a loose three-car convoy, two plain vehicles flanking the ambulance for protection. Personnel included eight men, plus three more in the ambulance, all well-armed. However, as Tino had suspected, the informant in the ambulance service had leaked the itinerary to a rival drug importer—who was a dirty cop to boot, with access to a helicopter and trained shooters—resulting in the ambush from the sky and three carloads of bloody, tattered men. Their best efforts to guard the ambulance weren't enough to hold off a professional air assault.

Tino shook his head to drive the gory scene away from his thoughts and back to the business at hand. "Well, I asked you the question." He laced his fingers behind his head and leaned back. "And you damn sure gave me an answer, disgusting as it sounds. Oh, by the way, we've used your driveshaft trick since then, and it worked. They even put two dogs on the vehicles a few times, but found nothing."

"You think that trick is wearing thin?"

"I don't know, but I got word that my cross-town competitor is using it. Not in ambulances, just Ford vans built on the chassis that has those big fat driveshafts. Hell, Brujido Ramos probably can't *spell* ambulance unless he sees it printed on the side of one."

Carlton shook his head. "Tino, I think the real strength is in the ambulance concept. We both know Border Patrol agents don't really care if they inconvenience a delivery van driver, but even those guys are reluctant to hold up an ambulance with a patient in the back while they take a driveshaft out and disassemble it. It takes a cutting torch or a drill to check out the inside. And a good welder to put it back together. Then it's got to be balanced and re-installed.

"Oh, and if you get any indication that the feds are using the new imaging technology at the control check points, you have to start lining the inside of the shafts with lead. That's an extra step, but it's only got to be done once on each drive shaft."

"You mentioned that before. How do we do that without spending a lot of time and money?"

"Easy. You've got all those old wheel weights at the tire shop. They can be melted and poured inside the shaft before it's welded up. Then, the guys have to spin it up like they do when they balance it, and re-heat the outside with a cutting torch to re-melt it and distribute it evenly, so it coats the interior. After that, they can cut one end off and put the product inside, re-weld the yoke, and they're done. That will defeat the imaging technology."

"Damn, Carlton, where do you come up with this stuff?"

Carlton shrugged. "That one's easy; it's the same reason the dental technician puts that heavy vest over you when she X-rays your teeth. It's lead-lined, to protect you from the X-rays being absorbed in excess amounts. Anyway, I'm recommending that you use every possible avenue to ensure the driveshaft trick stays in play. The feds can't be given any reason to start looking, and the ambulance ploy is a good one."

"I think you're right, but if one of his guys gets nailed, they're going to be jerking driveshafts out of every Ford Van, ambulance or not, so I'd like to have an alternative method. But what you're suggesting means I need to buy a mortuary service, right?"

Carlton thought for a moment. "Maybe, maybe not. I saw a news story about individuals trying to bring bodies back to the States for burial. The Border Patrol checks them out closely to determine if they're the victim in an open murder investigation. They showed the fed guys opening up the casket and unwrapping the body, but not cutting into it. Another reason they check is to determine where that individual's identification documents ended up, like his green card or birth certificate. Those need to be cancelled for dead people, or they'll end up voting for Democrats in the next election."

Tino laughed at Carlton's cynical observation of politics. "I don't care if it gives Republicans some grief, but it sounds like they check too closely for pulling off a contraband smuggling operation. Wouldn't they see a big incision down the stiff's chest and wonder what the hell might be in there?"

It was Carlton's turn to laugh at Tino's vivid description. "Maybe. But remember, these are individual citizens, just Juan driving cousin Pablo's corpse back over here in their Chevy pickup. A real ambulance service would be treated differently. I mean, patients die sometimes in ambulances, don't they? And I suppose an ambulance service could legally haul corpses for burial in another location. Probably a permitting process to go through, fees to pay. But yes, if you had a legitimate mortuary or funeral transport business, the gig would work better. How many guys want to pull a body out of the mortuary van and check it for contraband?"

Tino frowned. "Not me, for damn sure! But they might let the dogs sniff around longer if the passenger is already deceased. Not like the patient is going to complain. Nor can a dead patient take a turn for the worse, or sue the Border Patrol."

"That's a possibility," Carlton agreed. "But the formaldehyde smell should mask things pretty well, no matter how scent-specific the dog is trained to be. And if the dog points, then what? They going to cut into the corpse and take a look around?"

Tino made a face at that comment, then stood and turned to the air conditioner humming softly behind his desk. He turned the temperature control all the way to the left. "Damn, it's September and still hitting a hundred degrees every day this week." Peering at the controls, he thought for a moment. "I need to get a handle on how many people die here and need to be transported to Laredo, Del Rio, Eagle Pass, or the Valley for burial. And how many coming back this direction."

"You can bet the Border Patrol has access to those numbers now that they're a part of Homeland Security, even if they've never thought about a reason for using them. And the DEA too. Hey, maybe you can contract with your friend at the funeral chapel you've used. What's his name, Rafael Villa? He'll know. You could set up a small company to buy his transport vehicles and take over all the body shipments, going and coming. Maybe not have to buy the entire business, just contract to do the body transports."

"Maybe. But Rafael Villa is getting up in years, and his sons will want to take over the business. Hell, I can just buy them out, keep them working for me. It's got to be a profitable business on its own, right? And the younger guys would be more likely to carry out a plan like yours than the old man. Rafael can retire and go fishing."

"Can it be arranged on the other end?" Carlton asked. "I mean, you can oversee putting cash into the bodies on this end, but will your supplier put the dope into bodies on that end?"

"Yeah, I think I can get everyone on board with the process and the logistics. I just don't want to take undue risk."

"Well, you could make a couple of trial runs and have the crews observe exactly what the reaction of the border guards is under different scenarios. But with the proper paperwork citing cause of death and so on, it would work. Remember, the piece I saw was about people trying to get relatives back over here with nothing but a dead stiff and a weak story."

Tino nodded his agreement. "Yeah, that's probably right. The system sounds good, even if it's creepy. Anyway, I've got to do something. Brujido Ramos is kicking our ass. He's also giving us all a bad name by using violent, strong-arm means to push his product into new territory."

"Who's he?" Carlton asked, more out of courtesy toward the conversation than wanting to know any more about Tino's business competitors.

"A mid-level supplier—and violent jackass—who brings in product, steps on it a bunch, then distributes it in the suburbs and smaller communities, where they don't know the difference between quality blow and flour. Pretty big market in places like Somerset, Lytle, Pleasanton, China Grove—"

"That sleepy little town, the one that's down around San Antone?"

Tino looked at him, annoyed with the pop-culture reference, something Carlton did with disturbing frequency. "The same. Ramos used to work only the east side and southeast into Wilson County, but lately he's really increased his presence in South Bexar County. That's edging into my territory. Your success in throwing the local DEA office into a frenzy has helped him."

At the mention of Tino's upstart competition, both men stopped again to reflect on the nature of the business under discussion. A conflict with a rogue DEA agent, aided by Tino's own treacherous employee, had resulted in the recent bloody melee. When it was over, four men were dead and three wounded, and the entire community under Perez's oversight severely impacted. One of the dead had been a young man Carlton had worked with and grown to like, a rare occurrence in Carlton's solitary lifestyle. The next three days were spent consoling families and attending funerals.

A few days after the shooting, Perez and a vengeful Carlton Westerfield devised a plan to have the traitor use a car containing a potent fire bomb, another result of Carlton's long-past military training. As it occurred, the informant was joined in the ill-fated car by the lead DEA agent, resulting in a major setback in the investigation of Faustino's operations. For the past few months, drug smuggling interdiction had taken a back seat to a murder investigation, a favorable scenario for Perez—but a temporary one.

No business fills a vacuum faster than one involving supply and demand, especially if it generates large amounts of money. Thus, the competitor—who had been a minor player, no threat to Perez's profits—had entered the picture and upped his game considerably, bringing into focus all the horror depicted by the news media regarding conflicts between rival drug dealers. Oddly, the stories put forth by the media—print, digital, and television—were inaccurate, and not for being too sensational. If anything, the stories and pictures usually failed to impart the true extent of the violence employed in order to garner one's market share.

Like most people, Carlton was well aware of that facet of the industry, having been treated to hours of television documentaries and news stories about violence in the drug trafficking industry. His own career of performing murder-for-hire had inured him to most of the gritty fare shown by the news media, but even his years as a professional killer had failed to prepare him when his employment caused him to cross paths with the drug kingpin in whose office he now sat.

Carlton's long-time employer, Randall "Big Mo" Morris, had taken on a contract to kill Faustino Perez. When presented with the job, Carlton took a pass, citing too much blowback from popping a local crime figure. But even after declining the job, Carlton had been caught up in the whirlwind of events beginning with Big Mo's untimely death: two competing drug lords, the DEA, and a pretty woman who turned out to be Perez's half-sister. Now, months later, he found himself discussing the finer points of a tawdry business he would never have dreamed of entering…until Paula Hendricks came along.

Paula was the most seductive—and unfathomable—woman Carlton had ever met. Their bizarre relationship had been forged during a frightening war between competing drug lords, including her own half-brother, Tino, and the Drug Enforcement Agency. In the eighteen or so months since he'd first heard of her, Paula had gone from being a nameless rumor to a runaway companion, friend, lover, enemy, stalker, thief, informant, flight risk, and almost a victim of a car bomb constructed by Carlton himself. Most recently, she had been his travel companion on a two-month escape to Rio de Janeiro. He thought both of them had crammed a full lifetime of joint adventures into less than two years and figured Paula shared his feelings.

Carlton's musings about how he ended up being an advisor to a man he'd once been hired to kill were interrupted by his cell phone ring. Pulling the cheap burner phone from his pocket—his second in as many weeks—he flipped it open and checked the number before accepting the call and speaking.

"Hi there."

"Hi! Where are you?" came Paula's cheerful voice.

"Talking to your brother. What are you doing?" Despite changing phones and numbers weekly, Carlton tried to keep his phone conversations short and devoid of names and places. It served to eliminate prying ears being able to pinpoint his activities. At least that was the point of it. Like many of his old habits, keeping a low profile was a hard one to break and one he'd done a poor job of lately. Even with the attraction to Paula, he sometimes felt a longing for his former lifestyle as an overly cautious loner.

"Sitting here wondering if a handsome man would take me to dinner."

"I know a guy who can arrange dinner. Don't know about the handsome man, though. You might have to settle for one who can just afford to pay."

"Well, okay, Mr. Deep Pockets. I'll just have to hope for the handsome part. Pick me up at eight?" The question was followed by a seductive laugh.

"I'll be there."

Paula's laugh had its usual effect, and Carlton felt himself moving into a better mood than he'd been in since…well, since the last time he'd talked with her. Flipping the phone closed, he looked up at Tino, who stood gazing out the window of his portable building office at the rows of vendor stalls.

"I've got an invitation to dinner with a good-looking woman. Considerably prettier than you, so I think I'll take her up on it."

"Can't blame you for that. How is Paula, anyway?"

"She's fine, as far as I can tell. With her, who knows?"

"Yeah, my sister can be a mystery."

"Paula? *A mystery?*" Carlton responded with mock surprise. "That's like calling World War II a disagreement between neighbors."

Tino laughed without humor. "Yeah, I guess you should know a little about her by now."

"Yeah, Tino, you're telling Noah about flood water." After a moment, he asked, "By the way, why did you keep it such a secret—that y'all are siblings?"

Perez shifted uncomfortably from the window and retreated to his chair, a move Carlton saw as a delaying tactic, giving him time to formulate a response. When he was seated again, he spoke. "She and I haven't always been that close through the years. In fact, we've been on opposite sides of the fence from time to time. She really didn't seem like my sister when we were at odds so often. And by the time you got really involved in all this…well, we had other fish to fry, as you recall. It wasn't the time to open up another can of worms."

"I like your fishing metaphors, Tino. So while we're using them, I guess we can call me a sucker, right?"

"Who fell for my sister, who is a piranha?"

"Yeah, hook, line, and sinker," Carlton added, laughing in spite of himself. He was getting used to Tino's snappy comebacks, even enjoying the ones aimed at him. Likewise, he didn't pass up a chance at tossing a barb or two in Tino's direction, now that he'd learned he wouldn't end up dead for a tiny verbal slight against the powerful drug kingpin. Tino was a clever man with whom Carlton had formed a strange bond. Despite the drug lord's ruthless reputation and Carlton's penchant for secrecy, the circumstances that had thrown them together served as a catalyst for an unlikely alliance.

After returning from a year of lying low, Carlton had been approached by two DEA agents and coerced into working at Perez's Southside operation, supposedly to spy on his activities. At the same time, the Agency had enough goods on Perez to force him to hire Carlton in order to avoid indictment. Both men later agreed the setup was simply to keep close tabs on both of them while the investigation continued. Had the DEA foreseen that "encouraging" the two men to work together would lead to an uneasy partnership of mutual respect, the tactic would have been abandoned soon after its inception.

From the first time they'd met, Carlton was intrigued by the disparity between the man's appearance and his verbal skills. Faustino Perez was stocky, barrel-chested and swarthy, with a flat, impassive, peasant face clearly linking him to his ancient Indian ancestry—in contrast to an up-to-date intellect reflected in a wide vocabulary and dry sense of humor. His diction and enunciation belied his peasant farmer countenance, his speech—while speaking English—lacked any hint of his obvious Hispanic heritage. And when the situation called for it, his Spanish was equally superb; or so it sounded to Carlton, who had struggled for years to learn the basics.

When queried by Carlton, he'd confided that he copied his speech patterns after distinguished Mexican-Americans like Henry Cisneros, a former mayor of San Antonio, and the actor, Ricardo Montalban. He opined that their success in a predominately Anglo environment was due to their ability to conquer the divide that a limited vocabulary or a harsh foreign accent often creates, rightly or wrongly. Afterward, he had seemed embarrassed by the admission. Carlton, whose Spanish skills remained weak, had to admire Perez for accomplishing that measure for success, drug kingpin or not.

In any event, Carlton could see that Tino wasn't being forthcoming with a good answer to the question regarding the secrecy of his half-sister. Neither had Paula, not during the two months they'd spent together lounging on beaches in South America. In fact, she'd been less than forthcoming about a number of things Carlton had wondered about, not living up to her pledge as they departed on the trip to tell him "*every last ugly bit of it. As long as it takes.*" Oh, she had cleared up most of the inconsistencies, and Carlton could see how she had been caught up between her crime-boss half-brother, a cheating, abusive spouse, a manipulative sister-in-law, the DEA, the IRS, and their own former employer, Randall (Big Mo) Morris, now deceased. Carlton knew enough about the latter to know that the obese pawn broker/contract hit arranger wasn't squeaky clean in all his dealings, no surprise there. But combine his sleazy style with Paula's gender and physical attractiveness, and Carlton understood why he'd had a much easier time dealing with Big Mo than she had.

Still, it irked him that he could not get entirely comfortable with Paula, attraction or not. That had led to a wistful parting of ways when they returned from their trip, he to his apartment and she to hers. They still spent time together, like the spontaneous dinner date they'd just made. But Carlton felt sure that, at the end of the day, he'd best remain a solo player.

As to his relationship with her brother, Carlton rather enjoyed being on the fringes of Tino's diverse business operations, at least the legal parts of it. And when Tino wanted to discuss a matter in the not-so-legal department, he had no problem in being a team player—strictly in an advisory capacity. (The "advisory" caveat had been added soon after the car bomb incident)

However, some days Carlton had a hard time trying to justify in his mind any involvement, advisory or otherwise, in the bloody, nasty industry of illegal drug importation. It was a younger man's business, he knew. He had recently marked another birthday and grimly realized he had years of experience that left him ill-prepared to do anything marketable that passed muster for being legal. On the plus side, his needs weren't great, and he had amassed a tidy sum from his career as Big Mo's hit man. So tidy, in fact, why do anything risky, he wondered? Well, what else was on the agenda? *Nothing.* On those days when he mentally wrestled with the problem, he felt a lot like the moth drawn to a flame...which led to a comparison of dying from foolishness or boredom. Neither prospect was appealing.

Carlton abandoned his musings, rose from the uncomfortable chair, and stretched. "I think I'll go home and take a nap, Tino. I've got a hot date tonight, and I slept like crap the last two nights."

"Probably a guilty conscience," came the sardonic reply. "Anyone who knows about stuffing a corpse with nose candy can't expect to sleep like a baby. Anyway, I'll check on the mortuary setup, and we'll talk again after I visit with Rafael Villa."

Carlton stood and headed for the door. Hand on the knob, he stopped and turned to Tino. "One question about Rafael Villa. Does he really have a son named Pancho?"

"Yes, the oldest boy's name is Francisco. The nickname caught on for the obvious reason. I've known him since he was a kid. That's who I'll be dealing with when the old man leaves the business."

"So, you'll be doing business with *Pancho Villa*. Can I call you Lefty?"

Tino rolled his eyes at the remark. "That song's not about *the* Pancho Villa, is it? Who the hell was Lefty, some gringo invention?"

Grinning, Carlton opened the door and stepped out into the heat.

CHAPTER 2

Carlton pulled his Cadillac into a visitor parking spot at Paula's apartment building and walked past the pool toward number 236. As he climbed the stairs to the second floor, Paula came around the corner, carrying a big handbag, a pale yellow sundress flowing around her in the sultry breeze funneling through the stairwell. She was in a rush, looking into the handbag instead of in front of her, and nearly collided with him. Carlton stopped on the fourth step from the top and smiled at her as she finally raised her eyes to check for traffic on the stairs.

"You in a hurry?" he asked, the smile breaking into a grin as surprise registered on her face.

"Oh! Hi!" She pulled up short, her big brown eyes made even bigger by the near collision—with her dinner date, no less. "You scared me. I was kind of in a hurry, forgot to look where I was going."

"So I noticed. You trying to get away before I got here? Change your mind about going to dinner with a man of questionable handsomeness?"

"No, I left my cover-up down at the pool, along with my favorite wine glass. I was headed down to get it and get back before you came. And I certainly wouldn't change my mind about going with the most handsome man I know. Plus, I heard you can afford dinner."

"Barely, after our little excursion down south. But maybe we can find some cheap tacos somewhere."

"Sounds good to me. Let me get my stuff, and I'll just put it in the car. I'm hungry."

Carlton went back to the parking lot and clicked open the doors while

Paula retrieved her things. When she emerged from the pool area, she got in and placed her cover-up and glass on the seat between them. Walking around to his side, Carlton failed to notice a silver Dodge Durango with Mexican plates backed into a slot at the end of the lot. Neither did he see the Dodge pull out of the lot and follow them from a half-block behind, nor the black Mercedes that pulled out of the Valero station at the corner, accelerating in behind the Dodge.

Carlton drove north, exiting at Military Highway and going east, almost to New Braunfels Avenue before pulling into the lot of an orange-hued building with garish red trim housing a large Tex-Mex restaurant. It was one of the best on the South Side.

"This place okay?" he asked, knowing the answer without asking. It was popular with everyone on this side of the city and a number of people from other areas. And Paula, like Carlton, liked good Tex-Mex food, the standard fare at this place.

"Yeah, I love this place. Remember, I'm the one who took you here first."

"Nope, you've gotten me confused with that handsome guy you're always looking for," Carlton replied with a straight face. "You probably brought him here as part of your plan to seduce him, get him to spend a lot of money on you."

Paula sighed. "Okay, you've got me. But he didn't spend much money on me. This place has the best food and cheapest prices anywhere."

"Well, that seduces me."

The pair walked toward the front door of the restaurant, continuing their banter as they walked hand-in-hand. They paid no heed to the silver Dodge Durango and the black Mercedes turning into the lot and converging on them from opposite directions. While they were still twenty yards from the entrance, the back doors of both vehicles popped open and four men spilled out and rushed the unsuspecting couple. Carlton swiveled his vision between the oncoming attackers, trying to make an evaluation of which he should take on first, but their movements were too fast. The decision was taken from him before he could drop Paula's hand and raise his own in defense. Two of the men zeroed in on him and grabbed his arms. It felt like a pair of vises had encompassed his arms with overwhelming strength and pressure. The other two grabbed Paula and quickly manhandled her to the Mercedes, using their enormous arms to pick her up like a bundle of dried sticks. Her feet were dangling uselessly a couple of feet above the pavement, and though she screamed and shook her head wildly from side to side, it had no effect on her captors. They calmly carried her to the Mercedes, shoved her into the back seat head-first, and followed her into the car, slamming the doors behind them.

Meanwhile, Carlton struggled without success with his two captors, who seemed intent on holding him in place and making no move toward either vehicle. Both were large, muscled men, with shaved heads and tattoos of black barbed wire intertwined with orange flames snaking out of Tee shirt tops and sleeves, traveling up their necks and down their arms. The arm portion of tattoo patterns ended at the men's wrists, the only part of the body decoration he could see. As Carlton continued to fight, he managed to get his left arm free of the iron grip. Before he could take a swing, one of the men pulled a length of pipe from his pocket and slapped wildly at the side of Carlton's head. Fortunately for him, the blow glanced off his skull behind his right ear. But it was enough to deck him. After a brief flash of stars and sparks behind his eyes, Carlton's vision blurred and swayed, then faded slowly to gray. The men dropped him like a sack of cement, and he noticed the gray color advancing on him, blurry, but still getting closer, filling his field of vision and moving fast. At the last instant, he realized that the gray color was the pavement coming up to meet him.

He hit the asphalt hard, not having any ability to break the fall. The impact seemed to revive him a bit, and he tried to look around, but the parking lot, the restaurant, and the fleeing vehicles seemed surreal, almost cartoonish. It felt as though his brain were disconnected from his body, and he was watching the scene from elsewhere. He blinked his eyes a few times, but the blurriness was still there. He had a sudden thought about an episode on Discovery Channel describing each part of the brain and what function it served. He concentrated on where the blow had landed and wondered if the area now throbbing behind his ear housed his brain's vision center. Unable to recall, he chastised himself for not paying more attention to the educational presentation. Later, he would have no memory of how long he followed the off-the-wall line of thought, but it wasn't long. He became too spaced-out to concentrate on anything. Then he briefly lost consciousness. The entire attack and kidnapping had taken less than fifteen seconds.

A few minutes later, maybe longer—Carlton lost track of time—a group of diners, possibly a celebration party of some kind, came out of the front door of the restaurant. Spotting the dazed Anglo struggling to sit upright in the parking lot, they dodged him and averted their eyes as they made their way to their respective vehicles. Clearly, they wanted no part of this outsider who was either drunk or stoned, now trying to regain his footing.

When Carlton was finally able to stand, he wobbled over to the steps of the restaurant and dug around in his pocket for his phone. His vision was still so blurred he couldn't see the keypad. For a moment, he panicked, thinking the damage might be permanent. Then his thoughts flashed to the last sight he'd had of Paula being shoved into the car, and he simply stood holding his phone, unable to think of anything but her. At least she'd been taken alive, and now he could only hope she stayed that way.

A couple of months before, he'd thought Paula had died in a car explosion of his own making, and the thought of losing her had devastated him. When she turned up alive and well, he was ecstatic. So his concern for her was extreme and real, and whether it was founded in attraction, passion, friendship, or love, he didn't know. However, Carlton dealt in reality, blurred as it was right now. Fretting over her was a waste of time, and calling the police was out of the question. He needed—*Paula* needed—the best help available to get out of this. He had to get Faustino Perez, and now.

He shook his head, trying to clear the cobwebs. It didn't work right away, but in the next few minutes, his vision cleared a bit, replaced by a throbbing headache. He tried to scroll through the contacts list and remembered that he'd quit using that function, another safety habit imposed after his recent experience with the DEA agents. Struggling to recall Tino's number, he punched in the digits and hoped his impaired memory was right. He waited anxiously while it rang, becoming concerned that a new group of three diners exiting the restaurant might call the police. He tried to stand up straight, forcing himself not to look like a guy who'd just been slugged with a pipe. From the looks on their faces, he failed.

"Tino, it's Carlton."

"You need me to help you with your dates now? I have to do everything for you?" Tino's voice jokingly mocked him.

"I wish it were that easy," Carlton began without preamble, speaking quickly and surprised that his voice sounded strong. *"Some guys have taken Paula. Grabbed her while they held me, threw her into a black car, a Benz I think. Four guys, big strong ones, two held me and the other two grabbed her, threw her into a car..."* His voice trailed off as he realized he was babbling, repeating the story without giving any relevant details.

The garbled explanation didn't seem to faze Tino Perez. *"Shit! Where are you?"* he snapped.

"Uh, La Perla, over on Southwest Military, near—"

"I know the place. Stay there. Go inside and ask for Sara. Tell her I'm on the way, and I want you to sit tight for a few minutes."

The conversation ended, Carlton snapped his phone shut and slowly made his way up the steps and into the restaurant. Inside, the place was busy, and no one looked his way for a moment. Then a waitress approached him and asked in halting English if he wanted a table or a booth.

"I'm looking for Sara?" Carlton intoned questioningly, pronouncing the name in Spanish as Tino had.

"Ah, sí, espere un momento," she instructed, turning toward the kitchen area as the words left her mouth.

Carlton's still-foggy brain and marginal Spanish abilities combined to cause a slight delay in the message getting through, but he vaguely recalled "*esperar*" meaning "to wait," so he did. Seconds later, a middle-aged woman emerged from the kitchen and approached him, an inquisitive look on her face.

"Puedo ayudarle?" Clearly, she was not accustomed to having an Anglo man, a disheveled, battered one at that, asking for her, but "can I help you?" seemed a logical place to start.

"Yes, please—" Carlton stopped and began again, much as he didn't want to try his poor Spanish right now. *"Sí, por favor. Mi amigo, Faustino Perez, me dijo preguntar para usted. Yo necesito esperar aquí para diez minutos, mas o menos. Está bien?"*

The effort was worth it. Carlton knew he'd probably bungled the attempt to tell her that his friend, Tino Perez, told him to ask for her and that he needed to wait here for ten minutes or so. But his faulty Spanish didn't matter; it was trying to use her language that pleased the woman. (Plus, dropping the name of the man who probably owned the place, or had some vital connection to it, didn't hurt)

The woman, Sara, smiled broadly and started babbling in *Español* so rapidly that Carlton scarcely caught a word. All he could do was nod and smile, which seemed to work just fine. He asked for a glass of tea and was ushered quickly to a private booth near the kitchen. He dropped heavily into the booth and leaned back. When the tea arrived, he gulped half the glass and took a deep breath. Only then was he able to try to piece together the events in the parking lot.

He had no idea who would have orchestrated such a bold daylight grab. He and Paula had only been back in the city for a few weeks, and during that time nothing of any importance had occurred with either of them, and Tino hadn't voiced any concerns or warnings, other than bugging Carlton about catching the Zika virus while in Rio. Clearly, the kidnapping was connected to the unsavory line of work he'd been associated with, along with Paula and her half-brother. But why had they taken only Paula and not him? To make sure Tino got the story and would be prepared to round up ransom money? Or were they certain he wouldn't be able to shed any light on the well-executed grab and weren't worried about leaving him behind? Maybe his attacker thought he'd swung hard enough to finish off the only witness. It had certainly seemed a possibility to Carlton out in the parking lot for a few minutes.

Kidnapping was a capital offense, one that would draw some serious slammer time or possibly a ride on the needle, so something important was behind it, money for sure, maybe something else. Since being around Faustino Perez, his competitors, and the DEA, Carlton had learned that anything was a possible catalyst or incentive for strange occurrences, many of them falling into the capital offense category.

The "capital offense" phrase rattling around in his mind conjured up Eric Clapton singing about shooting a sheriff, and the tune wouldn't go away for several seconds. He pushed the ridiculous thought aside and tried hard to concentrate on the short event, trying to recall anything about the men or the cars, but other than the black Mercedes gobbling up Paula and taking a hard shot to the head, he was drawing a blank.

Recalling the blow from something hard, he touched his head gingerly and flinched when his fingers found the injury. Then he remembered the arm swinging the weapon and the tattoos flashed before him, black barbed wire and something orange. *Flames*, that was it. Both of them had sported orange flames intertwined with barbed wire running down to their wrists. He also vaguely felt both of them were shaven-headed. Of the two who'd grabbed Paula, he didn't know. He'd been too focused on her being tossed into the car like a bag of laundry. All he could remember was the look of terror he'd glimpsed on her face as she disappeared into the back seat.

Carlton's thoughts again moved to her, and he wondered if she were okay. Since the guys grabbed her and made sure Carlton saw it, they had plans for her in live condition, of that he was fairly certain. For now, he had to cling to that hope, ignore other possibilities and concentrate on getting her back alive.

It took Tino less than twenty minutes to make the half-hour drive. He strode into the restaurant and his eyes darted around until he spotted Carlton in the booth next to the kitchen door. Carlton spotted him at the same time and started to rise, but a wave of vertigo set in, followed by nausea. He slumped back into the booth while Tino went quickly to the opposite seat and slid in.

"Damn, buddy, you look paler than your usual gringo self," he opened, a look of genuine concern in his eyes. "You alright? We need to get you to the doctor first?"

Carlton shook his head. "Yeah, I feel pretty pale. I thought I was better, but standing up is going to be a challenge for a while, I think. Let's hold off on the doctor for a bit. First, what do we need to do?"

"I called some guys on the way over here. They're standing by, ready to go, and I've got people manning the office phones in case I get the call there instead of one of my cell phones." He patted his shirt pockets, demonstrating his heed of Carlton's advice to use different phones for different callers and to change them often. "Now tell me everything that happened, everything you can remember."

Carlton wasn't sure what good recounting the exact play-by-play would do, but he complied. "I pulled into the parking lot, and we were walking toward the front door. Two cars came at us from opposite directions and slammed on their brakes about twenty feet from us. Two guys bailed out of each car, two grabbed Paula and hustled her back to the car. It was a black Mercedes, late model, the big sedan. The other two grabbed me, one on each side, but didn't try to get me into their car. They just held me in place. Now that I think about it, I think they wanted me to witness Paula being tossed into the car unhurt."

Tino nodded. "Yeah, that sounds right. That's why I wanted to hear it step by step. They wanted you to be the messenger. And the message is, 'we're rough, we're serious, but Paula is alive.' What happened then?"

"I kept struggling, trying to get an arm loose to swing at one of them, but they were really big, strong guys. Kept me nearly immobile, but I finally got my left arm loose. Before I could swing, the guy on my right popped me behind the ear with something pretty solid. I went down faster than Monica Lewinsky did on Bill Clinton. I was out for a few seconds, I think. Next thing I remember, I was trying to sit up and the cars were pulling away from the parking lot. In a hurry, but not enough to draw much attention or hit another car."

"They were Latino, right?"

"Yes, all four appeared to be. All had dark skin, and I think they had shaved heads. Oh, and the two that held me had tattoos on their arms, orange flames and black barbed wire twisted in it. All the way down to their wrists. That's about the only detail I can recall seeing. I don't think it took over twenty seconds from beginning to end."

Tino nodded again. "Big, strong guys who are quick and professional. Flames and barbed wire, huh? I'll have somebody check on the tatts, but I'm sure it had to be Ramos' guys."

Carlton looked at him, surprised. "The guy you said is kicking your ass in business? If he's doing such a good job beating your business, why would he jeopardize a peaceful existence? He's got to know this is going to bring major heat down on him. You told me once that taking harsh action isn't always the best plan, you need to pick the time very carefully before you do something that could result in a major conflict."

Tino grimaced and shook his head. "I'm glad to hear that you listened to me on a couple of things I told you, but not everyone has my philosophy about stirring up trouble when it's not going to gain anything. Ramos isn't like that. He's tough and wants everyone to know it. He relies on violence to get respect. He wants everyone frightened, all the time. That's *his* business philosophy."

"Okay, so what's our plan?" Carlton asked. "Do we do anything right now or just wait for the phone call?"

"We won't have to wait long," Tino replied. "He may be rash in starting things, but he's not stupid. He doesn't want this to drag on for a long time. Whatever he wants, he'll make the demand pretty soon. The good news is, Paula will probably get reasonable treatment. He knows if he kills her he won't get squat, or if he and his guys mistreat her, the retaliation afterward may not be worth it, no matter how much he likes violence."

"Will it be money, or will he want some other business concession from you?"

"Both, probably. Oh, there's not much way he can force me agree to anything after he lets her go. He knows I'll just come back on him with some retaliatory move once she's safe. Kidnap his kid or something. So it'll probably be money, and lots of it."

"What's to keep it from happening again?" Carlton asked, knowing the answer.

"Not a damn thing," Tino sighed, shaking his head again. "In addition to costing me a lot of money, he may tell me to close up shop, or he'll do it again. That's a possibility, even if he can't easily enforce it."

"And there's nothing we can do to prevent it?" Even as he asked, Carlton wondered why he stubbornly clung to a return to normalcy.

"Sure, if we all want to live like the narcos in Mexico and Colombia, holed up in some compound and being surrounded by an army every time we want to go to Walmart or go out to eat." He emphasized the last part by gesturing toward Carlton and the restaurant around them. "It's bad enough having to watch out for the law. But at least they have some rules they're supposed to follow. Not those gangster cartel guys, their only rule is having more guns and more protection than the other guy. And they have to be on their toes every minute. I don't want to live like that. I like being low-profile, just doing my other legal business and having this as the big money-maker. *Tax free.* It would appear those days are over."

Carlton thought for a minute about what Tino had just said. "Well, would you quit if you could afford to? Just concentrate on all your other businesses and leave this crap alone?"

Tino leaned across the booth and spoke quietly. "You mean not have to watch my back and everyone around me for traitors? Not have to worry about getting shot by a bunch of teenage gangbangers when I'm spending my Social Security check? Not have to buy a damn funeral home to stuff the stiffs with dope and cash? You mean, would I do *that*?"

Carlton just nodded, not having to answer the rhetorical questions. Tino's tone had told him everything he needed to know. For the next few minutes, both men sat silently, each immersed in his own thoughts, worrying about Paula's fate, wondering when the ransom call would come, and if they could raise the money to spring her, and how the deal—whatever it was—would go down. And when it was over, what next? Start worrying about the next time?

Carlton had come to the same conclusion about his own life soon after his employer, Big Mo, had died violently. While taking a year-long sabbatical to escape the revenge of the man seated across from him plus his main rival kingpin, along with the DEA and various other law enforcement types, Carlton had realized his career of being a murderer-for-hire was not a profession he wished to pursue to retirement; mainly, because there *was* no retirement. As the years added up, the odds increased that he would slip up, or that one of his assignments would become aware of his fate and be waiting for his assassin and pop Carlton before he performed his usual quick, thorough job. In that regard, it was not unlike the gunfighters of the Old West; *someone* out there was always faster, or a lawman could get lucky, or the sun would get in your eyes at the wrong time.

Carlton had stashed enough money to make it to home plate if he lived reasonably. Now, sitting here pondering the dicey situation he was in—correction, *Paula* was in—he wished he had taken a different path the minute he and Paula returned from Brazil. Too late now, he told himself. But if they could just get this resolved and get Paula out alive, he might re-think that part about dying of boredom.

His reverie was interrupted by Tino's voice. "Hey, you don't look so good. Let's get out of here and get you to see Dr. Morales."

Carlton pulled a ten-dollar bill from his pocket and placed it on the table as they stood and turned toward the door. He noticed Tino discretely waving and gesturing to a couple of the tables before ducking his head and striding forward purposefully to avoid a conversation. Before they reached the door, Sara rounded the corner from the kitchen and gave Carlton a big smile, which he returned gratefully.

In the parking lot, Carlton started for the Cadillac, but Tino pointed toward his own vehicle, a red Ford F-250. "Let's go in mine. I got a couple of guys watching your car to make sure it doesn't get any added accessories. Put your key on the right front tire, and they'll take care of getting it back to my office or your apartment. You don't look fit for driving anyway."

On the way to the small clinic Tino had used for his crew after the shootout, the crime boss again waxed philosophically about his lifestyle and what to do in order to enjoy his senior years. "Hell, yes, I'd get out of this business. After going to a bunch of funerals for friends and their children, I'd quit this racket and try to make enough money from my other stuff. How about you? You had enough?"

"Yep. The car bomb was enough for me. I didn't like Dennis Bradford or Tim Hunnicut, but my rule was never to take out anyone I had a connection with. I broke the rule on that one, and I've regretted it since. Besides, I thought I'd killed Paula and nearly passed out when I read it. I nearly passed out again when she showed up at the Corpus Christi airport alive. I just hope she makes it through this one alive," he added.

Tino looked over at his companion. "Yeah, that was a tough one. But you seem to be cut out for this business. You took care of my inside traitor and that meddling DEA *pendejo* at one time. It put a stop to the investigation and gave you an excuse to go to Rio de Janeiro for six months. And it only cost you an old car."

Carlton looked hurt. "It was *two* months, Tino, not six. And I liked my old Honda, even if you did replace it with the Caddy. That's a nice car, by the way."

Tino nodded in agreement, but persisted in his quest to analyze Carlton. "You worked for Big Mo for a long time. You never had a change of heart during those years?"

"Yeah, when I finally made a hit that was connected to me, or at least *became* connected to me. I couldn't have known that Don Fulton was Paula's cheating husband, but after everything started shaking out, it got really complicated. I've decided I'm too old for that crap, I can't foresee complications like that." He turned back from the window where he had been watching the cityscape roll by and looked straight ahead. "I'm checking out, Tino, leaving this stuff behind."

Tino cocked his head and thought for a moment. "*Checking out*, huh? Leaving it behind? You're always quoting some song or something in history that's apropos to the situation at hand."

Carlton turned in the seat to look at him, wondering where he was headed with this.

Enjoying himself, Tino continued. "You know, like your smart-ass remark about Pancho and Lefty? Well, I've got one for you in just a few more seconds. Listen, now."

He reached for the volume knob on the pickup's radio and turned up the sound just as the *Eagles* crooned the last verse of one of their most popular hits. Carlton could only stare at the radio as Don Henley and Glenn Frey offered sage advice about checking out any time one liked, but never being able to leave. Carlton shook his head. Just because the song was referring to an illusory hotel, not a lifestyle, the line still seemed like a bad omen, one that mocked his earlier lofty declaration.

He looked back at Faustino Perez, who was grinning from ear to ear despite the current situation—knowing his sister had been kidnapped and was being held against her will and in a lot of danger. He had to admire this example of the crime boss' extraordinary ability to channel his thoughts and actions in directions that seemed at odds with the mood of the moment.

In response to the timely verbal jab, Carlton tried to mimic the drug lord's earlier display of dismissiveness by rolling his eyes, but the effort made his head hurt.

CHAPTER 3

Dr. Morales straightened and removed his stethoscope from his ears, frowning as he did so. "Your pulse is still slightly erratic, not unusual after taking a blow like that on the head. I think you suffered a mild concussion, also normal after getting a hard jolt to your skull. At that point, just behind the ear, it could have been much worse. The blow must have been a glancing one, not a direct contact. You are lucky, Mr. Westerfield."

"Glad to hear it. I didn't feel so lucky stumbling around in a daze while ago."

"It barely broke the skin, but you still took a good hit. You may have trouble with your vision for a few more hours, but I think you will be alright after a good night's rest. Call me if the headache doesn't go away after tomorrow."

"Thank you, Dr. Morales. I appreciate this. Hope it didn't spoil your evening too badly."

"Sure, no problem with my evening. But yours will be a bit woozy, I'm afraid, so get lots of rest over the next few days. And drink plenty of fluids, but no alcohol for twenty-four hours. And don't drive a car or operate machinery. Also, in spite of how you feel, try to eat something."

Carlton nodded his acknowledgment of the instructions. Tino rose from the chair in the corner where he'd been watching the examination. He thanked Dr. Morales in English, then switched to Spanish for a quick exchange before leading Carlton out of the clinic and back to his vehicle.

As they pulled out of the parking lot, Carlton turned to Tino. "Should

I send a note to Dr. Morales, thanking him for coming here so late in the evening? And maybe stick a couple of C-notes in it?"

Tino shrugged. "It would be a nice gesture, but unnecessary. Dr. Morales knows the entire story about the gun battle and your part in coming to Encinal and picking us up. He knows you pay your dues in the community, and then some. Tonight's office visit is his way of paying his dues."

"Still, it's nice of him to show up so quickly. He said something about eating, right? I am a bit hungry. I seem to recall that dinner was interrupted."

"Yeah, he told me to get you to eat something, so let's go where we can talk. We need to start preparing for what's coming."

Tino didn't need to explain. In the past two hours, Carlton's thoughts had never strayed far from Paula's predicament; he felt a pang of guilt mentioning his hunger at a time when Paula had not only missed their planned meal, but might not even be alive. He had to push the thought aside and concentrate on what was logical and what Tino had predicted; that she was going to be kept in good shape, even if only for practical reasons. Thin as it was, it was the only encouragement available right now.

Tino pulled into a small taco stand where both men ordered and carried their meals to a corner table. Tino pulled the two phones from his pockets and checked to see that both were turned on and charged before setting them on the table in front of him.

Carlton pulled his phone to check on the offhand chance that Paula had been able to text him. As he thought, there was nothing. Ramos' men would have taken her phone immediately and would likely use it to make the initial ransom demand, not worried about tracking the burner phone to her location. Things would be set up to take place quickly, not much time to mount a retaliatory attack, not even a recon mission for that matter. Carlton could only hope that he and Tino could raise the necessary ransom money and make the exchange safely.

Carlton's hunger dissipated quickly as he nibbled at his meal, but across the table, Tino ate with gusto, seemingly oblivious to the dangerous events building around them. On the outside, he gave the appearance of entertaining another normal business deal, but Carlton knew better. Two months earlier, after both of them thought Paula had been killed in the car bomb, Tino had been morose and depressed that his half-sister had become the latest collateral victim of his chosen lifestyle. Even though Tino and Paula had plenty of differences, the Latin penchant for attachment to family remained intact.

Carlton hadn't seen Tino's reaction to the news that she had escaped harm, but he knew the relief and gratitude had likely matched his own.

Carlton wondered what Tino would come up with, what he wanted to talk over while eating. After five minutes, he hadn't said a word, just continued eating. But Carlton could almost hear the wheels turning and knew he'd be filled in when it was time. After all, Tino had been attached to Paula for a long time. Plus, he knew this ugly business and how to operate when it became messy, of that Carlton was certain, and it didn't get much uglier than having a loved one taken, her life threatened. Still, the uncertainty of the outcome was weighing heavily on Carlton and he hoped his confidence in her crime boss half-brother wasn't misplaced.

A few minutes later, Carlton pushed aside his half-eaten taco plate and wondered about his own attachment to the alluring and mysterious Paula Hendricks. Notwithstanding the fact that she was physically attractive, sexy, and seemed genuinely attracted to him, there remained a gap in Carlton's understanding of his feelings for her. He knew that could be due to his own shortfall in the attachment department; he'd never had more than a few-weeks' fling with any woman before meeting Paula. Oh, the flings had been numerous over the years, but never serious enough to think about settling down to one woman and certainly not marriage. The brief relationships invariably stalled, faltered, then faded away, leaving nothing more than memories; however, the memories were generally good ones, and Carlton never sought to alter his course.

At this moment, he was willing to take any action to rescue a woman he didn't understand, and worse, didn't fully trust. It seemed an odd emotion, this all-encompassing sense of responsibility for her safety, something with which Carlton had little experience. All his adult life, he'd been on his own and responsible only for himself. Even while in the Army in Southeast Asia he'd never fully signed on to the "protect your buddy's six" doctrine. Instead, he concentrated on watching his own back, doing his job, and returning home.

Now, he felt differently, like his entire purpose in life was to see that Paula got back unharmed. Not knowing why he felt that way caused him to wonder about his motives, or even his sanity. In short, she seemed a poor choice for changing one's entire life, but that had occurred the minute she entered his life, so there was no backing up now. He pushed the useless thoughts aside and tried to eat some more of his food. Two more bites and he gave up, waiting for his hungrier companion to clean his plate.

Finally done, the crime boss drained his tea glass before looking Carlton in the eye. "You got any problem with being involved in the exchange? Like being the bagman?" he asked quietly, leaning in toward Carlton and watching his reaction closely.

Carlton was surprised, but hesitated only an instant, then shrugged. "I'll do whatever's needed to get her back, obviously. You think I'm the best choice, though? You think they'd trust a gringo in the exchange?"

Tino shook his head. "They don't trust anyone, just like I don't trust any of them, so it's a moot point. But an exchange has to be arranged so we can get Paula back alive, and that takes some negotiation over conditions, timing, and logistics, which is where I come in. But I won't deliver the money personally, just like Ramos won't deliver Paula. It's the way this business works, Carlton. Bad as it sounds, we get somebody else to do the shit jobs."

"Sounds like the military," Carlton observed. "And that doesn't especially bother me. I guess no one wants to risk their top brass being in the line of fire. It makes sense."

Tino nodded. "Yeah, that sums it up as to personnel. Bottom line, though, they're just going to want their money, or whatever, they don't give two shits about who shows up with it, just like we don't care who delivers Paula, long as she's safe. I've got other guys, but I think you'd be good at dealing with it, given your experience."

"Tino, my experience doesn't include dealing with kidnappers who speak a different language than I do." Carlton's tone was one of exasperation, borne of an acute awareness of his weakness in picking up the Spanish language, even though he was around it to some degree every day.

"I meant that the work you did for Randall Morris was pretty…uh, nerve-wracking and demanding. And dealing with sleazy people. Just like this exchange will be. And I like the way you dealt with the last sleazy bunch. Hell, I even admired the little package you put together for me to find in the warehouse. You're pretty good with that tricky exploding stuff." The last remark was accompanied by a sly grin.

"You mean you're thinking about putting a little something extra in the ransom money?" Carlton asked, shocked that Tino would suggest a bomb or similar device when his sister's life was on the line. "Shouldn't we wait till we get her back and retaliate later?"

Tino shook his head. "Yeah, that's just wishful thinking. I'd like to add to the ransom package, but I don't know how we'd pull it off. Ramos will insist on everything being checked out before he releases her."

Carlton thought for a minute. "Maybe I'd be best at that phase—planning something for another time. I'm just concerned that I might screw up the ransom exchange, get Paula hurt or killed."

"You won't screw up. We'll have specific instructions, you just follow them, do what they say. We get her back, we'll come up with something for later."

Carlton shook his head and tried a different tack. "Won't it be a disadvantage to have me do it? Or dangerous? I don't speak Spanish very well and understand it even less. What if they say something I need to know, or I need to answer a question?"

"I've thought about that, and it may even be an advantage, odd as that seems. If they want to discuss much of anything, they'll immediately see that they need to do it in English. So the language barrier cuts both ways. You'll be more adept and they'll be off balance having to carry out the transaction completely in English."

Carlton nodded, seeing the logic of his remark, but wondering if it were indeed correct. Maybe a language barrier would only serve to frustrate or anger someone, someone who had the authority to pull the plug. *Or the trigger*, he thought morbidly.

A thought occurred to him regarding logistics. "Are they going to run me all over town, from one spot to another? I may not know the section of the city well enough to get to the next checkpoint or whatever. At least that's what I see in the movies, and they may not read the same script I do."

"Another advantage of not being Latino or from this side of town. I plan to tell them that when they call with the exchange information. They may have you move to one or two other spots, but I'll make it clear that you'll be looking at a map, not using a Smartphone GPS app."

"My car's got it, but I don't use it often enough to do it quickly. And I prefer looking at a map that doesn't move in and out, changing the viewing perspective. That's what I have eyeballs for."

"One other thing," Tino added, ignoring Carlton's technology complaint. He leaned closer to him and pointed an index finger at the ceiling. "I can trust you to get there with the money and exchange it for Paula, not stop off along the way and buy magic beans or something."

Carlton looked closely at Tino's face, waiting for further explanation. After a few seconds and seeing none was forthcoming, he simply nodded in agreement with the trusting comment. He wasn't about to ask about trustworthiness among the drug lord's troops; he'd dealt with that only a couple of months before and didn't want to risk getting caught up in another search-and-purge mission for Faustino Perez, or anyone else. He hoped Tino had taken the earlier hint that he regretted killing anyone he had any connection with. Plus, he was serious about checking out of the life, despite Frey and Henley's classic observation regarding hotels in the desert.

After a prolonged silence, Carlton gave up the debate and confirmed his earlier nodding gesture. "If you think I'm best for the job, then I'll do it. I want some specific instructions, just as soon as we hear from those bastards. I just want Paula back, safe and unhurt. I'll need a tutorial on how to accomplish that."

"They'll have some hoops for us to jump through, and I'll know more about how to do it when we hear—"

One of the phones on the table buzzed, interrupting the conversation. Tino grabbed it and answered in Spanish. *"Bueno?"*

The opening conversation on the other end was short, too short to be the kidnappers making a ransom demand and giving instructions. Then Carlton heard Tino ask about tattoos and give terse instructions to the caller before ending the call. He snapped the phone shut and looked at Carlton. "They contacted my office, left a message for me to call Paula on her phone. Assholes don't even want to use up a burner phone to make a ransom demand. They didn't say, but I'm pretty sure it's Ramos. I got Arturo working on the tattoos, just to make certain."

He flipped the phone open and dialed, then pushed the CALL button. Within seconds, the phone was answered, but it was not Paula's voice Carlton could hear on the phone across the table. A male Hispanic answered by beginning a conversation in Spanish, apparently seeing that Faustino Perez was the caller. After a few exchanges which Carlton couldn't follow, he began to pick up on the words, at least the ones coming from Tino. In a brusque interruption of the party on the other end, he inquired after Paula's safety and demanded to talk to her. The conversation went silent for a few seconds, then Carlton could hear Paula's voice sounding shaky and scared.

"Tino, I'm alright. Just scared, that's all. Do you know what's going on?"

"They're going to demand money for your release. You've got to stay calm and let this get worked out, okay?"

"How long?"

"I don't know yet. They're going to tell me pretty quick. Are you being treated okay?"

"Yes...I think so. I've been really sleepy, I think they gave me a shot or something. But I feel okay, just dizzy, that's all."

"Do you know where you are?"

"No, they put a cloth over my eyes. I haven't seen anything—"

Paula? Paula? You there?"

Tino frowned and stared at the phone. Evidently, the kidnappers had been listening for anything in the conversation that might reveal their location, and upon Tino's asking her whereabouts, the phone was quickly snatched away from her and the call ended.

Tino slowly closed his phone and looked at Carlton, the relief clear on both their faces. "At least she sounded okay, for the moment, anyway," he informed him needlessly, not realizing Carlton could hear her voice across the table. "But I should have known they'd be listening and not let her tell me where she is, if she even knows."

"Is it Brujido Ramos?" Carlton asked, still wondering why the opposition drug lord would risk an all-out war by kidnapping a competitor's sister.

Tino nodded. "Yeah, just as I thought. I guess it's a waste of time for Arturo to chase the tattoo identification." He sighed deeply and leaned back, fatigue showing on his face, replacing the earlier look of relief.

"At least I'll know what to watch for in the future," Carlton quipped. "If I see tattoos of flames and barbed wire, I can safely assume it's okay to shoot?"

Tino grimaced. "Absolutely. Those jackasses have the upper hand right now, but after we get her back..."

The look on his face said retaliation was already being considered, even before this first dangerous stage played out. Carlton felt helpless, unable to do anything, or even suggest anything that Faustino Perez hadn't already thought about. Plus, as Carlton had witnessed after the interstate shootout, the crime boss surrounded himself with capable people, notwithstanding the bloody outcome on that day. As Carlton had earlier determined, Perez's group would be able to handle this better than anyone else, so long as Brujido Ramos didn't make a foolish—and fatal—error in handling his victim.

Another minute of silence passed, while both men worried over Paula's condition despite hearing her voice moments before. Given the mental state of someone who would dare grab Faustino Perez's sister, it was possible that her status could change instantly.

"Will they call back?" Carlton ventured, worried that Tino's inquiry of her location had been a blunder the kidnappers would take out on Paula.

Tino opened his mouth to speak, but the ringing phone on the table answered the question for them. He waited two rings, then answered again in Spanish. This time, he listened, then asked a couple of questions, of which Carlton could only pick up the words for "when" and "where" with a lot more detail thrown in than he could understand. Then he heard Tino saying his name, followed by a lengthy explanation. Next, the inevitable word "*dinero*" arose, followed by quick exchanges Carlton couldn't follow. Apparently, an argument ensued, judging by the tone of the conversation. After two or three minutes of heated exchange, Tino's tone became calmer, more conciliatory. Evidently, a deal was being struck, and Carlton hoped it was going the way Tino had envisioned. He couldn't think of anyone else who would be better equipped to handle something like a kidnapping ransom and exchange.

Another two minutes of quieter verbal exchange crawled by before Tino snapped the phone shut and took a deep breath. "Shit! He wants a half million dollars."

"Ouch!" Carlton didn't know what the going ransom was for the sister of a mid-level drug kingpin, but a half mil seemed a lot. "I don't know that much about your business, but is that an amount that's always lying around just for emergencies?"

"Hell, no!" Tino spread his arms in frustration. "The public has this picture of all crime bosses rolling around in bales of money, like something in a movie or a *Miami Vice* episode. That may be true at the very top of the chain, say Joaquín Guzmán, or somebody like him, but in real life for most downstream distributors, money has to be reinvested, kept moving into inventory, and preparing for price increases and unforeseen expenses. Just like any other business. But no, I don't keep that kind of cash in my pillow case, and Ramos knows it."

"I've got some cash. We've got to get Paula out safely, so don't worry about that part."

Tino smiled, relief on his face. "I was too embarrassed to ask, but I figured you did. I've got about three hundred grand at my immediate disposal."

Carlton nodded. "I can cover the rest."

"And the news isn't all bad, he gave me a discount."

"Huh?" Carlton was having trouble understanding how any of this was good news.

"Yeah, he wanted a million at first, and I refused, said I absolutely couldn't afford that amount, Paula's life or not. I even told him a sister was only worth so much. He pushed back hard at that, so I told him the truth; Paula's my *half*-sister. He laughed and said, 'so you only want to pay a *half* million?'" Tino spread his hands to indicate something beyond his control before continuing. "He started yelling about returning some body parts to convince me, but I held firm about simply not having the money, no matter what he did. A risky move against somebody like Brujido Ramos, but it worked."

Carlton thought about it for a moment. "Why would he agree so quickly to drop the amount? Why not wait until you sell something and come up with the full amount?"

"Again, people only know what they see in the movies, the tough gangster demanding an outrageous amount in, oh, twenty-four hours and not budging on it. Says he'll kill the victim, pay up or else. In reality, if Ramos kills Paula, he knows that I will turn the earth inside out until he's died a most unpleasant death. Plus, he doesn't want this to drag on very long. He wants what he can get, and quick. That amount is five hundred thousand dollars in cash."

"Yeah, and even if a half million bucks is chicken feed, it would feed a *lot* of chickens. So did he say when and where? And how?"

Perez locked eyes with Carlton. "*When* is the tough part. At three o'clock tomorrow morning. About...he paused to glance at his phone...five and a half hours from now."

Not for the first time that night, Carlton was stunned. "*Are you serious?* Are you sure it's not three A.M. *tomorrow*, uh, make that *Monday* morning? How the hell are we going to do that?"

Tino was shaking his head even while Carlton spoke. "Nope. That's what I was telling you, he wants money now and is willing to take less in order to collect immediately. It leaves us no time to plan anything, to stall, to notify anyone who could, or would, help us. Not even time to try to grab someone important to him and turn Raul Vega loose on him. Come on, let's go to my office and get started on this."

During the drive, Tino was talkative, making instructive comments about exchanging the money for Paula. Listening carefully, Carlton asked a few questions about the process. It sounded simple enough on the surface, but within minutes the simplicity faded and he became doubtful about success. He frowned at the pang of apprehension invading his stomach while he envisioned the actual steps: Paula being drug from a car, blindfolded; he, getting out of a car and carrying a duffel bag full of money; handing it over to some armed scumbag (and waiting while the kidnappers counted it); then, the feeling of helplessness as the parties retreated to their respective vehicles (hopefully) and left the scene. A dozen things could happen during the exchange, most of them bad.

He dreaded the thought of facing this unknown task alone, despite Tino's assurances that all the kidnappers wanted was the money and a smooth transfer. By the time Tino pulled into the flea market parking lot and circled the darkened stalls to park in front of his office, Carlton was regretting his agreement to be the solitary bagman, but there was no time to make alternate plans. He could only hope something would change, something would turn up to make the prospects of the dangerous rendezvous less daunting.

Recalling what Tino had said about Raul Vega, he wished the old man were able to go with him. Maybe even his wife, Caterina, too. A couple of months before, the couple had practiced for hours with Carlton planning a diversion inside the upscale restaurant where Carlton had set up the crooked DEA agent to be eliminated. As it occurred, the situation changed at the last minute, and they hadn't needed to implement the diversion—but they were there and ready all the same. In fact, their quick adaption to the changing plan enforced Carlton's confidence in the pair.

The men walked into the building, and Tino flipped on the lights while Carlton fiddled with the air conditioner, just as Tino had fiddled with it only a few hours before—a few hours in which a lot had changed. Carlton's life had once again been thrown in disarray: his friend and lover violently taken, his head smacked, a visit to the doctor, an offer made to spend a big chunk of his retirement money...plus, he'd been "volunteered" to act as the bagman for the kidnapping exchange.

Carlton decided to try to change things again, this time in his favor. "Did they insist that only one person deliver the money?"

"Yes, Ramos was firm on that part. When I told him about you, he balked, but settled down when I told him you'd had lots of experience, no problem in your coming alone."

"Gosh, thanks, Tino! I always appreciate an endorsement like that!"

Tino frowned and ignored the sarcastic remark. "Why? Who did you have in mind?"

"Well, since you ask, I really liked working with Raul and Caterina. They played out their parts perfectly inside Ernesto's Restaurant, adapted to the last-minute change like pros. I could tell they had some past experience with dangerous situations, but the time never seemed right to inquire where they learned or practiced it. Without spending too much time we don't have, tell me the story on those two."

Despite the tension of the moment, Tino smiled, but shook his head. "Not a chance of using them for this job, Carlton. I was nervous enough when you used them inside that restaurant."

"I just think I need some professional help with this assignment," he argued testily.

"Nope, but Raul will be useful for the retaliation plan. Anyway, not enough time to give you the whole background, but the quick version is this: Raul and Caterina aren't originally from here or Mexico. They came from Cuba—Castro's Cuba. When things really went to shit for the people during the late seventies, they worked for an underground group that specialized in supporting some kind of guerilla activity. They weren't successful overall, since they never got organized enough to launch an overthrow movement, but they caused enough trouble with Castro's goons to bring relief to their little town and the surrounding area. They learned some pretty harsh lessons during that time."

Carlton nodded. "I knew they were something when they were younger. Too bad we can't enlist Raul's help on this. By the way, how would you 'turn Vega loose' as you put it?"

Perez didn't hesitate to give an example of his old friend's utility. "A few years ago, we had trouble with a group who were terrorizing some of the merchants at the flea market, extorting money from them. Raul Vega went undercover and finally managed to be in a stall when two guys came in and cornered the female owner, demanding protection money. Raul sauntered over and told the two to get lost. As you know, he's a small guy and was well into his sixties at the time, so the two assholes laughed at him and pushed him. It was their last time to push anyone around, no matter their size or age."

When Tino paused for effect, Carlton took the bait. "What did Mr. Vega do to them?"

"He knifed the bigger man, killing him instantly. Then he threw some kind of punch into the other guy's gut that immobilized him. He called for help, and we took him to a warehouse out back, and Raul…um, *extracted* information about who was behind the protection racket. The guy lived and took home a story that stopped the problem."

"*Extracted*?"

"I didn't stick around for the entire session, but I know it involved a pair of water pump pliers and the guy's testicles."

Carlton made a face and quickly crossed his legs. "Jeez Louise! And I think Caterina may be even tougher than Raul!"

"She is, believe me. Now let's get busy. We've got to round up the rest of the money and get you to the dance on time. By yourself, amigo."

Carlton gave up lobbying for assistance and steeled himself for the uncomfortable task ahead. After all, he'd done dozens of jobs entailing more risk than handing over a bag full of money. All of them had been solo gigs, at his insistence. But it didn't make him like doing something with which he had no experience, without backup, without anyone to turn to if things didn't go as planned. He felt like Gilbert O'Sullivan singing *"Alone Again" (Naturally)*, but couldn't remember any words except the title, which was enough.

Even while finishing the story of Raul Vega's run-in with extortionists, Perez had been dialing the combination to a squat floor safe in the corner of his portable building office. When he swung the door open, he motioned for Carlton to hand him a tattered suitcase stored under his desk. In short order, he scooped up stacks of neatly banded bills from the floor of the safe and tucked them tightly into the suitcase. Then he closed it and snapped the clasps as he stood.

"That's all I keep in there, two hundred thousand," he announced, pushing the safe's thick steel door shut. "I've got some more over at the safe at your apartment building."

Carlton looked surprised. "You keep big money at your other sister's apartment complex?"

"Yes. Marta has a wall safe in her office. It's fireproof, probably a longer burn time than this old thing," he said, gesturing to the ancient block of steel at their feet.

Carrying the suitcase, Tino led the way out of the office to his pickup. Five minutes later, they pulled into the apartment complex, where Tino used a key to unlock the front door, another to enter Marta's office.

Carlton, carrying the suitcase, looked around the spotless office. "Your sister keeps a lot nicer digs than you do, Tino. I live here, but I've not been into her back office until now."

"She can afford to. She's got less overhead in her operation. Bring that suitcase over here." Tino dug out more banded stacks of money, quietly mouthing the running total amount as he placed them in the suitcase. "Three hundred, three-twenty, three-forty…um, three-sixty. That's it, the Perez cupboard is bare."

"Okay. Three-sixty. I need to get one-forty, so I'll have to hit two places at least. You still driving?"

CHAPTER 4

Carlton gave Tino directions to the nearest of his depository locations, an alley behind a restaurant on Loop 410, near Fredericksburg Road. He knew that location would contain about sixty grand, all that remained in a sealed, four-inch diameter PVC pipe buried behind a utility pole.

Tino pulled into the back of the restaurant parking lot and killed his headlights. Carlton carried a short gardener's spade into the alley and took a look around. Ambient light from the adjoining strip mall revealed that no one, not even a drunk or a panhandler from the nearby street intersection was spending the night there; nothing except a mangy cat leaping from the dumpster, which scared him witless and sent his pulse rate into the stratosphere. It reminded him why he preferred to visit his hiding locations in broad daylight, wearing coveralls and carrying a clipboard. That way, his actions appeared to be those of a maintenance person, a lot more innocent than slinking around in the dark. If confronted in daylight, he could always explain some vague checkup process being conducted on the pole or the soil around it. Tonight, he didn't have that option.

He went straight to the second utility pole, the one nearest the dumpster, and started digging behind it. Just before reaching fifteen inches in the hard caliche, he struck the PVC pipe and expanded his digging area to clear the dirt from around it. Tugging it from its hiding place, he placed it on the ground and shoveled dirt back in the hole before jumping into Tino's pickup and tossing it on the floorboard.

The next stop, the San Antonio Water Supply headquarters building off U.S. Highway 281, held just over a hundred thousand dollars. Carlton sprinted through the darkened lawn and counted bushes adorning the base of the building, starting from the southwest corner. Under the fifth bush, he again worked up a sweat digging; this time, almost two feet of earth covered the sealed pipe. He worked feverishly to pull the pipe from the moist soil and just as quickly to refill the hole. Before running back to the pickup, he surveyed the lawn and surrounding street scene, but saw nothing of importance. A couple of late-night joggers huffed up Alvin Street towards North St. Mary's, but they paid scant attention to the figure dashing across the manicured lawn and jumping into the idling Ford pickup.

"Okay, this bit of banking withdrawal business is done. We may have to use a hacksaw to cut into this pipe. I put a lot of glue on the caps."

"You glued them on? Makes a partial withdrawal a bit difficult, doesn't it?"

"Well, you know how SAWS likes to water their lawn while prohibiting everyone else from watering theirs. I didn't want soggy currency."

Tino laughed at the local truism and made the turnaround at Hildebrand to head back toward the south side of the city. As he exited McAllister Freeway to merge with I-35 South, Carlton decided to start on specifics. "You're sure they won't tell you where this exchange is happening?"

"No, he's saving that for later. Supposed to call me back at 2:00 A.M."

"Keeps us from coming up with much of a plan."

"That's the idea. If he calls at two, the exchange place can't be very far away, though. Brujido Ramos wants this to work just as much as we do."

"What will I drive?"

"Take your Caddy, bad GPS unit or not. Oh, Raymond texted me that he parked it in front of the snack bar, keys on the right front tire. If it's the same guys who grabbed her, they'll recognize it from this afternoon, help smooth any suspicions they might have, at least a bit."

Carlton nodded in the dark, agreeing with the reasoning. In the tension of a kidnapping exchange, it wouldn't hurt to have things, even small details, as familiar as possible to the parties pulling off the trade. The kidnappers already knew it was his car, they'd likely memorized the license plate to make the grab, so looking for the same vehicle to show up made sense all around.

Carlton thought of something that might prove helpful. "I've got an unused burner phone. I'll call you just as I pull in to the exchange site and put it on speaker, full volume. That way, you can hear what's taking place. If something goes south..." He let the phrase hang, and Tino Perez nodded affirmation. If the exchange turned violent, Tino would be aware of it in real time and move in on the scene.

"Yeah, I need to call and update the men, get them ready to move from their locations. As soon as I get the call for the transfer location, I'll text them the info. They can leave individually in their vehicles and converge on the spot."

"Will they all know how far back to stop?"

"I'll tell them two to three blocks, no closer to you and Paula. Unless I hear something go bad, that is."

Carlton tried not to think about that phrase, what it might imply. But he knew that a single gunshot or word of alarm from him or Paula would result in Faustino Perez releasing the equivalent of hounds from Hell, and from that there would be no return to normalcy in anyone's foreseeable future.

When they pulled back into the flea market, Carlton noticed his car was indeed parked in front. He went to the front tire and pocketed his keys, then carried the two PVC pipe sections into Tino's office. Tino followed him in with a tool box, and the pair proceeded—with some difficulty—to unscrew the caps and extract bundles of currency, counting out one hundred and forty thousand dollars and placing it on the floor. Carlton's remaining twenty-five thousand-plus dollars went into Tino's safe and the suitcase got the big chunk. Adding the money to the suitcase, Carlton noticed it was now about three-fourths full, and it weighed around eighteen or twenty pounds. Since most of the bills were one-hundred dollar bills, along with some fifties, there were almost six thousand bills weighing in at one gram each. That would amount to just over thirteen pounds, not including the suitcase.

Carlton had to smile at an earlier memory of Paula trying to convince him that the same sum of money, a half million bucks, was tucked neatly into a small briefcase—in twenty-dollar bills, no less! It was only a small example of her propensity to weave a story that suited her needs; however, that time her story failed due to what Carlton would have categorized as a useless piece of trivia he carried in his brain: the weight of a single Federal Reserve note, plus some math skills. He shook his head at the memory, recalling that scene ending with Paula pointing a gun at him and pulling the trigger. Luckily, his suspicious nature had led to his disabling the gun hours earlier...his smile turned to a shake of the head. *This was the woman he was going to save?*

Carlton hefted the load and checked the latches while Tino began making calls, never speaking for longer than a few seconds before stabbing the END key and dialing another. Carlton placed the suitcase on the floor, handle side up, and perched on it, trying without success to decipher Tino's rapid-fire phone instructions. After three or four minutes, the wait became maddening, but there was nothing to do but wait and worry.

Finally, Tino snapped his phone shut and looked at Carlton. "Okay, I've got six guys ready to roll. Four of them you know already from the Encinal trip, including Raul Vega. You feel better now?"

"Well, I don't feel any worse. But I'm plenty worried about Paula. We have no control over what those bastards do to her, and I won't know her condition until she's turned over to me. And even then, I can't do anything about it." Carlton's voice was rising, and by the end of his tirade, the volume of his voice made him realize that the tension was getting to him.

Even before he finished speaking, Tino was motioning with his hands to calm down. "I know, Carlton! I understand, and I agree with you. But remember, they just want the money, and the quicker it takes place, the less time there is for anything to go wrong, or for them to change their mind and do something stupid to her. Believe me, I'm worried too, but I know how this works. You've got to calm down and trust me on this."

Carlton took a deep breath and tried to concentrate on what Tino was telling him and what he already knew—Faustino Perez and his men were well-versed in the ways of the opposition drug smugglers-turned-kidnappers residing here, near their own turf. And why not? They all played the same deadly game while importing contraband narcotics across the Texas-Mexico border. They all plotted, schemed, and killed to achieve the goal of distributing illegal drugs to ready users across South Texas. They were all Latino, steeped in the culture and language that made the Border a dangerous—but profitable—place to do business. And, like Carlton Westerfield, none of them was a candidate for sainthood, so he'd do well to listen to the logic of one of the top guys, the half-brother of the kidnap victim to boot.

But at this moment, nothing was making him feel any better about Paula being in the hands of a bunch of men of the same ilk, largely due to her being taken from him in broad daylight, and he moved to get that point across to the crime boss. "Look, Tino, it's my fault she was grabbed in the first place. I'm not an expert on your line of work, but I know something about this life in general. I should have been on guard against something like this happening. I should have been carrying a piece and—"

"And gotten both of you killed? You think you can outshoot two teams of guys who are armed and ready to kill? Nobody expects something like that to happen when you're on your way to eat tacos."

"Well, it appears I'd better get used to expecting something like that, every minute of every day. Until I can get out of this mess and get Paula out of it. For *good*."

Tino paused and took a breath himself, apparently hoping to ease the mood of the moment and give Carlton a chance to collect his wits and prepare for the upcoming exchange. "Okay, okay. Look, I know this a bad position for you to be in. The timing couldn't have been worse, especially if you've been considering leaving the life and doing something entirely different, never encountering any crap like this for the remainder of your days. But we're in it right now, and we've got to see this through and be smart while we're doing it. It's the best chance Paula has."

The last part made Carlton wince. He had suspected all along that Tino was soft-pedaling the dilemma a bit in order to soothe his concerns, but now, alluding to her "best chance" reminded him of how her life hung in the balance. Despite Tino's earlier assurances that Ramos simply wanted the ransom money, the fact remained that he was a man of violence, and Paula's situation was precarious, to put it mildly.

"You want somebody else to make the exchange?" Tino asked quietly, breaking almost a full minute of silence. "Despite what I said earlier, I've got guys who can do it." As if to drive home the point, he added: "Hell, Raul can do it if necessary. I just didn't want to put a seventy-plus-year-old-man in that spot if I can help it. Besides, he might start the retaliation phase before Paula even gets in the car."

Carlton had to laugh at that. "From what I saw of him, he just might. No, I'll do the exchange. I'm the right guy for the job, because in my mind, Paula's my responsibility."

Tino shook his head. "No, you're the right guy for the job because you're older, but not too old, you think things through, and you're not as likely to fly off the handle if they shove her toward the car with more force than necessary. You don't know Spanish well enough to be insulted by things they may say, so your emotions won't come into play. You can see the end result we want and not do anything to screw it up. And yes, maybe, because you *think* she's your responsibility, you have an attachment to her, so you'll be careful and do it right," he conceded.

Carlton sighed. "Okay, I'm the right guy, we're agreed on that. So what time is it, anyway?" he asked while pulling his own phone and looking at the screen. "Just past midnight. Wish this show could just get on the road."

"Lie down on the couch, get a few winks," Tino suggested, gesturing toward the ugly thing against the side wall. "It's worked for me many times in the past, that very couch. I'm going over to Raul's for a while, see if we can come up with anything useful. Not too early to start planning on getting back at that bastard. I'll call you when it's time. Oh, and let's put that suitcase back in the safe."

Carlton took him up on the offer and moved over to the Holiday Inn castoff. "Good idea. Maybe I can catch a few winks. But wake me as soon as you hear anything, okay, Lefty?"

Tino grimaced and headed for the door, mumbling as he reached for the light switch. "Damn gringo thinks he's a comedian."

CHAPTER 5

Not surprisingly, Carlton fell asleep the minute his head touched the arm of the couch. As he had informed Tino earlier, he hadn't slept well the previous night, and now his tired brain skipped stages three and four sleep, going straight into stage five, the REM stage. For a while, he was drifting in and out of the early dream stage, with short, disjointed dreams in which he realized he was dreaming, making the action all the more surreal.

Then the drama at hand came to visit dreamland. He was driving through South San Antonio, looking for the rendezvous point and unable to locate it. The clock on the instrument panel of the Cadillac crept closer to 3:00 A.M., and he was starting to panic, despite the fact that he felt certain he was only dreaming. After all, Tino would have awakened him, right? Faustino Perez knew how this worked, he knew where the exchange was, that it had to be on time. He had all the answers, explaining the process to Carlton as though he were a child who didn't pay close attention, trying to mollify his feelings, placate his fears—

Carlton awoke with a start and sat up. He squinted at his phone face and saw that he'd only been on the couch about thirty minutes, asleep maybe twenty-five, if he wanted to count the goofy little dream sequences at the end. His REM stage sleep had ended quickly, and he'd awakened with an elevated pulse and respiration rate. Something was amiss, he knew it, and he could feel it throughout his body.

This entire drama, right from the beginning—it was wrong. The kidnapping, the men holding him, the pop to his head, the Benz leaving with Paula. Then, Tino showing up in minutes with his calming effect in full swing, words and action, *El Jefe* at work. His correct call about Brujido Ramos being the kidnapper, his prediction about how the demand would come, the timing of the exchange...on and on, the flow of weird occurrences, Tino's projections, remarks, phone calls, money gathering...right up to a few minutes ago, when he had suggested Carlton catch a few Zs before showtime...all *too* choreographed, not enough confusion and doubt for the situation at hand.

Carlton took a deep breath in the darkness and wondered if the earlier crack to his skull was impairing his judgment. He touched the side of his head and flinched at the tenderness of the wound. He still had a slight headache, having declined Dr. Morales' offer of pain medication. Still, he could think clearly, and one thing was certain: tonight was not what it seemed, or maybe not what Perez was wanting it to seem.

Faustino Perez, drug lord, kingpin, crime boss, *patrón* of an entire area of the city, would not willingly let Brujido Ramos—or anyone else—control the flow of events as was now happening if there were any alternative. While Tino had informed Carlton of Ramos' violent nature and the ramifications of escalating a conflict without prior planning, it seemed inconceivable that nothing could be done short of handing over a half million dollars to his competitor for five minutes work by four muscle men with bad tattoos. Did this Ramos guy have another card in his hand, something that held Perez at bay, something beyond holding his half-sister for ransom? If so, could he, Carlton, do anything about it?

Still, like most people, Carlton's knowledge of kidnapping and the resulting ransom and exchange process was limited to what he had seen in movies and read in books. Maybe, just maybe, this was the way these things actually went down. Or maybe not. He leaned back on the arm of the couch and tried to collect his thoughts, put tonight's events into a timeline and apply logic to each one, starting *after* the kidnapping itself.

Upon learning of Paula's kidnapping, Tino had been quick to arrive and assess the situation. He allowed that the grab was professional, probably ordered by his main rival in the drug business. After a visit to the clinic and some discussion, he quickly nominated Carlton to be the bagman, before he even heard the ransom demand. When he spoke with the kidnappers, he had to argue the point with them, finally getting them to agree. He had cited several reasons, all of them valid—up to a point.

Primarily, Carlton believed Tino trusted him to remain calm in the face of a dangerous situation, something he'd done many times while performing work for Big Mo. That had to be a big plus in the crime boss' mind; that and trusting him to drive away with a half million bucks in untraceable cash. Also high on his list of qualifications had to be the emotional connection he knew existed between Carlton and his half-sister. Carlton Westerfield had serious skin in the game, no question.

The review of events did nothing to ease his mind, and though he was unable to come up with a solid reason for his discomfort, he still felt more was afoot than he'd been told. Abandoning that train of thought, he began to ponder his own position in the unfolding drama. What to do when the time came, how to handle his assignment, how would Paula react, what to tell Tino afterwards...all those questions deserved answers. Instead, his mind wandered to an evaluation of himself—as seen by others.

Tino's reasoning had been based on his knowledge of Carlton collected during the past year and a half, eighteen months of an odd melding of their personalities, skills, and attitudes. Along the way, mutual respect for each other's abilities had developed into some kind of uneasy partnership; but just what level that alliance was, it was unlikely that either man could verbalize it. On Carlton's part, he appreciated that Tino was exactly what he appeared to be: a tough *patrón* and crime boss who took care of his people and neither made nor accepted excuses for the successes and failings that occurred around him. Tino undoubtedly appreciated Carlton's unwavering willingness to rise to the occasion at hand, as he had on the day of the interstate massacre and in dealing with Tino's inside informant to the DEA.

Even though Carlton had not changed appreciably in his overt actions during the past couple of years—really, his entire adult life—there remained things that Tino Perez did not know about his part-time advisor in crime techniques and law enforcement evasion. Of course, he knew Carlton had worked for Big Mo, carrying out contract work. And he had seen first-hand how Carlton could build a car bomb, figure out connections between seemingly unassociated people and events, and launch into action as he had on that horrible day in Encinal. He was dependable and no stranger to action and violence, no matter how much he proclaimed to be inexperienced in such matters, using his unassuming demeanor and physical appearance to support the modest self-image. And while mild-mannered, middle-aged Carlton Westerfield had another, darker side, one that Paula and Tino were aware of, neither of them knew *how* Carlton came to be the poster boy for someone not being exactly as he appeared—nor *what* that dark side was when conditions called for it.

The *"how"* occurred soon after Carlton returned from overseas, following military service and a brief stint that bordered on being a mercenary. The young man had gone to work for a local newspaper selling advertisements, when his job placed him in contact with an unsavory insurance broker who bragged to him at length about selling worthless, over-priced life policies to old people. As it occurred, the scam hit close to home: Carlton's mother had been victim to such a ruse, possibly the same obese slimeball now regaling Carlton with tales of his deceptions, outright proud of his feats. Carlton made his opinion of the guy's practices known and, upon returning to his workplace, was immediately fired from his job for losing the ad account.

Three nights later, the crooked insurance man walked out of his usual watering hole in a seedy section of downtown. His body was found the next day in a nearby alley, two gunshot wounds in his forehead. His killer was never caught. Only one person had witnessed the execution-style murder: Randall "Big Mo" Morris, a local pawnbroker, bookmaker, and handler of stolen goods was, as befit his classy persona, relieving himself in the alley when he heard a disturbance. He watched as a man jerked the repulsive scammer into the alley and reminded him who he was and how much he despised his business practices. When the fat man responded with his well-used bluster, his tormentor calmly produced a small handgun. The blabbering turned to begging, then pleading, but with a slight shift of the gun, the insurance crook's life ended. It happened so quickly Big Mo scarcely had time to stumble back to his car and watch the killer get in his own vehicle and drive away.

He managed to follow the killer until he stopped, engaging him in conversation far from the scene. There, he made the man a job offer that was to set the stage for the rest of his life. The interview process was short. Big Mo didn't bother to ask Carlton Westerfield how he could shoot his target in the face so quickly and dispassionately. He only asked him if he could do it on request, on short notice, and repeatedly—for money. The answer to all three was affirmative.

But Tino and Paula—or even Big Mo—didn't realize *what* the transformation process entailed when Carlton Westerfield held a gun in his hand. For starters, Carlton was the rare Texas male who didn't fit into the gun culture so prevalent throughout the Lone Star State; indeed, much of America. He didn't own guns, at least none that he kept in his possession and cherished as valuable items of intricate mechanical genius or collector-grade treasures. He didn't have a license to carry a concealed weapon, he didn't practice marksmanship; nor did he worry about caliber, bullet weight, powder load, casing crimp, barrel twist, muzzle velocity, or any of the dozens of arcane details that typical gun fans pored over at length and discussed *ad nauseum* at gun shows, coffee shops, and on internet forums. In short, Carlton wasn't a gun guy in the traditional sense.

However, at the moment of truth—objective defined, assignment clarified, subject identified, target in sight, *gun in hand*—Carlton was possessed with a single-mindedness and concentration that approached supernatural. Nothing mattered but the task at hand, completing the kill as quickly and efficiently as possible.

And there was more to the picture. Though Carlton did not consider himself a great marksman, he was blessed with remarkable hand-to-eye coordination, a genetic gift enabling him to send a bullet to the target with unfailing accuracy. It was as though he willed the bullet to its mark rather than pointed the gun in the correct direction. He took no time to aim, but his shots—usually three rapid ones—were unerringly placed close together. Furthermore, he possessed an economy of movement that would make the act seem even faster to an observer—if ever there were one. Not since Big Mo had seen Carlton commit his first execution had anyone seen the calm, non-descript man pull the trigger on a gun—except his victims, none of whom lived to tell about the experience.

Now, as Carlton mentally arranged the facts surrounding another strange day in the life of an aging loner with a unique gift, it became clear that he could only prepare to act in the same manner that had served him well for a long time. His history said that would probably result in more victims having a chance to witness their own demise.

Carlton sat up and struggled to control his breathing. Relying on his time-honored method of going over and over needed preparations in his mind, he calmed quickly and began a mental countdown. First, he had to leave quickly. Next, he had to get his hands on a gun. With those two items off the list, he could concentrate on variables that might arise when Tino got the phone call for the exchange location. That train of thought made him feel better than he had since being cracked on the head a few hours earlier. Already his pulse and respiration were back to resting rates.

Pushing himself off the couch, he strode to the office door in the dark, then opened it and glanced around outside. Nothing in the lot except his blue Cadillac, gleaming under the security light. He slipped outside quickly, pulled the door shut, and trotted to the car. Within minutes, he was nearing Old Castroville Road and the large cemetery that served as the final resting place for thousands of human beings—and the temporary resting place for a Colt .45 caliber automatic pistol.

Carlton parked in the quiet neighborhood on the south side of San Fernando Cemetery and walked to the perimeter fence along Morelia Street. Walking east, he soon spotted a familiar break in the fence, heavily used by lovers and kids to access the graveyard after hours. He didn't know why the hole in the fence hadn't been repaired, since the immaculate cemetery was well-kept and secure otherwise. Tonight he didn't care; he was glad it was still available to him. Climbing the fence after midnight would be a lot more noticeable and surely draw unwanted attention.

He squeezed through the gap in the fence and walked due north for about two hundred yards. As he neared the north boundary along Old Castroville Road, he turned west until he saw the statue of Jesus Christ towering over the northwest portion of the park. Squatting at a park bench under the gaze of the Savior, he leaned forward and reached toward the base of the statue to pull back a section of turf. Digging under the edge of the foundation and into the soft soil about six inches, he felt a familiar plastic bag and tugged it from the hiding place. The heft told him the Colt and a full box of ammo were there, just as he had wrapped and left them soon after Tino had given it to him as a present. The gift had been a joke between them, a reminder of his clever switch of a similar weapon with a drunken, drugged DEA agent months before. As with other weapons he'd used through the years, Carlton had deposited the piece here, preferring the watchful eyes of Jesus Christ to those of law enforcement types.

Without checking the gun, he stripped the dirty outer bag from the package and replaced it in the hole, then covered it, complete with the section of turf. What he now held was clean, and he tucked it into his shirt. He rose and trotted back to the hole in the fence and walked calmly to his car. First two items taken care of, he thought.

At this point, Carlton grew nervous. He didn't like carrying a gun, didn't want one in his car or anywhere near his person. He didn't "own" a gun in the sense ownership usually implies; he kept a few in hiding places such as this one, waiting for the occasion that he needed it. Sometimes it might be weeks or months before the need arose for one of the pieces he'd picked up through individual sales (never a gun store) and that was fine. The longer an undocumented weapon lay unused, the better. Individual sellers of cold weapons either didn't keep records, or they lost them, they forgot the buyer, or they simply moved on, died, whatever.

In fact, since Big Mo's untimely death, Carlton hadn't needed a gun for his usual line of work. Only when he had planned to kill Gregorio Molina with a DEA agent's weapon had Tino procured one much like he now carried with him. That one he had carried in a rented car for only a few minutes; on normal assignments, he had a gun on his person only for the time required to do the job, ditching it within minutes of completion. He firmly adhered to the theory of less time holding a gun meant less chance of being caught with it during a routine traffic stop, a car breakdown, or something else unforeseen. Tonight, that wasn't an option. He cruised out of the neighborhood, turned right on Cupples Road, then left onto Highway 90. At the I-35 interchange, he turned south and pulled into his apartment building ten minutes later.

Back in his apartment, Carlton unwrapped the gun and checked it thoroughly, giving it a good wipe-down with the cloth he'd deposited inside yet another plastic bag inside the package. He did the same with a handful of the huge cartridges and loaded the clip, then slammed it home into the grip and jacked a round into the chamber. The action felt good; worn enough to be slick and smooth, oiled and well-maintained throughout its life. He pulled the pistol up quickly in a double-handed grip, arms extended, slightly bent at the elbow. Swinging the muzzle around the room, it felt heavy and secure in his hand. The balance was there, enough weight and size in the grip to keep the shooter in control, the trigger guard big and accessible. As the rounds were fired and casings ejected, the weight effect would decrease, but still a well-balanced piece.

Carlton normally didn't care for automatic pistols. The ejected brass flew everywhere, providing crime investigators with a valuable evidence item that could be matched to the weapon itself, and tied to the shooter who was foolish enough to keep the weapon around. While it was theoretically possible to collect the casings or to alter a firing pin or barrel land-and-groove wear pattern to fool forensic investigators, he preferred to avoid the problem altogether: use a different type of gun or get rid of an automatic very quickly.

In his long career as a mechanic, he had always used revolvers. The brass stayed in the cylinder and could be disposed of later, each casing buried in a different field or tossed into separate storm drains, miles from the hit. But tonight, he wanted the heft and enormous power of the venerable military auto-pistol. As its official designation of "Model 1911" implied, it had a long history, much of it bloody and all of it dependable. As to the ejected brass and evidence issue, the gun might have to go back under the hem of Jesus' robe for a long time. Or, in keeping with the tone of that setting, using a familiar Christian term, an eternity.

From under the kitchen counter, he retrieved a box of thin rubber kitchen gloves and put on a pair. Then he popped the clip, ejected the chambered round, and pushed it back into the magazine before re-inserting it. He wiped it and the remaining cartridges carefully and laid them on the counter. Handling the gun with gloves was a bit cumbersome, but not nearly as inconvenient as riding the needle or, worse, going to prison for a long time. He'd carry a pair of the gloves tonight, he thought, as he gave the gun a final wipe, re-chambered a round, and clicked the safety button.

Checking the time, he took a quick shower and exchanged tailored slacks and silk pullover for cargo pants and a long-sleeved safari shirt. Lightweight desert hikers completed his clothing ensemble, and he plopped down in his recliner to mentally sift through all the variables he could imagine arising at a kidnapping ransom exchange. All the other questions, the tricky matters that would arise later, faded from his consciousness. Right now, Carlton was concentrating on the task at hand.

CHAPTER 6

The call came at 2:05 A.M.

"Where are you?" Tino began by way of greeting.

"I came home and took a shower, changed clothes. But I did get some sleep on the lovely couch," Carlton added, hedging a bit on his recent activities.

"Good. I just got word from Ramos himself. The first rendezvous is going to be at a car wash on the east side of the city. It's next to a little city park, Dorie Miller Park on, uh...Martin Luther King Drive. You need to be there at three o'clock sharp, no sooner, no later."

"Hold on, let me pull up a map." Carlton had already Googled a city map, and he quickly typed in the street name. "Okay, I see it. The park's not far off of I-10."

"I told him you'd be in your blue Cadillac, the same car you were in this afternoon. When you pull into the last wash stall on the right, get out and put enough money into the box to run the car wash for at least five minutes. It's supposed to be an old-school car wash, one that uses quarters. They'll be watching you, timing the wash cycle. Right at the end, you'll get a call on the phone you're using now. They'll send you to the next location."

Carlton waited for the next step. After a pause, he asked, "That's it for now? That's all the info we've got to work with?"

"Yep. Like I said, they want to keep us in the dark, check you for a tail, and give out only the next step, with no time for planning anything on our end."

"Okay, I've got the other burner that I'll have on speaker. When they say the next location, I'll repeat it so you'll know and be able to direct the guys."

"See, I told you that you were the right man for this job," Tino replied. "That's a good idea with the other phone on speaker, even though they're probably aware of that trick. Anyway, repeating the next location aloud shouldn't raise a question, since their guy will undoubtedly have an accent. Repeating it will seem reasonable as long as you just go along with their instructions, get to the next location on time."

Carlton scrambled for a comment to take the conversation another direction. "Okay. Just one other thing," he intoned gravely, waiting a couple of beats for Tino to inquire.

"What?"

"Should I use the spray wax or just the soft rinse on the Caddy?" In his mind, Carlton could see the grimace on Tino's face, the rolling of the eyes. The sarcastic snort in his ear told him he was right.

"Yeah, I can tell you're real nervous about this, my gringo comedian friend," came the caustic reply. After a brief silence he added, "I'll be in your parking lot with the suitcase in about one minute. Try to have another wise-ass joke ready for me, will you?"

Smiling, Carlton printed the area map, used a cloth to pocket the gun, and headed for his car just as Tino pulled into the parking lot. He got out with the suitcase in hand, and Carlton popped the trunk button. Neither man said a word until the trunk lid clicked to lock position. Carlton turned to his companion and saw, to his surprise, an expression of concern he'd not witnessed before on the crime boss' face. "Okay, I guess I'm set," Carlton said lamely, wondering if he should say something reassuring, given this odd switching of roles. An hour earlier, Tino had been the calming one; Carlton on edge and nervous.

"That was the worst joke you've ever had, gringo, but go with the spray wax," Tino quipped, the look of concern replaced by a grin. "Call me and put it on speaker when you get near the car wash. We'll be close by, but not too close."

Carlton didn't reply, but pulled his spare phone out and turned it on. Ten seconds went by without a word between the two before Tino broke the silence. "Good luck, Carlton. *Vaya con Dios*, and bring Paula back. I'm counting on you." His tone said he meant it.

Carlton nodded and got in the car, placing the map on the seat beside him. At least the first stop was easy; if they sent him to another back street in the sprawling city, he'd have to hope the old-fashioned city map in the glove box would suffice. If not, he'd have to deal with the car's GPS and its touchy input screen. He gently gassed the Caddy out of the lot and accelerated toward the north, engine purring and the radio emitting something classical. He was on his own, back in his element, and it felt good to have the powerful vehicle around him.

Earlier in the day, he had checked the car for operation of the lights, brakes, tires, turn signals, and the fuel tank level. Almost full, the way he kept it. Everything was perfect, lessening the possibility of a traffic violation or breakdown at a critical moment. All the precautions borne of habit came into play despite the reliability a relatively new luxury car should have, especially since he routinely checked those items on a weekly basis. It was an obsessive compulsion from days past, unlikely to change.

By 2:39 A.M., he was driving east on IH-10, headed toward the first ordered point. He kept his speed just below the posted limit and arrived at the MLK exit with eight minutes to spare, less time than he'd hoped for. But as soon as he turned left toward the tiny city park, he spotted the car wash on the left side of the street, so he'd be early, just as he wanted. Reaching into his back pocket, he withdrew the gloves and quickly pulled them on. Taking a deep breath, Carlton gave another left turn signal and eased the car up the street, murmuring aloud to himself: *"Okay, this is where I leave the script behind. It's show time, Carlton style."* He reached into his shirt pocket and turned off the spare burner phone.

The clock on the dashboard read 2:56 A.M. Despite the precise instructions, Carlton pulled into the lot and headed around the line of stalls, toward the vacuum cleaners, which were positioned beneath utility poles. Each pole was topped with a trio of floodlights which cast a glare over the entire operation, designed to deter coin machine smashers in this less-than-desirable area. Looping around the machines, he stopped briefly, then drove directly for the nearest stall to his right—the one at the far *left* from the street-side perspective. He got out, fished in his pockets for quarters—and found two, not enough for five minutes. Rather than walk to the change machine, he stalked around the car, feigning irritation, and opened the passenger door. Leaning down in the floorboard, he looked the part of a man searching for loose change. He remained there for about thirty seconds before hearing a car engine, then the voice. Relieved and tense at the same time, he knew his intentional screw-up had thrown Ramos' men off their plan to watch, wait, and make a phone call. They were undoubtedly curious about his mistake, and curiosity...well, *almost* everyone knew what that caused. He forced himself to stay bent over inside the car, butt sticking out, until he heard a voice.

"Hey, pendejo, jew don' know lef from right?" The voice, male and obviously Hispanic, had a jeering tone. *"Jewer in the wrong damn stall, man!"*

Emerging from the car's interior, Carlton blinked and showed confusion on his face, then anger. "It depends on where you start from, dumbass. This stall was on the right when I looped around the vacuum cleaners. Besides, you're supposed to call me on my mobile communication device, aren't you? Not come blowing in here criticizing my sense of directional acumen!"

The barrage of less-than-common English words worked. The man got out of the car and walked toward him a few paces, then stopped, squinting in the glare. He looked about twenty, maybe older, but he had a buzz haircut, not shaved. From Carlton's vantage point, the car wash lights behind him gave him the advantage in vision. Glancing toward the car, a Ford Crown Victoria, he tried to determine how many opponents it held. There appeared to be two men in the back seat, and the driver remained behind the wheel. Next to him in the middle, Paula sat stiffly erect, fear evident in her rigid posture. Something covered her face, a blindfold of sorts, it appeared.

Carlton's heart literally stopped, skipping not one, but several contractions. He took a deep breath to settle down and contemplated how to get Paula safely out of the front seat. He had known this wouldn't be simple, but all four were likely armed to the teeth, so he had to hope for a lot of luck to make his plan work with three of them staying in the car.

Seated next to Paula, the driver was poorly illuminated, and Carlton was unable to determine much about him, but he had the right build for one of the muscular kidnappers. None of the other men had moved, but it was possible they already had weapons drawn, holding them low. Also, the glaring light wouldn't impede their aim; for them, Carlton was a perfect silhouette target.

The first man spoke again. *"Who jew callin' a dumbass?"*

"Some guy who called me a *pendejo.* I think the two words mean about the same."

"Man, jew got some balls on you, gringo! I gonna' kick jewer white ass back to the nort' side." The last statement came out with increased anger and a much heavier accent. He clenched his fists and advanced on Carlton in exaggerated steps, making his threatening statement seem more like a confidence booster than a declaration of intent.

Carlton reached in the left front pocket of his cargo pants and pulled out his billfold. The move stopped the man in his tracks until Carlton called out:

"Hey, I've only got two quarters, and the change machine is out of order. You got change for a couple of singles? My instructions were to wash the car for five minutes."

He made a show of extracting two one-dollar bills and stepping toward the young thug who, now thoroughly confused, still squinted in the harsh glare of the car wash lights. If he wondered why this Anglo was wearing gloves, he didn't ask, but it may have added to his vacillation. His hesitation had the desired effect; the back doors opened and two more men got out, walking toward Carlton with menacing expressions and the same gait.

But the major concern was the driver, who remained behind the wheel with Paula seated next to him, unable to see what was happening. Carlton had little time to act; he'd have to deal with the driver and his near proximity to Paula as best he could—later. For now, it was time to handle the three men approaching him in gangsta-style swagger. The anger building on their faces left little doubt as to their serious intentions, despite their ridiculous baggy-pants walk. Carlton shrugged and put the billfold back in his left pocket, the dollar bills in the right side. The gangbangers continued advancing, spreading out slightly in an arc in front of him, now less than twenty feet away.

When he withdrew his right hand from the roomy pocket, he saw the expression on all three faces undergo a rapid transformation as they realized their error in underestimating this comical Anglo, this bumbling fool who obviously didn't understand how dangerous they were. They reacted quickly, scrambling for their own guns tucked into waistbands under their baggy shirts. But not quickly enough.

Carlton was already pulling the .45 up in the two-handed grip he'd used in his apartment; elbows slightly bent, leaning forward in a crouch. He pulled the trigger smoothly, swinging the gun right to left, never bothering with the sights. Brass cartridges spit from the ejection port onto the concrete, each tinkling sound lost in the roar of the succeeding blast.

The leader and apparent spokesman died first; the other two went down almost simultaneously as the big auto-pistol roared five times in quick succession. Turning quickly to his right, Carlton saw, as he had hoped, the driver abandoning Paula and exiting the car. Carlton stepped forward and shifted his aim while the man was swinging his gun over the roof of the big Crown Vic. The move was professional, offering Carlton little target save his head and arms. The glare shone off his shaved head, and his extended arms clearly displayed the barbed-wire tattoos. Seeing the shining head and tattoos re-focused Carlton's actions, amplifying the calm resolve that emerged in him at such critical times. For an instant, he recalled the thugs pinning his arms, Paula being tossed into the Mercedes, and the blow to the side of his head. He could only hope this one was the culprit who'd given him a headache, but it didn't matter. If it wasn't, he'd get the message anyway.

The shining pate was sufficient target, and when the Colt spoke again, the man's head nearly disappeared as the big slug tore through his face from thirty feet away. The impact drove the man back a few feet, where he tumbled to the pavement. His gun clattered as it struck and skittered across the lot, the racket replaced by eerie silence. The four ransom collectors—rather, collector *wannabes*—never got off a round. Their cocky attitudes, their arrogance upon witnessing an older man appearing to bungle the payoff instructions had cost them their lives.

Carlton dashed to the Ford and leaned forward to grab Paula's wrist. She was already scrambling toward him, and nearly pulled him over as she leapt out of the car and threw her arms toward him clumsily, her lack of eyesight nearly resulting in landing a strong right hook to his face. He ducked, regained his balance, and put an arm around her as he reached for the makeshift blindfold and pulled it off.

"Are you hurt?" he asked, looking her over and realizing as he said it how foolish the question was. Had she been injured to any degree, she would not have been able to exit her captors' car as she had, like an ICBM heading to Moscow, blindfolded or not.

"I've never been so glad to see anyone in my life as I am right now," she said tearfully. "In fact, I'm glad to see anything." As if to prove the point, she grabbed him again and hugged him so tightly he staggered again.

"I'm glad to see you, too, but we've got to get out of here."

The pair dashed for the idling Cadillac. Paula jumped in on the passenger side while Carlton was already pulling the car in gear. As he whipped the wheel to avoid the Ford, he contemplated tossing the Colt toward the three bodies. As always, he hated having *any* gun in his possession, and especially a hot, smoking piece like the one now lying at his feet. Maybe the police would simply label the piece as "found at scene, no prints, sub unknown." But he didn't know where Tino had gotten the gun, and not knowing its provenance, he couldn't take a chance that it could be traced back to a friendly. He'd have to disassemble the gun and toss the pieces over a wide area—still a risk if he didn't find a lake or storm drain—or make a quick diversionary trip by Jesus' place and pray to Him that he didn't get stopped in transit. He tugged off the gloves and shoved them into his back pocket, hoping he could dispose of them quickly. No need to try out the current law theory regarding gunshot residue—GSR—as court-acceptable evidence of having recently shot a weapon.

He retraced his route, accelerating up the on-ramp of IH-10 West, while his other phone began ringing. He didn't have to check to see who was calling.

"Where the hell are you? You okay? Is your other phone on speaker?" The bombardment of questions got a smile from Carlton despite the tension of the moment.

"I'm pulling back onto the ten, I'm okay, and so is Paula. She's sitting beside me. I don't know what happened to that cheap phone. You saw me turn it on, but when I tried to call you, it went haywire."

"What? You've got Paula already? How'd that happen? The exchange was at the first rendezvous?"

"The exchange took place at the car wash, but I used something besides money. It's complicated, Tino. Let's meet and I'll explain everything then. How about the IHOP on thirty-seven south, the New Braunfels exit?"

"Okay, okay. Um…we're headed there now. Do we need the rest of the guys?"

"No, everything's cool. Just tell them it went better than expected and they can go home. You can tell them the entire story later. Look, I got to go, see you in ten."

Carlton snapped his phone shut to avoid any more conversation until he could look Tino in the eye. Then, recalling one of Tino's many questions, he reached into his pocket and turned the spare phone on again. Beside him, Paula was wide-eyed and nervous, literally quaking while gripping his right arm with both hands, as though he might try to escape her grasp.

Carlton reached for her knee and spoke without looking over. "Are you really okay? I know you're shaken up; so am I. But are you hurt?"

"No, no, I'm fine, I really am. Just scared, that's all. Make that *terrified.* It's just that I've never seen…uh, anything…like *that.* And I didn't even *see* it, but I could hear all the talking and then the shooting, it was crazy! What just happened, I mean, was crazy. It was so loud, and I didn't know what to do, how to stay out of the way. I was confused, but when I heard your voice, I almost yelled out for instructions." She took a deep breath, realizing that she was babbling pure nonsense. After a pause, she quietly added: "I didn't know you could do that…what you did. I mean, I know you did things for Big Mo, but I thought it was always one person who got killed, just an assignment for one person. How did you…"

Her voice trailed off, and Carlton almost smiled at her dodging the utterance of truly descriptive words to impart what had occurred. Instead, he looked at the road ahead and spoke quietly to her. "I know, Paula. It's not very pretty watching someone get shot, seeing someone die. But that's what had to happen back there. Tino wanted me to pay the ransom and make the exchange as they demanded, but I thought I might screw that up, regardless of what he thinks my skills are." Turning his head to face her, he added, "So I did it differently. You'll learn more when I discuss it with your brother."

She nodded and remained silent for the rest of the short trip to their destination. Tino's red Ford pickup was already parked near the front door when they arrived. Carlton got out and reached for Paula's hand, helping her out of the car. He noticed she was still shaking as he escorted her to the front door, but her expression was calm, and she ceased clinging to his arm so tightly. As they approached the front door of the restaurant, he guided her ahead of him and discretely dropped the gloves into a trash can.

Tino was already seated in a booth, Raul Vega across from him. Both men's faces betrayed no emotion whatsoever until the pair approached the booth. Tino's look changed to relief, then outright happiness at the sight of Paula; Raul simply nodded at Carlton and raised his eyebrows in questioning. Carlton returned a smile and extended his hand. "How are you, Mr. Vega? And how is Mrs. Vega?"

"We are both well," he replied, his lined face breaking into a grin as he rose to shake hands. "And Caterina asked about you today. She will be glad to hear that you are okay," he added quietly, looking around at the sparsely populated seating area for prying ears. But they had chosen well; the few other patrons were not in hearing distance of their booth, and anyone observing would view the four as friends reuniting for a late—early?—cup of coffee.

Tino rose to give Paula a hug and murmured a few words in her ear. She shook her head, then smiled tentatively and scooted into the booth beside him, while Carlton sat beside the old guerrilla fighter. An awkward silence descended over the table until a tired waitress ambled over and took their order. As she waddled away, Tino leaned over toward Carlton, his usually inscrutable face now awash with animation. Even the veteran Raul cocked his head in the direction of the anticipated story.

"What the hell happened?" Tino hissed. "I kept waiting for the call, checking to see if my phone was on, but didn't hear from you. I waited until three-fifteen to call you."

Carlton resisted the urge to tell him the spray wax took longer than anticipated. Instead, he opened with a question of his own. "Tino, why would a guy like Brujido Ramos send amateurs on such an important job?" He watched closely as Tino processed the remark, but saw only a touch of confusion, quickly replaced by a questioning look.

"What are you talking about? Who did he send? I mean, how many? And how did you determine they were amateurs?"

"Because three of the four were just baggy-pants gangbangers. The fourth guy may have been from this afternoon—make that yesterday afternoon—but he stayed in the car until it was too late to help his buds."

The look on the crime boss' face said he was still confused, but his quick wit covered for him. "So you gave them fashion advice and they gave you Paula? I'm confused here, Carlton! How did the exchange go down? Did you give them the money?"

Carlton started to reply, but Paula interrupted, leaning in toward the center of the table and speaking in a hushed, quavering voice. "He killed all four of them."

The look on Tino's face matched the expression he'd had months before, when Carlton informed him of his plan to blow up his own car—with Tino's hated traitor behind the wheel. While the look didn't tell Carlton all he wanted to know, he felt reasonably sure that his recent assignment had been on the up-and-up, not some cock-eyed test or screwy joke that was intended to leave him in the dark. In his peripheral vision, he could see that even Raul Vega was dumbfounded by Paula's explicit report. The old man's eyes were wide, locked onto Carlton, and he sat stock-still in his seat, clearly measuring the impact of this turn of events.

Finally, Tino was able to speak again. He shook his head and turned his face toward Carlton. "You are a real piece of work, my friend. I don't know how you did it, even if you're right about Ramos sending incompetent guys. Apparently, there's a lot we don't know about Mr. Westerfield."

Carlton shrugged, deciding to keep some of his thoughts to himself for now. "I just prepared for another outcome besides handing over the money to those jackasses just because they said to. If they had come prepared and handled it like pros, I would have followed the script, done what they said. It didn't work out that way."

Tino grinned. "I take it that means you carried a piece and blew away four of Ramos' guys—"

"*Punks*," Carlton interrupted. "The first three out of the car were just *gangster wannabes* with baggy pants. They didn't wait five minutes, and they didn't call me. I felt I had the upper hand as soon as I saw how they reacted to my intentional screw-up. Instead of waiting and watching, they drove up and jumped me for pulling into the wrong car wash stall."

"*Huh?* You mean you didn't pull into the one on the far right?"

"Nope, no way," he said, shaking his head emphatically. "That one had a sign that said the spray wax was out of order."

Dawn hadn't even thought about visiting the eastern horizon when Carlton pulled onto the lot in front of Tino's office. It was the third time for the Caddy in twelve hours; he hoped it was the last for a while.

After talking briefly at the IHOP, the group had broken up; Tino took Paula with him and Vega, while Carlton left for San Fernando Cemetery to re-deposit the gun. Much as he would like to have altered, cleaned, and oiled the weapon first, he couldn't take a chance on keeping the gun in his possession. In fact, he would have preferred to simply dump it in a storm drain, but during the restaurant meeting Tino told him it had belonged to a "friend of a friend" and didn't need to resurface *anywhere*...so, back under Jesus' benevolent gaze it would rest for a long time, probably forever.

Carlton felt a huge weight lifted from him as he pulled back onto the street, minus the gun. By now, the police would have swarmed the car wash; any witness' report of a blue Cadillac being seen in the area around 3:00 A.M. could result in being stopped and searched, even on the other side of the city. And how does one explain a recently fired .45 caliber handgun—oh, and that suitcase with a half million dollars! He'd forgotten about the money and remained nervous until he pulled into the flea market.

As he got out of the car, Carlton's jitters were overcome by fatigue. Except for a few minutes of restless sleep on the old office couch, he hadn't slept in almost twenty-four hours. Combined with being popped on the head and the worry and tension of the night, he was exhausted. He clicked the trunk open and retrieved the suitcase. Staggering alongside Tino's pickup, the office door opened, throwing a shaft of light into the darkened lot and momentarily blinding him. Seeing him squint, Paula pushed the door shut and stepped to take his arm.

"My God, you look beat!"

"Nope, never better. Top of my game," came the tired response. He was glad to hear her giggle at his absurd claim.

Inside, Tino was opening the safe while Raul Vega watched from the ugly couch. "Well, you look like you've had a long night, my friend," Tino observed quickly before returning to the safe combination.

"I've had quieter days and nights. The gun's tucked away, and I thought we should get this back into a safe somewhere. We can re-distribute it later. Right now, I'm beat."

He set the suitcase on the floor as Tino pulled open the old safe door, then reached for the still-full suitcase. He opened it and began removing bundles and placing them back onto the safe's shelf, just where some of it had been only a few hours before. When the suitcase was empty, he shut the safe and spun the lock.

Standing, he spoke quietly, but with the strength and authority Carlton had heard during the shootout crisis. "Tomorrow, I want the whole story, every detail. But right now, let's all go get some sleep. Make that a *lot* of sleep. I'll take Paula over to the Vegas' house. She'll stay there with Raul and Caterina for a couple of days until we see what's going to take place. If you're going back to your place, I'll put a couple of guys over there."

Carlton nodded gratefully. "I wouldn't mind that. I'm going to sleep for as long as I can, so watchers won't hurt my feelings." Glancing at Paula, he sensed that she was on board with the idea. Whether suggested by Tino or not, he didn't know and, right now, was too tired to care. She seemed okay physically, and while he was still concerned about the possibility of mental trauma, he figured their relationship had survived plenty of rough patches in its time; a few nights of separation wouldn't hurt either of them. He reached for her hand and gave it a squeeze, getting a big kiss on the cheek in return.

Suddenly, Tino came around the desk and briefly embraced Carlton. Then he stepped back, clearly embarrassed. "Thank you, my friend. Not only did you get Paula back, you saved me a lot of money, a lot of trouble in the community. Tonight could have gone very badly for us. Instead, it went very badly for Ramos."

Carlton was shocked by the embrace and embarrassed by the words. Both seemed out of character for a drug kingpin who dealt with harsh reality every day of his existence. Despite the inevitable "godfather" comparison, it was the first time Carlton had noticed such emotion from this inscrutable crime boss, and he fumbled for a response. "Yeah, well, some of it was my money. And as for Paula, we're both happy to have her back. Not that she wouldn't have been worth every dime in that suitcase!" he added quickly, drawing a laugh from everyone.

Now it was Paula's turn to be embarrassed. She cleared her throat and addressed the men nervously, wringing her hands as she spoke. "I can never thank both of you—" she turned to include Raul Vega—"*all* of you for saving me. I've never been so scared in my life. I've heard what happens to some kidnap victims, especially women. So please tell everyone that I appreciate them, Tino," she added. "I know all your men were ready to do whatever was needed to get me out of that."

Tino and Raul both murmured something in Spanish, an acknowledgement of her thanks it sounded like. A few seconds of silence set in, and Carlton thought it time to leave. As he headed for the door, Tino thought of something. "Hey, you want a receipt or something for your money that's now sitting in my rusty old safe?"

Carlton laughed. "I don't think that's necessary. I've been driving around with it in my car for hours, so you trusted me with your share. Besides, if we don't trust each other by now, I don't know when we will."

"That's true," Tino admitted. "I told you trust was a big reason I wanted you to make the exchange, remember?"

"Just hang on to it, I might need it. It'll be a while before I can put it back into my private banks."

At that moment, the usually taciturn Raul Vega spoke up, something he rarely did. "Hell, Faustino, he doesn't need a receipt. Who would be foolish enough to deny this *pistolero* entry to the safe? Not me!"

"I agree, old friend. I was just trying to be as business-minded as he is."

Raul wasn't done with his evaluation. "I think you were right earlier; there is more to *Señor* Westerfield than we know. My wife and I discussed it after the night in the restaurant. There was no violence that night; only business, but I think the business of violence suits him better," he declared. Then, turning to Carlton he added, "I wish you had been with me and my wife in our country's struggle for independence. We could have used your skill with a weapon in the old days."

Embarrassed again by the two men's banter, Carlton hedged. "I'm not sure it's a skill. I think tonight was a combination of luck on my part and poor training on the part of Ramos' men. I'm just glad it's over."

"*Por supuesto*, but we will see," came Raul's ominous response before falling into his usual silence.

Carlton, seeing this as his cue, waved and left. Sitting down in the Cadillac, he sighed deeply and stretched his arms before closing the driver's door. Then he rolled his neck and shoulders to alleviate the tightening muscles and reached for the ignition. He was backing out of the lot as the others were exiting Tino's office, the rectangle of light from the door spilling out and silhouetting each of them in turn. He slowed and watched Paula take the two steps down to the parking lot, her slim jean-clad figure accentuated by the light behind her. Even in his state of fatigue, he had to admire her shapely form...something about the scene, alluring as she was, was disturbing to him, but he was too tired to pin down what made it so.

He dropped the Caddy into gear and left the parking lot. Within minutes, he was pulling into his apartment lot. Only ten more minutes passed before he was in bed, asleep, and dreaming of extending his arms and shooting the big Colt .45. Suddenly, to his horror, he noticed his arms were covered in tattoos, a combination of flames and barbed wire. While examining himself, the gunfire continued, and he noticed blood running down his arms, completely engulfing the tattoos in red.

He awoke with a start, sweating and breathing hard. He got up and paced around the apartment, trying to shake off the vivid nightmare. At the same time, he wondered what his fatigued brain was trying to piece together in the free-wheeling state of stage-four sleep. Was it a premonition of what he was facing? Was it a warning to do what he'd intended: get as far from this life as possible? Or was it nothing more than a replay of last night's grisly shootout, with reversed roles?

He was tired to the point of exhaustion, but not sleepy. He sat in front of the television for a half hour, surfing the channels and barely noticing what was on. He finally gave up and headed back to bed, but it was a long time before he went back to sleep.

CHAPTER 7

The next day passed uneventfully for all until late in the afternoon, with the exception of an interesting phone call from Brujido Ramos to Tino Perez. At nine in the morning, Tino's phone rang, indicating the caller was Paula. She'd not mentioned having her phone returned to her, so he assumed the caller to be his rival. Glancing at the screen, he hit "Talk" and spoke evenly.

"You don't even have the decency to return my sister's phone? Are you that hard up for money?"

The response on the other end was also even, but had a decidedly tense edge to it. *"You think you're pretty damn smart, sending an old gringo to fetch su hermana? One that kills four of my helpers instead of handing over the money? I found out who he is, or was, your gringo pistolero, what he did for that fat pawnshop asshole. We shall see how this plays out, pendejo!"*

The rest of the conversation went downhill from there, Perez's voice rising to Ramos' level, asking what the hell he could expect when trying to extort a half million dollars from Faustino Perez, and Ramos' sputtering reply to the effect of "business interests." Perez's response of incredulity to such reasoning was met with a barrage of profanity from Ramos which, was duly met with the same from Perez. All in all, a futile waste of both men's time except to clarify the growing hatred between them.

As he hoped, Carlton managed to sleep for several hours even after the sun rose. Exhausted from her ordeal, Paula did likewise at the Vega household. Meanwhile, Tino showed up around noon at his office and fielded several calls and visits from his men, all inquiring about the previous night's mysterious events, which had culminated in their being dismissed before taking part in any action. Tino could only give them the basics and inform them that a big backlash was likely in the offing, adding instructions to "take special care in your movements and especially those of your families." When he could thoroughly question Carlton, he said, he'd know more about the nature of Ramos' failed kidnapping/ransom plan. That would give him more information on what to expect, he told them. His response was met with varying degrees of curiosity about the actions of the mild-mannered Anglo in their midst.

And though it remained largely unexpressed, there was another common reaction to the boss' news report—a grudging admiration. Tino's entire hand-picked crew consisted of men who were well-versed in the harsh practices of their chosen occupation. They had, to a man, experienced the violence and brutality—along with the rewards—of drug smuggling. In short, they were all tough guys, genuine hard cases when the time came, although much of the time it was hidden under a façade of legitimate work and family life. Understandably, they'd had strong reservations about a single, polite, older Anglo man thrust upon their group—by the Drug Enforcement Agency, no less—as had Tino.

At first, their mistrust had been strong, almost palpable. However, having no say in the matter (and likely upon Tino's order), Carlton was politely tolerated as a fellow worker in the flea market operation, a common laborer not unlike themselves and others in the community during daytime hours. After a while, he even developed a friendship with one of theirs, Mauricio Avila, who was killed in the interstate shootout.

But after the shootout, their attitudes changed. A few of them witnessed first-hand Carlton's assistance on that dark day and during the sad funeral days that followed. They learned more of his clever plan to enable contraband to be hauled undetected while thumbing his nose at the DEA and his part in exposing and eliminating the traitor from their ranks. Carlton Westerfield came to be accepted in the community as a stand-up guy, Anglo or not, who would do his part. Oh, plus, there was the boss' sister who had the hots for him...

But the brief outline they received of last night's ransom exchange surprised the men. A middle-aged man who acted mild-mannered to the point of being meek might be able to bag stiffened, mangled bodies, ferret out a traitor, or build a car bomb, they thought; but shoot down four of their rival gang's members? Recover the crime boss' sister, unharmed? Hold on to all the ransom money? This older *white guy* was edging up there with the likes of Raul Vega! And since it was almost certain that the conflict with Brujido Ramos' bunch was about to explode, they were glad to have both the older men included as friendlies.

Pulling into the lot late in the afternoon, Carlton noticed the Sunday shopping crowd was larger than usual, likely due to the weak cool front that had blown in from the west earlier in the day. The people seemed energized by the weather change, something for which Carlton envied them. He wasn't energized at all; in fact, quite the opposite. Last night's excitement and adrenaline had gone, and even the extra sleep had done little for his mood. Recalling his plan to retire from his dark occupation, last night's events now left him feeling like a recovering alcoholic who had fallen off the wagon. And since Tino hadn't set a specific time for the tell-all meeting, he decided to stall for a while and people-watch. Right now, he just didn't feel like talking, so temporarily boycott the meeting he would. He spent the time contemplating his lot in life.

It was not the taking of four lives that fueled Carlton's malaise; at this moment he did not dwell on commission of an act universally regarded as wrong. That was an area with which he dealt with on an entirely different plane than most human beings. He was an intelligent man, moderately well-educated, and oddly, not entirely lacking in religious upbringing. He knew right from wrong in the Christian sense, as well as from a secular viewpoint. But he had long since compartmentalized his morals—albeit subconsciously—into beliefs and *actions*. Had he been questioned under hypnosis, for instance, he would certainly opine that murder was inherently wrong. But as the moment of action approached which would result in the intentional death of another human, Carlton Westerfield underwent a transformation, one that left him a flawed person who saw, felt, and heard only those movements and thoughts necessary to eliminate the target.

The "moment of action" had been prompted by the lure of money for an entire career; the previous night's murders were prompted by self-preservation and the need to free Paula from her captors (who themselves held no reservations regarding murder) For Carlton, the difference was negligible, even non-existent. He only knew that, when the time came, the decision had already been made in a part of his brain over which he took no conscious control, much as his marksmanship was a result of natural movements rather than a developed skill.

He sat in the car for a while, mulling over his recent past and his possible future, watching as some of the shops began pulling shades and partitions, signaling an end to business. As was customary, most had attended church in the morning before opening around noon, and as sundown approached, evening Mass would call for an abbreviated work day. The exodus occurred quickly, and within a half-hour the place was almost deserted. A line of vehicles stretched across the big parking lot toward the highway as the patrons left for home and church.

Perez's pickup and two other cars were parked in front of his office. Carlton hesitated, almost knocked, then simply pulled the door open and stepped inside. Raul was there, along with a couple of Tino's other men, both of whom Carlton recognized from the interstate shootout. He nodded, raised a hand in greeting, and was met with nods and grins. Tino had apparently told them the story, or what he knew of it. By the expectant look on their faces, everyone in the room looked forward to hearing every detail of the saga.

"You get some sleep?" Tino asked.

"Yes, more than I usually get. And thanks for the watchers. I didn't have to keep one eye open."

Tino dismissed the thanks with a wave of his hand. "Least we could do under the circumstances. You remember David and Enrique," he said, gesturing toward the two additional men who nodded again and murmured greetings.

"Sure I do." He stepped over and shook hands in the traditional Latino manner, a single deliberate down-stroke, rather than several hand pumps used by most Anglos. He recognized David Avila immediately; he was Mauricio's brother. The other man, Enrique, he recalled had also lost a brother—Marty?—in the interstate bloodbath.

Turning back to Tino, he saw a chair had been strategically set for him to address the group. He took his seat and looked over at Raul Vega who was seated on the couch, same as the night before, making Carlton wonder if he had ever left it. Exchanging smiles with the old guerrilla fighter seemed to suffice, so Carlton turned to face Faustino Perez: *patrón*, drug kingpin, Paula's half-brother and, at this moment, a man seeking answers.

"I told the men the basic story, what I know as of now. Please tell us the entire story, exactly what took place from the time you left this parking lot until pulling into the IHOP."

Carlton took a breath and launched his narrative, including every action and detail he could recall, but leaving out for the moment his *reason* for turning off the cell phone which was to have provided a live link to the back-up team. Even with details and asides, the telling didn't take as long as the actual event, short as it had been. When he finished, he raised his hands in a gesture that told the group he was done. He waited expectantly for the inevitable question and wasn't disappointed.

"Why did you turn off the phone without telling me?" Tino's tone wasn't unfriendly or challenging; more curious.

Carlton didn't hesitate. "I felt there was more to the story than I'd been told, for whatever reason. Everything leading up to the ransom exchange was happening so fast, so structured, that I thought I was being played. It seemed too structured, too scripted; if not by you, then by Ramos, or both of you. I couldn't imagine anyone being able to pull your strings that easily."

Tino nodded, but said nothing.

After a moment's silence, Carlton continued. "Is that the way kidnappings work these days, or was it just some circumstances with which I'm not familiar?" He paused, waiting for his words to get a reaction before concluding. "Anyway, I decided to do things my way." Saying this, he held eye contact with Tino, looking for any hint that he was right, but the crime boss' level gaze told him nothing.

Finally, Tino leaned forward in his chair to address Carlton. "Why would you think that?" This time the tone was more than curious; worried, maybe. "What made you think you were being lied to?"

"I'm not sure, but I didn't survive this long by ignoring events around me that make me feel uncomfortable."

Perez nodded in agreement with that explanation. "I can understand that attitude, but I don't know why you would think I would be involved with Ramos or any planned charade to get you into a dangerous situation. As I told you from the beginning, it was just Ramos trying a quick extortion scheme to get money—a lot of money—in short order. In a way, that told me something: that Ramos thinks I'm more successful than I am, that a half million would be chump change to me. Just hand it over, get Paula back safely, and move on until we face each other again. And, that was my thought process, so I guess he played me. Of course, at some point, we're going to war, no question about that after last night's event."

After a brief pause, he went on to recount his earlier phone conversation with Brujido Ramos. "Ramos did some research and found out about your past employment with Big Mo. He's actually pissed that I sent a professional hitter, whom I described as a middle-aged white guy who felt responsible for Paula. He had the gall to be upset at my *misrepresentation*, even though he kidnapped my damned sister! *Can you believe that?* I told you he was nuts! And I told him the same thing!"

Glancing around at the other men, Carlton saw they were entertained by their boss' animated narrative regarding his competitor's warped sense of reasoning. Both David and Enrique laughed and, with typical young men's bravado, offered comments on handling Ramos' attitude. Even Raul sat smiling and shaking his head in disbelief. Carlton grinned but said nothing, hoping his silence would generate something additional.

Instead, Tino changed gears, leading the conversation another direction. "Speaking of your past job, I still want to know how you managed to kill four guys at a car wash, all of them armed, all of them used to violence—even if they weren't very good at it. I didn't think the, uh…*work* you did for Big Mo required such marksmanship. Weren't most of the jobs close-range?"

"Yeah, usually. In fact, I always tried to keep the job as uncomplicated as possible. Research the target's movements, plan for close range encounter, no conversation beyond verifying the target, quick shots, quick exit. There was seldom even a need to aim."

"The hits were point-blank, you mean."

Carlton spread his hands in a "so what?" gesture in acceptance of Tino's observation. "Yes. I didn't get paid extra for long-range shooting." He paused to get Tino's full attention. "But to answer the question you're itching to ask outright, I took a few handgun training courses in the military. My job allowed me opportunity to work with guys who were specialists in that area, so I took advantage of it. I was pretty good at hitting the target, but they kept saying my technique was wrong. They put me back in an ordnance unit, to work on munitions and explosives."

"How the hell can your technique be wrong if you hit the target? Isn't that the bottom line?"

"You don't know the military, Tino. It has to be the Army way, or the Marine way, whatever the training manual says, no more, no less. Training doctrine means more than results, strange as that sounds. But yes, for some reason, I could point and shoot very quickly and accurately. When I did jobs for Big Mo, I didn't see the need to try out my natural…um, *skill*, though. I just did the job and collected my fee. Last night was different. I fell back on my old ability and just hoped I hadn't lost it."

"Four kidnappers dead, and Paula doesn't think they even get off a shot. I guess you haven't lost it." Tino eyed him closely, as though to gauge the remark's impact.

Carlton shrugged. "I guess not. But like I said, a lot of it was luck and poor competition."

Tino seemed to accept that and leaned back in his chair, changing the direction of the meeting once again. "Well, we've got some planning to do. And we've got to change our movements, have full-time protection, and watch where and when we go anywhere. Especially all the women. The wives, kids, anybody that could become a kidnapping target." He gestured toward the other men in the office, the directive aimed at them.

Carlton stirred in his seat. "Exactly what we talked about earlier when you said you didn't want to live like that."

Tino sighed deeply and leaned forward in his chair. "Just because I don't like it doesn't make it go away. *I hate it.* Not only for me, but for everyone else. I've got some family and other, uh…*friends* who don't even live here, but I've got to see to their protection, just in case Ramos can find out about them. It's no way to live. There's not enough reward to live like those big cartel guys with twenty-four hour guards and a lifestyle like a crooked politician."

Carlton couldn't resist trying to put a little levity in the gloomy conversation. "What other kind of politician is there?"

Everyone got a chuckle, and the somber mood lifted a bit. Perez stood and appeared to be preparing an end to the meeting, though Carlton knew better. "David, I want you and Enrique to instruct all the others to watch their movements. No one going anywhere alone, especially the wives and kids. Get Pete, Freddy, and Alberto to take turns at school drop-offs and pickups, starting in the morning. They work for me, so they don't have to arrange anything with their boss about being late.

"I don't think Ramos has that much intel on our local bunch, not yet, at least. But I'm not hopeful that the crazy son of a bitch will forget about us and move on to his next nut-case idea, so we have to be extra careful for at least a couple of weeks, see how this shakes out."

He turned to Carlton. "Better park the Caddy in that garage behind stall eighteen. There's a Mazda pickup in there now. The key's in it. Use it for a while. The Caddy's too well-known, not only by Ramos, but the cops will be scraping the neighborhood over there for anybody who saw something happening at the car wash. Hell, they may stop every blue Cadillac in town."

"That's for certain. I was going to ask for something less attention-grabbing than the Cadillac. What's been said on the news, by the way? I slept late and haven't even turned on the TV."

"There was a piece on KENS 5 noon news. It's being pitched as a gang-related shootout. Apparently, one of the guys had the tattoos, but the others didn't, so they may speculate that the four dead were members of rival gangs. That would be good for us. We don't have any affiliation with any of that gang crap."

"Maybe the paper will have more detail tomorrow. Monday's edition is always thin, needs something to pump it up."

The other men made for the door and Carlton let them pass first, each cautiously exchanging friendly remarks with him. Clearly, he was fully accepted in the group now. Last night's gunfight had elevated his status in the community to a new level, but it wasn't something he was proud of, or even pleased with. He would have preferred not to have been involved in this end of Perez's business. Instead, he wished he still were spending a few hours each day doing grunt work with a cheerful Mauricio Avila—alive and well—not exchanging clever verbal jabs with a brother still grieving his death.

When the other men had filed out, Tino motioned for Carlton to take a seat, something he had expected. "Now that we're talking privately, you care to tell me more about why you thought you were being set up or something?" His voice was less friendly than it had been a few minutes before while making the same inquiry.

"If there were more—now that we're talking privately—I'd tell you, believe me. And if you'll stop and think over the chain of events and the timing, you'll understand why I got such an idea in my head. The entire drama took about ten hours, Tino, from the time they grabbed Paula until we met you at IHOP. Can you sit there and tell me that's a typical timetable from the *grab* to the *payoff* and *exchange*?" Carlton's voice had risen during the statement, and as he cited the three elements at the end, he was clinching his jaw to keep from shouting.

Tino didn't change expressions, but he did put up his hands in mock surrender. "Okay, okay, I get it! Calm down, will you? Alright, I suppose it did happen pretty quickly; bam, bam, bam, now that you point it out. Maybe I was too worried about getting the money together and arranging a successful outcome to notice how everything must have seemed so…" he searched for the right word until Carlton supplied it.

"Choreographed."

"Good choice of a word," he agreed. "It could have seemed like everything was going too smooth, too fast to be real. But that was not the case," he added with a bit more force.

Carlton wasn't done. "And as I said earlier, I don't know how kidnappings are supposed to work. Guess I've seen too many movies where the kidnappers call and tell you the victim will be killed if you call the police. Then they call back and tell you the amount of the ransom. It drags on for days, then the victim's family demands a picture of the victim holding up a current newspaper with the date proving they're still alive. This thing was over almost before it started. Plus, I thought you took his demand a little too easily, but I didn't understand the phone conversation you had with him."

Tino thought for a moment before responding. "Yeah, I countered his initial demand pretty hard, but maybe I let it happen too fast. As to the usual warning about not calling in the police, Ramos knows I wouldn't do that in a hundred years, just as he wouldn't, so he didn't waste time telling me something I already knew. And just like I thought he would, he called soon after the grab with no more than a demand amount, so I judged the best possible outcome was to get Paula back as soon as we could, then figure out how to pay him back. In fact, we're already working on that."

"I assumed so. Raul Vega is bound to be a big help in that area."

"Oh, he is, for sure." Here, Tino paused for a moment before continuing. "And you? Are you on board with helping?"

Carlton fidgeted in his chair, not sure how to answer. He now realized this second part of the meeting—in private— had been planned all along to gauge his willingness to fight in an all-out war between the two San Antonio traffickers. Within seconds, he knew his stalling tactic wouldn't work and he'd have to respond, so he chose his words carefully. "It appears that my performance last night has cemented me into your group, Tino, but I'm not sure how much help I can be. I assure you that last night's outcome was a fluke. Okay, I can shoot a bit, and those guys were overconfident, but the bottom line was still having luck on my side."

Tino was shaking his head while the words hung in the air. "Look, I know you're not the most open person in the world concerning your background, your personal life, and some of your abilities. I respect that, I like it. You know how most of these young Latino guys have that macho chip on their shoulder? I put up with it because it's in their nature, but I don't like it. I like someone a bit more modest."

"I don't know if it's modesty or just wisdom, brought about by age and reality."

Tino waved aside the explanation. "Anyway, in using a weapon, the results are what matter here, not some military training manual. And no matter what you say, the bottom line was taking out four guys who snatched my sister and would have killed her for a song. That's quite a night's work. I need a repeat performance, maybe several of them."

"What about the rest of your staff?" Carlton argued. "They did a helluva job against an air attack, took out two or three of their guys and repelled the chopper. That's the reason y'all were able to survive at all. I'd say they were plenty competent."

"They are, but truthfully we need additional manpower. Besides, you know as well as anyone of our losses that day. I haven't replaced those individuals because I didn't want to recruit other young men from the community so soon. It'd look too mercenary.

"I was serious when I said I'd like to get out of this business, but it's easier said than done. I could recruit any number of young men in a couple of hours. They see the smuggling life as glitzy and glamorous, despite what happened to their friends and relatives. I don't want to get any more of them involved—"

"You just want to keep an *old* guy involved. You remember, I told you I wanted out, too. And I *can* check out *and* leave, no matter what the *Eagles* say."

Tino laughed without humor. "I know. But I'm asking you to stay. I'll pay you well."

The offer surprised Carlton, only because he hadn't really thought about his mechanic services being for sale, not any more. In his current "advisory" capacity, Tino fronted him with little more than walking money. After Big Mo's death and the fiasco with the Drug Enforcement Agency in which they had promised him money to keep tabs on Faustino Perez—and didn't pay him—he'd dismissed the idea of doing others' dirty work for a living. His past life had left him with a tidy nest egg and, combined with doing some honest work, he managed to live as well as he wanted.

But now, confronted with an offer, he was intrigued. He decided to play this one slowly, see what the offer entailed before turning it down. "I don't even know how you pay your other guys. And I don't know if I'm worth more or less, but I wouldn't want to cause a problem with your pay scale just because you think I'm a gunfighter. My work doesn't come with a warranty. I could only guarantee you that I'm your *oldest* gunman."

Tino shrugged and waved away his concerns. "It's none of their business what I pay someone else, just like it's none of your business what I pay them. We can discuss whatever money you think is right. All I can do is say no—or yes. Those years you worked for Randall Morris, he paid you by the job, right?"

"Yes. Some paid more than others, of course. A lot of them were five to twenty grand, my cut, but some commanded more, a lot more."

"I figured. You didn't end up with stashes of money by doing only nickel-and-dime stuff. This could be the same. I'd pay you a regular salary, say a grand a week—cash, of course—and extra for taking out individual members of Ramos' bunch on a job-by-job basis. But those jobs would have to look like random hits that have nothing to do with me or a retaliation for kidnapping Paula. They'd have to look like an old grudge being settled, or a follow-up to a bar fight or a jealous lover reaction."

"Pretty hard to come up with that info and *very* hard to arrange those circumstances, but it could be done. Are you sure Ramos wouldn't see through it, know you're behind his, uh...staff decreases?"

Tino again waved his hand dismissively and continued with his original train of thought. "That would leave him in a weakened position, sort of like I am, with inadequate personnel to do much in the way of conflict. Maybe he'd just stick to running his drug business and stay away from kidnapping, or screwing with us at all."

Carlton tucked the response away and decided not to pursue his concerns out loud. He changed gears. "How do you decide who to take out? You know any of his crew?"

Tino shook his head. "Not personally, and a couple only by reputation, plus Ramos. I'd have to get intel on key members of his staff, and we'd decide beforehand how much the job is worth."

Carlton thought about that. "Using that logic, why not go to the top and kill Brujido Ramos? Or better yet, why not set him up to go to prison for a long time? That way, he's out of business, but our hands stay clean. And you don't risk an all-out war, which is a pissing contest with no winner."

Tino looked at him questioningly. "You think it's impossible for us to win such a pissing contest?"

Carlton shrugged. "I don't know, but I know what they say about pissing contests: 'usually, everyone just gets wet legs.'"

Tino smirked at the gringo saying before asking, "And how might you arrange for Ramos to go away and avoid getting our legs wet, my shifty friend? Or should I ask? You've never failed to come up with some crazy idea and, so far, they've worked…sort of."

"I'm not sure," Carlton answered slowly. "But there's bound to be a way to find out a lot about his organization and use the information to take him off the board. And maybe it could be done without starting a bloodbath."

Tino started warming to the idea. "That would be a major plus, to get him put away, out of business, without getting anyone killed." Then, as if re-thinking it, he sighed and leaned back. "Don't get me wrong Carlton; I'm delighted with the way this worked out, but earlier I was hoping that paying the ransom would give me time to reorganize and gain some competent guys before going to war. Now, in addition to being crazy, he's really pissed, and we may not have much time, unless he finds something else to occupy his mind in the next day or so."

Carlton waited a moment before replying. "Maybe we can help with that. I wonder if my pretty friend at the DEA knows about Ramos' Ford vans with the fat driveshafts, the ones that have a lot of storage room inside."

Tino's face slowly organized into a grin, seeing the possibilities of Carlton's plan unfolding and giving Brujido Ramos a giant headache. "I might be able to get information on the vehicles he's using, but not the times and schedules of his runs. You think the DEA is patient enough to watch him for a while and pop him when the time is right?"

"Oh, yeah, they can be patient; why shouldn't they? They're getting paid whether they're making a bust or making a pot of coffee. Let's just hope Ramos carries on as usual for a couple of days, hauling contraband, and doesn't start something violent with your group right away."

"*Our* group, my gringo business associate who handles a gun very well—without following the training manual."

Carlton smiled grimly. "Okay, *our* group. Anyway, we all have to be extra careful, even though I don't think he'd try another kidnapping in the next day or so, do you?"

Tino shook his head emphatically. "No, not likely. The next time, it will be just as quick, but a lot more deadly than grabbing someone to hold for ransom. They will shoot to kill, no doubt about that. He lost four men last night, and whether they were good or not doesn't matter."

"So you think he's going to try and even the score, man-for-man?"

"Absolutely." Tino stabbed his desktop with an index finger to make his point. "Right now, I'd bet everything I own that he's set on killing four people in our community."

CHAPTER 8

Tino's prediction was right. That night, two men were killed in a drive-by shooting, leaving the bloody retaliation game only half settled. Two members of Perez's crew, Gabriel Fuentes and Tony Esparza, had pulled into a drive-in beer barn just after sundown. As they waited for a break in traffic to pull out of the parking lot, a gray Taurus swept by and blasted Tony's Chevrolet pickup with dozens of shots; handgun, rifle, and even a shotgun blast which took out the windshield and Tony's head. Gabriel "Gabe" Fuentes lived long enough to give police a description of the car, then died en route to the hospital.

Also predictable, Faustino Perez was livid. He raged and stomped around his small office while Carlton and Raul sat quietly, waiting for the storm to subside sufficiently to hear what he deemed a proper response. Listening to him bellow, Carlton figured nothing less than a platoon of storm troopers converging on Ramos' headquarters would satisfy the crime boss.

The tiniest of blessings was the familial status of the two slain men. Both Gabriel and Tony were bachelors, young men in their early twenties who had performed some work for Perez in the past. It wasn't yet clear how Ramos' group had made the connection or how they had gotten the intel to locate and follow them to the beer barn, but Tino's attention turned to that matter after ten minutes of raving about the event itself.

"That son of a bitch found out about Gabe and Tony working for me, but I'm damned if I know how. Their parents live in El Paso. The guys moved here about six months ago and worked in the tire shop and the muffler shop. They went along on a couple of runs to Laredo after the shootout because I needed some backup. They weren't given any details so they couldn't break under pressure if they were apprehended at the customs inspection station, but they must have babbled about the Laredo runs to someone with connections to Ramos. Either pillow talk or drunk talk. Both will get a man killed."

Carlton and Raul both simply nodded at the explanation. It made perfect sense, hiring the men and using them in a limited capacity, something Tino would have done while short-handed. The only good news for him was not having to face an anguished *local* family, especially wives and children. Of course, Tino would still pay respects (and some compensation) to the families in El Paso, but at least the local community wouldn't have two more funerals of their own loved ones to attend.

Another easy prediction was the splash on the front page of the newspaper. A total of six dead by violence in one weekend was a huge story, even in a big city. The articles combined the two shootings, and speculation abounded regarding a connection between the victims and the shootings. Carlton passed the paper over to Raul and remained leaning forward as Tino wound down his tirade.

"You think putting the bug in DEA's ear will help any?" he asked during a break in Tino's verbal onslaught.

"Shit! I don't know, but how can it hurt? When it got down to it, I would have probably used Gabe and Tony in a hit against Ramos' bunch. Not that I don't—*didn't*—value them, but no wives or kids is a definite plus when it's going to get bad. Now, those two with almost zero connection have been killed, and recruitment will be harder than ever, at least for guys I'd want to depend on. It's easy to get tattooed boneheads anytime; they think they're bullet-proof, so they sign up for anything. But real help is hard to get."

Seeing a chance to escape Tino's renewed rage, Carlton pulled his billfold out and searched for the scrap of paper with Heather Colson's encoded private burner number, the number she had given him months before, during his supposed "employment" with her agency. Soon after, he'd had a couple of private talks with her about her immediate supervisor and his inexplicable hatred for Carlton, which trickled down on his subordinates. The conversations had provided a basis for an uneasy but useful coalition, and Carlton hoped to use the connection to stir up trouble for Ramos.

"Hello?"

"Agent Colson? Hi, it's Carlton Westerfield."

Silence met his introduction for a few seconds. Then, *"Well, hello there,*

Mr. Westerfield. I see you've lost another phone, since I didn't recognize the number. And what mischief are you up to these days?"

"Same as always, I'm afraid; not much at all. I'd like to have a conversation with you regarding changing that. Is this a good time for you?"

"Good as any. Are you going to report on your old bud, Faustino Perez? He's still spreading snow on the streets, isn't he?"

"I don't know anything about what he's spreading, but I'll bet it doesn't smell as bad as what your boss was spreading a while back." Again he waited for her response, not wanting to let her know that he was even aware of Tim Hunnicutt's violent demise. As he figured, she knew better.

"You're perfectly aware that he's not spreading anything these days, unless he's spreading his wings in heaven—"

"Really? Well, given his personality, I doubt that's happening. But that means he's working at that Big Agency in the Sky? With his attitude, I can't say I'm surprised, but I didn't know he'd moved on. I'll bet he can't call himself Agent-in-Charge while he's there. I hear Someone else has that title."

On the other end, he heard Heather stifle a giggle before reverting to her stern agency voice. *"You know damn well he died in a car explosion along with another shady character in Perez's employ. Somehow, explosions seem to happen around you pretty often, Westerfield. Ever notice that?"*

"Nope, I haven't."

"Well, the Agency has. And you'll screw up one day, trust me."

"Not a chance of my trusting you. In the first place, you're too pretty. Secondly, you work for the government. Third, I—"

"Save it, Mr. Smooth. Just tell me what you're calling about, even if it's not your personal snowman, Mr. Perez."

"Forget Perez. He's not even in the drug business, and you know it. You tried for months, but couldn't get anything to stick. But I've run across some info on another guy who's a regular blizzard. And I know how he's getting it across and into our fair city." Carlton paused to gauge the impact of his words, waiting to see how long the pretty DEA agent would wait before nibbling at the hook. He judged it to be about four seconds before she couldn't contain herself.

"Oh, so you're a weather prognosticator now! How lovely! Well, tell me more. Maybe you can finally give us some intel that we can put to good use."

"And maybe you can finally get me paid with some money that I can put to good use. I'd really like to collect what I was promised, you know," he countered, ribbing her about the money he'd been promised to keep tabs on Perez—but never received.

"Paid informants need to produce good stuff these days. I'll need some product that results in arrests and convictions, not a rumor about some slimeball taking a leak in public or your boss being nominated for Citizen of the Year."

"Look, let's get this straight: I don't hang around slimeballs, I don't have a boss, and I've never even seen the snowman I'm talking about. But the intel is worthwhile; it's timely and accurate—

"Really? You mind telling me how you happened to come on to this earth-shaking info? And why?"

"How? By keeping my ears open and my mouth shut. As to the 'why,' you told me before that information would be worth some money, but Perez was never involved, at least that I could see. So now that I have information on a real *drug dealer, does your agency want it, or do y'all want to keep on sitting on your government butts, drawing a paycheck without doing jack? In other words, business as usual."*

"Screw you, Carlton!"

"How about the horse I rode in on?"

"Huh? Look, cut the crap and tell me, okay?"

"You ever heard of Brujido Ramos?"

"Yes. A competitor of your buddy Perez. Mid-level, lots of street-action distribution. But he likes the outskirts better than inner city. He's been the main supplier in Lytle and Somerset, plus he's now out in Elmendorf and China Grove area."

"Whoa, ho ho, are you talking about China Grove? That one?"

"Okay, Doobie Boy Carlton, I get it. Anyway, what about him?"

Surprised that she had made the connection with his dated pop culture reference, Carlton told her. *"Driveshafts. The dope's being carried in the driveshafts of Ramos' delivery vans."*

The remark was met with silence, about another five seconds worth. *"Oh, yeah? How informative! And just what is a driveshaft?"*

He proceeded to give the agent a quick lesson in automotive construction. After a few minutes in which he heard the scratching of a pen on paper, she asked if he could get details on the mysterious delivery vans with some "hollow shaft contraption" underneath. He assured her that would be possible, but not immediately. Following a few more verbal jabs—mostly friendly—the conversation ended with a promise to call as soon as he could pinpoint a specific vehicle and possibly, a date for a trip with contraband aboard.

Carlton looked across at Tino, who had sat quietly during the phone call listening to Carlton's side. "She sounded interested, but like all government employees, she wants someone else to do most of the hard work. As soon as we can get a firm vehicle description and a possible date or dates, I'll call her back."

"What did she say about paying you for the information? Same as before?"

"Probably, but I played that up as a reason for doing this. Don't want her thinking I'm involved except for needing a paycheck. And she's bound to know that I'll be pretty stingy the next time I call; I'll try to hold out on the good stuff until she commits to pay me, whether she really intends to or not. And if I can supply her with good intel, she may actually initiate a bust without trying to figure out what I'm up to, or that I'm connected to you in any way."

Tino nodded, agreeing with Carlton that it made sense to offer information for money and try to recover some of what he'd been promised before, but never received. Both figured Heather Colson may not be the most experienced agent in the shop, but she was smart enough to know Carlton wouldn't call and offer information simply from a sense of civic duty. Tino looked at Carlton and voiced his own plan. "Okay, I'll put a couple of guys on getting the exact vehicle information. Maybe they can stake out the vans, see if they see any movements that look like they're being loaded with money for a run."

"Good. And I want to talk with Paula about her stay in the enemy camp. If she can remember how long the drive was to the car wash, maybe we can get a handle on where Ramos' operation is."

Tino shook his head. "She said they kept her blindfolded the entire time. The first time she saw anything was when you pulled her out of the car. She said she was scared out of her mind, so I wouldn't count on her being able to recall much."

Carlton thought about it for a moment. "Still, I want to give it a shot. Now that I've got that Mazda pickup, we can go undercover and just check out the area where they held her." He didn't want to reveal exactly what he had in mind and hoped Tino wouldn't want details about his upcoming plans, but the crime boss' response blew away that prospect.

"The pickup is better for that than your flashy car, but I wouldn't push it. Where are you thinking about doing this undercover work?" Tino asked while making quotation marks on his last two words, his expression clearly conveying his suspicions regarding Carlton's use of the plural pronoun 'we.' "You're not thinking about hauling Paula over to the east side and trolling that neighborhood near Dorie Miller Park, are you? That wouldn't be very smart."

Carlton silently cursed himself, wishing he'd not disclosed so much. Instead of responding to Tino's observations, he turned to Raul, who had been sitting quietly, listening to the phone call and the discussion between Carlton and Tino. "Is Paula with Caterina today?"

"I think so. You want me to call Caterina? I think they were going to get Paula another phone today."

"Please, Mr. Vega. And if Caterina would bring her over here when they're through phone-shopping, I'd appreciate it."

Raul reached for his phone, and Carlton turned back to Tino. "I'll be careful, a lot more careful than the last time I took her somewhere. I can't imagine any of Ramos' bunch watching closely for me to show up in their territory. Besides, it may not be their territory; maybe they just used it for the first meeting place. Why would anybody pull off a ransom meeting in their own backyard?"

"With Ramos, who knows? We're all agreed that this entire mess was a stupid idea on his part, but that didn't stop him." Tino paused for a minute, apparently reconsidering and recalling that Carlton had indeed come up with good ideas in the past. "But if you think we really need to check out that neighborhood, I can send a couple of young guys over there to look around."

"Young guys like Gabe and Tony? It didn't work out too well for them, and they weren't even in that part of the city. Like you said, they probably just talked to the wrong people, drinking and bragging about working for Faustino Perez. It cost them their lives."

"My point exactly. I don't think it's a good idea to risk *anyone* else, but certainly not you."

Carlton couldn't argue with that, but he had one more card to play, one he hoped would point out an obvious advantage to his checking out the neighborhood instead of sending any of Tino's younger employees. "Look, Tino, you're knowledgeable about this stuff, and I'll do what you say on this. But no one over there will recognize me, because the last time I talked to any of Ramos' bunch, they were pretty quiet by the time our conversation was over."

Tino scowled, but offered no further advice; nor did he question why Carlton would pursue such an avenue if he really doubted Ramos was based in that particular east side neighborhood. As for Carlton, he figured the crime boss was simply in a foul mood; therefore, it would be best just to escape his wrath, even if it meant leaving poor Raul with him to suffer another rant about the previous night's tragic event.

Caterina and Paula showed up within the hour. It was the first time she and Carlton had seen each other since leaving the market before dawn on Sunday, and Carlton was surprised when he realized it was now only Monday afternoon. He wondered about his feelings, but pushed it aside as simply too much happening in too little time.

Giving her a hug, he was quick to exploit the time-warp feeling. "Seems like I haven't seen you in days. How are you feeling? Oh, and how are you Mrs. Vega? Thank you for bringing Paula over here."

Caterina acknowledged his thanks with a big smile, and headed into the office. Paula fielded his concern with a roll of her eyes, something Carlton was now beginning to see as a family trait. "Well, I'm glad you missed me, but it's only been yesterday, smooth talker," she said, returning his hug. "But that's okay, keep telling me that," she added, giving him her own trademark smile.

Carlton took her hand and led her for a stroll through the stall area, waiting a few minutes before beginning. "Look, I wanted to ask you about your time with those thugs, see if you can recall anything that might be helpful in locating their headquarters. You feel up to it?"

She stopped in her tracks, and The Smile was replaced with the cloudy look women reserve for entry into any forbidden conversation. "I was so scared, I don't know if I can be much help. And I was blindfolded right after they threw me into the car."

"Yeah, I know, but I was hoping you might remember how long the ride was from where you were held until you got to the car wash."

"Car wash?" Her blank look told him that she'd not even realized where the shootout had taken place.

"Yes, that's where it all ended. I pulled you out of their car at a car wash on the southeast side of town." Seeing the worried look increase he added, "Sorry, I didn't mean to bring up a bad subject, but I was hoping you might be able to help pinpoint where they held you by judging the time it took to get there."

Her face brightened. "Oh, it doesn't bother me to talk about it. I just feel bad because I was so helpless then, and I'm not doing much better now." She paused for a moment, thinking. "We weren't in the car very long, I know that. I'd been kept in a house, I know that much. It was old, I think; you know how old houses smell. Not bad, just...*old.* And the door creaked, I think it was an old-type screen door, you know, the wooden ones?"

Carlton did, and he nodded but kept quiet, hoping her jaunt down memory lane would reveal something more. He wasn't disappointed.

"Oh, and I don't think there was any furniture, because it had that empty sound, hollow. And they led me into a back room where I was told to sit down. I didn't know where they meant for me to sit—remember, I was blindfolded—but one of them shoved me down, and I ended up on the floor. I scooted away from him and backed up to a wall. I didn't run into any furniture..." Her voice trailed off and she spread her hands to indicate an end to her recollection of the inside of the house.

"Sounds like you got it right. An older, smaller house would sound hollow like that with no furniture or carpets. And the "old house" smell is standard, too."

"That's about all I can remember about the house. I wish I could help more. Everyone did so much to get me out, and now I can't give you any help at all," she said, her voice quavering.

Carlton put his arm around her and squeezed. "Don't worry about that. Besides, what you just said gives me something to go on."

They resumed their stroll through the market, Carlton waiting a few minutes before trying again. "So you were kept there the entire time, from Saturday evening until about three o'clock Sunday morning?" he asked, not wanting to push too hard, but trying to move the story along while she was replaying the event in her mind.

"Yes, we didn't leave there until they came and got me to go...uh, to the car wash, I guess. But they brought my phone back to me when they had Tino on the line. The rest of the time, they stayed in another room. They were talking and laughing, and I think I heard cards being shuffled, but I'm not sure."

"Okay, Paula, try to remember this part: How long was the trip from when they put you in the car until they pulled into the car wash and opened the doors, when that first guy got out?"

She thought about it for a moment. "It wasn't long at all, maybe five minutes? God, I'm so sorry, Carlton. I just can't judge time like that. Maybe it was seven or eight minutes..."

Her voice trailed off again, and then Carlton heard her sniffle. Clearly, revisiting the horrifying event was tough, and he hurried to ease her distress at not being able to pinpoint details. "Hey, it's okay! Look, everything you've said is helpful. You're doing great. I know you were blindfolded, and that's incredibly disorienting, would be for anyone, man or woman, no matter how tough they were. That's why victims are always blindfolded, it ruins your sense of time and space. Although those jackasses didn't *know* that, they just saw it in a movie," he added.

That got a small laugh from her, and the weeping spell was broken. "I'll try to remember the blindfold trick next time you stay with me. I've never seen you disoriented or even shaken up."

"Careful—I might be so disoriented that I don't know whose house I'm in," Carlton replied, putting one hand over his eyes and reaching out with his free hand. "Carol, is that you? Oh, it's Michelle! How silly of me! I should have known the feel of those puppy dogs!" His free hand was now obscenely fondling imaginary "puppies," resulting in a swift punch in the ribs from Paula. Carlton flinched, but the pain was worth it; she recovered from her funk, and they continued walking a big loop until arriving back in front of the office.

He turned to her and placed his hands on her arms. "Paula, that was a big help, believe me. Your brother and Raul are doing the big-picture planning, but I'm trying to get a handle on where their operation might be located. What you remembered will be a big help."

"Are you going back over there?" she asked, the Worried Look returning.

"Yep. With the information you gave me, I'll try to find vacant houses within a five or ten minute drive of the car wash. All the houses are likely to be older ones, but vacant ones should narrow it down. Can you remember anything else that might be of use?"

She thought for a long moment, then looked up sharply, her big eyes even bigger with a welcome mental connection. "I heard bells, school bells! You know, the ones that ring at the beginning and end of classes."

Carlton looked confused. "Paula, it was Saturday night, Sunday morning. There's no school at those hours."

"Silly! The bells ring anyway, twice every hour; a short one to end class and the longer one to signal tardy about ten minutes later. That pattern was how I knew it was a school bell. They're set to some kind of timer, I guess. We used to play on a school playground on weekends, and I remember the bells rang twice every hour or so, just like when class is going on."

Carlton was pleased with the news. "I didn't know schools still had those, but that's an old neighborhood over there. Why wouldn't they? Paula, that's great information! I can find all the schools that are ten minutes or so from the car wash and narrow the search down to vacant houses near them."

The look on Paula's face said she was even happier. "I'm glad I was able to come up with something good. There can't be that many schools located within ten minutes, right?"

"Who knows? I didn't even know school bells sounded after hours. When

I was a kid, the last bell was the signal for me to leave and not return until absolutely necessary."

"Well, is it absolutely necessary for you to go back over there? I mean, if that is their base of operations or whatever, they might see you driving around. They can't be very happy with you, so that might be a bad idea right now."

"You sound like your brother. He's got his panties in a wad about my plan, but I'm going to be extra careful. I'll wear sunglasses and a golf cap."

That got a smile, and he wondered if the silly line would work on Tino, change his foul mood a bit. He was considering the thought when the office door opened and Tino, Raul, and Caterina emerged. The earlier scowl had been replaced with his moderate frown and the Vegas seemed placid, so he took that as a good sign. Paula joined Caterina, and the two women began talking as though they'd not seen each other for months, while Raul and Tino sauntered over to Carlton.

"You still got that crazy idea of going over there for *undercover work*?" Tino asked, putting sarcastic emphasis on the last two words.

Clearly, his mood wasn't that improved, Carlton thought. "Yes. Paula was able to recall some good information. But I'll be extra careful, I assure you. I'll try to blend in. I might even put one of those magnetic signs on the door of the Mazda pickup. One that says "Lefty's Plumbing."

Surprisingly, Tino broke into a grin, but not at Carlton's clever remark, not directly anyway. "That's a good idea. But it's going to be 'Medina's Plumbing.'"

Carlton looked at him questioningly. "Oh? Why?"

"I've already got a sign like that. It's leaning against the wall in the garage, right in front of the Mazda pickup. It's the same pickup Manny Medina used in his plumbing business. And I still don't think it's very smart to go over there poking around."

Carlton had to laugh at the irony as he beckoned for the two men to come closer, out of earshot of Paula and Caterina. "Well, you know what they say about plumbers; like me, they may not seem that smart, but they know three things for sure."

The expectant look on Tino's face was matched by the one on Raul Vega's. "Okay, I can't wait for this bit of gringo wisdom."

"Crap runs downhill, payday's on Friday, and the boss is a sonuvabitch."

Raul Vega laughed out loud, and even Perez, shaking his head, had to grin.

CHAPTER 9

Carlton waited until the next day, Tuesday, to cruise the neighborhood around Dorie Miller Park. As he had determined from a city map, the area he wanted to study was squeezed between IH-10 to the south and East Houston Street to the north. He exited on MLK and turned left under the freeway, then drove the three blocks toward the car wash. Barriers stood at the left end of the parking lot, still holding streamers of yellow crime-scene tape flapping in the breeze. He slowed, but barely glanced over, then pulled away to check out the rest of the area.

Daytime hadn't improved the neighborhood's appearance. Just like during his quick nighttime evaluation, the old neighborhood was quiet and shabby, comprised of short, narrow streets, with a couple of longer east-west thoroughfares heading toward downtown. The houses were old, and most of them looked worn-out, with peeling paint, broken windows, and sagging doors. However, a few tidy dwellings were scattered among them, their owners' pride and determination evident in their appearance. The smattering of neighborhood churches, mostly Baptist, would be the Sunday hangout for those residents, he thought. Some decent homeowners were clearly fighting a losing battle here in this ghetto.

Driving around the car wash's immediate vicinity, he realized that Paula could have been describing almost any of the houses, since most of them looked old and empty. He noticed a small school building immediately, but it was located almost within sight, not a five or ten minute drive away; more like one minute or maybe two. The little school shared the run-down look of its neighbors—well past its prime.

Branching out to the north, away from IH-10, the houses improved, but not much. Cruising along in the drab little pickup, he looped farther away from the car wash, making big rectangles and looking for a school located five to ten minutes' drive away. After forty-five minutes of driving around and making a show of checking addresses as though scouting for Medina Plumbing's next job, he was ready to call it quits. Nothing looked promising, with too many of the houses looking vacant or simply trashed beyond livability. Still, any of them would have made a decent place to hold a kidnap victim, but there were too many to narrow down the search. He decided to give it fifteen more minutes before throwing in the towel.

Taking the next street to the north, he went two blocks, then turned left onto Houston Street. He spotted one small school, an elementary level by the looks of the playground equipment, and another larger facility only three blocks from it. Using Paula's information, he had to assume both were good candidates for housing the class bells she heard while in captivity. He made his way back toward the car wash, but took a wrong turn and had to go around a long block to correct his course. Even so, it took only nine minutes to make the drive, well within her admittedly wide time frame. Carlton began to feel better about his task, mentally thanking Paula for her audio-observational powers.

He returned to the schools and started looking for vacant houses, but as with the rest of the area, there were too many to determine in which one she might have been held. In all, he spotted eight possibles, three of those very near one of the schools, surely within hearing distance of ringing class bells. One had a For Sale sign in the yard. He took down the address and realtor's number and headed back toward the interstate.

On the way, he realized that he had not seen a single car or individual who looked like they might be a part of a successful drug-running operation. In fact, it didn't even look like an area where drugs are prevalent—no young, militant-looking thugs with baggy pants, no used-up hookers standing outside dank beer joints, and no jacked-up, "big heavies" on twenty-two inch wheels. Instead, the entire area was occupied by older people, predominately Black or Hispanic, who looked retired—and tired—or simply poor and unemployed, shabby as the houses. The cars—few of which appeared to be in running order—were old and dilapidated. In summary, he thought the house used for holding Paula was a one-time, temporary base, used only for that phase of Ramos' recent ill-fated operation. It seemed highly unlikely that Ramos used the gritty old neighborhood for anything except a holding pen for his kidnap victim and a place to arrange the first ransom exchange meeting at the nearby car wash. Discouraged, he turned right onto the IH-10 on-ramp and headed west toward his apartment.

"What did you find out?" The question was posed by Tino Perez as he leaned back in the chair behind his battered desk. It was Wednesday afternoon, and Tino had insisted that Carlton come by and deliver his report after Tino had spent two days making arrangements to ship Gabe and Tony's bodies back to El Paso for burial.

"Nothing useful, I'm afraid," Carlton replied from his usual spot in the straight-backed wooden contraption that passed for a chair, across from Perez. "I didn't even scare up any plumbing business, although every house there looked like it had a problem somewhere." He went on to describe the neighborhood structures and general atmosphere, crediting Paula with good information, but citing too many possibilities to nail down a particular house.

"Sounds like Ramos could have picked almost anywhere to serve his purposes the other night, but he happened to choose that one. It's almost certainly not his usual base of operations. And from what you're saying, it was a smart move, intended or not. Like trying to find a needle in a haystack made of needles."

"That's about right. You learn anything yet on Ramos' delivery vans?"

"Arturo Matamoros thinks he's spotted a common theme in his vans, they're all white Fords with metal grill-work to protect the windows. Plus, he took down four different license plate numbers, and three of them are consecutive, like they were titled or registered at the same window. The other one was only five digits off, indicating it was done at the adjacent window at the tax office. Of course, that's not iron-clad proof, but it's a good indication that he bought all four at the same time, went to the tax office with the title work and did it all the same day."

Carlton nodded at the logic. "That sounds right to me, from what I recall about doing car paperwork for the rental agency I worked for. Can we tell if those four are his only delivery vans? And what does he deliver, anyway?"

Tino laughed. "Well-diluted cocaine, usually. But between drug trafficking gigs, his men do hotshot delivery for a couple of car parts warehouses. Arturo said he followed one to several stops at garages and mechanic shops. The driver got out and took parts inside each place. When he followed the guy back to the warehouse, he spotted another one of them. Same as the first one, it made several stops delivering car parts, then headed back to the base warehouse. Arturo stayed at it all day; that's how he ended up with four license plates."

"Arturo must be a patient guy," Carlton said. "I think he did a good job, and I think his evaluation is correct. That arrangement gives them a good reason to be driving all over the city with boxes of stuff stacked in the back. Very common to be loading and unloading all day long, lots of stops, lots of back-tracking. It would seem like aimless driving around to anyone trying to stake them out."

"Yep. I told Arturo to take a day off, gave him a hundred bucks to take his wife for a nice lunch somewhere."

"He deserved it. That information gives us something to give to Heather Colson. She can run checks on the vehicles while Arturo is keeping tabs to see if he can pinpoint one of them preparing for hauling something besides car fenders."

"Yeah, but that might take a while, depending on Ramos' buying schedule."

"Well, what do you think, call her now, and give her something to whet her appetite, or wait until we see if Arturo can get more?"

Tino thought for a moment before responding. "I'm going to have Arturo see if he can spot any other vans. I'll put him back on it tomorrow. Meanwhile, it's a good idea to give the DEA something to do and hope they give Ramos something to worry about."

Carlton pulled yet a different burner phone from his pocket and dialed Heather's number, knowing he'd catch her off guard for a moment when she didn't recognize the number; plus, he could barely wait to get an earful over his constantly changing phones. He wasn't disappointed on either count.

"Hello? Who is this?" The irritation in her voice came through loud and clear.

"Agent Colson, this is Carlton Westerfield. How are you today?" Carlton carefully modulated his voice to project the epitome of courtesy and pleasantness.

"Oh, crap! I should have known when I saw another number I didn't recognize that it would be you. Not that many people have this number, and you change phones like most people change socks. What the hell is it with you and phones, Carlton?"

"I seem to have incredibly bad luck in hanging on to them."

"Sure you do," she responded in a tone that said she saw through his

bald-faced lie. *"I hope you don't have this number programmed into them before you leave them on the sidewalk in front of the homeless shelter."*

"Not to worry, Ms. Colson. I don't program anyone's number into my phone. That could create a real hardship for someone," he assured her in his most solemn tone. In fact, he memorized the numbers he needed often. Others he kept in a carefully coded written form on scraps of paper; to an observer, they would mean nothing. Additionally, he deleted every call and text from the log as soon as he was finished talking or texting. Therefore, in case a phone fell into the wrong hands, little information could be extracted from it. While he had only seen programmed phone numbers cause trouble in the movies, it seemed a sound practice. Amazingly, the movie hero always knew exactly how to ferret out the villain's contact with evil doers from a phone he'd never seen, much less used. Another misconception peddled by popular culture, Carlton thought.

However, Carlton *had* programmed the DEA's local tip-line number into a phone a few months prior and given it to a drunken man under an IH-35 overpass, telling him the number could be used to order free wine. Furthermore, he had warned the man to continue calling with his request, since the "free wine distributor" was extremely busy and forgetful.

Heather's response to his assurances sounded like something between a snort of derision and the I-35 wino clearing his throat. It was hard to attribute the ugly sound to the attractive woman on the other end. She sighed loudly before continuing. *"Okay, Carlton, what do you have for me? Something we can use, I hope."*

"Absolutely. I have license plate numbers and descriptions for four of the delivery vans Brujido Ramos uses."

"Are they registered to him?"

"No, I think they're registered under his company name: Ramos' Drug Smuggling and Trafficking, Inc."

"Okay, wiseass, I just wondered how you know they're his."

"I didn't say they were; I said he uses them. I truly doubt they're in any name that could be traced to him very easily. Probably in the name of...um, what's that legal term? A shell company? Anyway, if you want the plate numbers, I'll give them to you, and you can waste all the taxpayer money you want tracking them down. Alternatively, you can check them out at the auto parts warehouse where they make hotshot parts deliveries in their spare time. Sooner or later, all of them are used to import contraband hidden in the driveshafts."

"Sooner or later?"

"Yes, one of those time frames, I'm certain of it." Carlton was enjoying himself now, between listening to Heather and watching Tino's face across the desk.

"Damn you, Westerfield! I wish I'd never given you this number! Just call in your crappy tips to the DEA tip hotline like every other mutt in this town, will you?"

Carlton could imagine her face turning red with anger over his wordplay and thought she was going to hang up. He struggled to come up with something to keep her on, and thought of her clever ploy to get his phone number months before. *"Now, what if I'd not given you my phone that day in Galveston? You used me to get my number, didn't you? And look what our relationship has become since that lovely, memorable day!"*

Another snort, this one prettier, sounding like it was tempered by an embarrassed smile. *"Okay, wise guy. Seriously, does that mean you don't know when, or can you find out? Or what?"*

"Seriously, I hope I can find out, but it may take some time. Meanwhile, your agency has the resources to watch the vehicles, check out the ownership, all the things that you law enforcement types do, right? I just wanted you to know I'm thinking of you, that's all."

"Yeah, right. Well, think about me again when you come up with a timeline for this to go down. That's when I'll tell my boss and we'll set up something."

"You get a new boss? Hope he's more personable than the old one."

"Yep. His name is Stanley Ikos, just transferred here from the Minneapolis office. He's a hardass, but not too bad on the worker bees."

"A hardass on crime, then."

"You're pretty quick on the uptake for an old geezer, Carlton."

"Yep, a mind like a steel trap. Do I get to meet Agent—what's his name? Ikos? Is he going to see that I get paid for my hot tip?"

"Maybe. It depends on how hot your tip turns out to be. Just find out when Ramos is going for a buy, and I'll discuss it with Ikos. I recommend that you come up with more information than last time."

"I recommend it be handled more generously than last time."

"I'll take your recommendation under consideration. You going to give me those plate numbers?"

Carlton recited the plate numbers and the warehouse address, then hung up before he thought of another clever (and useless) remark with which to needle Agent Heather Colson. He didn't expect to be paid as an informer, but keeping the money motive clear in her mind wouldn't hurt. He wondered briefly why she hadn't seemed more excited to get the plate numbers for a known drug smuggler—until he remembered that she got paid whether she made a bust or not.

Upon reflection, her carefree, non-committal attitude shouldn't have surprised him; it was a standard ploy for all government agencies. He knew that calling the IRS with the simplest of questions resulted in dodgy, non-specific answers, like "page 104 of publication 1610 lists all instances whereby a taxpayer may claim a Burmese python as a seeing-eye companion, but for vision-impaired taxpayers, (except herpetologists) it would be page 18 of publication 458."

He shook his head and looked to Tino in frustration. "Hope they don't hurt themselves jumping into action so quickly."

Tino shrugged. "You gave them all we have for the moment. And I'll bet she is already checking the plate numbers. She just doesn't want to seem excited, or you'll start thinking your information is worth a lot."

Carlton laughed. "Maybe so. Anyway, if they check out the ownership of those vans, maybe something will wave a red flag. It'd be great if they clamped down on him by rounding up every vehicle at his disposal."

Carlton's ringing phone interrupted the conversation. It was Paula, and she wanted to know if the two of them could try again for an evening meal, this time at Jacala over on West Avenue. Carlton put the phone on speaker and asked her to repeat the question for the one who would make the decision.

In response, Tino shook his head emphatically. *"Not alone, Paula. Absolutely not. But I can send a couple of watchers. Get Caterina to bring you over here, and I'll have some guys ready. What time is this happening?"*

"How about six? That way, we'll be done before it gets too late."

"Okay, good. I can't have you keeping your guardians out too late. I have to pay overtime, you know."

On the other end, Paula giggled and said she would be there at six, then hung up.

Carlton snapped his phone shut and leaned back in the increasingly uncomfortable chair. "I appreciate your taking care of us, but I hate for you to have to send guys out. You were making a joke, but I know you really do have to pay them. I wish there were an end in sight for all this."

Tino gave his usual dismissive wave of the hand. "What I pay a couple of guns to go out on a date with my sister is like a drop of ice water for a man in Hell. Don't worry about it. Think of all the money you saved me—us—when you got her back for free the other night."

"Didn't do Gabe and Tony much good," Carlton said. "And if your theory is right, Ramos is still owed two lives."

"I'd bet on it. He wants to even the score, show me and everyone else that he can't be bested. Oh, and get this: a few of his street workers have started handing out pamphlets in my territory, advertising the quality of his product over mine. *The way he cuts his stuff?* Can you believe the gall that nut has?"

"Man, that is pretty weird, alright." Carlton agreed. "He seems to be getting worse every day."

"Seems like it. He has to be sampling his own miserable product. He must cut it with Ajax."

Carlton reflected for a minute on the situation at hand. A seemingly unstable competitor who reigned with terror on his side of town, now trying to make inroads in Perez's territory by a wide variety of means, from threats and kidnapping to gunning down people...and handing out notices on street corners? And so far, the best option to rid themselves of him was by giving information to a government agency and depending on its personnel to act on it. Not the most efficient plan of action, he thought.

He rose from the chair and strode across the room to the window, irritation showing in his movements. "Shouldn't we be planning something that doesn't leave us dependent on a bureaucratic government agency that doesn't give a damn about how many people in your community are killed by Ramos?" Matching his restless movement, Carlton's voice had an edge to it.

Hearing the tone and the mild profanity—a rarity from Carlton—Tino looked up sharply. "This mess is wadding up your panties, isn't it?" Without waiting for a response, he continued. "Well, it's got mine wadded up too, I promise you, but I have to be careful about how I display my concern."

Carlton nodded, still irritated. "I didn't mean to imply that you weren't sufficiently concerned. It's your job to handle everything that comes along without anyone seeing you sweat. I get that. But I think we should be working on Plan B before Plan A even takes place. *If* it takes place."

"I agree, and so does Raul. He's pretty skeptical about the DEA throwing a wrench in Ramos' operation, even if they nab a van or two with cash or dope. Ramos is a *jackass*, not a dumbass. Loony as he is, he'll still have his ass covered nine ways from Hell. All it will do is cause him some financial pain and make him re-evaluate how he makes his runs."

"Not much then, possibly. How could we really wreck his operation, short of going in with guns blazing? What if he lost his credibility on the street?"

Tino thought for a moment. "That would be tough to do. He's got street guys to move his product, guys he just pays through intermediaries as they produce profits. The street guys don't know who Ramos is, and their customers don't know the connection, so bad or poisoned product wouldn't hurt him. Dopers can't report bad product to the Better Business Bureau. He's protected by market forces on that count."

"How about his procurement process? No big deals set up in advance, like on *Miami Vice*?" Carlton asked, grinning. "I always liked seeing Crockett and Tubbs setting up a deal, then getting the dope, the money, *and* the bad guys all within an hour, including commercials."

"Afraid real life is tougher than writing a screenplay," Tino said sourly.

Carlton stared out the window for a long time before speaking again. "What if someone had the clout to set up a big buy for Ramos, then pulled the rug out? This person could end up with Ramos' money *and* the product. Then he could stand by and watch the DEA haul him away."

"What kind of 'someone' would that be?" Tino asked testily. "Remember, our local chapter of the DEA doesn't have guys like—who'd you say your TV heroes were? Davy Crockett and Ernest Tubb?"

Carlton burst out laughing at Tino's mismatched mayhem with celebrity names, including San Antonio's own historical hero and a county-western singer from decades gone by. He was about to straighten out the crime boss' recollection of the popular eighties television program, but a glance at Tino's face told him that his own chain was being jerked. Once again, Faustino Perez had illustrated his ability to bridge the cultural gap—at Carlton's expense.

"I'm supposed to be the wise guy comedian, remember?"

"Just trying to compete, my gringo friend. But tell me more of this plan to clip my competitor of his money and his inventory."

"It would have to be somebody in your industry, someone you could trust. And he'd have to be big enough to set up the big score with suppliers in Mexico, or have that kind of inventory on hand. Plus, he'd have to be unknown to Brujido Ramos, probably not from this part of the market, or he'd have to lie low during the job. And finally, he'd have to be willing to go through with this for the potential profit."

"Either that, or I'd have to pay him like a movie star."

"Exactly. Know anyone who fits that description?"

Thirty seconds went by with no sound in the office save the window-unit air conditioner, struggling to combat the September heat. When Tino leaned forward, his chair creaked loudly, causing Carlton to look around. "I know who can do it. And he will, too. He owes me from way back in the day."

"He fits all the criteria?" Carlton asked, somewhat doubtful that his laundry list of requirements was fulfilled from Faustino Perez's mental directory of acquaintances in less than one minute. "Who is he? And where is he?"

"Reynaldo Gomez. And he's in North Texas, in Wichita Falls when he's not flying around getting richer."

Something clicked in Carlton's mind upon hearing the name of the small, bustling North Texas city, situated too near to Oklahoma for most San Antonians to take seriously, even if it did actually have a waterfall on their version of the Riverwalk. He couldn't place where or why he would have heard about anyone from Wichita Falls until Tino launched into a profile of his fellow narcotics importer.

"He's a major mover in North Texas. He had a great deal going for several years, importing pottery from Mexico. He had an arrangement with the pottery supplier to pick up a few random pieces from his contact. Those pieces were a bit different; they had hollow spaces that held cocaine. Mixed in with a big batch of regulars, it escaped detection for a long time, and Gomez made a lot of money."

The nagging thought in Carlton's mind coalesced into the story being told by Tino. "Is he the guy who had his pottery shipment taken by mistake? By a tough character from El Paso who sabotaged his helicopter and killed his two shooters?"

Tino stared at him in disbelief. "How the hell did you know that?"

"Big Mo told me the story about your…uh, acquaintance from North Texas having a good thing going with the pottery trick. His guys were a couple of shooters I knew a long time ago, Vince and Dan. I've forgotten their last names, but what they went by probably wasn't what was on their birth certificates.

"Anyway, a shipment gets picked up by mistake by a real pottery dealer from El Paso, a guy who turns out to be pretty resourceful. Vince and Dan were assigned to take him out, but the dude runs over one with his car, then jerks wires from the helicopter they were flying. It crashed and killed the other one. So much for Vince and Dan, but your friend survived."

"Randall Morris told you it was Reynaldo Gomez?" Tino asked incredulously. "No wonder that fat prick ended up dead. No one in his business should use real names, no matter who they're talking to. But I'm sure Big Mo had confidence in you to keep your mouth shut."

"He didn't mention his name, just that he was a big importer in North Texas. When you mentioned the pottery scheme, it occurred to me that Gomez must have been the one."

Tino apparently wasn't satisfied to leave it alone. "So why was Big Mo talking out of school? He trying to set up a class reunion among old hit men?" he asked sarcastically.

"No, he was just telling me what had happened to the shooters. Maybe he was going to sell me some life insurance." Carlton wondered about the grilling and thought it wise to leave out the fact that he'd heard the tale while Big Mo was trying to hire him to kill Faustino Perez. He tried to move the conversation to safer ground. "So, this Gomez guy is a long-time friend of yours?"

"Yes. I've known him almost my entire life. We both came from the same town, came to the States legally, but got into the same illegal business. He's been more successful than I have, though."

"Why? Is he just a bigger player?"

"Yes, and he doesn't have an entire community to look after, so he doesn't own other businesses to keep them all employed. Last time we talked, he washes his money through a construction company. It's simpler than all the small vendors I have, and the numbers work on a much larger scale, because his company does high-end home construction and remodels. Oh, and it's a real advantage to own a ranch in Mexico, one that operates at a profit. All I have in Mexico are a wife, two girlfriends, and some kids who spend money like drunken oil sheiks."

Carlton laughed. "Sounds like your problems are self-inflicted."

"Yeah, probably so," Tino agreed. "How's this scheme of yours supposed to work?"

"That's the hard part. You've got the right party, so now we need to figure out exactly how Mr. Gomez can set up a deal big enough to attract Brujido Ramos—and every dime he has—then stiff him for his cash plus the dope and wave good-bye as the Feds haul him away. You think he'll help us?"

"I thought you already had it figured out. Now you want me to help you with a screenplay worthy of a *Miami Vice* episode? So you can relive your misspent television-watching past?"

"I'm sure I can use some help. Even Pancho Villa needed an accomplice; remember?" Seeing Tino roll his eyes, Carlton quickly added: "But I know you've got plenty to do, so I'll try to come up with something on my own, Lefty. Just leave it to my capable imagination."

The answering snort made Carlton wonder if it was due to using Tino's new nickname or his self-inflated opinion of his imagination.

CHAPTER 10

The dinner date with Paula started out better than their previous attempt. She seemed to have recovered completely, the nervous rambling from the kidnapping aftermath was replaced with her usual amount of chatter. Plus, she treated Carlton to a couple of peeks of The Smile, her best feature, in his opinion. Carlton, for his part, was glad to have a chance to spend time with her without worrying about a replay of the last time, due to the watchers assigned them by Perez.

The two men entered the popular old restaurant less than a minute after Carlton and Paula had been seated. Like most bodyguards, they were big guys, muscled, with a no-nonsense air about them. Both had a couple of tattoos showing under stretched shirts, but they sported fashionable haircuts, making them a lot less formidable-looking than the skinhead kidnappers. Carlton had seen both men around the flea market, but he thought they worked in another facet of Perez's multi-layered conglomerate, maybe one of the auto repair shops or the big tire outlet. They were quiet and conservatively dressed, and they drew scant attention from anyone when they asked to be seated at a table between Carlton and Paula and the front door. Not aware of the protocol for having bodyguards, Carlton wasn't sure if he should acknowledge their presence, but when he looked toward their table both gave a discrete nod, which he returned.

"Nice to have your brother send those guys to keep watch over us," he commented. "I'm still pretty goosey over our last dinner date."

"Not as goosey as I am. That was the most terrifying thing I've ever been through. And Tino thinks it would be worse now, no more simple kidnapping. That Ramos nutcase just wants to even up the body count."

"If that's the case, he's only halfway to his goal. The two young guys, Gabe and Tony, probably didn't even know what had happened to bring about their own demise. And because of that, two more young guys are sitting here ready to pull triggers. I wonder if they worry about how tonight will end?"

Paula shook her head. "Probably not. Those guys who work for Tino all know the danger they're in, but I suppose it never really sinks in until something bad happens."

"Well, it's sunk in on me. I've had enough of this lifestyle already. I don't want to live like a cartel guy in Medellín or Cartagena."

Paula looked at him. "For a man who doesn't want to live like one, you seem to do quite well in the cartel environment. Not many people could do what you did the other night."

"That was survival. Doesn't mean I like it."

Paula picked up the tone of finality in his voice and dropped the subject. By the time their food arrived, both of them were glad to relax and enjoy a meal and the time together, thanks largely to the watchers a few tables over. The conversation had moved on to other topics, with Carlton describing, in vague terms, his meetings with Perez and some of his men and Paula describing her recent sanctuary at the Vega home. Due to the weighty matters afoot with Faustino Perez and company, Carlton was content to let her expound on her new-found friends all she wanted.

As usual, her mood and animated chatter told Carlton as much as her words. "I don't know what I'd have done without them. I was scared to death right after you got me away from those guys, but both of them made me feel welcome and safe in their home, especially Caterina. I really enjoy talking with her. She's so much fun and can talk about a lot of things. Did you know she and Raul were from Cuba? And they were part of a guerilla group trying to overthrow the Castro government?"

"Yes, I just learned that recently. Tino told me that and another story about Raul, how valuable and...*resourceful* he was. He and Caterina seem well-matched. He hardly says a word, and she chatters like someone else I know."

Paula smiled at him. "Well, it works just fine then, doesn't it?" After a brief pause, she added, "Do I really chatter that much?" The Smile was replaced by the Worried Look, and Carlton had to laugh out loud at the transformation.

He shook his head and reached across for her hand. "Just enough for me to like it. And it looks like Raul does, too. You don't see either of us packing our bags, do you?"

"Okay. Just checking. Anyway, I don't want to think about going back to my apartment, not yet. I talked with Tino about it, and he says he would have to use at least three watchers to take the place of my staying at the Vegas. But I'm worried about wearing out my welcome. Caterina swears it's not a problem, that she enjoys the company. Raul's been spending a lot of time doing something for Tino, so I guess it is a good thing for her."

The evening wore on, with Paula warming up and getting in fifty or so words for ten of Carlton's, just the way he wanted it. Time flew, and when Carlton checked the time, it was after eight o'clock. He glanced toward the watchers, but they seemed content to sip after-dinner drinks and talk quietly while surreptitiously checking the surroundings. Mindful of Tino's employee overtime expense, he took a final drink of tea and looked expectantly across the table. "I've really enjoyed this. Seems like it's been a long time since we spent time together. I wish it didn't have to be so structured."

"Me too. I wish we could go to my apartment and spend the night. Or yours." She glanced toward their bodyguards, then back to Carlton. "You think we could arrange that with our watchers?"

"I didn't hear Tino give any specific instructions or announce a curfew for us. I guess I could just go over and ask. I wouldn't want to put those guys at odds with any directives they've been given by your brother."

Paula sighed. "You're right, but I'm already tired of being watched. It's not that way when I'm at the Vegas' house. This is like being spied on. How much longer does this go on, anyway?"

Carlton shrugged. "I don't know. Tino seems to know Ramos' ways pretty well, and he's awfully nervous about any of us, but especially women and children, to be anywhere outside the immediate community without bodyguards. It goes on until Tino says it doesn't, I suppose."

"Well, when do you *think* this might pass? Or what will it take to get things back to normal?"

Carlton wondered about her persistent questioning. He wasn't about to disclose any of his recent planning meetings with Tino. And if he could, there was no way to ensure that intervention by the DEA would result in immediate relief from the state of siege under which Tino felt they should operate, so that wouldn't answer her question, no matter how often she posed it. For now, he thought it best to close out the evening, even though her suggestions about spending the night sounded very appealing.

He leaned in closer to her. "Paula, I can't think of anything I'd like better than to spend the night with you. I'll go ask the guys if they think it's okay with your brother to have them keep an eye on us all night. Or, better yet, maybe I should call Tino straight up, see what he says."

She giggled at his suggestion. "What, we call my big brother and ask him if it's okay for us to spend the night together?"

Carlton laughed at her analysis of the situation. "Yep. Sounds pretty silly when you cut through the fluff, doesn't it? But if we ask our watchers, I'll bet they have to check with Tino first, anyway."

Paula thought about it for a minute, the Worried Look again creeping onto her face. "I don't know if we should. He's got a lot on his mind right now. Maybe we'd be better off not to bother him with another management decision."

Carlton did his best leering act, leaning in at her with a suggestive sneer on his face. "Like one deciding whether or not his sister gets laid? That's a management decision?"

Paula burst out laughing, and Carlton followed suit. At that moment, one of the watchers rose from their table and approached them. Carlton thought for a minute they'd been so loud he wanted to warn them to stop attracting attention. However, nothing was further from the bodyguard's mind. He stopped a few feet away and awkwardly looked back and forth between them. "Uh, I'm not sure how I should say this...uh, do you want to go somewhere else? I mean, like to...um, be alone for a while?"

Paula and Carlton again laughed, but not as boisterously as before. Then Carlton answered the embarrassed young man. "We're laughing because we were just discussing that very thing. But the answer is no. Y'all probably need to just follow us back to the boss' office and see that Paula gets over to the Vegas' house."

Paula leaned toward their watcher, a grin plastered on her face. "We figured someone would have to call Tino to get an okay, but neither of us wants to. And we don't want to put you in that position, either. He's got a lot going on right now."

The relief on the man's face was evident. "Yeah, that's kind of what we thought. But I would not mind calling," he added quickly, apparently evaluating Paula's pretty face and its probable effect on the man sitting across from her, the one they'd been assigned to guard—a man who had already picked up the moniker "*pistolero*."

Carlton decided to seal the decision that all of them knew was better, despite the man's willingness to accommodate this gringo of whom he'd heard so much. "No, that's not necessary. But I—we appreciate your asking. Right now, I think we'll all be better off not bugging the boss about our personal situations."

The man smiled gratefully, shook his head at his co-worker, and returned to their table. Carlton signaled for his check and stepped around the table to pull Paula's chair. Their server, already scurrying over, delivered the bill in exchange for Carlton's money. While he was waiting for his change, Paula walked toward the front door where the two men already stood, one on either side, and began an animated conversation. Within seconds, the men were smiling, hanging on every word she uttered.

Carlton watched as she used The Smile to turn on the charm. The looks on the young men's faces—no matter how tough and capable they were as bodyguards—told him they didn't stand a chance. He thought they looked so much like puppies they would have wagged their tails if they had them. He thanked his server and left him a nice tip. The obligatory handshake closed the business end of the meal, and he headed to join the others.

The two watchers exited first, after telling Carlton and Paula to wait a moment. They would come back in after checking the lot and escort them to the Mazda pickup, one of them informed him. All business now, the two walked out several seconds apart, and scouted the lot for any suspicious activity. Two cars had occupants that needed to be checked; after watching for a minute and determining that they were departing restaurant patrons, the watchers re-entered the restaurant and held the door for Carlton and Paula.

The men walked on either side of them, about five feet away, with one slightly ahead of their charges, the other slightly behind. While walking, they continued to swivel their heads and check out the surroundings. Both men's hands hovered near their jackets. It was a standard escort pattern for personal bodyguards, efficient and generally unobtrusive to the clients while walking across any expanse of open ground; a tactic designed to protect their lives.

A dark-colored Chrysler 300 turned into the lot and down the row of cars just ahead of the four. As it approached, Carlton saw it was painted flat black, not shiny. Even the bumpers and trim were flat black in color. Both watchers instinctively edged in closer to Paula and Carlton. As the car came closer, they noticed the dark windows, darker than was legal for side glass, but still not an indication of a problem. Lots of car owners simply liked the "murdered out" look and ignored the glass-tint statutes. Law enforcement officials had bigger problems to contend with, so scofflaws only had a problem if they were stopped for another offense. It was worth the risk to the true car nuts who liked the darker tint look.

But when the car slowed quickly, the watchers went to full alert, squeezing in toward the couple and forming a tight formation of four people. The one on the right and behind them spoke quietly: "Be ready to drop to the pavement. I don't like this car slowing down."

Carlton grabbed Paula's hand and leaned toward her, speaking softly. "If they give the word, stay with me, and stay as close to the ground as you can. They'll be watching for a window to go down."

Even as the words left his mouth, both windows on the approaching passenger side started sliding down simultaneously, as though both were on the same circuit. Carlton knew what to do before he heard one of the bodyguard's warning instructions. "Down!" he yelled. "Get down on the pavement, close to a car!"

Carlton was already diving for the deck, pulling Paula with him. As the pair went down, he tugged her toward a big Chevrolet pickup and hunkered down behind and slightly under its massive rear bumper. No sooner had they made it did they hear the opening shots, four or five of them, all emanating from the open driveway in front of the row of cars in which they now cowered. A second later, they heard the return fire from their watchers; big bore pistols, by the sound of it.

Carlton thought about trying to count the shots fired, but gave up the insane idea almost immediately. Instead, he pulled Paula down against him and cradled her head against his chest. He couldn't see their attackers or protectors. A few more shots were fired, then he heard the big Chrysler engine accelerate as the car sped from the scene. He took a chance and raised his head just as one of the bodyguards knelt beside them, startling him. He hadn't known the young man was so near. Apparently, he had stood directly over them while the shooting was going on.

"Are you okay?" he asked, his voice nervous and strained.

"Yeah, we're fine, we're good here. How about you? And your bud? Anybody hit?"

The other bodyguard trotted over from his position, giving Carlton the answer he hoped for. He broke into the same line of questions, inquiring if both he and Paula were okay. After quick mutual assurances from all four, the larger of the two men suggested they leave quickly.

"Let's see if we can just get out of here before the law comes. We've got permits and everything, but I'd rather not talk to the cops."

"Me neither," Carlton agreed. He grabbed Paula's hand and tugged her toward the Mazda pickup, while the two men dashed across the parking lot toward their car, a white, late-model Chevy Impala. When Carlton gassed the Mazda out of the lot, the Chevy pulled in behind them and kept close on their bumper all the way to Tino's office.

The bodyguards had apparently called Tino en route. His red pickup was sitting in its usual daytime spot, and the office door was ajar, the light shaft streaming outside. All four of them trooped up the steps and into the office, where a worried Faustino Perez paced. As usual, he wasted no time getting down to business. "What the hell happened?" he shouted, his question aimed at the two bodyguards. He scarcely glanced at Carlton and Paula.

The one Carlton had identified as the probable leader spoke up. "A late model Chrysler 300, flat black, murdered out, heavy tint. At least two shooters, but not good ones. Everybody's okay, we split before the cops got there. We put some holes in the car, don't know about hits."

The other bodyguard chimed in, stepping forward slightly and addressing Tino directly. "The hit wasn't well planned. No one should use a car like that, it's too easy to pick out. When we saw it was murdered out, our attention was drawn to it immediately. I think the hit was amateur work, maybe contracted with local nobodies."

Tino's scowl didn't lessen with the news. Instead, he slammed his hand down on his desk, his anger growing amidst the frustration. He glared at the two bodyguards again, and they remained silent, hands at their sides, faces expressionless. They stood motionless; the only sign that they were nervous being slight darting glances left and right as they waited out their boss.

Carlton stepped in, admiring the professionalism the young men exhibited under the crime boss' verbal onslaught. "Tino, the guys did a great job. They saw the hit coming at us. As soon as both windows started down, they knew—we all knew—to hit the deck. Sounded like the shots were pretty wild, another sign that the guys weren't pros. They got us out of there in a hurry; like he said, before the cops showed." He looked to the bodyguards to confirm this and got nods from both in return. "And I want to thank both of you, now that I've got a chance." He stepped toward them and shook hands, getting a grateful smile from both of them for speaking up to Tino and verifying what had occurred. "And before we go any further with this conversation, I want to actually meet these guys who saved our bacon. My name is Carlton Westerfield," he said, then needlessly pointed to Paula. "I'm sure you know this is Paula."

The bigger guy, the one Carlton assumed was the leader smiled tentatively and said, "I'm Sergio Estrada. That's my brother Estéban. And yes, we know who both of you are. We've heard all about you, even before getting the assignment tonight."

"Yeah, I've seen both of you around, but didn't get a chance to meet you," Carlton said casually. "Nice to finally meet both of you. And thank you again." He turned to Tino. "Well, this has turned out exactly like we spoke of. We're having to live like cartel people. What do we do now?"

Tino had been fuming while Carlton was going through the niceties of introductions, the conversation aimed solely at putting his young employees at ease, since they obviously had already known a lot about their charges. Still pacing, he stopped and leaned back on his desk. "I'll tell you what we do. We put together a group and take out that bastard Ramos and about half his crew. That's the only way I see this thing headed."

"He's making it hard to do much else, isn't he?"

"I'm not sure there's time for the plans we discussed earlier. Just like before, when you had a chart and outlined all the connections between Dennis Bradford, Timothy Hunnicutt, and all the players, it's come down to taking action."

Carlton put up his hands in surrender. "Hard to argue with that one. And you're right, the chart and analysis of those people didn't help last time. You still got caught up in a gun battle, people got killed, and we retaliated with a surprise for them. In hindsight, it made my chart look pretty silly. My thoughts about a plan to have someone else take Ramos off the board were designed to avoid bloodshed, that's all."

"I know, I know," Tino retorted irritably, waving his hand in his usual dismissive gesture. "And I wish it could work out, but I don't see how we can survive without striking back."

"You know I hate to start carrying a weapon, but it looks like I have no choice if I want to step outside."

"I'm glad you see the obvious." Tino opened a couple of desk drawers before finding what he wanted. He pulled out a revolver, flipped open the cylinder, and checked the loads. "Full house, and I've got another box here somewhere. Meanwhile, keep this handy, okay?"

"Yep. *Handy.* Will do," Carlton quipped, reaching for the pistol and stuffing it in his belt.

Sergio spoke up timidly "Uh, Carlton? Uh, I—*we* were talking tonight, Estéban and I, and we wondered why you didn't carry a gun. After what you did, you really didn't need any protection from us, did you?" He glanced nervously at Tino as he ended the question, clearly concerned that he had overstepped with his boss and this near-legend Anglo. Tino's passive gaze said nothing, but everyone in the room could hear the wheels turning in his head.

Carlton came to his rescue before Tino could react. "You probably heard a wild tale about my shooting, but in reality, it was like tonight: the shooters just weren't very good. I had them confused with the circumstances and my reaction to their instructions for the car wash, and they hesitated. I got lucky."

Sergio nodded, a look of mild disappointment on his face. Clearly, he had heard a much different account of this middle-aged gringo standing before him. The look said he was now wondering how he had earned the nickname "*pistolero*."

Tino chose the moment to make his re-entry in the conversation with a theatrical groan. "And our gringo friend is full of shit, Sergio," he intoned tiredly. "He got the drop on Ramos' guys, but still, he shot four of them dead before they got off a single round. Our Carlton is simply being modest. But to answer your concern, he doesn't like to carry a gun. Says he doesn't like guns. Plus, I wanted him and my sister to have a peaceful evening without having to pack heat. That's why I sent you and Estéban—"

"I wasn't questioning our assignment!" Sergio interrupted quickly, embarrassment on his face. "I—we—appreciate the work, we really do. I was just curious, that's all, because…"

"Don't worry about it. You did well. Carlton and Paula are safe—for the moment, anyway—and no one on our team is injured. I understand your curiosity. But don't spend too much time trying to evaluate our gringo *compadre*. Like I said, he's full of shit."

Carlton smiled at the Estrada brothers and shrugged helplessly. "It's nice to be loved."

Thus put at ease, the men grinned and relaxed, then turned again to their boss to hear more of his plan to deal with Brujido Ramos. But, if Faustino Perez had a specific retaliatory plan at this time, he wasn't expounding on it. Instead, he gave the bodyguards instructions for the night, including taking

Paula to Raul and Caterina's house, with Sergio spending the night in a guest cottage, while Estéban, was assigned to return to the office and go with Carlton to spend the night in his apartment.

Paula, who had remained silent during the men's discussion, rose to go and spoke up for the first time. "Sergio and Estéban, I want to thank both of you for tonight. It seems that's all I do lately, thank someone for taking care of me. But I really appreciate it."

The young men waved off her concerns and herded her out the door, with Estéban assuring Tino he'd be back as soon as his sister and Sergio were safely deposited at the Vega household. When the door closed, Tino motioned to the chair in front of his desk, then settled back in his own chair.

Carlton sighed and took his usual seat in the uncomfortable wooden contraption in front of Tino's desk. "If I have to spend much more time sitting here, I'm going to buy you a better chair," he complained.

"If you spend much more time sitting there, I'm getting rid of it completely. I'm as tired of seeing you there as you are." The snappy remark was followed by a sly grin. Tino had finally cooled down and seemed content to banter with Carlton for a few minutes, but Carlton knew it was a prelude to another serious talk about what to do with Brujido Ramos. He didn't have to wait long.

"That bastard is not going to quit until he goads us into a full-scale street war. And I'm ready to accommodate him."

Carlton thought for a moment before responding. "What if we continue to be careful, keeping everyone under guard for another week or so? Is it possible that he will get tired of using men and resources to get even?"

"Who knows? Maybe. But do I want to take a chance? No! Going into action against his group will put him on the defensive, make him spend time guarding his own people."

"Is there any word on the vans? Any movement that might indicate he's ready to make a run?"

"Damn, Carlton, that was only this afternoon that you called your girlfriend at DEA with the plate numbers. I told you I gave Arturo the evening off to go have a nice meal—with bodyguards, of course. I'll get him back on it tomorrow, but we can't count on finding out anything for a few days, at best."

Carlton blinked, thinking "*my God, that* <u>*was*</u> *only this afternoon! This crap is warping my sense of time.*" He shook his head, embarrassed at being reminded of how recently they'd had anything to go on. Of course it was too soon to hope for any additional information. It was a vivid reminder that time was against them, that their enemy was working all the time to even the score for his, Carlton's, recent night of victory. Right now, after surviving another shootout, that victory seemed a long time past, though it had only been four days ago.

He still had hopes that he could pass along information to Heather Colson that would result in a devastating blow to Ramos' operation. Whether everyone else in Perez's extended community/family would survive that long remained to be seen. Certainly, Gabriel Fuentes and Tony Esparza hadn't. Despite rescuing Paula and saving a half million dollars in the process, Carlton couldn't help but wonder if he'd made the right decision by changing the agreed-to plan for ransoming Tino's sister. But the nagging thought came back to him that something had been amiss with that entire scenario, beginning with the kidnapping itself...

His thoughts were interrupted by Tino's next proclamation: "I'll talk with Raul and David before making a final decision on all-out retaliation. But meanwhile, we've got to change some things. I'm going to talk to Marta about her apartments. I know she's got a couple of units that she's in the process of refurbishing. I'm going to move into one and put Sergio and Estéban in the other. I think there's an efficiency unit just over the office, and I'm going to put Paula there."

Carlton nodded. An argument could be made against having too many people concentrated in one spot, but the idea made sense in this case. Faustino Perez was no stranger to violence, and the bodyguards, though youthful, seemed quite competent. And, as he had voiced earlier, it was time for him to start carrying a weapon, distasteful as it was to him. Sergio had been right to question why he, Carlton, would have needed protection while being tagged with the nickname "*pistolero*." When it came down to it, Carlton felt certain he could protect himself and those around him.

Tino wasn't done. "I'm going to call Reynaldo Gomez tomorrow and see if he'll help us. He may have some ideas about how to pull off a sting on Ramos. But I want you to give it some thought, too. I'd rather it be our plan that saves our asses, not his."

Carlton snapped a quick Boy Scout salute. "I agree. I've got an idea or two about switching out the product and leaving Ramos with fairy dust and handcuffs. It will work, depending on the usual process for carrying out a buy between parties that don't know each other. Your friend Gomez can enlighten us on that part, and I think he'll like the idea I've got."

"Okay," Tino sighed. "I'm going home. You wait here until Sergio gets back. I'll make those other arrangements first thing in the morning." He got up and headed toward the door, but stopped as he reached for the doorknob. "Oh, one other thing. What the hell is a "murdered out" car? I didn't want Sergio to know I wasn't up on the latest buzz word."

Carlton gave his boss a quick rundown on the fad among car aficionados that favored an all-over flat-finish paint job and heavily tinted windows. "That's the look that some guys are liking these days. Usually, the paint is flat black, but I understand there are other colors available. I don't know how it got a name like 'murdered out.'"

Tino listened carefully to the explanation, then shook his head. "*Murdered out*. How appropriate. Shit."

CHAPTER 11

The next day, Thursday, was a flurry of action for Faustino Perez and those closest to him. He and Marta surveyed the entire complex, concentrating on three vacancies she currently had. Two were in the initial stage of renovation, and Tino arranged to have a small home-improvement company—the principals of which were in his employ, of course—come over and begin a hurry-up completion of the work. Incredibly, by the end of the day, all that remained was paint work and a few trim items. The third apartment, an efficiency unit, was tagged for Paula, and she and Caterina spent the day relocating her belongings to the new digs, working around the painters who were happy to watch her and warn her repeatedly about wet paint areas.

Carlton already lived in the crime boss' other sister's apartment complex, so he didn't need to be involved. Instead, he quietly slipped out before noon in the plumbing pickup and rounded up a few basic plumbing tools, then drove back to the area where he'd encountered the four inept kidnappers a few nights before. He turned north at the car wash and once again cruised by the small elementary school he'd spotted on his last recon, the one that had been too close to the car wash to qualify as a possible place where Paula had been held. Just as his phone indicated 1:00 P.M., he pulled to a stop sign by the school playground and rolled down the window of the Mazda. Less than a minute went by before he heard the sound of a ringing bell, the class-end/class-begin signal still used at some community schools.

The sound was fairly loud here in the adjacent street, and it served its purpose on the schoolyard. A small army of kids swarmed from the playground equipment toward the building entrance, the boys dragging their feet at the prospect of being cooped up for the rest of the warm September afternoon. The girls moved to the front of the pack, glad to chat up friends and head to class where they would pay closer attention and be smarter than their male counterparts. Carlton grinned to himself at the memories of his own reluctance to head into class and realized nothing changes, certainly not the boys and their poor attention thing, and girls being smarter.

He drove east from the school, slowly cruising the neighborhood until he spotted a vacant house, this one with a For Sale sign in the yard. Making ever-widening blocks in the area, he determined that it was the only one that fit the description Paula had given—vacant and empty—except for the fact that the drive to the car wash was less than two minutes, not the seven or eight minutes she thought the drive had taken. Of course, nothing said the kidnappers couldn't have taken a circuitous route…

Wrong house or not, something nagged at him about it and he drove by again, then stopped, backed up and parked across the street. Checking the realtor's sign, he saw what had gotten his attention, albeit subconsciously. It was the name of the realtor representing the realty company, a woman named Brenda Ramos. Her photo was on the sign, an attractive woman of indeterminate age that Carlton thought looked the part of a friendly, aggressive, well-informed house peddler—just like every For Sale sign photo in the world, he reminded himself. It was the name "Ramos" that had stuck in his mind, same as Tino's bloodthirsty competitor and, by all standards, an incompetent kidnapper. However, Ramos was a very common Hispanic name, and he discounted the name as a coincidence. After a few minutes spent pondering his reason for being here again, he started the pickup and left.

Heading back toward the freeway, he chastised himself for doing this again, but turned back toward the vacant house, this time parking right in front at the curb. After noting the street and house number, he pulled a clipboard with a tablet of invoices and quickly scribbled a makeshift work order for the residence. Carrying the clipboard, he strolled to the front door and found a realtor's security key box hanging from the doorknob. Jiggling the apparatus, he found it to be secure as intended. He looked around for security cameras and saw none, so he stepped to the front window and pushed up on the frame. Nothing doing. Cupping his hands, he peered into the window. It was apparently the living area, though its emptiness and lack of any distinguishing features other than size gave no clue to its function.

He moved to the side, hoping no one would call the police, forcing him to go into his Medina Plumbing act for a supposed service call at this address.

Smiling as he recalled the three requirements for being a plumber, he tried the next window, then the next. Still no movement, but as he cupped his hands against the glare to look inside, he spotted something interesting. A folding card table sat in the middle of the room, this one presumably the kitchen. Three chairs sat in disarray around it, but otherwise the room was clean and devoid of any other items. His attention heightened as he remembered Paula's account of a possible card game while she was being held in another room. This was looking like less of a waste of time after all.

Moving to the back of the house, he passed on the back corner window positioned high in the wall. It was obviously a bathroom, the window small and too high to enter without a ladder, unlocked or not. The next window around the corner was for another bedroom. Oddly, it had a curtain pulled across it, makeshift by the look of it, almost completely blocking view from the outside. He pushed up on the frame, but it held tightly, just as the others had.

Carlton studied the window framework and pulled a pocketknife from his jeans. Using the tip of the blade, he pried the window edging material, brittle with age, from its hold between the glass pane and the framework. Working around the pane, he soon had removed all four edging strips. Then he gently pried on the edge of the glass until it gave way and fell into his hand.

He reached inside and flipped the lock up, then pushed the window open so he could hoist himself inside the room. It took more effort than he'd expected, but within seconds, he was in the house. Moving quickly to the back door, he unlocked it and trotted to the pickup, where he retrieved a workman's bag containing the plumbing tools. Back inside, scribbled a note that read "back door unlocked, please fix sink." He went to the front door and pushed it into the crack between the door and doorjamb, then went back to the rear door and stepped inside. He set the tools and clipboard near the kitchen sink and breathed easier for the first time in twenty minutes. Now, if he were approached he could use the service call story, saying the back door was unlocked as promised, and he would be done with the job soon. It was weak, but better than nothing.

He stepped through the musty old house quickly, checking in closets and cupboards, but found nothing until he got to the kitchen where the card table sat with three wobbly chairs. He looked around for cards, chips, empty bottles, or ashtrays, but found nothing to suggest a card game—or anything else—had taken place. It simply seemed out of place in the otherwise barren house.

Almost reluctantly, he moved to the front bedroom where he'd gained entry and stepped in facing the closet. When he opened the closet door, what he saw caused his vision to cloud and his mind went completely blank for several long seconds. Even though he'd gone to this trouble in a house that didn't fit all the criteria Paula had recited, he had hoped all along he'd been mistaken, that his intuition had failed him, that the pressure of that night's gunfight and killing four men had caused his brain to play tricks on his vision.

And it had.

Whatever he *thought* he'd seen dissolved before his eyes; his imagination must have fooled his vision for a brief instant, because now, only a single bare clothes hanger was suspended from the closet bar. It hung motionless, mocking him for coming back here and risking criminal charges—or worse—solely because of a dream.

Last night, he'd had a dream in which he and Paula were going to run on the beach in Rio de Janeiro; not unusual, since that very activity had occurred several times while they were absent for two months in Brazil's famed vacation spot. Usually, he ran in swim trunks and Paula trotted alongside him wearing whatever she'd had on at the beach earlier—shorts or swimsuit.

In the dream, Carlton was wearing his usual, and he trotted off at a slow pace so Paula could keep up. But she ran only a few yards, calling out that she "couldn't run in this." When he turned to see what she was talking about, he saw she was wearing a flowing, yellow sun dress. They were only a few yards from their beach cabana, so he pulled up and suggested that she change into something else, he'd wait for her. But as she turned to walk back, instead of a thatched roof beach cabana under palm trees, the structure was a small, dilapidated house—much like the one he now stood in.

Jerked from sleep, he had looked at the bedside clock. *3:18 A.M.* He lay there going over the dream for a few minutes before it hit him. Wide awake, a chill began in his stomach and wandered up to his throat, forming the feeling of dread he'd come to recognize whenever his judgement was proven entirely skewed by a new set of facts, or a revelation which changed everything.

In a flash of recall he understood why he had been troubled that night leaving Tino's office. When he'd picked Paula up for their dinner date at La Perla, she had been wearing that same yellow sundress as in the dream. Minutes later, she was kidnapped and thrown into a car by a couple of thugs, the terror evident on her face. Hours later, after the gunfight and rescue, she had recounted her tale of horror to Tino, saying she'd been blindfolded the entire time, pushed to the floor in a vacant house until the kidnappers loaded her into the car for the planned ransom exchange.

Undoubtedly, it hadn't been the best time or place to change clothes... but when he watched Paula step from Tino's office later that eventful night, he noticed she wore jeans, ones that accented her figure, something any man would notice—and Carlton did. For some reason, the scene had troubled him at the time, but he couldn't figure out why and was too tired to concentrate on it. She wore jeans often, what was the big deal? After a couple of days and another shootout, he'd forgotten about the event entirely.

That is, until he had the dream.

Now, Carlton stood as though his feet were nailed to the floor, staring at the empty hangar and recalling another part of the dream, where he'd stared at the house and wondered where their cute cabana and its paradise setting had gone. As if to compound the mystery, somewhere down the Brazilian beach a school bell rang and the dream faded.

Pondering that, he stayed motionless for a full five minutes, wondering if his sanity were at risk or if his entire world was about to fold up and smother him. Neither scenario seemed pleasant. He was shaken from his reverie by the sound of the real school bell ringing nearby and wondered if the expression "saved by the bell" applied to this turn of events.

Carlton shut the window, grabbed the tool bag and pulled the back door shut. Then he went to the side of the house and replaced the window pane before trotting to the plumbing truck. He pulled away from the curb, turned the corner, and made his way back to the interstate, watching the mirror and wondering what the hell was going on—both in reality *and* his over-active brain. He gassed the pickup onto the ramp and headed back toward his apartment building—make that *everyone's* apartment building now—determined to find out where and how Paula had managed to change clothes during the few hours that should have been filled with stark terror for her, not a concern about what she was wearing. But within a couple of miles, Carlton settled down and started applying logic to the matter, which settled his jangled nerves.

First, he recalled that Paula had her big bag with her, which could have carried a change of clothes, makeup, billfold, cell phone, hair brush...with enough room left for the inventory of a good-sized store. So it was conceivable that she had the jeans and a top with her. Second, it seemed impossible that a woman could make it two hours, much less ten or so, without a bathroom break. Her captors had allowed that, and she had convinced them to let her take her bag and change clothes. It made sense for them, too, to have her dressed for more activity than the sundress would allow. Third, Carlton's alarm at the revelation was based on a dream, and while he was pleased that his nocturnal subconscious brain power had provided clarity to his waking hours, it seemed a weak premise on which to base judgment of his…his what? *Girlfriend?* That thought made him feel a bit guilty, until he recalled a few other questions she had artfully dodged during their "tell all secrets" getaway to Rio.

Anyway, what could the clothes change mean? Was she working with the kidnappers? Had it all been a scheme to clip her brother for a half million bucks? (Not to mention that Carlton had kicked in a buck-forty of the cash himself!) Or was something deeper at work here, a power play between Tino and Ramos, in which Paula had become an unwitting pawn? The questions all led back to Carlton's inquiries about the brother-sister relationship, both with Paula in Brazil and more recently, with Tino. It continued to be a subject that neither sibling seemed willing to explain, and that bothered him.

Furthermore, Carlton couldn't shake the feeling he'd had when he awakened on Tino's office couch just before the ransom delivery. His intuition told him something was wrong with the entire situation, that he was being used by one or both of them. Later, he had asked Tino about it point-blank and was given an explanation designed to assuage his concerns; still; he hadn't been able to shake the feeling that the whole kidnapping thing was…what, a hoax? A charade to throw attention off of something else? In order to find out, he would have to be very careful about how he mentioned the subject and who, if anyone, he informed of his theory. Tino had acted so dismissively, even hostile, when questioned before, it would take some finesse to bring the subject to light again.

By the time he arrived at his apartment building he had decided to let the matter of the clothes change slide, at least for the moment. However, another thought had occurred to him while hunkering under the bumper of a Chevy Silverado, listening to bullets whining around them. Why had they been at Jacala's on West Avenue, far from the relative safety of the southwest side of town? Because that's where Paula had wanted to go. While it was plausible that they had been followed, it was a long drive through downtown, and followers of any caliber would have had their hands full. Given the incompetence of this second batch of shooters—like the first—Carlton had doubts. Still, not impossible…was it?

He left the plumbing tools in the pickup and climbed the stairs to his apartment, hoping to dodge everyone and get a nap. Slipping in his door, he headed for the couch and, for the next two hours, slept dreamlessly and awoke feeling a lot better. He fixed a sandwich and read a book for the next hour, thinking the day had been a success after all. Indeed, the afternoon would have been perfect if not for the light knock on his door around four o'clock. It was Tino, and he wanted to talk. "I called Gomez this morning, and he's coming down here to talk to me—to us, that is."

Carlton shot him a questioning glance. "You want me to sit in on the first meeting? What'll he think about that?"

Tino waved away his concern. "He wants to meet you now. I told him about you, that you'd had some good ideas and you were working on something to deal with Ramos. He'll want to hear it."

Carlton shrugged. "All I've got is an idea for a way to swap the product after Ramos' guy tests it. It'll take some coordination, and we need to use one of the ambulances in your fleet."

"Okay, that's not a problem. Reynaldo arrives here tomorrow at mid-morning, and we'll meet him and talk."

"He flying into SAT?"

"No, he flies his own plane and will fly into Hondo."

Carlton saw the wisdom of that plan. "Easier to spot a tail driving to Hondo than while fighting traffic to SAT."

"Right. He's pretty high-profile in some areas and doesn't want to be seen talking with us, especially if we're concocting a scheme to clip Brujido Ramos."

"Makes sense. I'm sure we can take a drive in the country without taking any company along."

"Yes. We'll take another car I've got back in a garage, just to be sure we're suitably non-descript. Oh, and both of us need to carry a piece. You'll want to bring along the one I gave you. It's cold and cheap. You see any pressure developing, just ditch it."

"Don't worry, I will. I hate carrying a gun."

CHAPTER 12

They left at 8:00 the next day. Hondo was on U. S. Highway 90, some forty miles west of the city limits. The U. S. highway was the main street, paralleling the railroad tracks for a couple of miles through the town. Across the tracks lay the town center, mainly commercial, but with several buildings serving government functions since Hondo, with its population of about eight thousand people, was the county seat of Medina County. To the south side of the highway were the usual restaurants, car lots, and gas stations, while an H.E.B. grocery store anchored the area.

The most interesting landmark was positioned on the north side of the main drag. A billboard festooned with the phrase *"This is God's country. Please don't drive through it like Hell"* had stood for many years, re-done a few times and withstanding criticisms from anti-religious groups and passers-through who had gotten a traffic citation and didn't appreciate the irony of the admonishment. Carlton had to smile at the sign and its message as they passed it.

The South Texas Regional Airport was beyond the west end of the town, north of the highway. Started as a military training facility during the Second Word War, it had undergone a number of changes through the years. In more recent times, the airport had become popular as a meeting place for flying clubs, mainly because of its location away from the crowded skies nearer the city with its busy civilian airports, plus several military runways. Also, word was that the airport's restaurant attracted private pilots looking for a weekend destination with good food, excellent coffee, and reasonable prices.

Carlton had heard the airport's advantages being heralded by a private pilot-turned-car shuffler during his driving days. The older man had since given up flying his own plane, but liked to talk to his fellow drivers about flying clubs and the allure small regional airfields had for them. "Yeah, you and your buddies can fly into a small airport just by checking traffic on the local UNICOM frequency, announcing your turns, and plopping that baby onto the runway," he'd told them. "No smart-assed junior tower operator to boss you around, tell you stuff you don't need to know."

Now, as he pulled into the parking lot, he noticed the airfield had a flight service and a flight instruction school…but no restaurant. However, he saw a sign announcing a recently-opened flight museum and plans for a restaurant, presumably a replacement for the one from the old pilot's tales.

"Guess all good things come to an end," he muttered to himself, getting a look from Tino that wouldn't go away until he explained. "A guy I used to drive with said they came here because of the location, lack of air traffic, and a good restaurant. It must not have been good enough to last, though."

"Reynaldo mentioned that he used to fly in here for that reason. That, and he needed fuel to make it on to his ranch. Said fuel was cheaper here than at the larger places. Too bad about the restaurant. I could use breakfast."

Checking the time, they decided to wait on Gomez and see if he wanted to go into town to eat. They sat in the car, an older Mazda 626, and watched several small aircraft circle and land, then take off, apparently students from the flight school getting in the required number of hours to obtain a private license. Watching the scene, Carlton wondered if he could develop an interest in something like this, a new hobby with which to pass the time—providing he could survive this ongoing drug cartel war he'd not wanted to be involved with in the first place. The thought made him irritated, both at Tino Perez and himself; Tino, for urging him to help, and himself, for tacitly agreeing to do so. He had to put the thought aside and speculate about this upcoming meeting with Tino's friend, the mysterious drug kingpin from Wichita Falls, purportedly a much bigger player than Faustino Perez. He wished he could ask about the tale he'd heard from Big Mo, when the pottery guy from El Paso had defeated his two enforcers and ending up saving Gomez' life in the process. He certainly couldn't bring it up; Tino had seemed surprised that Carlton had even heard the story from the now-deceased Randall Morris. Maybe the story will come up, he thought, but without much hope.

A little after ten, a twin-engine plane circled the airfield, then dropped into a final approach and touched down gently before taxiing to the flight service building. When the pilot stepped out, Tino nodded toward him.

"That's Reynaldo. I'll give him a few minutes to take care of refueling business before I call him."

About three minutes later, Gomez emerged from the building, phone against his ear. Tino's phone rang, indicating his friend was already ahead of him. Tino answered in English, and the conversation following was conducted in a mix of Spanish and English. Carlton saw Gomez look up and scan the parking area until he spotted them, throwing up a hand in greeting as he pocketed his phone.

As the man approached the car, Carlton saw that his appearance was a lot different from his boyhood friend sitting beside him. Reynaldo Gomez was about six feet tall, with a full head of salt-and-pepper hair, cut short and brushed stylishly back. His face was handsome; almost like a movie idol, with a fine sharp nose and strong chin. Otherwise, he had regular features set off by a perfect olive skin tone. His smooth face was accented by dark beard stubble, the only feature incongruous with otherwise impeccable grooming. Carlton wondered if the George Michael beard stubble advertised a penchant for being hip, or if he simply hadn't had time to shave.

He wore khaki pants and a white snap-button shirt, both with starched creases that looked sharp enough to cut string. Footwear consisted of gleaming cowboy boots, black, with pointed toes that could finish off a cockroach in a tight corner with no effort. On his left wrist, a subtle gold watch that looked plenty pricey peeked from under the stiff shirt cuff. All in all, Carlton surmised, someone every girl is crazy about, if *ZZ Top's* song were to be believed.

As Gomez neared the car, Tino stepped out and Carlton followed suit, stepping around to meet the visitor. Gomez and Tino were exchanging pleasantries—or possibly friendly insults, judging by their grins—before engaging in a hearty embrace. Carlton stood by, watching the two friends' display and noticing that Reynaldo also had perfect teeth, very white and even…of course. Then Tino stepped aside and presented his friend to Carlton in a formal manner. "Carlton Westerfield, please meet my lifelong friend Reynaldo Gomez. Reynaldo, this is the man I spoke of. Carlton has been a great help to me and the community, as I told you."

Both men stepped forward and shook hands while holding eye contact. "A pleasure to meet you Mr. Gomez," Carlton said. "I understand you've known this guy for a long time," he added, nodding toward Tino with his head.

"Yes, I've known Faustino since we were kids growing up in a little dirt-street town in Chihuahua. But fortunately, I haven't let that relationship sour me on the rest of the world," he said with a wink. "I hope you are able to help him as much as he has been saying, because he needs a lot of help."

Tino took the jab good-naturedly, rolling his eyes and gesturing for all of them to get in the car. For the next few minutes, both men carried on in Spanish, apparently catching up on each other's lives since their last meeting. Finally, Gomez broke and apologized to Carlton for the snub.

Carlton dismissed his concern. "Not a problem. Y'all have a lot of catching up to do, I'm sure. But is everyone ready for some breakfast?"

"Absolutely," Tino said, not bothering to consult Reynaldo. "Let's go to that place we saw on the other end of town, just this side of the Ford dealership."

Ten minutes later, the three men were digging into a South Texas breakfast and downing coffee with enough gusto for a TV commercial. The two teenaged waitresses wandered in and out of the kitchen, eyeing Gomez and using any excuse to approach the table. A minute later, they met beside the kitchen door, giggling, then murmuring among themselves. Reynaldo caught them looking and smiled at each of them in turn, which started another round of embarrassed giggling.

Carlton watched the show with amusement, and wondered about the relationship between Reynaldo Gomez and Faustino Perez. Tino wasn't likely to have women swooning over him, not after a first glance at his short, stocky frame, barrel chest, and flat, peasant-farmer face. The two were worlds apart in appearance, but he knew that Tino's calculating mind and sharp wit would enable him to hold his own in the long run anytime, notwithstanding his buddy's movie-star looks.

Breakfast was filled with idle chatter, mostly between Tino and Reynaldo, but the two occasionally included Carlton by switching to English for a replay of some exchange between them. Otherwise, Carlton was content to sit and listen, trying to develop an ear for the language. Listening to most Latinos, he thought it sounded like gibberish, but hearing Reynaldo and Tino converse, he could pick out individual words and phrases, something he attributed to the men's superior education and clear enunciation of words in their native language. Unfortunately, that was not the environment most aspiring language students lived in every day.

When they finished eating and went to the car, Carlton got behind the wheel again, and Tino sat in the back behind him. Reynaldo took the front passenger seat, turning sideways to address them both, and the meeting began in earnest. Carlton started the Mazda and drove toward the airfield while the two talked.

"So, Tino, I understand you have a problem with a competitor, this man Ramos, who oversteps the boundaries of good sense and common courtesy."

Tino frowned. "Yes, if kidnapping my sister and demanding a half million dollars in ransom goes beyond common courtesy. Oh, and payable in just a few hours, too."

Gomez opened his eyes wide. "You told me Paula was safe now, but you didn't tell me the terms or what took place. Did you pay the demand?"

The frown was replaced with a sly grin. "No. But I—*we*—" he gestured toward Carlton—"we rounded up the full amount, and had it together within the time limit. Carlton drove to the first rendezvous, prepared to make the exchange or get instructions for the next meeting point." He again pointed toward Carlton in front of him. "But when this crazy gringo arrived, he saw fit to change the plan."

Reynaldo glanced sharply at Tino's use of the word "*gringo*," first at his friend, then over at Carlton, the subject of the sometime pejorative term, as though to check his reaction. Catching the look, Carlton simply grinned and shook his head, letting Gomez know the term was okay between them.

Tino caught the look too, and hastily explained. "It's okay, Reynaldo, Carlton knows I call him that just to distinguish him from me, you, and the rest of the taco-benders he has to put up with."

Reynaldo nodded and grinned at Carlton. "You're a good sport to put up with this guy. But he's right. Many Anglos think it's always derogatory, but it depends on how it's used. In your case, his explanation fits—got to be able to tell you from the crowd of Mexicans he hangs out with. Anyway, just how crazy were you? What happened at the first stop?"

Carlton started to answer, but Tino stepped in, not about to be upstaged in the story-telling. "He shot all four of them dead, pulled Paula out of the car, and met me for pancakes about twenty minutes later. With all the ransom money safe in the trunk of his car."

Reynaldo sat dumbfounded for a few seconds. "Damn, Carlton! No wonder Tino wants to keep you around. How the hell did you do that?"

Carlton waved off the question and ducked his head, embarrassed at yet another recounting of the recent night. "Mainly, I got lucky. Ramos didn't send the cream of the crop on that job. They got confused when I intentionally pulled into the wrong place, and three of them got out like tough guys, swaggering toward me while holding up their baggy pants. When they got too close, I pulled on them. They were too slow. The fourth guy got out of the car then, and I got lucky with a quick head shot." He spread his hands to indicate the end of the story, or perhaps his lack of further explanation.

Gomez continued to stare at him for a few seconds, then looked back at Tino. "What the hell you need help for? Sounds like this guy's got your problem headed for a resolution."

"Yeah, well, it worked out fine that night," Tino said. "But I knew Ramos was a hothead and he wouldn't just admit defeat and move on to something like normal business. Sure enough, last Sunday evening, a drive-by took out two of my crew, a couple of younger guys who hadn't been with me for long. Then, Wednesday, Carlton took Paula to dinner. I sent a couple of my best to watch over them, and I'm glad I did. When they left the restaurant, another drive-by was attempted. Nobody on our side got hurt, though."

"So you're certain this guy's not going to give up, at least until he evens the score? What, kills four of your people? Or is it something else he may have in mind, something I need to—"

Tino quickly interrupted him. "That's the way I see it happening. He's halfway there, and I don't want to lose two more of my crew. Hell, Reynaldo, you know about me and my crew! I've known some of them since they were babies, I knew their parents and grandparents before they were born."

"I know, Tino. You run your business differently, like a mom-and-pop operation, not a drug smuggling enterprise. You told me about the big mess a couple of months ago, and you lost what, four or five of your crew?"

Tino nodded, a pained look on his face. "In four days, I attended enough funerals to preach a mass from memory. I don't want a replay of that. Luckily, the two guys who died the other night were from El Paso, and they had no family here. I sent the bodies back to their families and paid for nice funerals, and I'll send some more money later on. But that doesn't make it okay."

Gomez was silent for a while, mulling over the situation his friend was describing to him. When he started to speak again, Carlton listened very carefully, trying to catch the tone, as well as the words, being spoken to Tino. It would be interesting to hear the plan from another viewpoint.

"If I understand what you told me on the phone, you would like to set up a buy for this guy Ramos, a big one. Then, get him busted in the process, plus take the product *and* the money he just delivered to buy it with? And you're hoping it will put him behind bars and out of business, right?"

Carlton sat quietly, evaluating the brief description of the plan he'd presented to Tino. This time, the words were being spoken by a third party, not among themselves, and Carlton had to admit it sounded far-fetched when being verbalized by a professional in the same business.

As it occurred, Tino picked that moment to put him on the spot. "Carlton, give him a rundown of what you had in mind, and you can ask the questions about the logistics and protocol of a wholesale drug buy while you're at it."

Carlton took a deep breath. "Mr. Gomez—"

"Please, please, just call me Reynaldo."

"Okay, Reynaldo. I have some, uh, *skills* in a related line of work, but I don't know how a big wholesale drug purchase goes down. Who gets out of the car first, who shows their end of the action first, how does the exchange actually take place, and so on. But at some point during the transaction, when the parties don't know each other, the buyer wants to see, and probably test, the product, right?"

"Yes, no question of that."

"Okay. For delivery of the product, I envisioned using a work truck with those tool compartments on the side, or better yet, one of Tino's ambulances with all those compartment doors. Bystanders and passersby might be curious about what's happening, but no one would really think anything illegal is taking place beside an ambulance with a compartment door open, would they?"

"Not likely. The lettering and the lights would make an ambulance seem a legitimate vehicle to be sitting almost anywhere without anyone questioning it."

"Okay. The seller representative opens the compartment, the buyer takes a look, does his test, whatever. Just as he says 'okay,' we have a car load of our young guys drive up, looking and sounding drunk, with loud music going. That will create a distraction, with both parties afraid of drawing attention to the deal. Acting quickly, as if to keep the product from being seen, our guy quickly slams the compartment door. In the vehicle, that's the signal for our inside guy to open the *back door* of the compartment and switch the approved batch with flour, gypsum dust, or powdered sugar—whatever looks right. Exact same packaging, same briefcase, box, or whatever container is used, so long as it's identical."

Reynaldo nodded, his interest growing upon hearing this scheme laid out step-by-step. If it sounded too far-fetched, it didn't show on his face, but Carlton could tell he was mentally scrutinizing the plan. Aloud, Gomez responded in a guarded tone. "Okay, I'm following you so far."

Carlton waited a few more seconds for him to digest the scenario and ask questions—or point out a problem. Hearing nothing, he continued. "After only a few seconds, the distraction car drives on by, our guy re-opens the compartment, and the transaction goes on despite the slight interruption. Our guy inside the transport vehicle stays quiet, hangs on to the real stuff, and the buyer ultimately walks away with the fake batch. Oh, and if the buyer has poked a knife into one of the packets to test it, our guy inside the compartment will put that one right back on top of the fake batch, same spot it was in. That should seal the legitimacy of the deal, put the buyer's mind at rest."

Reynaldo smiled. "So the buyer gets *some* value for his money, yes? One packet out of thirty or forty?"

"Yes, that is a weakness in my plan," Carlton admitted. "The seller would have to sacrifice the tested packet, or the buyer might notice. Or, if our guy has time to spot the test packet, he could duplicate the cut on the corresponding fake packet." Again, he waited a moment before continuing. "On the plus side, when the DEA busts him a few minutes later, maybe it's best if he's holding some real stuff. He won't get off because the batch tests out as baking ingredients. The amount might make a difference in the charges brought against him or the length of the sentence. I'm not familiar with that part of the law enforcement procedure."

"Well, I am," Reynaldo replied. "Even if they bother to test the entire batch, every individual packet, I would be amazed if they admit any of it wasn't top-quality blow. It should come as no surprise to you that law enforcement likes to boost their numbers, so a bust for twenty kilos of cocaine sounds better than one kilo of cocaine and nineteen kilos of flour."

From the back seat, a derisive snort from Tino let them know he was in agreement with how law enforcement agencies worked when faced with such a dilemma as real contraband versus that which would result in a lesser prison sentence. He leaned forward in his seat to address his friend. "So Reynaldo, would such a switch tactic work in the real world? I've never bought under such circumstances. You know I have my own supplier, and we deal with each other like pros, have for years, so I'm in the dark about all this *Miami Vice* stuff Carlton dreams up. I know this plan is dependent on timing and communication with the guy doing the switch, but I have a man who could handle that part of it without fail."

Reynaldo thought for a moment before responding. "I like the idea. It has the potential to work, especially with the diversion car driving up and interrupting the deal. Carlton's right, all parties would want to slam the door, hide the product, and see what the hell was going on before continuing. So, it might work, if everything goes perfectly."

When nothing more was forthcoming, Tino pressed him. "Obviously, '*might work*' isn't exactly what I was wanting to hear, but I understand what you're saying. Are you saying it's too risky to try?"

"I'm like you, Tino, I buy from the same group all the time, we trust each other, and there's none of this 'movie intrigue' stuff going on." He made quotation marks in the air to express what he thought of movie plots being passed off as real life.

"What are the chances?"

Reynaldo shifted in his seat, uncomfortable at being put on the spot, even by his old friend. "I'd give it a seventy-five percent chance of working, knowing what I know about how the deals go down between parties who don't know each other, have no reason to trust—or mistrust—each other. Also, you've got to be coordinated with the law enforcement people to take down the buyer at the exact right time. And how do you know you won't get caught up in the sweep? They'd love to be able to take down all parties to a drug buy, and I wouldn't trust any of them."

Carlton felt he should represent this portion of the presentation. "I don't trust them either, Mr. Gom—Reynaldo. But I'm on fairly good terms with a pair of mid-level DEA agents who think I have a lot more information than I actually do. They stay connected only because they think I can advance their careers, not because they like me. But they will listen to what I have to say, and I'm certain I could get Ramos busted with the right timetable information. I agree with you about the possibility of getting caught up in the dragnet, though. That is definitely a risk."

"So, bottom line, Reynaldo." The request from Tino made it clear that he wanted to cut to the chase, determine if some scheme like this would work to put his rival out of business—and off the streets—for good.

Reynaldo shook his head. "Bottom line? I don't think I'd try it. There are just too many variables, too many chances for a screw-up, somebody getting trigger-happy..."

He shrugged and splayed his hands to emphasize uncertainty, a gesture unnecessary for Tino and Carlton. Both of them had already arrived at that conclusion during the discussion. A period of silence settled over the group as they drove up the street to the airfield. For the next few minutes, nothing was said, and Carlton pulled the car back into the same parking space as before. He shut off the engine and turned toward Reynaldo to see if he would elaborate or offer an alternative plan.

Reynaldo's next remark was a shock to Carlton and, judging by the look on Tino's face, a mild surprise to his long-time friend. "Tino, you want to get out of the business altogether? Maybe go into some part of the wholesale business, where you don't have to compete on the street level?"

Tino shook his head. "Sure, I'd do something else—" He paused, then changed his answer. "No, actually, what I'd like is to get out of it completely. I can make a living with my legal operations, do enough cash stuff to avoid giving it all to Uncle Sam and not have to worry about getting my friends and associates killed. Or myself."

Reynaldo wasn't through with his sales pitch. He turned toward Carlton. "Tino has told me you have good ideas, and the one you just mentioned is a good one. It just has..."

"Too many moving parts," Carlton finished for him. "Yeah, that's what I thought, even while I was explaining it to you. Too many things have to go exactly right, and that almost never happens."

Reynaldo nodded his agreement, then changed gears. "You have any more good ideas about getting product across from Mexico, like your driveshaft trick? I like that one."

Carlton thought for a moment. "Actually, I did come up with something a few days ago. You have a ranch in Mexico, right? Can you bring livestock across the border, say to a place in the U. S.?"

"Sure. The livestock might have to endure a quarantine period at the border, but that is not a big problem. In fact, in addition to my ranch in Mexico, I have a small cattle operation just west of here, in Sabinal. That's why I was familiar with flying into this airport. Sometimes I rent a car and drive over to check with my ranch foreman, see how the cows are doing. It's not much, just a hobby, really, but I enjoy it."

Carlton hesitated a moment before continuing, not wanting to make another dead-end suggestion. But when Reynaldo raised his eyebrows in question, he began. "Well...I saw a science channel presentation the other day about artificial insemination of livestock, and I had an idea. Couldn't the product be packaged and, uh...*deposited* inside a cow—or lots of cows—and be transported across—undetected?"

From the back seat, Tino gave a loud groan. "My God, Carlton, is there no end to your sick imagination? First, there's dead corpses with dope and cash stuffed inside, and now you want to shove packets of cocaine up a cow's—"

"Wait a minute, Tino!" Reynaldo interrupted. "I like it! As I said, there're checks for diseases and sometimes a quarantine period, but what he just said would work. I mean, I'd have to check again, but I don't think there's a reason for cows to be x-rayed like human mules at the airport."

Tino shook his head, a look of disgust on his face. "And even if they did, who's going to retrieve this package they've spotted on screen? Even ICE agents have some respectability—unlike somebody in this car."

That got a laugh from Reynaldo and Carlton. Reynaldo went quiet for a minute, going over the possibilities, while Tino sat in the back scowling at Carlton. Carlton, in a rare moment of jocularity, mimed the process he'd seen on the science program by slowly extending his arm over the seat, then thrusting his hand toward Tino and wriggling his fingers. Tino backed away, then scooted to the other side of the car, warily shaking he head in disgust.

When Reynaldo spoke again, he brought the conversation back on subject. "Seriously, Tino, if you want out completely, I understand, and maybe I can help. I would like for you to consider working in the wholesale end, you and Carlton both. You wouldn't come into contact with the likes of your current competitor, and I could—"

"But even so, that doesn't solve the problem with Brujido Ramos," Tino interrupted. "He's a maniac, and he won't rest until he's evened the score. So it's either wait until he kills two more of my guys, go to war with him and lose people in the process, or figure out a way to put him out of business for good, preferably behind bars for a long time."

Reynaldo started again, trying to calm his friend. "Wait, let me finish. What if I joined your retail operation and lowered prices at the street level to a point that would break Ramos' financially? It would mean accepting a lower margin, at least for a while, until Ramos either goes broke or moves his operation out of San Antonio. In the meantime, he'll be too busy trying to survive to spend time and money going to war."

"You think that would work?"

"Without knowing his financial reserves, I can't say for sure. He may be able to hang tough for a long time. I can try to find out for sure about his money situation, but tell me this: does he sell quality product, or does he step all over it?"

"The word I get is that Ramos sells crap, diluted so much it shouldn't even be illegal. But it enables him to cut prices, plus, he sells in some areas where the customers don't know good blow from powdered sugar. Trouble is, he's starting to peddle that shit in some of my territory. And sometimes, price trumps quality, no matter who the user is. We're dealing with dopers, not brain surgeons."

Reynaldo nodded. "I know, I've run into that problem before. But, in my experience, it tells me that Ramos isn't very strong financially. He's running a business that can be undermined by a lower-priced product, especially after the users learn that it's not only cheaper, it's better grade stuff. It would only take a few weeks, maybe less, for the word to get around. Dopers are nothing if not repeat customers, you know that. They can never take a break from looking for the next fix. It's what keeps us in business."

Tino thought about that for a long moment before speaking again. "So, in effect, I go to work for you, and you take over my retail end. Do you keep my street guys employed? All of them?"

"Absolutely. I would need all your team and maybe more. Oh, and I'm not talking about taking over your business, Tino. If you want, you could simply become a silent partner, and I would become the one Ramos competes with. Word would soon get out that you're not his problem, I am. He has connections for finding out about me, I'm sure, and he'll hear that I can hang tough longer than he can."

"And how does this work between you and me?"

"In return, I supply the product to be sold at a lower price—at least for a while, until Ramos gives up—so you and I share lower margins. We can even put a time frame on how long we try this, say six months. At the end of six months, if you don't like the arrangement, we dissolve and go back to our respective corners. Hopefully, by then, Ramos will be history."

"Forgive my asking, Reynaldo, but what's in this for you long-term?"

Reynaldo stared at him. "Well, first, you and I have been friends for what, forty-five, fifty years? That means something, doesn't it?"

Tino put up his hands in surrender. "Of course. That's why I asked your forgiveness in asking. But you're a businessman, and I know you need something in return to make it work."

"What I said earlier. You help me in the wholesale end. You have good contacts in Mexico that would be an addition to what I already have. Plus, you have Carlton in your employ." He looked over at Carlton to confirm this.

Not having spoken in several minutes, Carlton knew it was time to get some things straight. "I'm not really in Tino's full-time employ, Reynaldo. I agreed to work on this Ramos thing, but we never really ironed out any firm deal, did we Tino?" he asked looking back at him.

Tino shook his head. "No, we didn't. Our deal was just talk, not even a handshake, and it's evolved due to circumstances, things that happened really fast. Any arrangement you make with Carlton would be separate."

"Okay, I understand. Carlton, I would like for you to consider working for me. I don't expect an answer right now, but I want you to think over what we've been talking about. I could use a man of your…talents."

Carlton nodded his assent to think about it, then amended his gesture verbally. "I'll give it some thought, Reynaldo, but I'm a little long of tooth to be thinking about a new job. In fact, I've been thinking exactly like Tino; that I'd like to leave the business for good."

"I understand, because I've recently had the same thoughts. Everyone does. This business wears on you; it wears on me more every day. I envy you and Tino for coming to terms with it and, hopefully, we can put Ramos out of business first, then all of us can undergo some needed change."

"What will you do if you're not in the drug smuggling business?" Tino asked.

"For years, I've used a small construction company to wash money. The jobs have so many variables in costs and materials it's easy to change invoices and work orders to allow dirty money to be injected into the business. Anyway, the little company isn't so little anymore; it's starting to make serious money, so much that I have trouble washing currency through it. I could make a good living legally and not look over my shoulder all the time."

Tino laughed. "Must be tough having that problem of too much money, old friend."

"I'm sure you have something similar going on with all your associated operations," Reynaldo countered. "Don't tell me the flea market and tire and muffler shops don't do well. Plus the EMS transport business with those ambulances, let's not forget that!"

"Yeah, they do all right," he admitted. "And it would be even better if I had time to devote to running the other things, instead of worrying about that maniac across town wanting to kill people just to prove he's a tough guy."

"Well, we can best take care of him by busting him financially. Why don't you think about what I proposed and call me in a few days? And you also, Carlton; please give some thought to what we've gone over. Oh, and I'm going to research the possibilities of artificial insemination to smuggle product over and cash back. I really think it has potential. If I go forward and it's successful, I'll pay you a handsome bonus."

Carlton shook his head. "No, that's not necessary. It was just a thought I had while watching a television show. Just consider it a sample of Tino and me helping out in your wholesale operation."

"That's most generous of you. Please try to talk to your friend and mine, the wily Faustino Perez, will you? Get him to accept my plan." He reached over the seat to punch Tino in the arm.

In the back seat, Tino playfully fended off the jab, then leaned forward. "I've had enough time to think it over. Let's do it. When do we start?"

Reynaldo smiled, flashing his perfect teeth. He was obviously pleased with the outcome of the meeting, a swift decision from Tino to implement his proposal. "Good! The sooner the better! I'll get back from Mexico in two days and go by my place out in Sabinal. I can have product delivered there within a few days. What's today, Friday? By next Wednesday I can have product packaged and ready for delivery to your place. I'll call you and we'll go over details of how you want it delivered. Meantime, tell your street vendors to put out the word about some high-quality blow that's going to be in soon, for a great price."

After a few more minutes of conversation between the men, Reynaldo got out and strode toward the flight service building where his plane was sitting, refilled, and ready for him. He turned and waved toward the car, then disappeared inside the building.

Inside the car, Tino exhaled loudly and opened the rear door to get in up front. When he sat down, he looked over at Carlton and spoke as he buckled his seat belt. "What the hell did I just agree to?"

"I think you just agreed to let a big-time player come in and wipe out that jackass Ramos. At the same time, you can decide if you want to play in your friend's sandbox for a while, or retire completely and haul pottery and lawn decorations from Mexico, which is a lot safer than being a drug kingpin with someone gunning for you night and day."

"That about sums it up for me, and it sounds pretty damn good. What about you?"

Carlton shrugged. "I'll wait and see what's involved in his wholesale operation. Maybe I can do some piecemeal work for him, a contract from time to time. But I think I'd like to quit the life completely."

"Then maybe we both get what we want. By the way, what are you going to do about Paula?"

The question took Carlton by surprise, and he stalled by checking his mirror carefully before backing onto the street. When he pulled the car into Drive, he turned and told Tino the truth.

"I have absolutely no idea."

CHAPTER 13

Back in the city, Carlton dropped Tino off and got into the trusty little pickup at the flea market, then returned to his apartment. As he headed up the stairs, he noticed Paula at poolside and called out to her. She looked up, waved and smiled, motioning for him to come down. He signaled to give him a minute and ducked into his apartment to change clothes.

When he stepped out, she was standing below his apartment landing squinting up into the sun at him. "Would you get my phone and bring it down with you? It's on my kitchen counter. The door's not locked."

He skirted the upstairs landing until he reached her new abode, an efficiency directly above the manager's office. When he opened the door, the new-house smell hit him, and he looked around to check out the last-minute upgrade. Tino's construction guys had done a nice job of refurbishing the interior with new carpet, paint, and trim, despite the challenge of getting it ready within two days.

Stepping inside, he noticed Paula and Caterina also had done a good job of placing her stuff into the tiny space. With no room for a chair, any sitting would be on a beige love seat that took up almost an entire wall, facing a slim table with a flat-screen TV. The wall between held the folded-up Murphy bed, which would just fit the limited floor space when lowered. A couple of paintings she'd bought at the flea market had found a new home; one had been hung above the love seat and the other over a column between the miniature living space and what passed for a kitchen. Otherwise, furnishings were sparse, but there was little room anyway.

All in all, a sufficient place—and a safe one—for a single person who'd been kidnapped and whose life might be in danger, he thought. Then he realized that he had no idea what type of living accommodations she was accustomed to in her past life. He'd never heard her voice much about living standards, but he knew women were generally much more critical of Spartan surroundings than men. Furthermore, he knew that when she'd spent time with the crooked DEA agent, it had been at his home in Alamo Heights, which was undoubtedly much nicer digs than this tiny apartment on the south side of the city.

Carlton wondered how she was weathering the change; since being with him, she'd been camping in the Chihuahuan desert, stayed at his own modest apartment several times, and spent a few nights on the run at cheap motels. Then, after reuniting at the airport, she'd gone with him for a couple of months of luxury, staying in an upscale hotel in Rio de Janeiro, Brazil. Pretty wide range of habitat, he thought wryly.

He picked up the phone from the counter and idly flipped it open. He'd cautioned her about regularly erasing all texts and logs and not placing contact numbers in the directory. Of course, her directory was well-stocked with numbers—and names—just as he had advised against. He vowed to himself not to say a word; the precautionary measures were hold-overs from his past life anyway; probably not needed for her, even with the recent spate of violence they had endured. Besides, he had no business telling her anything, much less how to keep phone numbers.

Just as he started to close the phone, the first entry of the "Bs" caught his eye. The entry name was simply initials, and he didn't recognize the number as being one he knew, though it seemed vaguely familiar. He stared at it a few seconds, then dismissed it as being close to some number he'd taken time to memorize, as was his preferred habit for maintaining contact information. If he wanted to keep a number that wasn't used much, he scribbled it in his own code on a scrap of paper and kept it in his wallet. The efficiency of the code was tested from time to time and found overly sufficient; even *he* couldn't recall the significance of a couple of numbers he carried. Curious now, he scrolled through and found another with a single initial, but didn't recognize the number, not even the area code. He shook his head and closed the phone, more irritated at himself for being nosy than at Paula for being careless.

At poolside, he handed her the phone and stretched out in a lawn chair next to hers. "How was your day?" he asked.

"Pretty good, once I got all my clothes crammed into that tiny space of a closet. That, and the dresser that only holds a few pair of panties and six tops. That's all the room I've got to keep my clothes. And you know about my shoes."

Carlton let out a groan at the mention of this woman's footwear. Months before, when fleeing the city for the desert, he'd had to lug a monstrous suitcase around which he later learned was filled with shoes. Her penchant for shoes was renown, and he wondered where she had stored the remainder of her collection. It didn't take long to find out.

"I had to get Tino to let me put most of my shoes in one of the buildings behind his office."

"They fit in one building? When did you downsize your collection?"

The remark got him an obscene gesture combined with a stuck-out tongue. He leaned back and grinned, then closed his eyes for a quick poolside nap. But she wasn't about to allow that.

"Where did you and Tino go today? You must've left early. I got up before eight, and the little pickup was already gone. I called the flea market and Beatriz told me you and Tino had left together."

"We left from the flea market at eight. I left here about seven-forty-five."

"Where did you go?"

Carlton fidgeted in his chair, uncomfortable with her questions. While it was unlikely that Tino would keep the news of his visit with a childhood friend from his sister, he would have preferred that she ask her brother, not him. He hedged the answer.

"Hondo. We met an old friend of Tino's, and they spent the entire time talking over old times."

"Really? What was his name?"

Carlton turned to her. "I think his name was Gomez. You'd have to ask Tino to be sure. Like I said, I wasn't privy to much of the conversation, and they spoke Span—"

"Reynaldo Gomez? Why didn't you tell me? I can't believe you two met with Reynaldo! He's so handsome! I haven't seen him in a long time. What did they talk about?"

Carlton threw his hands up in surrender to the verbal barrage. "Whoa! Time out! Maybe you should just call your brother and make *his* ears bleed with all this interrogation." To temper his tone, he said it with a big smile plastered on his face, one that he didn't really feel.

As he feared, the smile didn't sufficiently cloak his stern admonition. Instead, her eyes got big, and The Hurt look began to emerge. He decided to backtrack and do his best to change the direction of her inquiry while saving himself from a lot of apologizing. Now that it was obvious that she knew Gomez, it was probably okay to disclose the nature, if not the content, of the conversation; however, Carlton had long understood the doctrine of "need to know," and he wasn't sure Tino would see the need in his half-sister knowing the plan to undo his competitor in the illegal drug business. He quickly reviewed his options and decided on comedy.

"And maybe Tino can tell you why he's not so handsome anymore, how he got that huge scar and gained a lot of weight—"

"*What?*" she fairly screamed. "A *scar*? And he's *fat*, too?"

"Not *real* fat, maybe two-ten, two-twenty. But it's all in his belly. And the scar looks like he got it when he lost a knife fight. It runs from his eyebrow around to his ear like this." Carlton traced the path on his own face with his finger. "Enough of a scar that I didn't notice the missing front tooth, not at first. I—"

"No way!" she shouted. "I cannot believe that Reynaldo Gomez—"

Carlton couldn't carry on any further. He burst out laughing, causing Paula to leap from her chair and give him several blows with her fists, a couple of which penetrated his feeble defenses. Still laughing, he had to retreat to the pool, swimming to the far end to escape her wrath. When she ran around the perimeter, he had to go to the middle and tread water while she glared at him from the edge.

"I can't believe you said all that! You're just jealous! I'm going to stay here until you drown out there."

"I can't believe you *believed* it. And yes, I'm jealous. What man wouldn't be? He's too good-looking for *my* own good. He *needs* a scar, just to make him more normal, like the rest of us. Oh, and I can tread water longer than you can stand there looking angry while you're laughing inside."

With her typical emotional shift—approaching the speed of light—she abandoned her attack mode and flashed The Smile while returning to her lawn chair, allowing Carlton to dog-paddle to the edge and cautiously hoist himself up. He approached her chair with caution, sliding his own out of her range before he sat down. However, one glance from her was all it took to send him into another round of uncontrollable laughter.

She stuck out her tongue again and issued a warning. "Don't ever do that to me again!"

"Okay. But it sure was funny to watch your face."

"It was funny to watch you run to the water, too." After a three-second pause, she continued. "So what did y'all talk about? I want to know."

"I know you do, Paula, but it's really not my place to tell. Please, just ask your brother. Or if you know Gomez, you can ask him."

She sighed and leaned back in the chair, pouting. "Okay, I know when I'm being shut out. Since that works both ways, I hope you know what that means for you." The warning was accompanied by a sidelong glance that left no doubt of what she meant.

Her warning proved to be false, though. Right after sunset, they opted for Carlton's apartment, watching television until after midnight, then sleeping in until after seven, when Paula's ringing phone woke them. She mumbled a greeting, then carried on a muted conversation for a few minutes while Carlton tried to go back to sleep. It didn't work, of course, and both of them rose and showered.

"That was Tino, and he wants us to go to breakfast with him. I'm to call him when we're ready."

Carlton was buttoning his shirt, almost ready, and hungry. "Good. I'm hungry. You?"

"Yes. And maybe I'll finally be able to learn what y'all talked about with Reynaldo."

"Gosh, I surely hope so!"

Tino picked them up in the parking lot. He had already been to the flea market and spoken with several vendors about their orders for Mexican pottery, art, and assorted junk which they sold from the rented stalls. He had a large written order and was planning to leave for Laredo as soon as he met with David Avila and Daniel Garza. He had told them to be at the flea market later, where he and Raul Vega would give them instructions regarding the changes to be forthcoming in the retail side of their drug business. With Carlton and Paula in the car, the conversation was less weighty, never touching on his earlier activities and instructions.

"What do you two have planned for the day?" he asked as the pair settled into their seats.

Carlton opened his mouth to speak, but never got the chance.

"Why didn't you tell me that Reynaldo was coming to see you?" Paula launched on him while buckling her seat belt. "What did you do? Just poke fun at each other like you always do? You could have invited me along, since I haven't seen him in years."

Tino turned to look accusingly at Carlton, but was met with a defensive glare that said he didn't like being stuck in the middle. "She pinned me down and did everything but waterboard me, Tino. I told her to ask you. And now she's asking, in case you didn't notice."

Tino shook his head, his ire apparently erased by Carlton's explanation, which he figured was accurate. He waited a moment, then began an edited description of the meeting. "We talked about our businesses, his and mine. I had called and told him about Ramos, what he had done, and we met to discuss it in more detail. I was hoping he had some advice about handling that maniac without going to an all-out war and getting more people killed."

"Why did you think he could help? Can't Raul and David and those other guys—Sergio and Estéban—take care of him?"

"Because Reynaldo's a lot bigger player than I am. He's dealt with some really big guys at the cartel level, and he knows more about the violence end than I do, more than I care to know."

"So, what did he advise?"

"That you can save up to fifteen percent on car insurance with Geico," Carlton quipped, trying to help Tino out of a jam with some humor.

The remark got him a punch in the arm, but she was laughing, and the punch lacked conviction. Even Tino chuckled at the witty remark. Paula wasn't through with her brother, though. "Do you think he can get Ramos under control?"

Tino grimaced, his usual expression for frustration. "I don't know. But he and I came up with something that will change the game for Ramos. And everyone else, for that matter. It'll take some time to tell if it's really going to work."

"But if you—"

"Dammit, Paula, right now, I just want to eat breakfast."

The remark put an end to her probing, at least for a while, and Carlton was glad for the respite. Much as he liked both of them, and perhaps even loved Paula, he was already tired of the verbal machinations between the siblings. While he recognized his own shortcomings in the relationship department, he would never be able to fathom the back-and-forth quibbling carried on by some people. His own life had simply been devoid of personal drama, and he didn't like being caught up in it. He felt justified in bristling at the look Tino had given him when he learned Paula had wrested information out of him, sparse as it was, about yesterday's meeting with Reynaldo.

Tino took them to a Jim's, and breakfast was a pleasant affair. The talk mostly centered on the new living conditions, how it was working out, and suggestions from Tino for additional precautions. "Sergio and Estéban like the new arrangement, which is good for all of us. Get them to go with you when you leave the apartment. They're good at what they do; plus, they're civilized enough that I don't mind their being around. One of them texts me every day with a report of what they observed, what action they took, blah, blah. It's overkill, but better than having a couple of guys who are too lax and let us get killed."

"They seemed plenty competent that night at Jacala's," Carlton said, repeating his earlier observation of the Estrada brothers' performance. "I wasn't just saying that when we got back to your office, I was serious. They knew instantly what was happening, and they knew what to do during and after the shooting took place. And you're right, they seem decent guys to be around."

"How much longer do you think we'll need bodyguards?" Paula asked.

"For a while, I'm afraid," her brother answered. "No matter what we do, it will take some time to determine if Ramos has given up trying to even the score, whether it's because he's broke, dead, or gone. I want to be certain that he's off the board for good before we lower our defenses in the least."

Fearing the conversation was getting back to the area Paula was so curious about, Carlton changed the subject. "What's on your agenda today?"

"I've got some shopping to do in Laredo. I think I can pick up everything on my vendors' lists at two places and not have to run all over town. You want to go?"

"Sure, why not? Are we taking a trailer? If so, Paula can ride back on top of the merchandise so it won't blow out."

Tino laughed, and she gave both of them a look that told them they were treading on thin ice, so Carlton eased off and finished his breakfast without any additional dangerous remarks. By nine they were on the road, pulling into Laredo before eleven o'clock. Tino drove to the first of his Mexican art suppliers and left a major portion of his order list with the proprietor, who was obviously a long-time associate, judging by the banter between them. Then he made two more stops, picking up several items from each, before returning to the first vendor. There, the biggest portion of the load was ready, and Tino supervised the crew loading the merchandise onto the trailer, making sure none of the other items became damaged in the process.

When he was satisfied that the load was securely loaded and tied, they left for lunch in a borrowed car. By two o'clock, they were back at the warehouse and Carlton was tasked with driving the rig back to the city while Tino indulged in a *siesta*. As he pulled out of the parking area onto the ramp leading to IH-35 North, Carlton checked the load in his mirror and resisted the urge to ask Paula if she would mind riding on top "just for a few miles to make sure it would stay." Just as well—within three miles she had joined her brother in a snoozing contest, and Carlton was left with a one-hundred-plus-mile drive on a full stomach and very little sleep the previous night.

Within a half-hour, he was nodding at the wheel, and started concentrating on the matters at hand to keep himself awake. Several events had continued to nag at him and, within the past twenty or so hours, a couple more things occurred to make him wonder if he were seeing everything he should. He began to itemize the points, hoping to discern some connection between them.

First, he couldn't fathom why Paula was so insistent about the security measure's endurance. What difference did it make how long Tino enforced the stringent security and close-quarters living conditions? It hadn't prevented her from doing pretty much what she wanted, so far as he knew. Yet, she had inquired of Tino exactly what she had asked Carlton at Jacala's, just before the parking lot shootout.

And second, what was the big interest in Tino's meeting with Reynaldo? Was it simply an interest in Reynaldo himself? That was understandable, given the man's charisma and good looks. How had she met him? Her mother had re-married her father after Tino and Marta's father died, and that marriage was in the States. Therefore, how could she have known Tino's boyhood friend? Of course, Carlton knew only the basics of the family's history, so there likely were connections he hadn't been made privy to; moreover, it wasn't anything that he needed to know.

A third item that still nagged at him was the house near the car wash. Although a weird dream was the basis for his checking it, something about hearing the school bell, the card table, the proximity to the car wash...well, okay, that item might need to be shelved. But what about the change of clothes?

For the next ten miles, he tried to organize the items into something that would connect the dots, but couldn't see it. He went back to the night of the kidnapping and went over Tino's somewhat odd behavior, the too-structured, too-accepting of the ransom demand. However, Tino had explained it away, and Carlton lacked the experience to refute it. His discomfort was based entirely on his gut feeling that something wasn't as it seemed.

Next, he thought about Tino's meeting with Reynaldo, his ready acceptance of the deal to undermine Ramos' pricing as a means to destroy him. Like the acquiescence to the ransom demand, it seemed at odds with Tino's reputation as a hardened crime boss. Offsetting that theory was Tino's reaction to recent events: the deadly interstate shootout, the funerals, the grief, the uncertainty as to what might lie ahead. As he had openly explained to Reynaldo, he was tired of seeing friends and kids of friends die. Despite the occasional bluster about all-out war with Ramos being the answer, he was considering a different approach, that the best way to protect himself and his loved ones was to get out of the business altogether. And since Carlton had had the exact same thoughts, he could find little fault with Tino bailing out, regardless of his past activities and his reputation as an experienced, no-nonsense kingpin figure.

The mental gymnastics did nothing to enlighten Carlton about the murkier aspects of life among the Perez drug business players, but it did make the miles slide by quickly. By four o'clock, he was pulling the trailer into the flea market lot a few minutes ahead of rush hour traffic, tired of driving and wondering how Tino and Paula had both managed to sleep almost the entire trip. Thinking ahead to the evening, he saw an opportunity to spend the night alone, using fatigue and the previous night as an excuse to get some sleep. But Paula chose that moment to lean toward him and brush her breast against his arm while stretching and blinking the sleep from her eyes.

She turned and gave him The Smile, albeit a sleepy one. "I can't believe I slept for so long! How did you stay awake?"

Carlton Westerfield was nothing if not quick. "By thinking about you."

The Smile widened and The Look told him that maybe he didn't need a full night's sleep alone after all.

CHAPTER 14

The next day, Caterina called Paula early and asked her to go to Mass with her. She accepted the invitation and, leaving Carlton with a quick kiss, went to her own apartment to get ready. Carlton took the opportunity to go back to sleep, something he rarely could do. Once awake, no matter the previous night's agenda, he was usually up for the day, but two nights in a row with Paula—meaning lots of exercise and little sleep—had taxed him enough to drift off again until after nine o'clock. When he finally rose and showered, he decided it would be a good day to spend alone, but not at home. He opted to look for a new depository site for the one hundred sixty-plus thousand dollars sitting in Tino's floor safe. Although he felt comfortable with its current location, he had a nagging feeling that he wanted to experience some part of his former lifestyle, even if it was only a quirky method of hiding large sums of currency.

Taking advantage of Sunday's lighter traffic, he drove to the north side of town and cruised the area north of Loop 410 between Blanco Road and Vance Jackson Road. At one time, it had marked the northern limits of the city and still remained nice, especially a central swath comprising the small city of Castle Hills. At just over four thousand in population, it was completely surrounded by San Antonio, but prided itself on maintaining a more upscale environment than its giant neighbor.

He checked out numerous business locations, commercial areas, and public parks where he could pose as a hard-hatted, safety-vested maintenance man, there to secret or recover a PVC pipe without fear of interference, while still being confident that he wouldn't be robbed of his stash on the way to his car. As he had figured, several spots seemed too affluent, where Crime Stopper neighborhoods housed paranoid, diligent (and nosy) inhabitants with nothing else to do but watch for any activity they deemed suspicious and worthy of a call to the police. Outside those enclaves were normal, everyday neighborhoods; decent enough, but without a gaggle of Cops on Patrol to make life difficult for a solitary man posing as a worker. Just as important, nothing in the area was run-down or seedy enough to harbor inhabitants who spent all *their* time watching for any opportunity to scam or steal. In short, it was the "Goldilocks area, just right" and, after noting several good possibilities for re-stashing his money, he turned back toward his current home, first stopping at La Madeleine's for breakfast.

While eating, Carlton felt himself slipping back in time a couple of years, wishing he were still living in this part of the city, leading his solitary lifestyle and working his low-profile job delivering cars. That line of thought led to a re-hash of why he had left in the first place. While he was satisfied enough with his current living situation, his move to the south side had been the result of violent events in the last two years, events that were beyond his control, and that was something he detested. He liked his surroundings predictable and within his power to govern, beginning with himself and his habits—even the ones that bordered on obsessive compulsiveness—and extending to the atmosphere of his neighborhood, its streets and businesses. As it was, he simply didn't feel the same sense of security and self-sufficiency that his previous life had offered.

Beginning with the bloody death of Big Mo, his murder-for-hire employer for many years, his life had spiraled out of his hands and hadn't returned, not entirely. Nothing had stayed constant for more than a few weeks since that fateful day. And, like it or not, he didn't have to analyze the situation very long before realizing that the common denominator behind all the turmoil was...Paula Hendricks.

Paula, who had arrived crying at his door months earlier, confirming Big Mo's demise and begging him to protect her from warring drug lords—one of whom turned out to be her brother. Paula, who had pulled the trigger on a gun he'd wisely disabled, thus avoiding being shot at point-blank range. Paula, who had nearly gotten him killed over the money she took from Big Mo's safe while his bloody body lay dead in the floor nearby. Paula, who *may* have tried to stab him at a restaurant in Mexico after he'd fled the city in a near panic. Paula, who had escaped death in a car bomb of Carlton's making and showed up at the airport, promising to tell him the entire truth during a romantic escape trip to Rio de Janeiro.

And yes, Paula, the same woman who'd left his bed a few hours before.

Carlton finished his coffee and cursed himself, aware that he had to do something to convince himself of his own sanity—or go crazy trying, he thought grimly. With luck, his doubts about Paula would prove groundless, a product of his own suspicious nature and his inadequacy in human relations. Maybe he and Paula would be able to achieve what they had discussed on several occasions, a departure from their lives of worry and uncertainty, a shift to a normal, peaceful existence that didn't include watching for people with guns or badges, people intent on killing or imprisoning them. Or maybe he would find that his instincts had been right all along: Paula Hendricks—attractive, vivacious, desirable—was trouble with a capital T. He pulled out of the parking lot, more confused than ever with the possibilities and unsure over which result he wanted. One thing *was* certain: he needed a lot more information to unwind the mysterious woman entrenched in his life.

Taking U. S. Highway 281 through downtown, he picked up IH-37 and headed south, back to the car wash where he'd managed to extract Paula from her kidnappers. From there, he slipped over a couple of blocks toward the small house he had broken into in order to confirm what he'd seen in a dream. Recalling that line of reasoning, he felt foolish; but he forged ahead and verified the address, committing it and the realtor's information to memory before leaving the run-down neighborhood and catching the on-ramp to IH-10 West.

As he drove across the south side of the city, he wondered if he should hire an expert to analyze his dreams. Weird as they sometimes were, he vowed not to ignore any information, regardless of the source. Now if he could just put what he'd learned to good use, he thought; inserting a puzzle piece that fits, or connecting some dots leading to an answer would be nice for a change.

By the time he got home, it was past noon and time for a Sunday afternoon nap. He plopped down on the couch and went out like a light. His ringing phone woke him just after three. Another rarity, he thought, looking at the time; an extended afternoon nap. *Not* so rare was being summoned by Faustino Perez.

"You sound sleepy. Did I wake you up?"

"Oh, no, I was just trying out some new scuba gear in the bathtub! The oxygen in those tanks makes my voice sound funny."

"Ha, ha. Amazing how you can be such a wiseass, even the instant you wake up. I talked to Arturo, and he's got some information on when Ramos' vans might be scheduled for a run."

Carlton was suddenly wide awake with the news. *"Good! How'd he find out? Or should I ask?"*

"He saw two of the drivers standing beside the vans outside the parts warehouse, taking a smoke break. He ambled over and joined them by bumming a light and started chatting them up about getting a job delivering parts. They told him he might be able to get some temp work because the vans they were driving were scheduled for another gig next Wednesday and Thursday. Then one of them said he didn't want to come back and work on Friday, so that would leave three full days that someone could probably get fill-in work."

"Man, that Arturo does good work. What an opportunist! Are we going to impart this nugget of intel to my pretty DEA friend?"

"I don't see why not. Whatever else we got going on for Ramos, it can't hurt to give him something else to deal with."

"Nothing on a location, I guess? Just tell her they will be making a trip to Laredo next Wednesday or Thursday? Or both?"

"That's about it. She has plate numbers for three vans, so they can just look for any or all of them."

"Yeah, we don't want to do all their work for them. They can just set up at the checkpoints for those plate numbers on white Ford vans. Or they can organize a dragnet or APB, whatever the current buzzword is."

Tino laughed. *"Right. Oh, and Reynaldo called. He confirmed that next Wednesday will be delivery day for us, too. Another good reason to call your sweetheart at DEA and make sure she's busy that day. All next week, in fact."*

"I'm all over it."

Carlton snapped his phone shut and thought about the information he was going to deliver to Heather and how to get the best reaction. First, he checked three different phones to find the one he'd last used to call her. This was probably not the time to aggravate her with yet another burner phone number showing up. Second, getting straight to the point and keeping the information spare would be the best approach, plus cutting the conversation short in order to dodge her attempts to find out his source or his reasons to be Mr. Concerned Citizen.

He felt good about getting the three-day lead time. If his take on government bureaucracy was correct, telling her early would give more time for all of the agents to be filled in, to formulate a plan, schedule meetings, go over everything again, give more input, generate reports, plan for contingencies… all the time-wasting hoopla favored by big business and bigger government. Which was fine; as Tino had pointed out; keeping the local DEA people busy all next week would be beneficial for everyone. Taxpayers might even get their money's worth for a change.

He dialed her private cell number and waited three rings before she answered.

"Well, well! My phone says this call is from a number previously used by Carlton Westerfield! Don't tell me you're using the same phone twice in a row! Did you run out of money or just get tired of buying a new phone every few days?"

"Nope, Walmart ran out of phones. I'll have a new one next time we talk. But I wanted to let you know that one or more of the vans are probably going to make a trip south next Wednesday or Thursday."

"That's as close as you can get? A forty-eight-hour window?"

"Well, gosh, I wish I could tell you the exact minute! Hold on while I make a call and get that info. I'd hate for the DEA to have to set up at a lonely checkpoint and actually do some work for a couple of days."

"An exact time would be helpful."

"Sorry, no can do. Wednesday or Thursday is the best I can get. If I were guessing, I'd say they're going down on Wednesday with cash in the driveshafts and returning on Thursday with a blizzard tucked in there. Early snowfall in San Antone."

"How poetic! I'll pass that part along to Ikos. Maybe it'll make him feel more confident in your intel."

"Confident enough to pay me, I hope."

"We'll see. He'll probably want to meet with you himself about this."

"Okay, should I wear my best suit?"

"You should be wearing orange coveralls, picking up litter on the highway. And if he gets his way, you will be."

"Nope. Orange doesn't work with my skin tone. Tell him that green works, though. As in money."

"I'll set it up and call you."

"'Bye."

Pleased with the call, Carlton considered how the DEA could play the information he'd provided. With its huge resources, it should be no problem to track the vans going, coming, or both. In fact, the government law agency should have the ability to monitor the money going down and dope coming back, maybe get some cooperation from the Mexican federal authorities. That would make their southern neighbors happy; the chance of seizing a large bundle of illicit cash would make their day better—provided it made it past the first group of *federales*' outstretched hands. In any event, knocking off a shipment of cash or product from Ramos' inventory would be good for Tino. And with luck, maybe Ramos would back off and tend to business instead of his vendetta against Perez's group.

With his assignment done, Carlton turned again to the slim cache of facts surrounding Paula and this entire mess. "Facts" might be pushing reality, he thought; instead, assumptions, clues, and gut instinct more accurately described the tools with which he was working. Moreover, his lack of experience with familial relationships and the ugly business of kidnapping and ransom put him at a disadvantage. He felt a lot like he had on his first night of perimeter guard duty in Vietnam, supplied with some sparse instructions, a weapon, and a shove in the back with the admonishment to "watch out for our own claymores."

For the next hour, he mulled over what he knew, or thought he knew, trying to make sense of it. He ended up formulating a plan to learn more about a possible player, one he didn't know and certainly was not going to inquire about. Then he gave up and turned on the television. After a couple of complete surfing trips through the channels, he settled on a Discovery Channel presentation showing graphic scenes of the mating rituals of cobras. Informative as it was, it only served to bring back hazy memories of teenage boys' expressions of lust. Halfway through, he surfed again and noticed that *Sponge Bob* cartoons were on one channel while congressional proceedings played on the next one. The mentality of both seemed comparable. He gave up and flipped over to a rerun of *Sanford and Son.*

Later that evening, he stepped out on the landing and saw Paula was again at the pool. He waved to her but received only a half-hearted response in return, and no sign of The Smile. Then she turned her head and looked the other way; a puzzling move, given the last time they were together. Not having known her to be especially moody, he wondered what might have occurred during the day to change her from the cheerful lover who'd left him snoozing that morning to the disinterested woman now sitting at the pool. He toyed with going down to visit, but thought better of it. If she wanted him to know what was bothering her, she would call him or come up to his apartment. If not; well, it would add one more mystery to the woman who already held the record.

Even though he chose to ignore Paula's mood swing, he was unable to escape the ongoing family involvement. Only a half hour passed before he got a call from Tino inquiring about his contact with Heather Colson. Carlton assured him that the conversation had gone well; only the pertinent information had been conveyed in a short, concise call, just as he had determined would be best. Tino sounded pleased at the report.

When the conversation ended, Carlton considered turning the phone off and salvaging the remainder of the day for himself, but changed his mind when he recalled the distracted look Paula had given him earlier. He put the phone on the kitchen counter and retreated into a book, disgusted with himself for wishing she would call.

CHAPTER 15

The next day started another work week, and Carlton was glad not to be included in the work force. However, he laid out some clothes from his stint of working at the flea market, since this day's activities called for looking like a working man, someone who would be comfortable in jeans and a slightly worn work shirt, not tailored slacks and a silk pullover shirt.

After a morning run and short workout, he showered and dressed in the work duds, then vowed to himself to face the day with renewed optimism. Paula had not called the previous night, but he reasoned that he had no control over what had caused her mood change, so there was no need to worry about it. Besides, he had rather enjoyed the evening to himself and getting a full night's sleep. That realization may him wonder if he were getting old, but recalling the previous two nights quelled the thought.

He skipped breakfast and opted for an early lunch. Eating alone, he hoped Tino wouldn't call and come up with some task for him, or want him to come by for a discussion. Also, it would be fine if Paula's distant mood would continue for a while. Ideally, she would spend the day with Caterina, and he might be able to accomplish what he needed in one day without making excuses or explanations for his absence. Either of them would instantly notice the work clothes, and Carlton didn't need any questions about his attire or his day's agenda. He wanted the time at a solitary lunch for rehearsing his approach to the realtor whose sign adorned the rag-tag house on the southeast side of the city. Then, hopefully, the rest of the day would be productive.

When he'd finished eating, he made good on his joke to Heather Colson, stopping at the nearest Walmart and heading to the electronics section. He bought a burner phone for twenty-two dollars and activated it with thirty dollars' worth of time. When he returned to the little pickup, he scribbled some notes regarding a loose batch of facts he'd come up with, including a few half-truths about himself, then dialed the number from his newly-acquired phone. It was answered on the second ring.

"Hello! This is Brenda Ramos. How may I help you?"

"Uhm, hi! This is Carl Weiss. I was looking at a house on Morningview Drive and saw your name and number on the sign. I was hoping to look at the inside of the house." Of course, that opening was like asking a hungry cheetah if it wanted to chase down an antelope.

"Oh, certainly, Mr.—"

"Weiss."

He hoped she wasn't a Louisiana history buff who would instantly recognize the name of Huey Long's assassin. On the plus side for using such a name, if she later Googled the name she'd be overwhelmed by information on the infamous Baton Rouge doctor and give up searching for her elusive prospect with the same name, the guy who was currently setting up a hokey house showing.

"Okay, Mr. Weiss. Yes, I'd be glad to show you the house. When would you be available to look at it?"

"Well, I'm off today and have time this afternoon. I was hoping to see it today. Would you be able to meet with me that soon?"

Carlton held his breath, counting on the fact that she was the listing agent and wouldn't be willing to farm out the task to another agent, thus opening up the possibility of sharing the sales commission. He also worried about the likelihood that she would bring another person with her for safety's sake, but couldn't do anything about it.

"Let me check my calendar."

A few seconds passed before Ms. Ramos verified her current day's appointment schedule and came back with the response he'd hoped for.

"Mr. Weiss? How about three-thirty?"

"That would be fine for me. I'll meet you there at three-thirty."

"Good! I'll see you then."

Carlton breathed a sigh of relief that she hadn't launched into any sales tactics like inquiring about his employment, his lender, his credit score, mortgage pre-qualifying, down payment, etc. Despite his notes and preparation, he might have been lost in the jargon and possibly responded in a manner that would arouse suspicion as to his motives behind looking at the house.

With the first part of his plan in place, he began thinking over the best way to get the information he needed. However, a few minutes of pondering the situation left him with little option besides winging it and counting on his charm—and a non-descript vehicle—to do the job.

He drove to a Jim's Restaurant not far from the house and settled in to finish the book he'd begun the previous night. By three-fifteen he had almost finished it, but opted to save the last four pages and headed toward Morningview Drive a bit early. He wanted to do a drive-by of the little house before Brenda Ramos showed in order to formulate a couple of pertinent questions.

The vacant house didn't look any better today than its occupied neighbors; nor did it look any different than when he'd visited and performed the fake plumbing repair a few days ago. The late summer period had brought little rain, and the sparse lawn was nearly devoid of grass. What little there was had turned brown and brittle in the sun, and the scrubby bushes against the foundation were struggling to survive. Even the house itself looked parched and thirsty. Driving by slowly and checking it out, he smiled as he again recalled the reason he'd come back to check on this place—his weird dream—but decided it might be in bad taste to tell the realtor it was his "dream house." Unable to think of any valid questions about the place except the price, he circled the block and pulled against the curb at a spot where Brenda Ramos would be likely to pull beyond him to park. When he got out, he removed the magnetic "Medina Plumbing" signs from the doors and stuck them behind the seat.

Promptly at three-thirty a maroon Nissan SUV pulled up and angled in front of him to park at the curb. Carlton took the opportunity to memorize the license plate number and noted some details about the car which could be used to spot it in a world filled with look-alike SUVs. It sported a nameplate that sounded more like a tropical disease than a car, but he suddenly recalled a Travel Channel presentation about some islands near Venice having the same name, clarifying why some corporate genius had borrowed it: it was supposed to bring the mystery and romance of a faraway island chain to the minds of prospective car buyers, thus enticing them to buy it. Still, it seemed a goofy moniker for a vehicle...until he remembered he was driving a twenty-plus-year-old plumbing pickup with "B2200" stamped on the fender.

That thought brought a smile to his face that was perfect for exiting the vehicle and greeting Ms. Ramos, an attractive, dark-haired Hispanic woman who looked to be in her well-preserved mid-forties. As she stepped from her car, he noticed she was wearing tasteful, expensive-looking clothes that flattered her middle-aged body very well without overdoing it. She was carrying a Louis Vuitton handbag that matched her shoes perfectly, and Carlton figured the designer made shoes to match its pricey purses. As she stepped closer, he saw she didn't scrimp on her hair and nails, either. Brenda Ramos was a very attractive woman, perfectly coifed and looking ready to earn her next sales commission—starting with a one-hundred-watt smile.

"Hello there!"

"Hi! I'm Carl Weiss. You're Brenda Ramos?"

"Yes, hello, Mr. Weiss! Nice to meet you." She extended a perfectly manicured hand—adorned with lots of glitter—for Carl to shake. "Thank you for calling me about this house. How did you learn about it?"

"I work for a small electric company. I was doing a job in this area and happened to see it was for sale. I saw your sign, so I called you."

"Fine! I'm so happy you did."

"First, I guess I should see if it's anywhere in my price range. What is the asking price?"

"The house is listed at fifty-seven five."

Carlton nodded as though the price made perfect sense. Inside, he was apprehensive; this was one area he wasn't comfortable with. He should have done more homework, he thought, pricing similar houses in order to have some kind of intelligent response. Instead, he stood looking at her with what he was sure was a dumb look on his face until he struck upon a saving tactic.

"Okay," he said slowly, nodding at her with uncertainty. He cleared his throat and, acting embarrassed, continued. "I must confess that I just started looking, so I'm completely unfamiliar with how much a house like this is supposed to cost. I've lived in an apartment for years. Please bear with me. I'm going to have to study this."

Practiced at putting people at ease, she smiled and touched his arm. "Oh, don't worry, Mr. Weiss. Please take your time and do a lot of research before you do anything. It's okay to be uninformed, but quite another to *stay* uninformed. You'll learn very quickly how to compare houses and prices." Her expression said that she didn't think someone his age could learn anything about buying a house, a process normally experienced well before middle age.

Carlton gave her his best Smile of Relief and Gratitude. "Thank you!

I'm going to learn all about this business and make a decision. So, this one is fifty-seven thousand, five hundred dollars?" He made a show of pointing at the house as though there were others in question and wondered how long he could keep a straight face.

"Yes, and there are some associated closing costs, some of which you pay, and some the seller pays. And some of them, you split."

"Okay. But just for round numbers, sixty thousand dollars would probably be enough, wouldn't it?" As Carlton said the number, he realized he couldn't even replace his Cadillac for sixty large, and he was standing here discussing giving that amount for a dumpy little house. Still, a new Caddy would be a better buy than this dump, he thought, wondering if six *hundred* dollars would be closer to its actual value.

"Oh, I'm almost certain that sixty thousand dollars would get the deal done!"

"Good! I'll talk that part over with my wife."

She gave a big smile of approval for that move, while stifling her realtor's natural instinct to ask if he could actually get that amount of money. She opted to set the hook and talk finances later. "Well, let's go inside and take a look, okay?"

She stepped onto the porch and produced a key for the lockbox. After she had unlocked it and retrieved the house key, she noticed a paper wedged between the door and doorjamb and reached to pull it out. As she unfolded it, Carlton watched her expression and noted the look of mild surprise as she read it. "Oh, it says the back door is unlocked, come in and fix the sink. That's strange, I don't recall ordering any repairs since I've had the listing and my hus—oh, maybe the owners arranged for the repair and left this note."

She tucked the paper into her purse and within seconds had the front door open, holding it for her prospective client. Carlton stepped through the front door opening into the living room he hadn't seen since the previous Thursday and looked around a minute as though evaluating its size for furniture. The carpet was still beige and faded, the walls still off-white and scarred, and the smell was still that of an old house. Moving to the kitchen, the card table and chairs were in the same place, and he stepped to one side and turned slightly in order to watch her face as she entered the room.

It was there; the subtle double-take, the slight narrowing of her eyes as she took in the appearance of the furniture. She recovered quickly, and Carlton looked away, then down at the table as though he had only just noticed it. "Looks like we're a bit late for the card game. Too bad."

"I wasn't aware that the owner had left anything in here. When I take a listing, I always insist that the house either be completely empty or has enough real furniture to show better than without. This old stuff makes the house look like it was occupied by beggars."

Or kidnappers, Carlton thought, although he couldn't imagine how the folding table and chairs could possibly tarnish the appearance of the run-down little house. Aloud he said, "Maybe they had one last pizza here after moving day. They probably deserved it, and were so tired they forgot to load the table and chairs."

Brenda smiled thinly in response and strode to the tiny kitchen closet, probably to check for any trash or other remnants of whomever had left the furniture items. Except for the hanger in the bedroom closet, Carlton already knew there was nothing. That made it easy to observe her now, moving into rooms ahead of him, obviously concerned about what else might have been left behind. He couldn't quite understand her concern; as a realtor, she surely had seen a lot worse than a shabby table left behind and, in this case, it wasn't any shabbier than the house. He decided she was just surprised to see something that wasn't supposed to be there and would be relieved when she found nothing else. And Carlton thought he knew why.

The little house wasn't big enough to take a long time studying, nor was there a lot to stand and marvel about. After ten minutes and a few questions regarding any recent maintenance or additions (there was none, save the sink repair), Carlton headed toward the front door and held it for Ms. Ramos.

"Thank you so much for your time, Ms. Ramos."

"It's Mrs., but please call me Brenda, Mr. Weiss. Here's my card."

"And I'm just plain Carl. My dad was Mr. Weiss." He put on his best smile and pocketed the business card, then extended his hand. "I'll give this a lot of consideration and do a bunch of research before I get back with you."

"Thank you so much, Carl! Have a nice afternoon!"

She stepped briskly to her car, and Carlton figured she had another appointment, one that held much better possibilities than the shaky showing she'd just performed. As he had hoped, she never glanced toward his vehicle as she clicked open her door and got in. She was already on her cell phone, probably chatting up her next prospect as she pulled away. He moved quickly to his pickup and gassed it away from the curb to keep the realtor's Nissan in sight. She turned back toward the freeway and moved up the on-ramp so fast Carlton had to give the pickup all it had to stay up. Finally, she approached highway speed plus ten, and he was able to drop back to a safe distance. Now if he could just keep up with her for the rest of her day without being seen, he had a chance at seeing whether or not Brenda Ramos was a link to the mystery or simply another sharp realtor with her face plastered on a yard sign.

Carlton lucked out with the realtor's schedule, and the afternoon wasn't as long as he had feared it would be. He circled the block a couple of times before finding a parking place north of downtown and watched from a distance while she met with a couple in a restaurant parking lot. Judging from the smiles and hugs, it must have been a satisfactory meeting; for Carlton, it was blessedly brief. Then, after another showing of a two-story in the area east of Broadway undergoing gentrification, she headed north, then caught Austin Highway into Terrell Hills. She turned left at the art museum and continued into the nice neighborhood adjoining Alamo Heights to the west and Terrell Hills to the south, an area Carlton assumed to be in San Antonio proper. At slower speeds in the quiet neighborhood, he had to hang back and almost lost her in the winding streets. Finally, she hit her brakes and wheeled into a wide driveway, punching the garage door opener on the way. Carlton went by with his head turned away, an unnecessary precaution. She was back on her phone and timed her approach with the rising door, a move so practiced it had to be her home. He shook his head, grinned at the antics of the hard-charging realtor, and headed for Loop 410 and his apartment.

He had an address and car description, and he knew what Brenda Ramos looked like. Now he had to figure out why her phone number was listed in Paula's phone, in the contacts list, but with only the initials "BR." Whatever the connection turned out to be, he was fairly certain that his feeling of unrest the past week was about to be justified.

CHAPTER 16

Traffic was heavy, and the trip across the city took more than two hours because of a major wreck on 281 and two stalled vehicles on IH-35. Carlton arrived at the apartments just before seven, cranky and tired from the tedious drive. As he climbed the stairs he saw that the pool area was deserted; an oddity, since it seemed someone always was out enjoying the still-warm early fall weather. In fact, the entire apartment complex was quiet and sounded as though it had been evacuated.

He went inside, plopped down in his chair, and wondered where Paula had spent the day and where she was right now. Then his mind returned to the problem of how he was going to approach the Brenda Ramos matter with her, the umpteenth time he had agonized over that subject since leaving the realtor's neighborhood. The feeling of accomplishment over having gotten what he wanted was short-lived; he had the information on her, but it had to be deciphered in order to be of any use. And to do that, he had to confront Paula.

On the drive home, he had considered going straight to Tino and explaining what he'd first suspected, what he had learned today, and what the possible explanation was according to his gut instinct. However, recalling his troubled feelings about Tino's reaction to the kidnapping, he nixed the idea, for the moment anyway. By talking to Paula first, maybe, just *maybe* there was a reasonable explanation to all of this, but he didn't hold out much hope for that. The dilemma left him unsure where to turn and what to do next. And much like his first perimeter patrol at a Vietnam basecamp, there was no one to ask.

He tilted the chair back and turned on the television. Not much was on, as usual, so he settled for a Nat Geo re-run documenting the mating habits of honey badgers…fascinating stuff. So fascinating, he awoke at eight-fifteen and wondered where he was for a minute before he could unfog his brain. The reason for the interruption from a deep sleep stage turned out to be his other phone ringing, and it took him a minute to find it on the dresser in the bedroom. By then, it had quit ringing and he checked the number of the missed call: *Paula.* He started to hit redial, but the phone rang in his hand, startling him. He checked the number: *Tino.* Well, so much for wondering where everyone was, he thought.

He called Paula back first. She answered on the first ring, and he could tell by her voice something was wrong.

"Are you home?" she asked without preamble.

"Yes, I got here…um, an hour ago and fell asleep in my chair. Are you okay?"

"I need—we need to talk to you. Okay if we come over?"

"We? Who's—"

"Tino and I."

Carlton was wary of what was happening, trying to gauge her degree of distress and what it meant. Also, Tino had become involved, both of them dialing his number, so it had to be serious; this call was *not* a prelude to a pleasurable visit from an attractive woman. He answered, hoping his response was quick enough to divert any suspicion about what he knew.

"Sure, come on over." He also hoped his voice sounded like he meant it.

He opened the door and looked over to the landing where her apartment was. The door was already opening, and she and Tino were on their way. Three minutes later they were all seated, and an uncomfortable silence settled over the room. He looked from one to the other for a few seconds; Paula was nervous and fidgety, while Tino's normally impassive face seemed tight and apprehensive, almost angry. The silence continued.

"Anybody want to tell me what's going on?" Carlton asked, trying to keep his voice casual.

Paula's fidgeting had ceased, replaced by tension that held her stock-still on the couch. She looked like she was holding her breath, and when she spoke, it seemed to take every ounce of her energy to deliver the simple declarative phrase.

"He's got my daughter at his house."

"*What?*" Carlton's response, in the form of a question, was automatic, but unintended and unnecessary. He didn't need a repeat of the words; he'd heard her clearly. He just needed clarification—lots of it—in order to understand what she had just imparted to him in seven shocking words.

"Brujido Ramos has my daughter." She took a deep breath and plunged on. "Her name is Cecilia. She's eleven years old, and Brujido is about to wreck her life."

Carlton opened his mouth to speak, but she boldly held up her hand like a traffic cop, shutting off what she assumed would be words of surprise, shock, anger—whatever emotion might be likely to surface under such circumstances—and began to set forth answers for questions without being asked.

"When I had her, I couldn't keep her, Carlton. My life and my health were in total chaos, so I arranged to have her adopted by a close friend. I went to college with her, a girl named—"

"Brenda Ramos." Carlton interrupted her with the answer.

Paula stared at him and nodded. "Brenda *Vara* then. Her family is from the Valley. She married Julian Ramos, Brujido's brother, right after we graduated. How did you—"

"And Julian's brother just happens to be a maniac smuggler who kidnaps women and girls just to jerk everyone's chain, or pick up a half million bucks here and there?"

Paula nodded numbly. Carlton looked at Tino, but his face told him nothing more, so his next remark was posed to both of them, delivered with sarcasm. "So, what does Julian do for kicks? Throw kittens into a threshing machine? Put baby chicks in a blender? Make porno snuff films?" With no aforethought, he was taking his anger out on both of them with outrageous words, lashing out in an attempt to cover his embarrassment at being played for the last nine days.

Tino wisely took it as a sign that he needed to step in. "Carlton, as far as we know, Julian is a pretty normal guy who does maintenance work for his wife. He repairs houses that are up for sale, does upkeep on their rental properties, stuff like that. He and his brother are not alike, best I can determine. But they are brothers, so that's the connection that certainly played a part in Cecilia being caught up in this. Brujido knew the arrangement Brenda made with Paula before the baby was born. And yes, he was probably *unknowingly* involved when Paula was kidnapped."

Carlton thought for a moment, trying to calm down and analyze the connection. "So Julian has access to the lockbox key, he can get into the listed properties. He let his brother use the little house on Morningview to keep Paula tied up until the ransom exchange."

Tino looked at him, puzzled. "Morningview? How did you find that out? And where is it, anyway?"

"It's where I've been today, over on the east side," he said, answering the last question first. "I met Brenda Ramos there to look at the house." Tino and Paula both stared at him in amazement, so he explained. "I posed as a possible buyer. I had looked at the house before and saw a couple of things that tied in with what Paula had told me about where she was held captive. And Brenda's phone number is in your contacts list," he added, looking at Paula's stricken face.

"How do you know…I mean, what did you do…" Her voice trailed off, unable to formulate the pertinent question. She even fumbled in her pocket for her phone, as though to see if it had the answer she wanted, but she stopped with his next words and held the phone in her hand without looking at it.

"I *snooped*, that's how, I'm embarrassed to say," Carlton explained. "Remember, I told you—correction, I *advised* you not to keep a contacts list on your phone. But I sneaked a peek and saw that you did what everyone does: you keep too much information for someone else to see. Well, I saw it."

"But how did you know what the number was?" she asked, apparently relying on the weak code she had used.

"I vaguely recognized the number from the sign in the yard of that little house. It rang a bell, but I couldn't place it until I went back over there and checked. Of course, I could have done that online, but I wanted to take another look at the house. Anyway, the number matched, and the name, Brenda Ramos; initials, BR. *BR, Paula, for cryin' out loud!* You think I'm an idiot?"

"You're the last person anyone would think that of, Carlton. What did you want at the house? I mean, why look at it?"

"I wanted to look at the inside of it. There were a couple of clues that led me to believe it's where you were kept by Ramos' men. Oh, and where you changed clothes the night you were held." Then he added, "While you were tied up and blindfolded, no doubt."

She opened her mouth to speak, but nothing came out, and Tino stirred in his seat.

Rather than explain, Carlton turned to Tino. "I've been thinking about this since the night of the kidnapping. Your response to the ransom demand, the setup of having me be the bagman. I told you I knew nothing about doing it, but you insisted. And your explanation made sense in a way; the language barrier, my age and appearance, my interest in Paula making me feel responsible. It added up to my being an easy choice, even if not the best one."

Tino nodded in agreement. "Yes, for all those reasons and more, you were the best choice. You proved that a few hours later, but not in the way I anticipated. When you popped those four assholes, it changed everything, it—"

"Maybe you could have let me in on how it was *supposed* to go down!" Carlton was nearly shouting, and he struggled to maintain his composure. Glancing down, he noticed his hands were steady, but just barely. He took a few deep breaths and glared at Tino.

Tino looked down, then back up to Carlton's face and locked his gaze on him. A few seconds went by before he spoke calmly. "You might recall that I *did* tell you how it was supposed to go down. And don't get me wrong, I was delighted that you handled it the way you did. Hell, I wish Ramos had been there. We wouldn't be having a problem now."

"Well, he *wasn't*—and we *do*."

At that, Tino actually grinned at Carlton's succinct and clever summation. "Yep. And Brujido has notched up the stakes since last time. So I guess it's time you heard all of it."

Carlton had used the brief delay to calm down, to tell himself there were several possible outcomes and arriving at the best one wouldn't be unearthed by anger. He didn't come up with anything specific in the short span, but seeing Tino's grin, he reverted to a standard fallback position—sarcastic comedy—when he responded. "You really think so, Lefty?" Then he turned to Paula with a look of inquiry on his face and motioned that she had the floor, along with his undivided attention.

Paula took a deep breath and began. "I was separated from Don at the time. We hadn't yet been married, but we had been seeing each other for over a year when things just fell apart. We went our separate ways, and I didn't think I'd ever see him again. Too bad that wasn't the case.

"Long story short, I had an affair, I got pregnant. I had some health problems; nothing life-threatening, but enough to keep me on edge during my pregnancy. Late in my pregnancy, the doctor said everything was going well with the baby, but I was a wreck. I was a little heavier in those days, but I had lost weight during pregnancy instead of gaining. I was so weak I could barely get out of bed or stand up for more than a few minutes without being exhausted. I didn't know what I was going to do with a daughter that I couldn't even stand up and hold. When the time came, I couldn't deliver naturally. Afterwards, I was out for two days.

"One of the few people who came to see me was Brenda Vara. And I don't mean to sound like 'oh, poor me, no one loves me;' I simply didn't know many people; I had lost touch with all my old friends and taken up with Don's. Of course, with what was going on, they didn't feel comfortable around me anymore."

Tino interrupted her tale. "I came to see you, *Hermanita*. So did Marta."

She smiled at him. "Yes, you did, Tino. I haven't forgotten, I guess I'm just editing this tale for brevity's sake."

Carlton held up his hand to interrupt the narrative. "Before we go further, is Cecilia alright?" he asked. "I didn't mean that my being fully informed was more important than getting her back. We can continue this later if we need to be doing something right now to get her back."

"No, I don't think she's in immediate danger, not physical danger. Her uncle is crazy as a loon, but I don't think he'd hurt her, not if we pay the ransom."

"Why does this story sound familiar? What is it this time? A million?" Carlton was losing his temper again at hearing this replay of Brujido Ramos' terror-inducing game plan, as well as deviating from the story he wanted to hear.

"He hasn't said a number yet, but that might be possible," Tino said, catching his tone and taking over for Paula. "I spoke with him once today, and he reminded me that we would have to pay a penalty for what happened last time."

Carlton rolled his eyes and said nothing for a moment. "Has he given a time deadline yet?"

"No. Right now, it seems everything is on hold. He's going to call me back at nine tonight, and I assume we'll get the complete demand then."

"How did this happen, anyway?"

Paula took over again. "Brenda and Julian live fairly near Brujido and his live-in, a young woman named Myra. And Brenda tells me that it's not unusual for Cecilia to go visit them. She gets along well with Myra, because she's young, maybe mid-twenties. I think Cecilia looks up to her, likes to spend time with her."

Carlton shook his head. "If only she knew Uncle Brujido better, she'd know that his squeeze isn't likely to win the Presidential Medal of Freedom.

Or maybe not; hell, I don't know what kids admire. Certainly not what I did when I was eleven."

"Brenda tells me that she's a pretty ordinary kid," Paula responded, sounding defensive. "Makes good grades, helps around the house, and doesn't get in any trouble."

Carlton nodded in agreement. "I didn't mean to imply anything bad about her, Paula. I just meant times are a lot different, and she's certainly growing up in a different environment than I did. My hero was an all-American boy from Oklahoma who could hit a baseball a country mile. Hers is probably some singer or actress who can't *spell* baseball *or* Oklahoma, or maybe a drug importer who kidnaps on the side." Despite the opening disclaimer, his tone of voice left no doubt about his opinion concerning modern celebrities—and their fans.

"Well, we can't do anything about that. I don't think Brenda and Julian can, or want to. They love her just like she is. And so do I, but I..." At that point, she looked about ready to burst into tears.

Carlton rushed to repair his clumsiness. "I know, I know. I'm just angry at this whole mess and taking it out on everything I dislike in the world. It doesn't help anything, and I'm sorry. Anyway, have you been able to talk to her?"

Paula glanced at Tino "No, I haven't been able to."

Carlton caught the look and suspected he was still being kept in the dark about something, but let it slide for the moment. She paused, as though gauging her next comment. "In fact, Cecilia doesn't even know she's been kidnapped; she's just staying at his house for a few days, with him and Myra."

"*Doesn't know she's been kidnapped?* So Uncle Brujido doesn't have her tied up in the basement? How do you figure she doesn't realize she's being held for ransom? You know for sure she's okay?"

"Yes, dammit, I know for sure! Okay?"

Now Carlton knew he'd been correct; his barrage of logical questions had pushed her into the defensive outburst. He leaned back in his seat and waited, looking from her face to Tino's with his eyebrows arched in inquiry, determined not to give up until he heard all of it.

She took a few deep breaths, then dropped the next bombshell. "I stay in touch with Brenda and keep up with my daughter, but Cecilia doesn't know about me, Carlton. I've never seen her, never held her."

Carlton struggled to keep the perplexed look from his face, but failed. He waited to hear her out. Seeing his look, she explained. "That was the condition

Brenda and Julian insisted on, that she be given to them with no strings, no attachment, no recourse, no future contact with me. Brenda and Julian were to be her parents forever. I don't even exist for Cecilia."

He was dumbfounded, feeling like he had earlier when discussing a house purchase with the realtor. He didn't know whether to express condolences, ask a question, or give advice, so he settled for ignorance. "I didn't think there was a way to do that, not legally. But what do I know about adoption?"

"Most people don't. Brenda's parents were quite wealthy, and they used a team of lawyers in handling their business and personal transactions. One of those was a malpractice suit against a doctor who recommended that Brenda have a surgery when she was seventeen, a procedure that left her unable to have children. Later, another doctor was stunned that she'd undergone the surgery; said it was totally unnecessary, and he testified to that in court. The Vara family won the suit and was awarded over three million dollars in damages, so they got wealthier.

"Of course, Brenda had access to the family legal team through the years and had learned about the importance of good legal work, even before that happened. When she came up with this plan to have a child—my child—she called on them to make it ironclad. I was in no position to negotiate. Besides, I knew my daughter would have a chance at a good life with Brenda and Julian, a lot better than with me, even if my health had been better."

Carlton nodded, seeing how it had been arranged and agreeing to her logic, no matter how odd it seemed now. But wondering about its permanence, he asked, "This is a big city, but how could all the parties be sure you wouldn't run into each other? Maybe at a shoe sale, or something?"

The remark got a brief smile and broke the tension a bit. "They moved to Dallas a long time ago, but last year she had an opportunity to open her own agency here and moved back. Soon after, Brujido contacted his brother and wanted them to find a home for him, here in San Antonio. What could she say?"

Again, Carlton didn't know what to say, and he chose his next words carefully. "So they're afraid Brujido will drop the dime on the arrangement, tell Cecilia she's adopted? I don't claim to know anything about human relationships, but..."

"And he might actually harm her, but I don't think so. Hopefully, Myra has enough power over him to prevent anything like that from happening. But he'll hurt her more than physically by telling her about me. And yes, it will kill Brenda and Julian, too; worse, they might hold me responsible for her being told about me. In other words, they think if I—we—just pay the ransom, she won't be told, and our little..."

"Deception?" he supplied the word and immediately regretted how it sounded, not even close to reality.

"*Lie.* And my little *lie* will stay untold," Paula said harshly, and Carlton admired her for it.

He was quiet for a moment, thinking back to an earlier conversation with Tino. He turned to him and asked, "And just like before: what's to keep Uncle Brujido from doing this again?"

Tino stirred in his seat and fielded the question. "And just like before: nothing. But this time the ransom will also include my giving up the business for good, or he'll tell Cecilia—or worse. That's what he's been angling for, and he's figured out a way to do it and keep it working, at least during her childhood."

"You really think that's been his plan all along? By kidnapping Paula, and now this?"

"Yes, I'm certain of it. In the future, if he hears a word about my infringing on 'his territory,' he'll tell her immediately. I'm certain that will be the deal when he calls. He'll claim that's the *penalty* for last time, in addition to a large sum of money. He wants to destroy me and has for a while. But lately, he's become obsessed with it. I think he's been listening to his cartel buddies about terror and extortion."

"And use an eleven-year-old girl to do it. What a prince of a man our Brujido Ramos is."

"He's gotten worse in the past year," Tino agreed. "Success in the drug business has made him crazy; he thinks he's like some big drug baron in South America who can take over any facet of the trade he doesn't already control.

"He contacted Paula through Brenda a couple of weeks ago and asked about my business. Of course, she doesn't really know anything about day-to-day operations, and she told him so. He demanded that she convince me to drop my business, to turn over my entire area to him, or something bad would happen to her."

Carlton turned to her. "How did you react?"

"I told him I would pass that along to Tino and, of course, I did. Then we heard nothing, not until last Saturday evening when they grabbed me. I had no idea what was going on, I'd never seen any of those guys. In fact, I had almost forgotten about the threat and didn't realize that Ramos was behind it until he showed up at that house. And I *was* tied up and blindfolded until he got there. I recognized him from Brenda's wedding, and I realized he was carrying out the threat he'd made over the phone. They left us alone to talk, and they put the blindfold back on me and tied my wrists as soon as he left. But you're right, while he was there, I asked if I could close the door and change clothes, and he let me. I can't believe you noticed something like that."

"You're pretty noticeable in a pair of jeans, you know. Or anything." He restrained himself from adding "or nothing," given the fact that her brother was sitting there.

Paula gave him an embarrassed smile. "You'd think I'd learn about you after all this time. You seldom miss anything."

Carlton shook his head. "No, I miss plenty, and this is proof of it." He turned back to Tino. "So, when I called you about the kidnapping, you already knew what was happening."

"Yes," he sighed. "Except for you getting popped on the head. I hadn't anticipated that. Another sign of Ramos turning more violent and passing it along in instructions to his crew. I can only apologize for that happening."

Carlton waved away his concern. "That's okay. One of the guys at the ransom exchange looked like he could have been the one who used my head for an anvil. I used his for a target. I hope it was the same guy, anyway."

Tino nodded an acknowledgment and couldn't help adding: "One good rap on the head deserves one in return?"

"Something like that."

"Anyway, Ramos told me that paying him a half million would represent profits that I should be sharing with him. I knew then that he was crazy, an absolute maniac. But he said if I would pay him the money, he'd return Paula, leave us alone, and withdraw the demand that I give him my area for good, that—"

"Which you knew was a crock, right?"

"Of course!" he retorted. "I would have been insane to think I could trust him. I was just trying to get Paula back quickly and figure out a way to take him off the board before he came up with something crazier."

"And he didn't have to come up with a crazier scheme; *I did.* I capped his ransom team."

"Yes, dammit, you did. All of them!" The look of glee on Tino's face said that he still relished that outcome, no matter the trouble it was now causing. "But as I said, it was going to cause repercussions, I knew that for sure."

"The first of which was killing Gabriel and Tony, neither of whom had any idea that any of this was going on."

Tino shook his head, misery showing on his face at the reminder. "I should have launched on him immediately, while he was still staggered from losing his four guys, but I wanted to think it out sufficiently so I wouldn't lose more people in a bloodbath that was poorly planned and executed. Also, I'm short on personnel, thanks to the crooked DEA jackass and a spy in my midst."

Carlton nodded. "He was counting on that factor when he came up with this, no doubt about it."

"Of course. That's why your plan to rat him out to the DEA was a good one, but now time has run out on us."

"So he's now come up with his Plan B, which is destroy several people's lives by running his big mouth. *Again.*"

"That sums it up nicely," Tino said grimly. "And now we wait to see what he demands this time. I should have gone to war with that bastard the minute he threatened me through Paula. Win, lose, or draw, it would have been better than this."

A lengthy silence settled over the room as everyone stole a peak at the clock in the kitchen, sliding toward nine o'clock.

CHAPTER 17

At five after nine, Tino's phone rang. He looked at the number display and nodded at Carlton before pressing "Talk" and answering in Spanish.

"Bueno?"

Carlton strained to hear the voice on the other end, trying to get an image in his mind to fit what he already knew about Brujido Ramos. He couldn't come up with anything, though, except the man was obviously driven by more than just greed and violence, the primary ingredients required to carry on in the highly lucrative—and illegal—business of smuggling contraband narcotics. Clearly, something was amiss in the guy's mind to motivate him to spend time and resources to meddle with his competition in such a perverted way. It was highly unlikely that Ramos was going hungry simply because Faustino Perez controlled an area of the city's drug trade—on the other side of town.

Tino spoke for about three minutes before snapping his phone shut. He exhaled loudly and leaned back on the couch. "Well, it's what I expected. He wants a half million dollars and all my inventory delivered to him, which puts me out of business. The way he cuts his product, mine will amount to a huge amount of money for him. He says if it doesn't happen exactly as he says, he'll sit down with Cecilia and tell her about her life in great detail. Plus, he said if that doesn't have the effect he wants, she might be harmed in another way. I didn't even ask what that might be." Capping the report, he added: "That babbling bastard needs his nuts cut off!"

Carlton nodded his agreement, then stole a look at Paula. She had a look of shock on her face, even more terrified than when she'd first come to Carlton's apartment to inform him of Big Mo's grisly death. He quickly looked away, reminding himself that that look had been fake, since she later confided that she had killed Big Mo herself. Recalling the incident, he reminded himself that nothing was likely to be exactly as it seemed, not with Paula or anything around her.

He turned back to face Tino. "What's the timetable?"

"Tomorrow night at midnight. He's smart enough to know I can't possibly round up all my inventory of product in that span of time, but I've got to come up with enough to make it look realistic, or talk him into an extension. I'll tell Reynaldo to hold the stuff he was going to have here by Wednesday. Ramos doesn't know about it, but it might leak that I've got more product than I turned over to that idiot. Plus, he raved on and on about what would take place if he ever got word that I was back in business. Brujido Ramos is an absolute raving maniac, and he proved it by his last demand, just before he hung up on me."

"Which is?"

Tino hesitated. "He'll call back with the meeting place, but he insists that you be the bagman."

Carlton laughed out loud. "Of course he does! Why didn't I think of that?"

Paula cleared her throat. "Carlton, please do this for me." Her eyes pleaded with him.

"Paula, I understand how important Cecilia is to you, and it would be a possible disaster for her to be told the truth about you and Brenda. But there is no doubt that I will be gunned down immediately by that psycho and his crew if I show up with the ransom—make that *extortion* money. He'll arrange a rendezvous point that will be impossible for Tino's crew to cover me and—"

"He's right, Paula," Tino interrupted. "Carlton can't possibly go. They will set it up to kill him, I know that. We've got to come up with something else. He's going to call back in the morning, and I've got to have something in place that will work. I'll meet with the entire crew tonight and get everyone ready, exactly what I should have done from the start." He opened his phone and started punching in numbers.

When he began speaking, Carlton figured it was Raul Vega on the other end. Listening to the rapid-fire Spanish, he could only pick up a few names; hearing Arturo, David, and Enrique mentioned among others, he knew the older veteran was being tasked to round up the entire crew. Struggling to understand more, he heard the word "*oficina*" and "*diez*," which must mean they were to meet at Tino's flea market office at ten. Otherwise, he didn't understand the conversation, but he had a good idea that the crime boss wasn't arranging anything pleasant for his nut-case competitor.

Tino finished talking and snapped his phone shut. All business now, he stood up quickly and headed for the door. Carlton didn't move, hoping he wouldn't be invited to the strategy meeting and depending on his poor Spanish skills to exempt him. It didn't work.

"Come on, ride with me," Tino barked. "I can conduct this in English, and I want your input. Besides, everyone will want to see I've got the *pistolero* with me."

Carlton groaned theatrically and rolled his eyes, but stood to go. "We don't need pistols, we need machine guns," he complained. "I hope your guys don't put too much faith in me on this deal."

"Well, they taught you about machine guns in the military, didn't they?"

"I know where the trigger is, if that's what you mean."

He stopped at the door and reached for Paula's hand. She was sitting stock-still, the worried look etched on her face. He leaned down and hugged her. "Don't worry, these guys will come up with something. Tino has been patient, trying to get something else to work, but Ramos doesn't leave much room for reasonable outcomes. It's time he learned the hard way."

Paula exhaled and leaned back. "I know. I just hope Cecilia doesn't have to suffer because of it."

Tino spoke up. "We'll do the best we can to prevent that, *Hermanita*. But Ramos is leaving me with no other choice. I won't be pushed around by that jackass anymore. If I've got to lose men, so be it. And if Cecilia hears something that shakes up her life, she'll have to deal with it. It will be easier for Brenda and Julian to handle it with Brujido off the map."

Listening to the sibling exchange, Carlton wondered if Cecilia would be better off hearing the truth about her background or hearing about her uncle's violent death. Either one didn't seem good but, as Tino had pointed out, Ramos didn't leave any choice. Besides, a man in Ramos' line of work wasn't likely to die of old age and be remembered as the kindly uncle who'd bounced little Cecilia on his knee and funded her college education. No, he would reside in Cecilia's memory as the uncle with the young girlfriend who turned her life upside down with shocking, unbelievable news—or as the oddball uncle whose closed-casket funeral she attended at age eleven, a weeping Myra by her side.

Nothing about these people is normal, he thought, conveniently putting aside his own chosen field of work. When the hypocrisy of his mental evaluation hit him, he justified it by his other choices: no family, no emotional attachments, no one to suffer at the hands of his mistakes save himself.

They left Paula at the apartment and met Estéban and Sergio in the parking lot where they all rode in the brothers' Chevy to the flea market office. Four other vehicles were there, and another pulled in beside them as they got out of the car. Carlton was surprised to see that about twenty men—plus the veterans Raul and Pete—were waiting for Tino Perez to instruct them in confronting the rival *contrabandista* gang threatening them from across the city. He figured this group must comprise Faustino Perez's entire crew, from street vendors, collectors, and transporters to enforcers and advisors such as Raul Vega and David Avila. As they all trooped into the makeshift office talking quietly among themselves, he was again impressed with the loyalty displayed. They were all keenly aware of the danger they were facing; each of them recalled the recent loss of friends and brothers in a similar situation; but a phone call had them here at ten o'clock sharp at the boss' little portable building office, about to plan another bloodbath.

Tino didn't waste any time. He opened with an update on Brujido Ramos' latest outrage, giving only sketchy details about Paula's daughter, who, he told them, "has lived with Paula's friends all her life, friends who have the misfortune of being related to Ramos." Leaving out details of the girl's parentage and her complete ignorance of Paula, Tino focused on the possibility that Ramos might physically harm the girl if his demands were not met, the first of which was a half million dollars in cash. Then he dropped the clincher, the demand that he relinquish his entire market area and never sell product again in southwest San Antonio.

It was enough to accomplish what he wanted.

At the end of the explanation a complete silence settled over the room for a few seconds; then the room erupted in murmurs among the men, some of whom expressed shock and anger, others incredulity. Their very livelihood was being threatened, their lives were being dictated by this guy across town? Unbelievable! Plus, given the fact that a little girl was the tool of leverage Ramos chose to use ignited the ever-present machismo attitude in the young Latinos.

The murmurs grew louder until Tino had to silence the group to continue his presentation. "We're going all-out against Ramos' bunch, and soon. Initially, I will try to meet his demand for cash and enough product to make him think we're going along with the demand. But as soon as the girl is returned to her parents, we've got to be prepared to carry out a few strikes against his crew, enough to draw him out. When that happens, he's got to be taken off the board, or we'll put up with another demand every time he forgets to take his medication. Besides, we're not about to be put out of business by that *hijo de puta* from the Valley.

"The demand for cash is set for midnight tomorrow, Tuesday, just a little over twenty-four hours from now. He's calling me back with the meeting place later and, just like last time, he's waiting until it's too late to plan anything. So I'm probably going through with his demand, unless I can convince him to give me a couple of days. As most of you know, we came up with some good information that Carlton has passed on to the local DEA that could throw a wrench in Ramos' operation, enough to make him change his mind. But it may make him angry enough to do something really insane; with him who knows?"

A hand went up in the group, and Tino nodded to the inquirer. It was David Avila, and he asked a good question. "If you can't get an extension on the time, who is going to deliver the money and product?"

Carlton stiffened in his chair, and Tino didn't hesitate. "He demands that Carlton deliver the money." Before anyone could comment, he continued. "Obviously, that won't work. We all know that he and his guys want to gun down our *pistolero* in a second, no matter what."

"If they could, you mean, *Jefe*!" a voice behind Carlton spoke out boldly. "That didn't work out so good for those *pendejos* last time!"

His bold outburst was met with more murmuring and a few muted cheers. Tino held up his hand for order and tried to maintain a stern countenance, but when silence returned he failed to restrain his grin and pointed to Carlton. "Ah, Arturo, you may be right, but we are not going to take a chance with our friend here. No matter what, Ramos will just have to settle for someone else."

Carlton flushed at the attention, but turned in his chair to get a look at Arturo Matamoros, the watcher who had gotten the info on Ramos' vans. He spotted a thin young guy about three chairs back, whose broad grin was accompanied by a thumbs-up for the *pistolero*. Carlton's embarrassment increased, but he acknowledged him with a smile and a wave, then returned his attention to the speaker.

Tino went on at some length about security for families, restriction of unnecessary trips, traveling in groups—all the smothering practices he had decried earlier and vowed to avoid, at least long-term. But for now, it was imperative that all members of Tino's crew protect themselves and their families; indeed, the entire community, until Ramos could be eliminated. A few men had questions, which were quickly answered, and the meeting drew to a close just after eleven o'clock. Everyone rose and exited the crowded little building, glad to escape into the fresh night air. Smokers lit up on the way to their vehicles, and the group quickly got in their vehicles and left, including Tino, Carlton, and the Estrada brothers.

On the way home, Carlton read the text message he had received while the meeting was taking place. It was from Heather Colson, and she wanted Carlton to meet with her and her new boss tomorrow just before noon. She gave the location of a taco shop on Broadway, near Brackenridge Park. Carlton showed Tino the screen before flipping the phone closed.

"Glad someone has good news. You get to meet with that pretty DEA agent, while I get to round up three-quarters of a million in cash and dope."

"Well, she going to have her new boss with her, a guy named Stan Ikos, so it can't be that good. I guess they want to know if I've heard anything additional about Ramos' intentions for Wednesday and Thursday."

Tino grunted in response, and Carlton knew he wasn't in the mood to be reminded that it would be helpful if Ramos could be convinced to wait a few days for his extortion money. He opted to go another route, one he'd considered bringing up earlier in his apartment. He waited a few minutes until Sergio had pulled into the apartment driveway and parked. He opened his door and stopped, looking over at Tino as though he'd just had the thought. "Do you think Reynaldo should be informed of this development?"

"Sure. I called him before you came home. Paula was in a frenzy, we didn't know where you were, so I called him with the update. He agrees that we're not left with many options, but when I told him about the tipoff to the DEA for Wednesday or Thursday, he stressed that stalling Ramos until that happens might put a new spin on things, and something different might present itself. Not necessarily good, mind you, but different. I assured him I would do my best."

The two men sat in the back seat with both rear doors open, mulling over the situation, watching while the Estrada brothers left them in privacy by splitting up and taking positions at each end of the small parking lot. Thinking about Carlton's text message from the DEA agent, Tino put aside his other front-burner issues and asked Carlton what else the federal agents could wanted to discuss. "I mean, hell, you called them and couched it in terms that you would like to be paid for the information, right? So if you had additional information, you'd be calling them back, trying to bump the price, or at least keep your payment on their minds. It's what snitches do."

"Yeah, that sounds right, so maybe it's something else. She's always wanting to know my source, so maybe she thinks her new boss can rattle me enough to give up some names."

Tino turned to look at him. "You think so? Damn, be sure you don't get rattled, then!"

Carlton knew he was joking, but felt compelled to remind him about her previous boss' attempts to browbeat him. "Timothy Hunnicutt tried to rattle me. I doubt this new guy will have any more success."

"If it means staying up with you half the night to build a bomb to blow his ass to hell, I hope he doesn't even try."

Carlton grinned. "That was a long night, wasn't it? And I drove to Corpus when we were done, got there about three in the morning. Anyway, I guess I'll find out tomorrow at lunch. Maybe the feds will spring for the check."

"Make sure you order extra guacamole on your taco. Probably all the payment you'll get for landing them a van full of blow."

"That would be sufficient payment if it diverts Ramos' attention enough to delay his extortion play."

Tino nodded in agreement. "That would buy us some time, allow me to get a few more guys, maybe see if Reynaldo can recommend some good contract help. I'd rather have guys I don't know get killed than ones I've known since they were kids."

"What do we do if Ramos changes his run schedule and the feds miss the shipment?"

Tino pulled his door shut and turned to look at him. "I sense a plan unfolding behind those shifty gringo eyes. In fact, that could be your new nickname: *Shifty*."

"More apt than *Pistolero*. We'd make quite a pair, Shifty and Lefty."

Tino's response was to roll his eyes and reach again for his door handle. When he didn't open it right away, Carlton sensed there was something more coming, and he was right.

"You still pissed about being jerked around?" he asked.

Carlton thought about it for a minute. "Not so much for being jerked around as for being jerked around by *you. And Paula*. Think about it, Tino; yes, you told me how it was supposed to happen, where to park, what to say, when to act uncertain, blah, blah. But if you'd told me this was just a setup deal, a farce of a kidnapping, I would have played along, handed them the dough, and we'd be taking our time to plot a response, not jumping through our hats and hoping that jackass doesn't pop that little girl's bubble about her background—or worse."

"I agree completely, my friend. It was a poor decision on my part. Again, I can only apologize."

"I think it might have been Paula's input that influenced your decision. She has a way of doing that."

Tino didn't answer, telling him he was right. Paula, the Black Widow, the consummate opportunist, depending on The Smile to get what she wanted. And what angered Carlton most was her confidence that she could get away with it; sway Tino, fool Carlton, and placate Ramos. Another successful manipulation of men, three at a time this round.

What she hadn't foreseen earlier was Carlton's ability to think on his feet, to change the game when the tide was running against him. In fact, he hadn't even had to think about what he was doing when the action played out at the car wash. It was similar to knowing he should file down the firing pin on the gun she had pointed at him those months ago. The real question was, why was he still in this mess?

Seething again, he turned his thoughts to the current crisis to cool down. He asked Tino something he hadn't dared to voice to Paula. "Do you think this is as big a deal as Paula says? If Ramos tells his niece that Brenda isn't her real mother, is it really going to wreck her life?"

Tino hesitated for a few seconds. "I'm not sure about that, and I sensed that you were doubtful, but didn't want to minimize the subject with Paula. But yes, I think it will be a shock, and it might take a while for her to adjust. Plus, we don't know exactly how that idiot will tell her, what he will say or how he'll say it. It's one thing to spring the news that Brenda and Julian aren't her biological parents; hell, that story line is on TV every night. But maybe he tells her that her real mother was a road whore who hooked up with a trans-gender Jamaican hairdresser, had a baby and tossed it in a dumpster. And now the State of Texas pays Brenda and Julian to take care of her, pose as her real parents. How does that play out in the mind of an eleven-year-old girl? I think that's what has Paula so concerned; that, and the possibility that he might lose his cool and do something physical."

"That's another thing, Tino. Would the guy who's been her uncle for over a decade really hurt her? For all intents and purposes, she *is* his niece, after all. And his young squeeze—Myra?—is Cecilia's role model. She would know if something bad was happening and put a stop to it. And Brenda and Julian would surely step in if they thought she was in danger, wouldn't they?"

"Of course they would, even though Brenda's probably terrified of him. You're forgetting that Brujido Ramos is crazy, and getting crazier every day. And just because Paula and Brenda are long-term friends, there's no way of knowing where Brenda's allegiance lies."

Carlton doggedly shook his head. "Look, I know zip about people's relationships and less about Ramos, but I just can't see him hurting her physically."

"Read the newspaper. Stranger things happen every day, right here in our fair city."

"True enough, I suppose. But the possibility of that seems like a very thin stick he's holding over your head to make you give up your entire business. Are you sure there's nothing else I need to know?"

Tino shifted uncomfortably in his seat. "I understand why you're suspicious after being lied to by omission. But to answer your question, Reynaldo will be taking over my business anyway, and my people will still have a job, I'll get a cut of the money. Ramos can just take it up with Reynaldo. He'll find out soon enough that Reynaldo has better connections than I do, he can jack with Ramos' supply lines in Mexico, cause him a lot of grief. And the price war he mentioned will put him out of business anyway.

"So, just between you and me, it's the extortion money I'm most concerned about. As we spoke of before, a half million isn't pocket change for me to hand over to that jackass. Oh, which brings up a perfect example of his craziness: his insistence that you be the bagman, and he's indicated he will be there in person. I told you last time, that's not a good business practice, for the head honcho to be at the tip of the spear."

Carlton nodded acceptance at the explanation, but he noticed Tino had wandered away from his answer at the end by commenting unnecessarily on Ramos' mental state. "Well, looks like he's re-writing the book, isn't he? By the way, do you need my money to make the deal? It's still in your safe, Lefty."

This time, Tino actually smiled in the dark at the use of his unsolicited nickname. "Yes, if I may, *Shifty*. As you know, I haven't exactly been on top of my game making money, so I'll need it. But I'll repay you. Paula's safety is one thing, her daughter's mental state is quite another, since we agree that the impact of telling her about her background is questionable. And losing my business is a non-event."

Carlton nodded his agreement, and the two men exited the car. They trudged toward Carlton's apartment to see if Paula was there and if she had heard anything further from her tormentor. When they went inside the apartment, she was gone. A note left on the kitchen counter said she'd heard nothing and was going home. Tino thought that was a good idea, and he left Carlton's, heading to his own apartment to think over the pending conflict by himself.

As for Carlton, he fell asleep watching a late-night re-run of *Miami Vice*, knowing that the hero vice cops would win out in the end; good guys always did on TV. But the strange dreams he had while tossing fitfully didn't turn out that way, and when he awoke unrested and irritable the next morning, he knew which outcome was closer to real life.

CHAPTER 18

A cold front blew in overnight, and a brisk, cool breeze blew from the northwest the next day, officially ending the hot summer, although everyone knew it wouldn't last long. The wind would die around sundown, and tomorrow would be mild and dry, the closest to traditional autumn weather one could hope to experience in South Texas. Warmer days would follow and be around until after Thanksgiving, but this reminder of the change of seasons elsewhere was pleasant, especially in San Antonio. There, the seasons range from hot to hotter, windy to windier, cold to damn cold...the traditional four seasons of North America didn't hold true in South Texas.

Carlton went for coffee, then returned to shower and shave, get ready for his meeting with Heather Colson and her new boss, Special Agent in Charge Stan Ikos. By eleven o'clock, he was headed north toward Broadway, hungry for what he hoped was a taxpayer-funded lunch and some insight into the Drug Enforcement Agency's view on using information supplied by citizens—and agreeing to pay for it.

During the time period he'd dealt with the agency under its former Special Agent in Charge, Timothy Hunnicutt, Carlton hadn't been paid a cent for his periodic reporting, despite Heather's promise to do so. Of course, he'd been instructed to report on unlawful plans of Faustino Perez; instead, he had given a few reports over the phone while Tino listened, both of them struggling to stifle laughter. He had to admit that he probably hadn't deserved payment.

While being paid a few hundred bucks by the DEA was nothing more than a personal joke with him, he still wanted to hold their feet to the fire and make them do as they had promised. Plus, his insistence on payment might establish his bona fides as a hungry private citizen who just happened to stumble on good intel and not someone personally involved in smuggling, although he knew that would be a tough sale to Heather Colson, much less her hard-assed boss.

In a recent phone call, Heather had already passed the buck on passing the bucks and informed him that payment would be up to Ikos. Recalling the contentious relationship he'd had with Hunnicutt, he doubted that SAIC Ikos would be any different, but he hoped this meeting would prove productive in a more important way: by making sure the agency was ready to act on his tip Wednesday and Thursday. Any payment he received would be a bonus.

He pulled into the taco shop at 11:42 and immediately spotted a plain SUV with government plates and dark tinted glass. When he stepped out of the Mazda pickup, the doors opened and Heather emerged, joined by a big blond guy with a ruddy complexion. Carlton waved to Heather and walked toward her as she offered her hand.

Shaking her hand, he was again struck by her blue eyes and flawless skin, her best features, which got the school librarian-looking woman a lot of second—and third—looks. As he greeted her, he reminded himself not to forget she was plenty sharp to boot; clever, quick…and dangerous. He liked her.

"Agent Colson! Good to see you again."

"Likewise, Mr. Westerfield. Glad you could make it." She turned to the big guy and gestured to him. "Carlton Westerfield, meet Special Agent in Charge Stan Ikos. Stan, this is Carlton."

Carlton stepped forward and shook Ikos' hand. It was like gripping the bumper of a '55 International Harvester pickup: hard and solid. He looked to be in his late forties, with rugged Scandinavian looks that said mid-west, and when he spoke, his voice said Minnesota.

"Good to meet you. Agent Colson's told me a lot about you, but I wanted to meet you for myself."

"Well, she told me a limited amount about you. Good to see you in person."

The trio headed for the front door of the *tacqueria* and took a booth just in time to beat the lunch crowd. By the time their waitress had delivered beverages, a steady stream of diners had descended on it, and the small place was crammed. Ikos' face took on a look that said this wasn't the place for discussion of undercover law enforcement activities. He glanced around nervously at first, then frowned as the crowd grew larger and louder.

"I didn't realize you'd picked the most popular eating spot in the city for our meeting," he said sharply to Heather, glaring around the noisy restaurant with obvious disdain.

True to her usual nature, she waved off the criticism, a trait Carlton had noticed on a couple of occasions when her old boss had tried to berate her. Her response provided proof that attractive women needn't be pushed around by anyone, including their boss. "You said pick a spot between our locations that wouldn't bust the lunch budget, and this is what I chose. I'm afraid every place that's worth eating at is crowded at this time of day."

"Well, next time remember that I come from an area that has quiet, out-of-the way places where three people could eat and hear themselves talking."

His reprimanding tone grated on Carlton's nerves. "I know just the place we could go, Agent Ikos, but it'll set you back about a hundred bucks for three of us to eat there."

"Who says I'm paying for three meals?" he asked. "We wanted to meet with you to get information, not hand out free meals. Besides, I saw that piece of crap you're driving, so I doubt you know much about expensive eating places."

Carlton shook his head. "Sorry, that's not the way this works, Ikos. Speak to me with a civil tongue in your head, or go back to your office. I didn't sign up to take tough talk from you or anyone else. You're going—"

"I make the rules for meetings with snitches!" he interrupted.

"Not this one, you don't, not while I'm sitting here," he replied calmly. "Because this meeting will no longer include me, and you can discuss whatever it is you want to talk about by yourself. Or with Agent Colson, if she's willing to sit here and listen to your arrogance," he added, giving her his best smile.

Ikos responded by glaring at him, but said nothing. Beside him, Heather Colson had to smother a look of amusement. Luckily, their food order came, and the three went silent for a few minutes while they ate tacos. Heather mentioned something funny she'd seen on Good Morning America, and the talk turned civil, almost friendly for a while.

Ikos finished well before Heather or Carlton and looked around as though he wanted to flag down the waitress for more food. Carlton took the opportunity to open up his end of the conversation. "Are you set for Wednesday and Thursday? Will it happen at the checkpoint on the thirty-five?" he directed the questions to Heather.

"Sorry, Agency operations and activities are not open for discussion."

"Even if I'm the one who made it possible?"

Ikos stepped in. "*Especially* since you're the one who made it possible. Surely you understand the need for secrecy. You have knowledge that could endanger the operation and jeopardize agents."

Carlton laughed. "And why would I do that? The main reason I showed up for this is to discuss my payment for the information I've provided. Why would I do anything to hinder the Agency's success or my getting paid?"

Ikos scowled at that and retreated behind standard bureaucratic double-speak. "It's Agency policy not to discuss active operations with anyone. As to your payment, it will depend on the value of this so-called 'hot tip' you've provided. What I want to know is how you got this information and from whom."

"Why?"

"Why what?"

"Why would you want to know from whom I got the information? I can tell you *how*; I keep my ears open and my mouth closed, same as I explained to Agent Colson. But *who* I heard it from is not important."

"It's important to the Agency."

"Sorry, Westerfield's operations and activities are not open for discussion. Surely you understand the need for secrecy."

Heather stifled a laugh, sounding as if she were choking on her last bite of taco. Ikos shot her a look and changed subjects. "Just what business are you in, Mr. Westerfield?"

"Minding my own, Mr. Ikos, and staying out of others'. This information I'm passing on to your agency is a new venture I'm trying."

"Okay, wise guy. I'll tell you this much about payment: the Agency doesn't pay out money to crooks, scofflaws—anyone involved with illegal activities."

"That's a relief, because I'm none of those."

"Well, what are you, then?" Ikos persisted.

"*Needy*. As you so rudely pointed out, I drove up in an old pickup that's retired from the plumbing business. And even so, there's a payment due on it next week. That's why I'd like to collect what the Agency normally pays for a tip that will lead to seizure of illegal contraband and several arrests."

Carlton was enjoying himself now, both at the bantering and the look of amusement on Heather's face at his outrageous lies concerning his financial status. She had very little insight into his personal finances, though she'd used all the government's prying resources trying to find out about one Carlton Delano Westerfield. What she'd learned wasn't much: name (his parents must have grown up in the Depression to hang such a middle name on their son), social security number, driver's license number (no accidents or citations on file), no concealed handgun license issued, income tax data (filed timely every year on a *very* modest income) military service (honorable discharge after attaining nominal rank), and current employment (unemployed).

Banking records showed a single checking account in a local bank with less than two thousand dollars, minimum activity consisting of irregular cash deposits and a few checks given for rent and utilities. No other accounts existed, giving her limited knowledge of Westerfield's financial means. What she did know, or strongly suspected, was that Carlton had considerable liquid assets from a long and shady career doing something for a deceased pawnbroker named Randall Morris. It wasn't likely that anyone could lay hands on those assets, save Carlton himself. As to his proclaimed poverty, the battered little pickup didn't quite jibe with his tailored silk/wool blend slacks and the Egyptian cotton shirt he was wearing. Those things came from someplace like Penner's, the venerable clothier located downtown on Commerce, known for quality goods, not bargain prices. Plus, she knew from experience that he spent more money on disposable cell phones than most people spent on rent and groceries.

Ikos wasn't done. "It can't be much of a payment, not on that pickup."

Carlton shrugged. "I'm looking to trade up."

The government agent actually smiled at that, then changed directions again. "I can tell you that we are assessing the information you gave concerning possible contraband movement on Wednesday and Thursday. We will act on it accordingly, and you'll get your money if your tip pays off. That's how it works: the Agency pays on proven intel, not speculation."

"I hope I don't have to wait long. Y'all will be licking your chops on Friday, when you've busted Ramos' vans and you're standing around posing for pictures with your 'seized contraband.' That would be a good time to pay me."

The smirk on Ikos' face told him something was coming. "I see you use the good ol' Texas term '*y'all*.' Makes me even more suspicious of your character."

"No less suspicious than I am of yours, since you can't verbally distinguish the difference between second person singular and second person plural. Makes me wonder who you're talking to."

"Huh?"

"*You* is second person singular. *You* is also used for second person *plural,* thus making it indistinguishable as to whom you're speaking. Ask Garrison Keillor; maybe he can explain that shortcoming in the English language that Texans have graciously corrected by inventing *y'all* for second person plural."

Ikos smiled at the mention of Minnesota's liberal radio celebrity. "You know, you're such a wiseass I may pay you for your tip on live television and have your name put in the newspaper story. That way, all your drug dealer buddies will see who's ratting them out."

"Let me know, I'll dress appropriately. Maybe we could appear on *Prairie Home Companion*, sing a duet of *Smugglers' Blues.*"

Ikos let that one slide and moved on to a different subject. "Why the big interest in having Brujido Ramos taken down? And don't tell me it's because you are you just doing your civic duty, because normal citizens aren't privy to a drug importer's transportation schedule."

Carlton leaned forward in his chair and locked eyes with Ikos. "Look, I overheard a couple of guys talking about driving Ramos' vans during the week. They run auto parts out of a warehouse, do hotshot delivery to various garages all over the city. I asked about getting a job there, and they told me I needed to have transportation, but the job would be open this Wednesday and Thursday because the vans they drive were going to Laredo to pick up stuff for their boss. I happen to know their boss is Ramos, and I know Ramos has been using the driveshaft trick to haul cash down and dope back."

"And I guess that information was given to you by some other dope runner, one of Ramos' competitors?"

"I saw it on the bathroom wall at the Tower of the Americas."

"Of course you did," Ikos smirked. "So like a good citizen, you decided to give the DEA a call?"

"More like I needed the tip money, and I could look at Agent Colson's pretty face, even if I had to meet her new boss to do it."

"Well, you've met me. And I truly hope your information proves valuable. Amazing how you just happen to be seeking a job at the warehouse where Ramos' guys use his vans during the off-season, then haul drugs on certain appointed days. And you just *happen* to find out that information, too."

"God works in mysterious ways."

"So does the Drug Enforcement Agency. Don't call us, we'll call you, Mr. Westerfield."

Recalling a similar remark she had made in the past, Heather spoke up.

"Uh, Chief, Carlton has a real problem with hanging onto a phone. He always gets a new one with a different number, so maybe we can have him call us. Say Friday morning?"

He shot her a look akin to daggers, but she held his eyes and didn't flinch, didn't even blink until he did. "Okay, fine with me," Ikos said irritably. "But I don't see why you cave in to this guy's silly demands when—"

"Because the last time I forced his hand on who-calls-whom, he threw his phone in the ocean."

Ikos stared at Carlton, but didn't ask.

The meeting ended soon thereafter, with Heather picking up the tab on her government credit card and Ikos leaving a tiny tip. Carlton rolled his eyes and made a show of adding to it, making it excessive. Outside, Carlton formally shook hands with both of them, Heather first. Meeting Ikos' departing smirk with a broad smile, Carlton hopped into the Mazda and headed south on Broadway, belly full and strangely cheerful. He wondered if it was the result of the lively tug-of-war with Agent Stan Ikos of the DEA, the prospect of derailing Ramos for a few days, or seeing Heather Colson.

Carlton wanted to go home and take a short nap, but decided to go by Tino's office first and report to him directly concerning his meeting with the DEA agents. When he pulled into the main entrance he angled around the row of vendor stalls on the right, then turned left toward Tino's portable building office. A late-model Lexus, the high-end sedan model, sat gleaming in front of the office's wooden steps. Against the backdrop of the flea market stalls, an outdoor restaurant with rickety tables, and Tino's makeshift office, the shiny blue luxury car stood out like Donald Trump at an NPR banquet.

Instead of knocking on the door, he pulled his phone and punched in Tino's number. He answered on the third ring, and Carlton figured he and the driver of the Lexus were having a discussion that might best be left uninterrupted.

"Bueno?"

"Tino, it's Carlton. You got a minute, or you want to call me back?"

"Hey, Carlton! No, no, now is fine. I'm talking with Reynaldo at my office. In fact, he just inquired about you, and we need you here. Can you come over to my place?"

"Sure, I'm right outside."

He flipped his phone shut and climbed the wooden steps, then knocked on the door.

"Come on in!"

The two men sat on opposite ends of the worn couch, apparently having been in a private discussion. Carlton was glad he had called instead of knocking on the door, leaving the drug kingpins a choice in whether to be interrupted. Reynaldo Gomez rose immediately and strode across the room to shake his hand. Carlton noticed he was again dressed immaculately, this time in denim jeans with enough starch to rub the hair off his legs and a pale blue shirt with dazzling silver cuff links and a matching belt buckle. The boots were tan and made from ostrich or emu hide, judging by the dimples left where feathers had once been. Carlton resisted the urge to ask why no one manufactured the boots with the feathers still intact.

"Carlton! Good to see you again."

"Likewise, Mr. Gom—Reynaldo. How've you been?"

"Busy! Tino and I were just discussing the plan we spoke of earlier. I understand our rogue friend has once again made outlandish threats and demands."

"Brujido Ramos is indeed becoming a major pain in the rear, to put it lightly."

Tino just grunted in agreement, and Reynaldo shook his head. "He's not leaving much room for flexibility. He called Tino this morning and, the good news is, he's agreed to hold off until Friday night at midnight."

"That *is* good news. I just came from a meeting with the DEA, and they hedged a bit on discussing details with me, but it seems they are going to use the information we supplied them about Ramos' vans."

"They wouldn't discuss it with you?" Tino asked. "You're the one who called them with the information!"

"I reminded the new Agent in Charge of that fact, but this is government bureaucracy mentality we're talking about here. Anyway, if everything goes according to the timetable we gave them, Ramos should have other things to worry about by late Thursday."

"Excellent!" Reynaldo was clearly excited by the prospect of his future competitor having a huge wrench thrown into his machinery.

Tino cleared his throat. "That's the good news. The bad news is, Ramos still insists that you be the one to deliver the money and the flake. In fact, the only reason he agreed to wait until Friday was for you to get back into town."

Carlton raised his eyebrows in surprise. "I'm not in town? Where am I?"

"Los Angeles. It was the only card I had left to play, Carlton. I told him you'd be back late Friday afternoon."

"Okay," he answered slowly. "I'll have to lie low for the next couple of days, not take a chance on being spotted. Also, maybe my Cadillac needs to be parked at SAT in case he sends someone to check on that."

"Good thinking. I'll have it taken over there in the next hour."

Carlton inhaled deeply and blew it out through pursed lips, trying to clear his mind and evaluate this turn of events. Tino took it as an expression of displeasure and hastened to explain. "Look, I know it's completely out of the question for you to expose yourself to that idiot for real, but this story gives us time to come up with something."

Carlton nodded, seeing the logic. With any luck, the DEA would nab both of Ramos' vans and cause such an uproar, Brujido Ramos wouldn't even recall his name by Friday night. If not, well, something else might present itself. But whatever occurred, Carlton thought it would be extremely risky for him to deliver the extortion payoff. Anyone erratic enough to threaten an eleven-year-old girl—his own niece—would be loony enough to take any measure needed to retaliate against the gunman who took four of his crew off the board. *However*...his train of thought was derailed by Tino's voice asking his opinion of Reynaldo's idea for eliminating Ramos by economics, as he had suggested during their meeting at the Hondo airport. Carlton agreed it could work, but might take longer than they wanted, depending on their competitor's tenacity.

Neither Tino nor Reynaldo commented; instead they moved on to a couple of possible strategies to co-exist with Brujido Ramos, then fell into a discussion of future business; how to carry on much as Tino had for years, plus expanding into other areas. And not just other geographical areas; the talk turned to smuggling weapons across the border to Mexico. Listening to them, Carlton recalled a recent news clip he'd seen about ordinary citizens in Mexico arming themselves against the violence of the cartels. Since individual gun ownership was extremely limited in Mexico, he wondered how the townspeople had done it and settled in to listen to the two kingpins give their views.

"If the weapons could be bought here and taken to my ranch in Sabinal, I think we could get them to my Mexico location by means of livestock trailers," Reynaldo offered.

"This doesn't involve some tawdry scheme about stuffing the guns into cows, does it?" Tino asked, looking straight-faced between Gomez and Carlton.

The remark and its dead-pan delivery got a laugh from both of them. "That might be a bit hard on the cows, my friend. But maybe Carlton has an idea on modifying the stock trailer to accommodate weapons." He looked questioningly toward Carlton for an idea.

Being put on the spot made him uncomfortable, but Carlton quickly covered the basics. "Without knowing the level of intensity at the checkpoints, I couldn't say for sure, but the obvious is a false bottom with lots of cow manure to discourage closer inspection. Or a false top might be better, less likely to be scrutinized, since they'd have to unload the cows or wade among them to access the center part. Either one needs a lead shielding in case they're using imaging technology. Given the curvature of most livestock trailer roofs, an open space up top would be harder to detect than a thicker floor and would accommodate a lead sheet.

"Either way, trailers' shapes don't leave much to the imagination, and weapons aren't as compact or pliable as cocaine. It'd be something to study and try out with some dry runs first, before you load up a trailer like an Al Qaeda convoy." He spread his hands to indicate that was the extent of his knowledge in the matter, confident he'd played it correctly by urging caution.

Reynaldo thought about it and nodded his agreement. "That's for sure. And I'd want to check on the profit margin before we launched into something like that. But it would be nice to create some problems for the violent element among the cartel people. It might help stabilize the flow of product and the price if normal, less violent operators could do business in peace."

Carlton told them about the news piece he'd seen and informed them that, according to the news story, the citizens' vigilante movement was expanding to other towns across the Mexican countryside. More weapons would be in demand, and prices on the increase. There had even been a suggestion that an armed citizenry might relieve the cartel folks of some product and trade it for more weapons...the classic armament escalation scenario.

After a few minutes of further discussion, Carlton excused himself and headed toward his apartment. He'd had enough discussion regarding drug running, kidnapping, extortion, murder, and gun running for one day. He hoped to talk to Paula and get some sense of what was likely taking place between Ramos and his sister-in-law. The discussion at Tino's office had given him an idea, perhaps a better way to rid themselves of their crazy cross-town rival. And more importantly, he had altered his thoughts about being the bagman; maybe it wasn't such a bad idea after all.

CHAPTER 19

When he arrived at the apartments, he went straight to Paula's and knocked. The door opened almost immediately. Paula stood there looking a bit dazed, and Carlton figured she hadn't gotten much sleep since the mess with Ramos began.

"Oh, hi. Come on in." Her voice sounded strained, matching her countenance.

"Hi! How was your day?" he asked, walking in and following her lead to the tiny love seat against the wall.

"Better than it could have been, I guess. Tino talked to Brujido, and he agreed to wait until Friday for his payoff. Can we do something by then that will change all this?"

"I'm not sure, but I think he's working on that right now. I stopped by his office, and he told me about Ramos' demand for me to be the delivery boy when I get back from L. A., which won't be until late Friday."

She looked at him, confused at first, then surprised when she understood the ploy. "Oh, so that's the reason he agreed to the extra time? Tino told him you were out of town?"

It was Carlton's turn to be surprised. She apparently knew of the time delay without knowing how her brother had engineered it. Now he felt uncomfortable for letting the news out. Not for the first time, he wished this bunch would get on the same page: either all the players know everything, or some specific instructions be given as to the need-to-know list.

He decided to hedge on what he'd said, modify the certainty of it. "That's what I understood, but maybe there's something else that your brother didn't tell me. Probably best if you heard all the details from him."

Paula laughed at that. "I've never known you to misunderstand anything, Carlton. You catch all the hints, the nuances, and the lies that people tell you. But I get what you're saying, you'd rather Tino tell me all this himself. Need-to-know, right?"

"Something like that. And speaking of needing to know, have you heard from Brenda?"

Her eyes clouded over at the mention of her friend's name. "Yes, she called me today. I was terrified when I heard her voice, but she just asked me what was going on between Brujido and Tino. Apparently, Brujido's raving on about my brother—maybe Julian told her—and she wanted to know what I knew about it. But I don't think she knows anything about his threats or the extortion demand."

"So she doesn't know about his threat to tell Cecilia about…her background?"

"Didn't seem like it. But she could have been pumping me for information by playing dumb. That's what I did, by the way. I told her I didn't know about a feud between them."

"She doesn't know about Ramos grabbing you last week? And holding you in the house she has listed over on Morningview?"

She shook her head. "No, I'm pretty certain of that. Her husband has access to all her listings and rental properties, he does the repairs and maintenance on all of them. Julian let his brother use the house, but he didn't let Brenda in on that part, I'm sure."

Carlton thought for a minute. "You said Ramos lives near Brenda and Julian. Do you know exactly where?"

She shook her head. "No. When she talked about Cecilia going over there, she said something like 'two streets over,' or something to that effect. Don't tell me you're going to pay him a visit!"

"No, not likely. I just like to be informed. It seems he knows where we live, since his crew was able to pick up on us and follow us to La Perla and Jacala's. They didn't just intercept us out in the street and decide to follow us."

"How did they get that information?"

"Probably followed us from the flea market sometime or another. It may have been weeks or months ago. Whatever else Ramos is, crazy or not, he likes to stay informed. Tino has his own observers, but Ramos is more thorough, or maybe he's completely obsessed. Remember, Tino mentioned that he liked to fancy himself as being like the big cartel guys. He probably has round-the-clock bodyguards who patrol his neighborhood."

"You're saying it would be impossible to take him out? Then what is Tino planning?"

Carlton hesitated. "It would be difficult if he really imitates the big cartel guys in all facets of his operation. But Tino knows all this, and I'm sure he's planning accordingly."

"You're making it sound as though Ramos has the upper hand. Is Tino's crew up to the task?"

Carlton waved off her concern, faking the confidence it conveyed. "Tino and his guys are well-versed in all this stuff, but Tino prefers to be less dramatic about his position. He hasn't let success turn him into some kind of movie image of a crime boss, but he's plenty capable."

"But can he win an all-out street war against Ramos?" she persisted.

"Well, it seems Ramos has notched his game up a few levels, trying to imitate the big boys in Cartagena, Medellín, and Mexico City. It might give his bunch an edge, I just don't know that much about it."

Paula was quiet for a moment and Carlton eased into a related subject. "Did Brenda say anything about Cecilia? I mean, is she okay?"

"Yes, she said she had called her a couple of times, but wants to stay over there through this week. Next week, her school is back on full schedule, and she'll have to come home, even though Myra has taken her to school and picked her up a few times in the past."

"I thought school was already in full swing. I see the parking lots are full and the school zone speed limits are in effect."

"Cecilia will go to a private school, starting this year. The schedule is set up differently."

Carlton just nodded. He knew nothing about school schedules or the children who attended them—nor did he want to. However, he wished he could learn the name of Cecilia's school and check out the story. Something didn't seem right, but what did he know about schools?

He decided to try his luck—carefully—at another subject. "Does Cecilia look like you?"

The question caught her by surprise. "Huh? Oh, I guess so, a little bit. Why?"

"Just wondered. She's only eleven now, but do you think she'll ever look in a mirror and wonder why she doesn't look like Brenda or Julian? Or does she have some features that look enough like one or both of them so it won't occur to her?" He waited for the provocative hint to sink in.

Paula sat quietly, digesting what he'd said. After a few seconds, he saw her lower lip tremble, then her composure broke. Tears came slowly at first, then more as she put her face in her hands and sobbed. "That was a lie when I said she looks a little bit like me. I really don't know, Carlton. I've never even seen a picture of her, my own daughter."

The last part was said with enough anguish that Carlton barely caught the words, but he didn't need to. Wishing he'd broached the subject differently, he slid across the small space and put his arms around her, pulling her tightly against him. "I'm sorry, Paula. I didn't know, and I didn't mean to make this worse. I'm just searching for a way that might lead us out of the mess without bloodshed."

She raised her tear-stained face from his chest. "How does her looks have anything to do with that?"

He didn't answer at first. Instead, he rose and went to the kitchen, dampened a paper towel and took it to her. She smiled tentatively and pressed it to her face for a minute. A few deep breaths and a nose blowing later, she regained her composure and thanked him with a weak smile. "How many times have you had to provide me with paper for the waterworks?"

He smiled at her and retook his seat. "It's what I do best; rescue damsels in distress."

"Well, you've got one in real distress, I'm afraid. And I'd already thought about what you just said; in fact, a couple of years ago it occurred to me. I mentioned it to Brenda, but she didn't seem all that concerned, and I have no input anyway."

Carlton nodded. "I understand that's your agreement with them—completely hands-off. Anyway, I don't know anything about children and less about human nature. But I'll bet one day she'll wonder about her physical traits, who she got her nose from, why her eyes are brown, and her hair curly or straight. She's probably already studying genetics in some biology class, or will be in the next year or so. It's natural and almost guaranteed that she'll wonder. Will Brenda and Julian be able to field the questions with good enough answers? Like, 'you got your height from your great-grandfather. He was seven feet tall!'"

Paula laughed at that, her distress packed away for the moment.

Hoping the time was right, he plunged on. "In the long run, as she heads into adolescence, what would be the impact of learning she's not their biological daughter? Isn't being her loving parents more important?"

"Yes, it's more important, but I don't know how she would react at this age. And I don't know exactly how Brujido will put it to her. He may—"

"I know, he could tell a sordid tale that makes Cecilia feel like rejected merchandise; Tino mentioned that. But what if she were told the absolute truth about who you are, why you had no choice, why Brenda and Julian—your friends—wanted her badly enough to obligate themselves to her—and you—for life?"

"You mean before he even has a chance to carry out his threat?"

He thought about that and answered with a question of his own. "If it would eliminate Ramos' ability to threaten you and Tino, take away the only weapon he has, could a lot of killing be avoided?"

"But what about his threat to actually hurt her? Have you forgotten that?"

Carlton shook his head. "Of course not. And he's obviously not mentally stable enough for us to rule out that possibility, but I have a hard time believing that Myra would not be able to see something like that coming down the pike, even if Brenda doesn't. She's younger and is bound to know about Brujido's lifestyle, what he does for a living. And she also knows that Cecilia looks up to her. Would a role model stand by if there were even a hint that something like that were possible?"

"I just don't know. I can't take the chance, though. And Tino doesn't want to, either."

"But we have no guarantee that paying that jackass will keep him from doing the same thing next week, or next month, whenever!"

"I've thought about that several times since Tino mentioned it. And when Brenda called today asking about the problems between her brother-in-law and Tino, I was actually encouraged. Maybe she'll start being careful about letting her be around him."

Carlton thought that over for a minute, wondering if Brenda's recent insight into her brother-in-law's contentious nature might provide an avenue of approach, a way to swing the real estate lady and her husband to Tino's side. He decided to keep the thought to himself for the moment and tried another track. "That'd be helpful, but still no guarantee he couldn't swing by and pick her up. Or send Myra. It's getting down to Brenda having to know what her brother-in-law really is. Cecilia may be exposed to that same ugly truth, harsh as it may be. And who everyone else in her life is; who really counts, versus who wants to use her."

"If we decided to do that, how would we do it? Without Brenda and Julian being on board..." Her voice trailed off.

"I don't know, Paula. I didn't say I had the answers. I just had some questions that might change how this thing is played. The positive side is, Ramos is using the ploy of telling Cecilia the truth about her background first, hoping that gets him the money and product from your brother. Even if he's completely nuts, I think physically harming her is a last resort kind of thing." Even as he said the words, Tino's negative comment on the matter came back to him. *"Read the newspaper. Stranger things happen every day, right here in our fair city."*

"I think you're right. I've kept telling myself that, anyway."

"We've got to come up with something before that happens, but the point I'm trying to make is this: Cecilia learning the truth about you, Brenda, and Julian probably won't scar her for life." He quickly added, "I'm not minimizing the immediate impact of that, but I'm trying to find a way to stay out of an all-out street war that will get people killed."

"What does Tino think?"

"I don't know," he admitted. "We'd have to ask him about taking any action. But he would surely like the least bloody resolution. That mess a few months ago was harder on him than you can imagine, losing those guys and having to face their families."

"I remember it all too well. My brother is a tough, harsh man. You know he's not a stranger to violence, and he accepts what has to be, death included. But he's loyal to his crew and their families because he expects that same loyalty from them. Those few days of funerals were pure hell for him."

Carlton didn't respond, but he had seen the effect on Tino—and himself. He leaned back and recalled the faces of Mauricio's children peeking from behind their mother's black funeral dress, the awkward hug he gave them, unable to speak even a word of consolation for fear his voice would break into a sob. He wondered how they were faring, the two kids and their young widowed mother. The memory reinforced what he'd already decided to do, on his own if necessary, to hell with what Tino, Reynaldo, or Raul Vega thought.

The pair slipped into a brief silence, the only sound being the north wind swirling through the stairwell outside her apartment. As the afternoon wore on, the wind would abate, leaving the evening crisp and still, a perfect time to enjoy the rare pleasant weather of early fall. Carlton put his arm around Paula and pulled her to him, feeling the now-familiar tug on his mind, body, and heart drawing him closer to her. While most of their encounters were filled with passion, this was different; somehow more and even better. It was a rare moment, and he wished they had time to savor it, but he knew better.

He went through his plan twice more in his head, then inhaled deeply. "I'm going to meet with Brenda Ramos and tell her the truth about her brother-in-law, that he's an unbalanced man in a violent occupation. If she doesn't get Cecilia away from him immediately, she may be in a lot of danger."

Paula pulled away from his chest and looked at him, her eyes big with fright and worry. "Are you sure that's the right way? When are you going to meet with her?"

He answered her questions in reverse order. "Tomorrow morning. And no, I'm not. But there isn't another way."

CHAPTER 20

Carlton woke early the next morning, his mind immediately moving to upcoming events, anxious to see how this day was going to play out.

It was Wednesday, the day Ramos' two vans were supposedly headed to Laredo. If the information Arturo had gotten was correct, today's trip south would likely have the vans carrying cash. However, that would depend on Ramos' financing arrangements with his suppliers in Mexico. Tino had opined that a mid-sized distributor like Ramos would normally be on a cash-and-carry basis, but who knew? However, if his suppliers had gotten wind of his erratic behavior, they would insist on cash, that was a given. No matter how the current brouhaha with Faustino Perez played out, instability was not a trait that encouraged big suppliers to extend liberal credit terms.

The return trip might take place as early as this afternoon, or as late as tonight, or even tomorrow. As Carlton had informed Agent Heather Colson, the intel didn't include a detailed itinerary. The timing of the risky return trip would depend on Brujido Ramos' evaluation of checkpoint efficiency. He might deem it best to go through in late afternoon, when a good traffic flow had the checkpoint personnel busy. Or he might think a late night passage best because the checkpoint agents would be lax, the darkness an impediment to searching underneath every vehicle, despite the availability of every kind of flashlight on the market, thanks to taxpayers.

Carlton reached for his phone and called Tino. After four rings, he was about to give up when Tino's sleepy voice mumbled something in Spanish.

"Tino, it's Carlton. Sorry to wake you, but I need to talk with you this morning."

"Uh, yeah. Um, when, now?

"Yes. I have a plan and I need to discuss it with you. Let's go to breakfast."

"Okay. Look, give me twenty minutes, okay? I gotta shower and dress."

"See you in twenty."

Carlton followed Tino's lead and jumped in the shower. He was out and dressed in fifteen minutes. When he opened his front door, he saw Tino walking toward him on the upstairs walkway. "Perfect timing. Good morning."

Tino opened his mouth to respond and stifled a yawn. "I hope so. For waking me up, you get to buy breakfast."

"Deal. I'll even drive."

As soon as they got in the little Mazda pickup, Carlton started giving Tino the background. "When I left you and Reynaldo, I came here and went straight to Paula's. We talked for a while about Cecilia and the threats her uncle is making, mostly just rehashing the same stuff we already covered.

"Then, Paula said Brenda called her yesterday and wanted to know what was up between you and Brujido. She heard there was some sort of big disagreement between y'all. Of course, Paula stonewalled her, said she didn't know. She said Brenda sounded concerned; she thinks it may be the first sign that she's seeing all is not well with letting her daughter spend time with Uncle Brujido. I agree, and I think the time is right to do something."

Tino grunted. "About time Brenda wakes up. I can't believe she doesn't see through him for what he is and keep Cecilia miles from him. I think she's scared to death of him, but she's in denial, doesn't want to admit that her brother-in-law is a cold-blooded killer who's gone off the rails."

Carlton continued his story. "I finally worked the conversation back to what would happen if Cecilia learned the truth about her life. Paula's still stuck on protecting her from the pain, but she agrees that one day she'll probably wonder why she doesn't look like Brenda or Julian and start asking questions. Mainly, I thinks she's worried that Ramos will tell her some horrific tale about her background and make the poor kid think she's rejected dirt."

"I know, I brought that up already, along with everything about this subject that we tip-toed around before. So what's new this morning and so earth-shaking that you woke me up?"

"I told her I was going to meet with Brenda and tell her the entire truth. I'll tell her about Brujido's threats and how he's using his niece to extort money from you. I may even tell her about Paula's failed kidnapping. And last, I'll tell her to go get Cecilia and head straight to a downtown hotel, check in, and stay until this blows over."

Tino thought for a minute. "I hadn't really thought about that approach. I guess I've concentrated too much on how to deal with Ramos directly. Paula agreed to this?"

"She didn't disagree. She realizes that Ramos can just go get her anytime and put everyone through the same drill again, no matter how much you pay him. Again, the same stuff we've talked about before. But now it's time to do something instead of letting him jerk our chain. We remove Cecilia from the picture, we eliminate Ramos' ability to threaten."

"How you going to do that? She's married to the jackass' brother. They're family."

"When I talk with Brenda, I'm going to recommend that she and Julian give some thought to telling her the truth about Paula. *And* her Uncle Brujido. And in the future, give him a wide berth, maybe a few hundred miles. It will buy some time to figure out how to deal with him permanently."

"So you want to go through with this right away?"

"I want to call her in about an hour. I'm going to get her to meet me at the house on Morningview, maybe later this morning."

"Think she'll do that?"

"Yes. She wants me to buy the little house. Realtors are nothing if not ambitious, so I'll bet she shows up to meet with me."

"Okay. So what do you need from me?"

"Approval, I suppose."

"Approval?"

"Don't play coy with me, Tino. I've watched and listened for the last ten days or so, and all we do is keep kicking the same can down the road. I don't claim to know anything about your business, but I know this: Brujido Ramos is bad news and he's not going away soon, not even if Reynaldo busts him financially. We're waiting to see if the DEA pours sand in his gears, we're hoping Brenda Ramos sees the light, we're hoping...what? He gets hit by a Via bus? So yeah, you're the boss and I need your approval. You got a better plan?"

"Even though you just mentioned it in a cynical manner—and I agree with your cynicism—we *could* wait and see how the DEA bust goes."

"I thought about that; if his vans get busted, he'll be so angry, no telling what he'll do. Who knows, maybe he takes it out on Cecilia, hurts her physically. If his vans somehow dodge the trap and make a successful run, he'll think he's the smartest guy on the block, and his arrogance will increase.

So, as it pertains to our situation, the DEA bust could possibly be a lose-lose event for us, at least in the short term."

Tino watched the road for a few seconds before saying anything. "I do have one question, Shifty."

"And what's that, uh, Lefty?"

"Are you going to pull into that Jim's for breakfast or keep driving all over town and hope I forget that you agreed to pay?"

The pair ate breakfast in silence, each going over the pros and cons of what Carlton had suggested. While Carlton paid the bill, Tino left a five on the table and headed for the parking lot. When Carlton got to the pickup, Tino was on the phone having a conversation in brisk Spanish. When he snapped it shut, he turned to Carlton. "Okay. Call Brenda and set up a meeting with her. You need any backup?"

Carlton shook his head. "No, I'm going to play it like I did the day I met her. I gave her my name as Carl Weiss, said I was interested in the little house and that I'd get in touch with her soon. Today's just sooner than I thought."

As they pulled into the apartment parking lot, Carlton had his phone out dialing Brenda Ramos' number.

"This is Brenda Ramos."

"Hi! Mrs. Ramos? I mean, Brenda? This is Carl Weiss. I spoke with you about the house over on Morningview. I'd like to meet you there and take a look at a few more specifics."

"Oh, sure, Carl! When would you like to do this?"

"Um, that's the problem. I have time this morning, but I can't get away again for several days. Could you meet me there this morning?"

"I've got several things going on this morning. How about tomorrow?"

Carlton paused a few seconds as though calculating the alternative. "Um, well...I guess I could go measure the rooms on the other two houses I'm considering. Then I guess I could call you back if they aren't satisfactory."

The silence on the other end lasted at least four seconds. *"No, I'll tell you what, Carl. I'll get my associate to handle a couple of these issues and meet you over there myself. What time did you want to come?"*

"I was hoping to meet you at, say, ten-thirty? It will only take me about fifteen minutes, and I'll be able to make a final decision today. You said the asking price is fifty-seven thousand dollars?"

"Fifty-seven five."

"Ah, yes, of course. Well, I'll see you at Morningview Drive at ten-thirty, then?"

"See you then."

Tino was shaking his head before Carlton snapped his phone shut. "Measure the other *two houses* you're considering? You really know the right bait for a realtor, don't you?"

Carlton smiled at him. "If you saw this house, you'd know why she can't let a possible buyer escape."

Tino laughed. "Okay, Mr. Carl Weiss, go look at that house. Oh, and take a tape measure." He opened the door and put one foot on the pavement, then turned around to face Carlton. "Carl Weiss? Wasn't he the guy who shot the governor of Alabama?"

Carlton shook his head. "Wrong governor. Arthur Bremer shot George Wallace in the seventies, I think. Carl Weiss shot the governor of Louisiana, Huey Long. That was back in the nineteen-thirties."

Tino acknowledged the correction with a nod. "Beats waiting for election time, I suppose." His brow furrowed for a few seconds before he spoke again. "Carl Weiss. Same initials as Carlton Westerfield." Without waiting for a response to that observation, he got out and closed the door.

CHAPTER 21

On the way across town, Carlton thought about how he would play the meeting with Brenda Ramos. There was no good way to soft-pedal the message he was going to deliver. He considered stopping to buy a tape measure to carry on with the charade as a prospective home buyer for the first few minutes, but nixed it. Once she arrived, he would immediately come clean and deliver the bad news in clear, concise terms, so there would be no doubt about the truth or gravity of his message.

By ten-twenty he was in front of the house. This time, he didn't bother to park where his vehicle wouldn't be as noticeable; by the end of his meeting with Brenda Ramos, she probably wouldn't remember much except the story he'd told her; at least that was his goal. She needed to be left with no alternative, no arguments against grabbing Cecilia and high-tailing it to safety.

Five minutes later, she pulled up in the SUV and emerged with her big realtor smile firmly in place. Carlton felt bad about being the one about to erase it.

"Good morning, Brenda. Thank you for coming." Before she could respond, he stepped toward her and continued. "What we have to do is very important."

Apparently she thought he was talking about measuring the rooms being critical to his decision. "Oh, I understand, I want you—"

"I will tell you what's going on, and you must go pick up your daughter and take her to a safe place."

He was standing directly in front of her, a few feet away when he interrupted. The effect of his words was instant and dramatic, which told

Carlton that she already had been aware that something was not right. Her eyes got big as saucers, and she shrank back from him, hands up as though to ward off any further information.

"Who are you?" she asked, her voice trembling. "What are you telling me? *I'm going to call the police!"* The last sentence was almost a shout.

"Please, Brenda, I'm sorry to be the one to deliver this news, but you already know that something bad is going on between your brother-in-law and Faustino Perez. Your daughter is being used to extort money and business inventory. Brujido is threatening to tell Cecilia about her birth mother if Tino doesn't deliver what he demanded."

"Who are you? How do you know all this?" By now she was truly shouting; the terror evident in her voice was now etched on her face.

Carlton cursed his bad judgement for starting this on the sidewalk, a clumsy effort to get the unpleasant task started without chit-chat about the house. "Please, Brenda, I'm here to help. I want your daughter to be safe. So do Paula and Tino. Let's go inside, and I'll explain everything, answer every question you have. *Please*."

She hesitated only a few seconds before stumbling toward the front door and unlocking the key box and door. Within seconds they were inside, but during the interval, she had regained her mental balance enough to be suspicious and angry. "Okay, now tell me who you are! And tell me the truth!"

"My name isn't important. What is important is the information I have—"

"I tried to find out about you online," she interrupted. "I always do that with new clients. I just like to know who I'm dealing with, because I meet them alone. And I couldn't find you on Facebook or any social media site. No one named Carl Weiss matched your description, but there were lots of sites about some guy named Carl Weiss who assassinated somebody a long time ago."

Carlton nodded patiently. "Yes, well, I'm not *that* Carl Weiss. And again, it's not important that you know about me. Cecilia is what's important here. You have to believe me when I tell you she's in danger."

She shook her head adamantly. "Her uncle knows it's important that she not be told about her real mother. It might hurt her, make her..." Her voice trailed off as she put together the consequences of that event with the threat this man had just described.

"I know. We *all* know, especially Paula. She's terrified of anything bad happening to Cecilia. I only recently heard the story, but she seems really pleased that you and Julian have her, and she's being raised by loving, caring parents.

"But her uncle is another matter. Even though Cecilia is his niece, Brujido is dealing with some dangerous, violent people in his line of business, and he wants to be like them. I don't know the man, but it happens to some people when they are exposed to something they want to copy; they stop at nothing to emulate them."

"But who would cause him to do something to his own niece?"

Carlton made a face at her. "He's tied in with drug cartel people, Brenda. You're bound to know that."

"Oh, my God!" Brenda's face crumpled as she heard a stranger confirm what she'd already suspected, or knew. *"What do you want?"*

The odd question took Carlton by surprise. "What do *I* want? I want you to go get your daughter and take her away. Maybe take her downtown to a busy hotel on the Riverwalk. Check in and stay around a lot of people. Don't let her out of your sight."

"Does my husband know?" she asked, changing gears and again surprising Carlton with a question beyond the scope of his warning.

"I don't know how much Julian knows about all this, but I think he gave his brother the key to get into this house."

The use of her husband's name, along with an allusion to his having a key lent credence to the tale, and Brenda's face lost most of the previous wariness. She turned squarely toward him with a more accepting body language, and Carlton pushed ahead. "Brujido's men kidnapped Paula a week ago Saturday. I believe she was held captive in this house." As if to drive home the point, he turned and pointed to the next room. "Remember the card table and the chairs you were surprised to see? Paula described what she thought was a card game while she was held there, blindfolded. She remembered hearing a school bell like the one across the street uses to signal classes."

"Paula was kidnapped? Are you sure? How do you know?"

Carlton sorted through the hysterical verbal barrage, recalling his promise to answer all her questions. "Yes, she was kidnapped, thrown into a car and brought here. I'm sure, because she was with me when she was grabbed. Two men held me while two more threw her into the car. They hit me on the head just before they drove off."

"But I spoke with her just yesterday—"

"She wasn't comfortable with telling you about that. I think she was afraid you'd take it as an attempt to break the contractual arrangement y'all have concerning Cecilia." The confused look on her face told Carlton he'd botched it, so he began again. "She thought if she told you such a dramatic story, you and Julian might think it was just a ploy to upset you, or somehow change what she'd agreed to eleven years ago: *not* to be involved with Cecilia in any way. Or maybe that you'd think she was crazy. Think about it, Brenda: This story *does* sound plenty crazy. That's why I wanted to meet with you and explain it all in person. And you've heard that Brujido and Tino have some bad blood between them, so now you're learning what's going on."

The woman sagged and looked around for a place to sit. Carlton stepped into the adjoining room and retrieved two of the chairs. She fell heavily into hers while he pulled his directly in front of her before sitting down facing her. "I know this is quite a shock, and I'm sorry I had to play it this way. But when I saw your name and picture on the sign, I put it together with the initials and phone number in Paula's phone."

"I don't know how you figured out who I was, who Cecilia..."

"Believe me, it wasn't easy," he said, stretching the truth. "Paula only told me about Cecilia when she received the threat from Brujido. She's been faithful to the agreement between y'all. But now it's evident that something has to happen, and you and Julian are the only ones who can do it."

She sat still for a few minutes, sorting through the facts, trying to reconcile what she had known with what she was now hearing. The mental exercise seemed to calm her, and she probed Carlton to learn more. "Then, who are *you*? I mean, why are you the one to deliver this news?"

"I'm a friend of Paula and Tino. I've done some...advisory work in the past, and they felt I would be best to do this. Now that I've upset you, I'm not so sure about that."

"I'm upset, yes, but I have to do everything to protect Cecilia. Julian and I love her very much. But it seems an odd thing for Brujido to threaten Paula's brother with. I mean, bad as it might be for Cecilia right now, it wouldn't be life-threatening or anything." She said the last part almost as a question, leading right to the area where Carlton worried about pushing her off the edge.

"I have to agree with you on that," he said, stalling for time. "By the way, do you have a picture of Cecilia?"

She opened her purse and pulled her phone out, thumbing through dozens of pictures in typical proud-mother fashion. She stopped on one, swiped to the next, and turned the screen toward him. Carlton moved closer and looked at the pretty girl smiling for the shot, obviously taken at a Spurs function from the background of posters, signs, and black and silver jersey-clad fans. Her own attire consisted of an oversized jersey with "20" under "Spurs" on the front. Though not a huge basketball fan, Carlton knew the name on the back was "Ginobili," a popular shooting guard on San Antonio's beloved team.

But the face drew his attention away from her clothes. Even at her tender age—eleven?—it was plain that Cecilia would be a stunning young woman in a few short years. Shiny black hair; full and stylishly cut. Her dark eyes were set perfectly in the flawless skin of her innocent face, her nose thin and fine, and a wide smile displaying perfect teeth. No orthodontic expense there, Carlton thought, scanning the photo for more detail.

Studying the photo a few more seconds, he wondered again if, told the news about her real mother, her life would undergo significant change. Or would it simply be another learning session in what appeared to be an excellent childhood for the young girl? The recurring hypothetical question shook his consciousness back to the subject at hand, the thought that Brenda had almost voiced a moment before.

"She's a beautiful girl. And Paula's told me that she's smart, makes good grades, helps out around the house. All reasons for everyone to be proud of her. I know Paula is. As to what you said while ago, I think you and Julian are too important to her for any news about her background to hurt her, certainly not long-term. When she's older, she will understand about people doing what they have to do when certain things happen. Life's full of choices, and a lot of them turn out to be wrong, but we make them with information we have at the time.

"But there's something wrong with her uncle, Brenda. And from what we've heard in his threats, we can't be sure he wouldn't hurt her, maybe take her away, especially if he thinks telling her about Paula won't accomplish what he wants."

He waited a few seconds for that to sink in. When it did, her hand flew to her mouth as though to stifle a sob. Tears appeared in her eyes, and he wished there had been an easier way to get the point across. But he needn't have worried; after a few seconds she lowered her hand, inhaled deeply, and blinked away the tears.

"I'll go get her now. Maybe he's gone, and I can just tell Myra that I have to get some things for her to begin her school year."

"She starts next week, right? At a private school?"

"Yes, classes start here next week, but she'll only be here for one week before the class leaves."

"Leaves? Where are they going?"

"Oh, her class will spend this fall semester out of the country. First, they go to Mexico City for two weeks, then on to Madrid, Spain. It's a very good school, lots of unique learning experiences."

"Oh! Uh, yes, it sure sounds like it. Um, does your brother-in-law know about her school? The trip to Mexico City, then abroad and all?"

"I'm sure he does. It's all Cecilia and Myra talk about."

"Brenda, go get her. Now!"

The pair walked out of the house together, but Carlton sat in his pickup for a few minutes after Brenda sped away. He dialed Paula's number and waited only one ring before she answered.

"Carlton? How did it go?"

"Pretty well, considering how badly it shook her up at first. She's going to get her."

"She shouldn't have been so surprised. Ramos is a nut case."

"I think she realizes that, but she doesn't want to face the fact, or she's too scared. But I was right, she tries to get some background info on all her clients, so she's not dumb about people; just her brother-in-law."

"She researches her real estate clients?" Paula asked, sounding doubtful.

"Sure. Probably trying to find out if they really have the ability to buy a house. Keeps her from wasting time if their Facebook page reveals they're a complete dud. Plus, she meets with clients in vacant houses, sometimes alone. She wants to make sure she's not meeting an ax murderer, so she probably subscribes to one of those investigative web sites to do background checks."

"Oh, Tino told me about you giving her another name. But she wouldn't have found much about Carlton Westerfield, so why did you give her a fake name?"

"In case my theory turned out to be nothing, I didn't want her looking any further, trying to find an address or phone number. I had no intention of buying this house and didn't want her looking for anything on me, whether or not she could find it. As of right now, she's never heard the name Carlton Westerfield and I hope she never does. I'm just careful that way."

"I can understand that. You didn't even want to leave her with a real name, in case she mentioned it later."

"Right. Who knows? Maybe she talks in her sleep. She didn't find much

about Carl Weiss, nothing that would fit me, anyway. If all this had just gone away, she'd just chalk it up to a lost sale, or a guy who wasn't serious. She'd forget everything in a few days."

"Pretty clever. So, she's going to get Cecilia away from Ramos? When?"

"She left here a minute ago, nearly smoking the tires on her car. So I take that to mean she's on her way right now."

"Good. Tino's here, I'll tell him."

"I'll be back there after while."

Carlton cranked up and headed back toward the other side of town, weighing all the possibilities he could envision as he drove. The information he had gained while meeting with Brenda was useful, he thought, but how to put it to use? He began by assembling upcoming events in chronological order, then considering how the players would react. First, Brenda was on her way to get the girl back. If she acted poorly—nervous or angry—and Ramos caught on, he could refuse to let Cecilia go with her. He might take Cecilia somewhere and simply hold her, then renew his threats to Tino and Paula. Longer term, he might take her away in order to prevent her leaving for Spain, where it would be more difficult to grab her. Either of those outcomes were bad; Carlton could only hope Brenda's acting skills were up to the task and she could get Cecilia away safely, take her somewhere long enough for Tino—or Reynaldo Gomez—to devise a plan.

Second, the DEA stop of Ramos' vans could occur anytime in the next thirty hours or so, possibly as soon as in the next six to eight hours. But the outside parameter, tomorrow evening at the latest, would be too late to interrupt Ramos' kidnapping plans if Brenda failed. On the bright side, it was possible that the DEA raid on his vans would result in a better outcome than he, Carlton, had predicted. Maybe Ramos' full attention would be directed at getting his crew out of custody, his vans returned, and recovering from a major financial setback. Carlton refused to rely on that; when Ramos discovered that he no longer had any leverage over Faustino Perez, all hell would break loose, DEA raid or not. Given his violent temperament, Ramos might simply declare an open street war out of frustration, something everyone in Tino's community had hoped to avoid.

One more event kept swirling around, dodging in and out of Carlton's consciousness. Reynaldo Gomez had shown up yesterday at Tino's office in a late-model luxury car, but it was impossible to know when he had arrived in town. He could have flown in an hour prior, the Lexus a rental from the airport. Or, the car might be his personal one, and he drove in from Wichita Falls. However Tino's buddy had gotten there, he was on hand for the upcoming showdown with Brujido Ramos. Carlton thought he knew why; what wasn't clear was the absence of any of Gomez' crew. Being a couple of notches above Tino in the drug traffic food chain, he surely had access to some highly qualified muscle; if *ever* they would be useful, now would be the time. Instead, Tino seemed stuck on keeping Carlton in the forefront—despite his opposition to repeating the bagman role—and holding strategy meetings with his own diminished crew. Maybe it involved some kind of drug-dealer protocol, something unknown to mere advisors, he thought. In any event, it was the least of his concerns.

CHAPTER 22

Mulling over the tangled mess of facts absorbed most of the quick half-hour trip back to the apartments. Carlton parked and went to his place, hoping for a quick bite to eat before reporting to Tino. Even though the call to Paula was made with Tino present, Carlton knew he would want a face-to-face recap, then an analysis of the new information. A clear outline of possible scenarios would be helpful in figuring out what to do, regardless of what happened…or so Carlton hoped. No matter how much speculation went into Ramos' reactions, nothing was certain. What if the loony drug importer did something entirely unexpected? As Tino had warned, strange things happened all the time, and Carlton didn't want to think about just how strange it could get.

He didn't get a sandwich made before a knock came on his door. Heeding Tino's repeated counsel about caution this time, he pulled a .38 revolver from a drawer before calling out. "Come in!"

Tino opened the door and stepped aside to let Paula enter first, then Reynaldo Gomez. Seeing the pistol barrel laid over the counter got a smile from Tino. "Good! I see you're being more cautious. Can't believe you actually took my advice."

"You gave me this thing over a week ago, but I've kept it in the kitchen drawer until now."

"So you didn't really take my advice, like keeping it handy all the time."

"Nope. Don't like guns. But it was *handy* just now."

Reynaldo looked surprised at the remark, but said nothing. Tino mumbled something that ended in "gringo comedian" before plopping down on the couch and rubbing his eyes. Carlton offered to make everyone a sandwich, and the next half-hour was spent eating and going over the morning's events. Carlton gave his summary of the possible outcomes between bites of sandwich and long pulls on a Sprite. When they finished, Paula helped clean up before the four of them settled into the tiny living room.

Reynaldo looked anxious, and Paula carried on with her usual nervous habit, twisting and wringing her hands. Only Tino remained his normal unperturbed self as Carlton looked from one to the other, hoping he would be let in on some new piece of information that would simplify their predicament, or at least give him a hint of what was going on. Seeing his questioning look, Paula turned toward him. "I texted Brenda just before we came over here, asking about Cecilia. She texted back, said she called her brother-in-law, but had to leave a message for him that she needed to bring Cecilia back home."

Carlton nodded, hiding his irritation at just now hearing this information. Though lunch had been short, she could have squeezed that tidbit into the agenda, he thought. He sat silent for a moment, then gave up his waiting game and spoke out. "I trust no one is going to enlighten me beyond that news flash and what I learned from Brenda Ramos."

"We don't know anything, Carlton," Tino said testily. "Why would I keep anything from you?"

"I don't know, I just feel like something's missing, something I'm not seeing. I was hoping someone could help me out, I guess." He let the comment sink in before turning to Reynaldo Gomez. "Reynaldo, give us your thoughts on this. Do you think we should do anything now, or just wait until Brenda gets back to Paula?"

Gomez shifted uneasily in his seat. "I can't think of anything we could do that wouldn't endanger Cecilia. I'm afraid we're completely dependent on Brenda Ramos."

"Seems that way. I was hoping somebody had a better plan, that's all."

Paula's phone made a noise, and she grabbed it from her pocket. After stabbing a button or two, she stared at the screen for what seemed a long time. When she looked up, it was clear that the message was unsettling. "Brenda can't find Cecilia. She went to Brujido's house. Nobody there. She called all their phones again, but gets nothing but voice mail on all of them."

"Maybe they went to a movie and turned off the phones," Reynaldo offered.

Paula visibly brightened at the idea. "I know she and Myra go the movies sometimes. I don't know if Brujido ever goes with them, though."

"He doesn't strike me as a movie guy," Tino said. "Dog fights would be more like it."

The group's speculation was interrupted by another text alert from Paula's phone. She punched the buttons and read the text aloud.

"Just got a message from Brujido. He has Cecilia and Myra with him, says he is keeping them safe, will let me know when she can return home. I'm getting scared."

"Damn! I was afraid of that," Carlton said, looking at Tino. "Brenda was scared and worried when she left. Ramos may have picked up on it when she left a message."

"He's just setting the stage for Friday night," Tino said. "That's when he thinks you're returning from California and will be the bagman."

"He's dreaming if he thinks I'm going to show up alone and get gunned down." Carlton said, shaking his head. A few beats later, he amended the declaration. "That is, unless he wants to follow my rules, meet at a location I choose." He looked at each of the three in turn as he spoke the last part.

Reynaldo saw what was coming with Tino getting it seconds later. "If the feds grab his vans full of blow, he *might* be more likely to have some flexibility to get his hands on the cash and product. If you talk to him directly and dictate the time and place..."

"At the last minute, just like he did last week," Carlton finished his deduction. "I might be able to pay him and get Cecilia dropped off somewhere in exchange. Regardless of what I think his mood will be after the feds pop him—arrogant, crazy, or both—we don't have any choice."

"It would be impossible to keep him honest," Tino protested. "He could have his guys follow him and pop you on arrival, no matter how you pull his strings."

Carlton disagreed. "Not necessarily. I can direct him to a public spot where I've got the money and blow with me, then get out of my vehicle and walk away. Of course, I'd only do that after receiving a call that Cecilia was safe. He can walk over, get the stuff and leave. I'll come back later, only get in my car if his is nowhere in sight.

"We'd have to count on his needing the money badly to go along with it. And yes, he could double-cross us, no matter how it's played, by leaving someone there to kill me. But I might have a plan to take care of that possibility without getting shot."

"Care to tell us about it?" Tino asked, knowing the answer. He wasn't surprised when Carlton said nothing. "I guess I had that coming," he added with a grin.

"I'm not being evasive. I'll have to think about it, that's all."

The conversation was interrupted again, this time by Tino's phone. He looked at the screen and put a finger to his lips as he flipped it open. All three watched silently as he answered in Spanish, then listened for about ten seconds before responding, still in Spanish. Carlton could only pick up a stray word or two, but the tone was unmistakable; it had to be Brujido Ramos. Several exchanges took place before Tino gestured to Carlton to give him his phone number. Carlton flipped it open for him, and went to the screen with information before turning it toward him. He read off the number in Spanish; a flood of angry-sounding Spanish followed before Tino closed his phone with a snap and tucked it into his shirt pocket.

Carlton looked questioningly back and forth between Tino and Reynaldo, eager to hear what had been said. The crime boss didn't keep him waiting. "That bastard has Cecilia with him and says he's going to keep her for as long as it takes to get you to deliver the money and product. He wants that to happen *tonight*. When I told him you were still in Los Angeles, he said he didn't believe me. He wanted your phone number, said he would call you with instructions to get ready to deliver tonight, or the girl will learn all about where she came from, how Brenda isn't her mother, blah, blah."

"So your end was just arguing about all that? I could only catch a few words, not enough to get the drift."

"Yes, I told him that was a shitty thing for an uncle to do to his niece. He said he wasn't her uncle, she wasn't his niece, and he would do a lot more to her if you didn't deliver the goods as instructed. Just a typical argument, mostly back and forth with no headway on either side."

Carlton thought about that for a moment. "Did he say why he didn't believe I was in California? I mean, did someone see me? Makes me wonder if he's having Brenda followed. I watched for anyone who looked out of place, but didn't spot anyone."

Tino was shaking his head before he finished. "No, I didn't get that impression. He was just raving and ranting, said I was talking bullshit about you being out of town. He ended up saying you'd better get a direct flight back if you were gone, because he wants the exchange to be tonight, not Friday, and he wanted your phone number to tell you himself."

Carlton nodded and leaned back in his seat. Listening to Tino, he had surreptitiously watched Reynaldo. The handsome man's face hadn't shown any indication of the conversation being different than Tino's recount. Not for the first time, Carlton wished he had tried harder to learn Spanish, although being fluent was a different matter…and to be fully bilingual would be the ultimate tool, he thought.

As if to confirm his observation, Reynaldo reached across and touched Tino's arm. "From what I could hear, I noticed he refuses to listen, wouldn't even hear you out before interrupting. That's a poor business practice in this industry. No matter what you're hearing, how disagreeable it sounds, it pays to listen to the entire sentence before interrupting. Sounds like he is completely unreasonable."

"And has poor manners to boot," Carlton quipped. "He may have—"

Another interruption, this time Carlton's phone. He opened it and turned the screen toward Tino to verify what he already knew. Tino nodded and grimaced. Carlton pressed "Talk" and put the phone to his ear.

"This is Carlton."

"This is Brujido Ramos. Where are you?" The voice spoke English with a heavier accent than Carlton had expected.

"None of your business, Mr. Ramos."

"That is too bad, Carlton Westerfield, you talk to me like that. Your boss tol' me you were in California, but he is a lying hijo de puta. I think you are here. In San Antonio."

"I don't have a boss, and I really don't care what you think, Mr. Ramos. But I'll tell you this much: your thinking is wrong. I'm sitting at a bar at Marina del Rey in Los Angeles. I'm happy to know you are in San Antonio, though."

"Oh? And why is that so?"

"Because it means I'm fifteen hundred miles from you, that's why."

A long minute of silence went by before Ramos spoke again. "You better get back here. You gonna' deliver some stuff to me tonight."

"What makes you think that? I don't take orders from you. Or anyone else."

"I tell this little girl about her puta mother! An' she's your puta girlfriend!"

"Sorry, can't help you. I get back to Texas on Friday afternoon. If I'm not too tired, I'll call you then. This number, right? Maybe we can set up something to meet and talk."

"Oh, yeah, Carlton Westerfield! We gonna' meet and talk. You think I forget what you did last time you deliver something?"

"No, I don't think you forget. Also, don't forget there were four of them. And only one of you, Mr. Ramos."

Ramos launched into a shouted response, but Carlton snapped his phone shut. Paula had a horrified look on her face, and Reynaldo looked even more anxious, his brow furrowed over narrowed eyes. Carlton thought it was the first time he had looked like an ordinary guy instead of a movie star posing for a poster shot. Tino sported a smirk, clearly entertained by the exchange.

Seeing the varied expressions, Carlton turned and addressed Paula first. "It didn't make any difference what I said to him, Paula. He's wandered off the reservation, and nothing is going to change what he thinks. He'll call back and go through the same song and dance. I'm going to rattle his chain and hope it trips him up. It's the best chance we've got at getting him to make a mistake. He already screwed up by implying he's in San Antonio. So he hasn't left the country with Cecilia, not yet anyway."

"I hope you are right."

The doubtful tone of Reynaldo's voice made Carlton turn toward him. "I don't know what's right or wrong here, Reynaldo, no one does when you're dealing with a maniac. There's a point where he could be pushed too far, and I'll try to avoid that. But we've got to keep him off balance. I was trying to set the stage for telling *him* where the drop is, not him telling *me*."

"The next time he calls, he'll already know you're not a pushover," Tino agreed. "Probably the only way to play it."

"That's the plan. But I have to be careful, walk the fine line."

A muted ring from the kitchen made everyone look in that direction. Carlton spun around on the bar stool and reached for another phone, one he had privately dubbed "Heather phone." He flipped it open and verified the incoming number before answering.

"This is Carlton."

"Well, your information paid off. Ramos' vans came through just after noon. We got about twelve kilos, all in one van. The other one was clean."

Carlton smiled at this first piece of good news and gave a thumbs-up to his companions. *"So he used one van as a decoy? I'd bet it went through first, clean as a whistle. The next one looked identical, should have gotten only a cursory look, but it held the snowstorm."*

"You got it. It worries me that you know so much about all the little tricks these guys use."

"Don't be. I read a lot. Plus, I know a bit about how people think and react, that's all."

"It will take some time to sift through all the information and paperwork, so it'll be a while before you get paid. I wanted to let you know, so you wouldn't get antsy with Ikos when you call."

Carlton laughed. *"Okay, I'll restrain myself. But I may need some help from y'all. It might land the main player."*

"Ramos? We played that tune with the van drivers, but they clammed up, said they had no idea what was in the drivershafter thingies and wanted lawyers."

Carlton laughed at her mangling of the automotive term. *"I'm sure they did. What I'm talking about will probably happen Friday night. You would need to be available and mobile, ready to go to a rendezvous point most riki-tik."*

"Huh? What was the last part about rat ticks?"

"Oh, sorry! Most riki-tik. Vietnamese slang for 'very fast.'"

"I'll speak to Ikos about it."

"You can't do this with a couple of helpers, leave your boss out of it? How about your buddy, Rex Baxter?"

"I'd have to clear any operation with the boss." Her statement had a note of finality, but curiosity won over after a few seconds. *"How's this going to go down?"*

"The location won't be disclosed until the last minute. As soon as I know, I'll call you. I could tell you what part of town, a general location beforehand," he added in a helpful tone. He waited patiently, knowing the ambitious agent was strongly attracted by a chance to take down a major player, trouble with the boss notwithstanding. He could almost hear the wheels turning inside the pretty head on the other end. When she finally responded, he was disappointed.

"Carlton, that would get me fired. Or maybe worse. This is modern times, no more cowboys, no Dirty Harrys."

"How about cowgirls or Dirty Harriets?" he asked jokingly.

She ignored his weak attempt at humor. *"It might even land me in jail. I'm serious, that rogue cop crap is for the movies."*

"Okay, I get it. How about this? Law enforcement personnel are always on duty, right? You just happen to see it going down, get out of your car and nail the bad guy. You'd be the hero of the day. Make that heroine," he added.

"Easy with that last word," she warned with a giggle. Another long moment of silence passed before she spoke again. *"That might work, but only if I were*

by myself. Another agent with me wouldn't fly with Ikos, he'd know what we were doing. It would be classified as an unauthorized operation."

"What about your bud, Rex?" he persisted. *"Is he out of the picture these days? I thought y'all were tight, maybe even a romance item. Surely you could be out in public with a friend, off-duty."*

"Um, we were…sort of. But he's a bit on the young side for me. Besides, he found other persuasions, more appealing than this girl."

"He's an idiot, then, because that's impossible."

"I think that's a compliment, so thank you. But I'm telling you he's not an idiot, he's gay."

"Oh! Well, that's even better. Neither of you can be reprimanded for fishing off the company pier. You two just went shopping for shoes, or went for pizza together."

"That might fly," she said doubtfully.

"Please think about it. You may come up with a better idea. Will you call me?"

"Sure. I'll let you know. I've got to go." She ended the call without a good-bye.

Carlton turned back to the group. "Good thing the feds set up early today to concentrate on the delivery vans. Both vans apparently went to Laredo real early, maybe even last night. They came back through today, and the feds nailed twelve kilos of Ramos' snow a couple of hours ago."

"Shouldn't be long before he hears about it," Tino observed. "Or maybe he already has. The drivers will contact the lawyer just like they've been instructed, without saying a word to the interrogation team."

Gomez shifted in his seat, still unsettled about something. "That's great news; it will give him something to occupy his time."

"Yes, and hopefully, forget about checking on my whereabouts," Carlton said. "I may not be able to lie as low as I had intended, so maybe losing a bundle will occupy his mind and his watchers. How much money does that represent, anyway?"

Reynaldo did the math quickly. "That amount represents about a half million bucks at consumer prices in this city, and a gross margin of a quarter mil. Not a huge hit to his pocketbook, but enough to make the cash flow tight for a week or so."

"Yeah, I'm surprised the haul was that light," Tino agreed. "But if he makes a couple of those runs a week, it represents a tidy profit. Especially the way he cuts his product for the street."

"But what do you have in mind for getting the DEA woman to take him down?" Reynaldo asked.

"I'm not sure how to work it. It will depend on getting Ramos to cooperate with my demand to pick up payment after I get a message about Cecilia's safety. Or maybe he picks it up without actually meeting with me. That may be hard to do. I'm counting on greed to do the trick, especially if his lawyer calls and tells him how badly he got bruised today."

"So it will be a balancing act of getting Ramos and company to show up for their extortion money and drugs at a particular place and time of your choosing, then notifying the DEA lady to be there and witness the pickup, then drop the hammer on him."

"Yes. And ideally, the feds would witness the drop-off of Cecilia, but that would be hard to do safely."

"Of course. That's what I'm worried about. If the DEA agents get the drop on Ramos and whomever he has helping him, there is likely to be a gun battle. With what we know about Brujido Ramos, I can't see him laying down his gun and putting out his hands for cuffs while he's got a hostage."

"No, I don't either," Carlton said slowly. "He'll keep his hole card—Cecilia—until he's certain there's no trap, or he's far away from the exchange point. And by then, he will have split from his crew and not have the money or drugs in his possession. He's too savvy for that."

"Exactly. And if you get him to release her beforehand, he'll be sure to change the drop off by at least a few blocks, give her a cell phone, and tell her to call her mom. The feds will be standing there scratching their...uh, *heads.*" Despite the tension of the moment, everyone had to smile at Reynaldo's polite word substitution for Paula's sake.

"Yes, and even if he chose to follow my demand and drop her at such-and-such, it would be hard to pin kidnapping charges on an uncle dropping off his niece—even with a dozen agents watching him. Providing he hasn't hurt her, of course."

Paula had been listening intently to the discussion of complicated tactics, but Carlton's last statement was too much. When she spoke, the strain was evident in her voice. "Can't we just concentrate on getting Cecilia back safely? Why do we have to use her to trap Ramos?"

"We talked about that, *Hermanita,*" Tino said patiently. "Because the next time he needs cash, he'll do it again. *Or worse.*"

"What if the loss of today's shipment is a bigger deal than we think, big enough to make him think about just getting the money? Maybe he'll just leave her with Brenda and go back to doing what he does."

"Tu hermano es correcto, Paula," Reynaldo said gently. "It will be great if Ramos gets the money and releases her. But sometime soon, Ramos has to go down for good or she will never be free from the danger he can bring."

Carlton had fallen silent while Tino and Reynaldo worked to quell Paula's fears, and he stepped forward to bolster their efforts. "Paula, you're right, of course. Cecilia is the priority here. Ramos is in last place. Sure, in a perfect world, he'd be taken off the board and we'd all live happily ever after. In the real world, I'm going to do everything I can to get Cecilia back safely and let the feds worry about Ramos. If I see it going sideways, I won't put her in danger."

"I know, but it doesn't sound very hopeful. I hate doing nothing but sitting here, waiting for something else to happen, somebody else to do something..."

Understanding her frustration, Carlton reached for her hand. "I know. This is driving all of us nuts, but there are too many moving parts to jump in and just hope for the best. We've got to wait and see how things develop.

"But we got some good news, the DEA busting Ramos' guys. Let's hope that shakes something loose. The next time Ramos calls me, he'll rave and rant again, but I'll bet the mood is different behind the scene. And Agent Colson is thinking real hard about my proposal, I'm sure of that. She just has to get comfortable with making a move without her boss' approval."

Tino spoke up. "*Paulita,* I have over two dozen guys on the street right now, waiting for the word to take it to Ramos' crew. If all else fails, we go to war against his guys and give him plenty to occupy his time. He's no more likely to harm Cecilia with a full plate; less likely, I'd say."

"I think Carlton is right." It was Reynaldo again. "And Tino has a good back-up plan that he can enact any time. I think everything possible is being done, Paula. Hard as it is, we have to wait and let the cards fall."

CHAPTER 23

By Thursday morning, everyone was wearing thin from the ongoing ordeal. The previous evening, they had talked until nine o'clock—"beating the same poor horse to death" in Reynaldo's words—before agreeing on breakfast in the morning and going separate ways. Tino and Reynaldo, accompanied by the Estrada brothers, went to meet with senior crew members, while Carlton and Paula shared a brief hug and kiss, but stayed in their own apartments.

The four met at the closest IHOP just after eight. Sergio Estrada strolled in a minute later after checking the cars in the lot and sat down a few tables away with Estéban, who had arrived a half-hour earlier. Even Carlton was packing heat, the .38 tucked into his waistband and covered by an untucked shirt. He hated it and didn't feel any safer, just foolish.

The morning was beautiful, the breeze cool, and the coffee hot. It should have been the perfect setting, but no one had slept well, and even Tino looked a bit worn. Everyone made an effort to steer away from the topic of the week; Reynaldo did his best to appear cheerful and Paula held up her end of the conversation despite the strain showing on her face. As the group finished eating, Paula said she would contact Brenda again and keep the others informed of any change in the status of the dysfunctional Ramos clan. Meanwhile, she and Caterina Vega were going shopping—for shoes, of course. Tino grumbled about safety until Reynaldo agreed to accompany them, leaving the Estrada brothers free for whatever Faustino Perez had in mind for them. Carlton smiled at Reynaldo, who winked to remind him he owed him one.

Carlton finished his light fare, then slipped away from the rest and bought a newspaper. He found the drug bust story below the fold, but still front page and read it a couple of times before texting Heather with congratulations. His text was only a few words and cryptic in construction in case anyone else had access to her personal burner phone, but he hoped it would serve as a reminder of yesterday's conversation. The remainder of the morning was spent taking care of the recurring-too-often bachelor tasks: laundry, grocery shopping, and cleaning the apartment.

Chores done, he prepared sandwiches for lunch, packed them with a couple of drinks in a backpack. At eleven o'clock, he again pulled a disappearing act and made his way to San Fernando Cemetery by using side streets. He wandered among the gravestones in the northeast sector, stopping for a few minutes at the graves of his mother and the aunt who had raised him after her early death.

Proceeding to the statue of Jesus Christ, he took a seat on the stone bench and ate one of the sandwiches. Afterward, he pulled a book from his backpack and leaned against the pedestal to read and sip a Sprite. About three pages in, he became drowsy, put the book away, and started scanning the area around him. On this Thursday lunch break, only a few people had visited, and they were now disappearing to return to work. An afternoon funeral carried on about a hundred yards to the south, the murmuring of the priest barely audible on the breeze. Otherwise, the big cemetery was quiet and serene, a perfect place for a loner like Carlton Westerfield to sort through the conflicting information surrounding Paula's kidnapped daughter.

First, he thought about retrieving the Colt .45 auto-pistol which was buried under a square of turf a few feet from where he now sat. He'd double-wrapped it in plastic and placed it there soon after the car wash shooting, glad to be rid of the damning weapon at the time. However, considering the possibilities for Friday night, he wished he could carry the well-balanced and powerful handgun. Any action occurring Friday would not be a quick identity verification and assassination; it could be more like the car wash scene, like it or not.

During his career as a mechanic, he had always preferred revolvers for keeping the brass intact, but the .38 now residing in his waistband seemed light and inadequate compared to the big automatic's weight, balance, and auto-loading design. On the negative side, the .45 had spit its spent brass all over the car wash apron that night, brass which surely had been collected, scrutinized by forensic ballistic experts, and carefully catalogued on several databases. Without some modifications, any future bullets fired (and brass ejected) by the Colt could be compared and matched within days, if not hours, to the deaths of four men. The thugs who had been killed at the car wash wouldn't be mourned over by law enforcement, but cops would jump at the opportunity to tie that night's shooter to any new activity to solve the case. Carlton couldn't take the chance that he might be connected to the murder weapon, much as he wanted to use it.

His thoughts were interrupted by his phone's text alert. It was Heather, acknowledging his congratulations and subtly inquiring about his Friday night plans. He texted back, asking for a time to talk when she wouldn't be interrupted or overheard. As he hit the "send" button, it occurred to him that he'd been foolish to worry about not having the Colt .45; he didn't need that weapon at all. A new idea hit him, and he texted Tino with a request for a different piece of firepower. Communications done, he leaned back to start what he'd come here for; to think in privacy and calculate every possible action and outcome.

Most bothersome was the nature of the threat facing Faustino Perez, his half-sister and, by extension, Carlton himself. It seemed highly unlikely that the possibility of Paula's daughter learning the truth about her background was sufficient reason to justify handing over a large amount of cash and valuable street product. So, the threat of actual physical harm must be the key, he thought. Evidently, Tino, Paula, or Reynaldo must have more insight into Ramos' predilection for violence than was being passed on to Carlton. But why keep him in the dark about it? They clearly trusted him, valued his expertise, and wanted him to help them solve the problem—why not tell him every snippet of information to help him do so? Why tip-toe around the subject of Brujido Ramos?

Carlton had managed to put together a few facts on his own. He now was certain that Reynaldo Gomez was not merely a quick, random choice made by Tino when asked about a possible helper in bringing down Ramos with a drug-cash switch involving the DEA. Nor was he *accidently* included in the plans to eliminate Tino's competitor, despite the discussion about taking over the retail end of Perez's business. But knowing the reason for Reynaldo's involvement didn't explain the secrecy surrounding this mess; in fact, Carlton thought the opposite should apply. His three associates would be well-served to fully inform him of all the facts regarding Gomez involvement, no matter what they might be.

Regardless of from what direction Carlton approached the problem, the answer always circled back to his being held at bay in the area of information.

And without full disclosure, it would be difficult for him to carry out what was needed, or even offer advice about it. After all, he was in the employ of Tino Perez for the purpose of advising him on certain things, like what was needed to maintain and further his business. In the case of the mercurial Ramos, he wasn't sure *what* was needed. On the surface, elimination of one's competitor seemed like a plus. But perhaps his replacement would be a tougher businessman—or woman—than Brujido Ramos. He or she would almost certainly be saner, he thought. *Or maybe not.*

Carlton glanced at his phone and saw he had spent almost an hour mulling over the same unanswerable questions. He hadn't come across any additional insight, or had a brilliant vision with which to return home. Still, the break from the siege mentality at his apartment had been worthwhile. He reached for his backpack and walked a big loop through the cemetery on his way to his pickup. The funeral was over; a few mourners, probably family members, stood staring at the fresh grave covered in bright flower arrangements. As he passed them by, he thought about the tens of thousands of people who had mourned in this place, himself included. It was traditionally a place of sadness, a parting spot for permanent good-byes, and a venue for humankind's ultimate transition. Still, it was beautiful and peaceful; a place where Carlton went to pay respects to his mother and aunt and to spend time by himself. Usually, it served as his own personal refuge from humanity and its problems. Today, he had brought others' problems with him to think about and straighten out. Now he seemed destined to leave with them intact and unsolved.

He also wondered how—and why—he had obligated himself to be the bagman for the second time in as many weeks. What had seemed an absurdity at first had changed and morphed into something he felt he had to do himself, mainly because he had seen the pain and concern on Paula's face and didn't know who else could do it better. Thinking back, he had scoffed at the idea, then simply taken the job by default. Tino had initially declared it too dangerous, but he hadn't mentioned anyone else, and his opposition to Carlton doing the job was perfunctory, bordering on listless.

On a positive note, Carlton's phone conversations had, hopefully, steered Brujido Ramos toward thinking about the money and product he would be receiving, and away from retaliating about his four dead crew members. The DEA bust had crimped his income, and it looked like greed would overrule Ramos' anger and caution, or so he hoped. Now it was time to come up with a logistics plan Ramos would accept while enabling Carlton to have some control over the action.

He left the cemetery through a gate on the south side and approached his parked vehicle from the opposite side of the street, watching all activity around it for anything suspicious. Seeing nothing, he got in and cranked up, anxious to get back and see if anything had happened. The drive home took about fifteen minutes, and he hoped he could sneak up to his apartment unseen for a quick nap. It wasn't to be.

Paula was standing at his door, phone at her ear. When she turned and saw him, her face brightened and she put the phone away.

"Hi! I knocked but got no answer, so I was calling you."

"And here I am! What luck for both of us. You find any shoes?"

"I did, but we had to cut it short. Brenda texted me back and said she's really worried now. Ramos has gone silent, she can't get through to Cecilia or Myra, and her husband is now missing."

"I was afraid it wouldn't get better as this thing unfolded. I wonder if she should do the normal thing, like go to the police, file a missing person report."

Paula looked doubtful. "She's been around too much shady stuff, despite the image she tries to give everyone with her super-realtor act. She probably knows that her brother-in-law would go completely off his rocker if the police got involved."

Her accurate observation made Carlton angry. "How the hell did she expect to raise Cecilia to be a normal kid? Surely she's known about Brujido's lifestyle and her husband's part in his business. She should have avoided him like the plague from the minute she got a daughter, and *not* find him a house a few blocks from her family."

"She didn't know then, Carlton," she explained, exasperation creeping into her voice. "He's recently gotten a lot worse, and that's the only side of him you've heard about. A couple of years ago, Brujido was a low-key player who didn't make waves, no violence, nothing to draw much attention. You know, kind of like, well..."

"He was like Tino? Yeah, your brother's pretty low-key from what I can tell, but he can get rough when he needs to. That makes a lot more sense than being over-the-top just to show how tough you are."

"Yes, that was my take on it, but I'd hate for my brother to hear me comparing him to Brujido Ramos."

"How did Brenda meet that idiot's brother?"

"I don't remember, but she's been married to Julian for about fifteen years.

She may have suspected Brujido wasn't exactly legal in everything he did, but he wasn't a threat to her or her family."

He nodded, having heard the story of Ramos changing to emulate the violent cartel guys. It made sense, but his earlier suggestion for Brenda was valid. "If things go really bad, Brenda and Julian will be looked at real hard if there's no record of them reporting their missing eleven-year-old daughter."

The meeting was interrupted by Tino walking up the steps to their landing, followed closely by Reynaldo. Carlton could tell by their expressions they weren't bringing good news. "Let's go inside," he said, opening the door for Paula and waiting on the men until they brushed by him muttering and cursing in two languages.

Once inside Carlton's apartment, Tino turned to him. "That bastard has killed another one of my guys, Jorge Villanova. Apparently, two of Ramos' street guys posed as new buyers and killed him when he drove up beside them in a parking lot. I'd told all my street sales staff not to work alone and to be really careful about new buyers. I ordered no transactions done in back alleys." He was growing angrier as he ticked off his standing instructions on his fingers. "But these young guys work on commission, so they make all the sales they can. This one cost him his life."

"I don't remember Jorge. Was he at the meeting the other night?"

"Yes, but so was everyone else. And I don't think you had formally met him. Good salesman, hard worker, always made his quota and earned bonuses for being top guy several times lately. But he tried too hard on this sale."

"You going to retaliate?" Carlton asked, guessing the answer from Tino's mood.

"Yes, tonight. We'll go over to his side of town with a couple of teams in lead cars, with two backup cars for each. I've got Arturo and Manny over there looking around for their street corners."

"Is that safe? Aren't they at risk over there, just two of them?"

"No, it's not safe, but it's not as risky as you might think. I sent them in a nice car, a new Ford Fusion. They're dressed nice, look like car salesmen or something. They'll play it cool by shopping for a connection to buy from, maybe even make a small purchase and see if Ramos' sales person will tell them where he'll be tonight. They can poor-boy it, say they've got to get more money and will come back."

"The prospect of repeat business. Always gets the attention of a sales person."

"Right. And Arturo and Manny are both family guys, haven't been seen on the street, so there's very little chance of being made. But if they are, they're heeled and have orders to pop anybody who looks at them cross-eyed."

"You think Ramos' guys will have received orders not to sell to any new customers? Won't he be expecting a reversal of exactly what his guys did to Jorge?"

"Possibly. Reynaldo and I had a long talk with Manny and Arturo, told them to watch for that and not press too hard if their sales people seem skittish. We coached them on acting like two inexperienced married guys out looking for action, girls, and coke. They'll ask about girls first, then dope. And I ordered them not to follow anyone to a remote location. Any buy will have to take place in the middle of a mall parking lot, a quick exchange away from other cars and people."

Carlton looked doubtful, but said nothing. Tino picked up on his disapproval immediately. "I've got to do something, and I can't run an ad on Craigslist. Those guys know their stuff, they look right, they know how to do it. Besides, they were good friends of Jorge's. They're determined to give some payback, just like I am."

This time Carlton nodded. "I know, Tino, and I'm certainly not questioning your logic or your plan. But Ramos' craziness might be catching, like the flu. All his guys may be as loony as he is."

"Maybe so. But if this business were easy, I'd be able to send a couple of girl scouts with notes pinned to their shirts."

"I wonder why he pulled this stunt now, one day before he's supposed to get money and leave us alone forever. You think he's given standing orders to his staff, and today was the first time one of his crew had a chance to do it? Or is he super-pissed at having his big purchase nabbed by the feds, wanted to take it out on someone?"

"That's what we were wondering," Reynaldo said. "I was hoping you had another explanation, but it sounds like we're all thinking the same way."

Carlton mulled it over. "I can't think of any way he could see a benefit in ordering a hit today, no matter how upset he is. It doesn't get his shipment back, doesn't get me back from L. A. any sooner, and it didn't make him any money. It just makes our guys angry, ready to jump at Tino's order to hit them tonight. It's just bad business."

"Nobody said Ramos was a smart businessman. He's just a damn lunatic."

Carlton turned back to Tino. "What if I called Ramos and told him I'd heard from you, that you were about to turn his end of town into a war zone." Tino opened his mouth to protest, but Carlton held up his hand. "Just hear me out, Tino. Let's say I tell him to cool his jets for another twenty-four hours, and I'll be back in San Antonio. And I just happen to mention that I've decided to be the bagman, but I'm going to call the shots about where, when, and how."

"I'm not following you completely, Carlton." It was Reynaldo seeing a glimmer, but wanting clarification.

"I tell him I can get Tino to hold off, but I won't do it unless he understands that I'm setting the agenda tomorrow night."

"And if he refuses?"

"If he refuses any part of what I propose, I promise him that I'll be on his side of town with three full clips, riding in the same car with Tino."

"You actually think you can intimidate that nutcase?" Tino asked. He sounded amazed that Carlton would even consider such a ploy. He looked at Gomez, who in turn, looked at Paula. No one spoke for almost a minute.

Reynaldo broke the silence. "Tino, put yourself in his position—forgetting for a minute that he's nuts. About two weeks ago, this same guy, Carlton Westerfield, killed four of your guys, and *they never got a shot off.* You may not be intimidated by this phone call, but you'd probably stop and think about getting the half mil and a lot of blow without taking a chance on losing more men."

"Yeah, but Ramos isn't me. I can't see him going for it."

"Then you've lost nothing, just five minutes of listening to me making a phone call," Carlton said. "Because if he doesn't agree, I'll ride with your guys, just like I said. Oh, and those three clips I mentioned? They'll be empty when I get back."

The tough talk made both Tino and Reynaldo smile. "Call him," they both said, almost in unison.

"Bueno?"

"Mr. Ramos, this is Carlton Westerfield. I got a call from Tino Perez, and he's mad as hell about losing one of his guys. May I ask why you would order such an action when you will get a lot of money tomorrow night?"

"Because I wanted to, that's why!"

"Well, it's caused quite a bit of trouble. I'm still in California, but I'll be coming back tomorrow. I was hoping you and I would conduct our business, and you and Perez would part and never cross paths again." The sentence construction confused Ramos, and Carlton scrambled to clarify himself.

"After you get paid, he doesn't ever want to hear from you again, not in any way, or for any reason."

"Yeah, that's good. But I still want to get even for the four guys you killed."

"Those guys weren't very good at their job, Mr. Ramos. They didn't take me seriously. They thought I was too old, demasiado viejo, and they were foolish and slow. And you would be foolish to try to get even on those four. They're not worth losing what Perez is paying you."

"Perez better pay, you better bring me all the money and all the flake he's got for sale, 'cause I'll know if you cheat me!"

"He won't have to pay you anything if he goes through with his new plan."

"His plan is shit! He has to pay me, or I tell Cecilia about her real mother, maybe mess with her head a little, no?"

Carlton forced a laugh. *"You think she won't learn that in a few years anyway? She doesn't look like Brenda, and I'll bet she doesn't look like Julian. When she's older, she will ask about that. Somebody will tell her anyway."*

"Maybe I will do something more, then. Something that will make Perez wish he'd never sent you to pay for his hermana."

Carlton laughed again. *"He didn't pay, remember? I took his bag of money back to him, along with his sister. So you'd be real lucky to get paid tomorrow night, because I've never heard him as angry as he was on the phone. He plans to go to your side of town and run up the score."*

Ramos was quiet for a few seconds too long, and when he spoke, his accent was heavier. *"How do you know this?"* came out *"how jew know dees?"* Carlton knew he had his attention.

"He told me, that's how. He called to tell me to take my time out here in Los Angeles, I didn't need to be back in San Antonio, because he's going to take care of you another way."

A string of obscenities in Spanish followed. Carlton held the phone out for Reynaldo and Tino to hear. Their grim expressions told him nothing.

"I'm calling you to save everybody some trouble," Carlton said at the first break in Ramos' tirade. *"I can get Tino to hold off, and no one loses any more men. Then you and I will do business tomorrow night. Just one more day, and you and Tino will have no reason to fight."*

"You and I do business tomorrow night? What do you mean?"

Carlton was growing frustrated at the language barrier, even a slight one that made him structure his sentences too carefully. Every word, every nuance and voice inflection had meaning in this type of environment. He decided to forge ahead and drop the news on him. *"Yes, I only care about the girl, so our business is this: you will deliver the girl to a place I pick. When I get a call that she is safe, I will hand you what you want. You get in your car, I get in mine, and we both drive away."*

"And if I don't want to do that, not your way? I don't like you telling me what to do!"

"Sorry about that, Mr. Ramos. Because that's the way I do business this time. I'm not going to a car wash and pull into a certain stall. I'm going to deliver it if you do what I tell you. You will get paid, but my way."

"I don't want to do that!" The tone was getting angrier, the voice louder. *"You don't do that my way, I'm going to do something else to the girl!"*

"Then we have nothing to talk about, Mr. Ramos, because you've got nothing else to sell but the girl. You do something bad to her, and then you have nothing, nada! And you're lucky I'm interested in the girl, because Tino is only interested in gunning down you and your entire crew. You killed one of his men without a good reason, and he will see you soon, unless I tell him to hold off. Then I will be seeing you tomorrow night anyway, because I'll be with Perez's men. And I'm going to bring lots of ammunition, Mr. Ramos, but no money. BALAS, PERO NO DINERO. Tu comprendes?"

He snapped his phone shut without waiting for a reply and hoped he hadn't mangled the Spanish too much. The looks on Tino's and Reynaldo's faces told him he had gotten the point across just fine.

CHAPTER 24

"I'm surprised he hasn't called you back," Tino said, reaching for the coffee pot. He liked the IHOP policy of delivering a pot of coffee to the table. It eliminated looking for a waitperson, but the restaurant charged enough for the pot to cover every refill in the place. Bargain coffee it wasn't, but he had insisted that the group meet at the same spot this morning as yesterday.

It was Friday, the big day for several reasons. First, Ramos had tacitly agreed to be paid his extortion fee tonight after being stonewalled for the past several days. Second, for that to occur, Carlton would "return" from Los Angeles and would be prepared to act as the bagman. And third, Tino was planning on carrying out a full scale attack on members of Ramos' crew in retaliation for another death, this one totally uncalled for in view of the pending delivery of money and drugs. Lastly, the four at the table—plus her parents, no doubt—hoped and prayed for Cecilia's safe return before this day was over.

"I don't think you left any doubt as to your intentions," Tino continued. "He can get paid, or he can add you to the long list of people gunning for him. He sounded a bit upset on the phone," he added dryly.

"Yes, but he can think about getting paid, and that should smooth his feathers a bit."

Paula wasn't so certain and made her feelings known yet again. "Was that the best thing to do? Don't you think he's mad enough to hurt her without goading him?"

"Paula, he's a maniac who likes hearing himself talk tough," Carlton answered gently. "He's used to having his own way by intimidating everyone.

If he is going to hurt Cecilia, he'll do it whether or not I poke him with a stick or not."

"And Carlton also mentioned the money, and how easy it would be for Ramos to get it by just playing along, Paula," offered Reynaldo. "I was concerned about talking tough to him, too, but I think Carlton is right; he's going to do what he wants, no matter what. At least now he knows he has to play ball with Carlton to get the money, at least without much fuss."

"And speaking of delivering the money, I got you the piece you wanted," Tino told him. "Any reason you wanted the Glock 19 in particular?"

"They're real popular, or so I've heard."

"So are nose piercings and tattoos, but you don't have either of those."

"Well, the day is young, I may get a tattoo after breakfast. Is the piece cold?"

Tino looked at him as if he'd asked about the moon being made of green cheese. "Of course! Stolen in New Orleans during the big hurricane. It's been out of circulation since then, but I had my guy take it to the range and run a few clips through it and clean it. He had a full box of ammo left after that, which was bought in a Houston Walmart about a year ago by someone else, paid cash. My man got it in a barter deal with his buddy, so there is no connection to anyone we know."

"That's perfect, because it will likely be tossed, and I won't have time to dismantle it."

Everyone fell quiet for a minute, no doubt thinking of the possible chain of events preceding a weapon being discarded in a storm drain or lake—and that would be a *good* outcome: Carlton alive and on the run. Less desirable outcomes were a distinct possibility, as everyone at the table knew.

Tino looked directly at Carlton. "There's still time to arrange for someone else to deliver the extortion money, no matter what Ramos demands. This time, I *don't* think you're the right person for the job."

Carlton shrugged. "I didn't like the idea at first, but I'm going to stress the part about his getting paid depending upon delivery of Cecilia, something he can't easily engineer while directing a firefight. Obviously, I can verify her return and still get bushwhacked afterward, but I've got something in mind for that."

"You need the full crew to be a couple of blocks away? We can do that, and if anything doesn't go the way you want it, we can be on him in half a minute. I mean that: less than thirty seconds, Carlton."

"That would be good to have. But if I can get the backup team I want—the DEA—you'll want to hang back a bit. The area might get real crowded."

Reynaldo raised his eyebrows. "You're going to deliver cash and drugs while the DEA is watching? I told you before, I hope you can trust them."

"I haven't forgotten your warning about that when we met for breakfast in Hondo. It's a valid concern, but I'm counting on this agent's desire for busting Ramos to keep me off the hook. That and my natural charm."

"You better keep that charm in check, Cowboy," Paula warned. The remark got a laugh from the men, but the look on her face said there was no humor intended.

"I'll only use it as a last resort," Carlton promised with a straight face.

The idle chatter was interrupted by his cell phone. He pulled it from his shirt pocket, checked the number, and held up a hand for silence.

"This is Carlton Westerfield."

"You gonna' deliver that money and the other stuff like I said?"

"Nope. Like I said. I told you that yesterday. I'm picking the time, the place, and the process for the exchange."

"You don' tell me what to do!" Ramos exploded, his voice able to be heard by the others at the table. *"Nobody tells me what to do!"* he added for good measure, in case Carlton hadn't gotten the drift.

"Just this one time I do, but you'll get over it when you get the money and other stuff. It will only take a few minutes, and we'll be done forever."

Ramos launched into something in Spanish, and Carlton had to wait until he quieted down. *"Look, Mr. Ramos, I'm at the airport now, and they're about to call my flight. I've got a stop-over in Phoenix, but I'll be in San Antonio about four o'clock. As soon as I get home, I'll call you. I've talked to Faustino Perez, and he has agreed to wait on starting a full retaliation for his man's death. But he's only going to wait until I tell him you and I have a deal to meet. If I don't report to him by seven o'clock, he's going forward with sending several cars to your side of town."*

"He's not going to do that! He will lose a lot more men if he tries!"

"That's what I'm trying to avoid, for everyone. But if you won't deal the way I want, I'll be with Tino, in the same car."

"Oh, yeah? That how I'm gonna know you? The gringo in the car?"

"Yes, and I'll be the one shooting at you and your men. You might recall that I've had some practice lately."

Some more curses flew over the airwaves, but Carlton snapped his phone shut on them.

"That's good," Tino grunted. "He calls you back and gets the same reaction; my way or the highway. That has to be upsetting to a guy who thinks the whole world bows down to him and his threats."

"Yes, and I hope I'm not misjudging him. I think it's the only way, though, because reason and logic aren't in his vocabulary."

Paula looked worried, and Reynaldo seemed preoccupied with his food, but the look on his face said he was more concerned than he cared to verbalize. Tino looked his usual self, but he was unsettled and fidgety, more than Carlton could recall seeing him. As he studied his table companions, he wondered if he looked any different than usual, but judging by the effect the past two weeks had had on everyone else, he didn't really want to know. Instead, he finished off his coffee and hinted that he needed to get organized and plan for the evening's showdown.

"I'm not sure where to try to make this happen, but I want it to be someplace he's not likely to be familiar with. I've got a couple of spots in mind, but I think I'll visit with Agent Colson, see who she has in mind for backup, and where she would recommend. I've got to have it all down cold before I call Ramos."

"You going to tell her the full story? What you'll be delivering to Ramos, and why?"

Carlton shrugged. "Yes, I don't see why not. It has to be enough for the DEA to be interested, and the chance to nab Ramos, along with a lot of cash and dope should do it. Right now, I've got some credibility with them, enough to tell them the whole story and have them act on it. I don't think we'll get a better opportunity to have Ramos taken off the board, legally and without a firefight."

"Don't forget the most important part of the exchange," Paula said. She was smiling, but the tension in her voice gave away her true feelings, that getting Ramos taken down was secondary to Cecilia's safe return.

"I won't forget, Paula. I told you she was first and foremost in this deal, and I meant it, even if Ramos ends up getting away clean. I'll do everything I can to get her back."

"I—we—know you will." It was Tino talking, but Carlton noticed his friend Reynaldo was nodding in affirmation across the table, reminding him that there was a lot more in play than just paying extortion money to a competitor. Carlton wished he knew the entire story, but there would be time for that later.

Reynaldo cleared his throat, then hesitated a moment before speaking. "I know you have good connections with those DEA agents, but they're going to think you're tied in with Ramos, or have been until recently."

"And now we've parted ways, and I'm trying to get him jailed or killed before he kills me, which he'd love to do if he found out I provided the info on getting his guys busted on Wednesday."

"Yes. That's how they will see it, no matter how good your relationship is with them. They would like to bag you at the same time, hoping you have inside information on Ramos' entire setup."

Carlton nodded. "I know you're right about that, Reynaldo. Believe me, I won't be hanging around long after this goes down. I'm not waiting for a pat on the back."

"Good, because the pat on your back would be to bend you over the fender of the police car, just before putting handcuffs on you. And I know I've told you this before, but I wanted to warn you once more about trusting the feds."

Carlton nodded again, thankful for the advice. He had no doubt that Heather Colson would do whatever advanced her career, including taking down someone who could provide more information to bolster the case against Brujido Ramos. Just because the pretty agent seemed to like him didn't mean he would fully trust her.

A half hour later, all four had returned to their respective apartments. Tino and Reynaldo didn't stay long, but left again with the Estrada brothers. Paula was unusually quiet and declined to come to Carlton's apartment while he made arrangements with the DEA and planned the critical evening down to the last detail.

He sat down with a map of the city and pulled up detail of several areas on his laptop. He looked for locations that had good freeway access, plus a number of surface streets for ingress and egress. He liked the north side because of his familiarity with it and Ramos' likely lack of knowledge of that side of town.

He had one in mind, Park North Shopping Center at Loop 410 and Blanco Road. He had lived near the big strip mall for years and frequented its restaurants and stores, so he already knew the layout. Recalling a covered parking area, he decided it would serve the purpose well, providing he could get Ramos to go along with his first pick.

He decided to have at least one option on the south side in the event Ramos absolutely refused his first choice. He studied an area on Southeast Military Drive, a shopping center called City Base Landing that fit the bill; busy with patrons who didn't pay much attention to what fellow shoppers were doing.

The name—City Base Landing—was derived from its location on a former Air Force base which had been taken over by the city in 2002, during the base closure period. For a few years, growth was slow in the transformed military facility, but in recent years, it had been developed into a mixed-used community with every type of business imaginable, from restaurants to office supply, apartment homes to vision centers and ice cream shops. Adjacent to the shopping center was the great American standby, Walmart. It was near Ramos' base of operations, had lots of ingress and egress points, so he would likely be in favor of it over a north side spot.

Mulling over the choices, he decided it didn't really make much difference where the exchange took place; Ramos would surely have backup, just as he, Carlton, would. Therefore, things could go sideways—harsh words spoken, threats made, guns drawn—no matter where it went down. The same applied to having too many choices; he decided two spots on opposite sides of the city would be enough. Ramos would simply have to be satisfied with one of them.

Any kidnapping or extortion payoff involved a small concession to mutual trust, a fair amount of precautions being taken, and a lot of greed for the parties to do the exchange. Carlton was betting heavily on the greed part, since Ramos had just lost a sizeable shipment, plus two vans and some crew members. Without the profits from that batch, a mid-size trafficker like Ramos would feel the pinch pretty quickly. He smiled as he thought about how Ramos would react if he knew where the intel had come from for the Wednesday bust.

Armed with two locations, he called Ramos' number. After five rings, it went to voice mail, and he left a message that he was still in Phoenix, but expected to be in San Antonio sometime around four, and would get in touch to discuss "business details."

Next, he called Heather's number (on the "Heather phone"), and she answered immediately.

"Can you talk a minute?"
"Sure. You find out about tonight?"

"Still choosing a meeting point. Can we meet at one of the choices and look it over?"

"I can get away for lunch any time after eleven."

"Great! How about the La Madeleine at Park North Mall? Blanco Road and 410; it's adjacent to the spot I'm going to use, if I can get an agreement from the other party."

"Eleven-thirty work for you?"

"Yep. See you then."

Both clicked off, and Carlton went back out to check on his temporary transportation. The Mazda pickup had been a pleasant surprise; it ran well and everything seemed to work; he'd actually enjoyed driving the beat-up little rig. However, it was an old work truck, so he went over every possible item that might cause a problem; lights, turn signals, brake lights, tires, fluid levels—he wanted nothing of a mechanical nature to go bad tonight.

He checked Southwest flights online and wrote down some information in case he had to wing it with Ramos regarding his schedule. Calculating a couple of scenarios, he memorized flight numbers and times before shutting down the screen.

He grabbed his kitchen gloves and cleaning equipment and drove to Tino's office at the flea market to look at the Glock. It was well-used, showing some shiny spots where the surface coating had worn thin. The action felt good; slick and smooth like the old Colt .45, but not as heavy. He practiced swinging the weapon up and onto various targets in the office while Tino looked on impassively. Then he donned the gloves and spent twenty minutes disassembling and cleaning the gun, the clips, and each individual round of ammunition.

Satisfied with the weapon, he laid it down on Tino's desk. "I like the Colt, but this one will be more useful if I have to use it tonight."

"DEA agents use these?"

"I read that they are standard sidearm issue, but each individual agent may get permission to use a personal handgun. Remember, Tim Hunnicut carried his own Colt."

"Didn't do him much good; he didn't get a chance to use it."

"Nope. I hope I don't have to use this thing, either, but if bullets start flying, I'd like to muddy the investigative waters a bit by using the same ammo as the feds. Ballistics will eventually reveal another gun on the scene, but it will take a while to sort out."

"You talk to your girlfriend at DEA yet?"

"Don't say that around your sister, Tino. And yes, I called her an hour ago. We're meeting for lunch at eleven-thirty. My best pick for an exchange location is right there by the restaurant, so we can talk and go check the layout."

"Where do you have in mind?"

"The parking garage at Park North Shopping Center. It's that shopping center on 410 that lies between Blanco and San Pedro. There's a Super Target store on one end and a Sears on the other, the San Pedro end. It has good ingress and egress, access to 410, or you can shoot down Blanco and catch any east-west streets to get out of the area."

"I hope you can convince Ramos to meet there. What if he refuses, wants to meet somewhere on his turf?"

"I'll play tough for a while, but that's mostly just to throw him off, give him the sense that I'm controlling the action. I want to set the tone for the actual meeting and exchange process. But if he balks too much, I'll tell him City Base Landing, the big center on Southeast Military. Actually, anywhere will do; it won't change what the DEA or your backup team does. I'll let you know the place as soon as I set it up with him."

I'll take Sergio and Estéban to that parking garage about two o'clock, then. We'll have time to check it out thoroughly, since I'm already familiar with that stuff over by Southeast Military and 281. I hope he goes for the one you're most comfortable with, though."

"Me too. Where's Reynaldo?"

"He drove out to Sabinal to check on some stuff at his ranch. Said he'd be back here about five."

"He was quiet this morning at breakfast. Looked a little spooked. You know why?"

Tino paused a second too long. "I think he's concerned about your being the bagman."

"Does he want to take the job?" Carlton asked the question with a grin to hide his ulterior motive. Reynaldo Gomez appeared to be a gentleman, courteous toward his old friend's advisor, but he hadn't known Carlton long enough to be overly concerned about his safety, except for how it related to his own agenda. Clearly, Tino was keeping that a secret.

"No, I think he wants to keep a low profile on this matter. Publicity is not a drug trafficker's friend, you know. Just because Brujido Ramos likes to grandstand, it doesn't make it smart business in this industry."

"Publicity is no friend to me either. But I'm not planning on issuing a press release."

Tino laughed at that. "No, but you have to understand this: old friend that he is, Reynaldo Gomez is a well-known player at a different level than Ramos—or myself. And he wants to keep it that way."

Carlton nodded at the explanation and didn't pursue if further, but he wanted to ask why a powerful trafficker like Gomez couldn't supply some muscle, at least temporarily. Maybe a better opportunity for the question would present itself; however, time was short, and the answer might be academic if Ramos' crew proved too strong—or if things went badly tonight.

Leaving the Glock in Tino's desk, he left for his lunch appointment. Heather was waiting just inside the front door at La Madeleine, which was drawing a big crowd this close to noon. They waded through the creeping line, placed their orders, and carried trays for the self-service of drinks and utensils. Carlton picked a deuce in the back corner which looked like it had been designed for this very type of meeting or, more likely, a lovers' tryst, since it was doubtful that restaurant management envisioned a lot of DEA agents meeting with their confidential informants.

He held Heather's chair while she sat down, but didn't hesitate or engage in polite small talk; instead, he launched into the subject as he was taking his seat. "I'm going to tell you everything that's going on, because I think you'll be more inclined to help if you know the entire story."

"Okay," she answered uncertainly. "It would be nice to hear the entire story, provided it's true."

"Deal. Let's eat first, and I'll tell you the story."

The next thirty minutes were spent eating and Carlton's listening to her stories about the life of a single female DEA agent. It was a welcome break from the drama and tension of the past thirteen days, which had been filled with threats, doubts, lies, tears, deaths, plans for retaliation…life on the wrong side of the law, he thought morosely. Thoroughly entertained, he asked her a few questions, made some comments, and found himself drawn to her snappy commentary and her appearance, which he had secretly labeled "naughty school librarian."

Finishing his grilled chicken breast sandwich, Carlton thought it time to get to the matter at hand, much as he would like to continue chatting about…nothing—and enjoying it. He waited for a pause that needed filling. "I wanted you to hear the whole story, and I want you to believe me. This entire mess is true, Heather. I don't have any reason to lie about it, and the timing doesn't leave much choice. You need to know everything in order to have a reason to help me, so here goes: first, Paula's eleven-year-old daughter is being held by Brujido Ramos—"

"She has a daughter?" she interrupted, skepticism on her face. "She doesn't look the motherly type."

"Yep. And I didn't know about the girl until a day or so ago myself. She lives with a lifelong friend of Paula's."

"Well, whatever the arrangement, kidnapping calls for the FBI to be involved."

"Just wait, let me tell everything first. She's being held, but not so much against *her* will as against her adoptive mother's will. Who, by the way, is Ramos' sister-in-law."

"Huh?" The confused look on Agent Colson's face made Carlton back up and start over. Five minutes later, she began nodding, getting the timeline and all the players straight. Carlton downplayed Faustino Perez, along with Reynaldo Gomez, as being sideline players, though he knew Heather would figure differently as the story unfolded. Instead, he stressed his own involvement as being tied to his relationship with Paula; hers to Cecilia, Brenda, and Julian Ramos.

When he had finished laying the foundation for his tale, he began again. "Brujido Ramos is threatening to tell Cecilia that Brenda Ramos is not her real mother, Julian is not her father, and he, Brujido, isn't really her uncle. He is using that threat against Paula Hendricks to extort a half million dollars in cash and a large amount of street product, which she has to get from her half-brother, Faustino Perez. Paula has me in the middle as the bagman—"

"Wait, wait a minute! Perez is handing over big money and his inventory to a competitor, just because Ramos is threatening to tell his niece about her background?"

Carlton held up his hands in surrender. "I know, it sounds like a weak threat to me, too, but I don't have a sister, I don't have kids, and I don't know how a little girl might react to that, especially if he tells her some sordid tale about her being conceived in a whorehouse, abandoned in a dump ground for rats to chew on." He held up his hand again to forestall any more interruption. "*Plus*—this prince of a man has threatened to do more than just tell her something too shocking for a little girl; he's alluded to physically harming her."

Heather looked alarmed. "That's pretty sick, even for a dope dealer. She's as much his niece as anyone could be, no matter who gave birth to her. Why can't her mother and her husband—Brujido's brother, right?—do something?"

"I think they're scared to death of him. Apparently, Ramos has been hanging with a tough crowd in Mexico City. Some of the big cartel guys, and their penchant for violence has rubbed off on him. Until recently, I understand he's been just your run-of-the-mill, mid-level trafficker. Kind of like Tony Soprano; a true gangster, but in terms of home and family, just a guy with everyday problems."

Heather smiled at the comparison to the TV series character. "I always thought that series was pretty hokey, but entertaining. Anyway, I get your point; he's wandered off the reservation, turned into a real violence advocate, instead of the neighborhood godfather figure Tony was."

"That's my take on it, but who knows? The point is, he will be in possession of some serious cash and dope tonight, and you can be there to relieve him of that burden, plus put handcuffs on him."

Heather studied his face for a long moment. "I'd love to do just that. But how in the world did you get this mixed up…oh, I remember!" She slapped her forehead as though recalling a forgotten Trivia game question. "The sexy Paula Hendricks and her skill at getting the little head to think for the big one? Am I right?"

The merry look on her face caused Carlton to grimace in fake pain, as though taking her verbal onslaught were body shots from Mike Tyson. "I know. And once again, you're right. But that aside, you can tidy up Wednesday's bust by rounding up the main man in possession of a snowstorm. The DEA needs him in the bucket."

"And that rids your squeeze of her problem, while making her *real* grateful to you and Perez, right? Grateful enough to repay her brother for his cash and inventory? Or is that task going to fall to one shining knight named Carlton Westerfield?"

"I don't have anything to do with what her brother chooses to help her with; I'm just the bagman. That should make her grateful enough, especially if I can get that idiot to hand over the girl to Brenda."

"Then what? What about next week, when he decides to do it again?"

Carlton was again impressed with the female agent's insight and savvy regarding criminal behavior. She was foreseeing immediately what he, Tino, and Reynaldo had spoken of early on, and he looked at her with renewed respect as he spoke. "If Brenda Ramos takes my advice, she and Julian will split for parts unknown, pick a time to enlighten Cecilia to her history and the fact that her uncle is a bad guy who should be avoided like the snake he is. Besides, he'll be in prison, thanks to Agent Heather Colson, right?"

She took the last bite of some quiche dish she had ordered and leaned back in her chair, thoughtfully chewing as she looked directly at Carlton. He held her gaze while he pushed his own plate away and finished his iced tea. It was a full minute before she spoke. "Okay, let's go look at this place where I can become Heather Colson, Super-Agent."

Leaving the Mazda pickup, Heather drove them in the same vehicle she and Ikos had used, following Carlton's instructions to the nearby covered parking area. It was large, the space comprising the entire area of the building above it, which was occupied by a theater and several other retail sales and service operations. They checked out the entrances and exits, finding that cars could enter and exit at the same doors, no one-way restrictions, no spiraling up or down ramps. The shopping center's driveways all led to the freeway loop to the north, or major streets to the east and west, both of which led to other freeways and interstate highways. A Target store's large parking lot to the south provided another avenue of evasion and escape via its southern driveway. There were security cameras at the elevators' entry/exit doors and stairwells, but any activity nearer the middle would not be picked up as anything sinister or illegal. At best, the cameras would only record a man handing something over to another one after talking on their phones. In short, it was perfect for conducting a quick, discrete handoff between two vehicles' occupants without drawing undue attention.

Ten minutes later, they had seen enough, and Carlton waited impatiently for her to give an opinion on the site and tell him she would be in place at the appointed time. She parked beside the pickup and put her government SUV in Park. Turning in the seat, she looked Carlton in the eye, a disquieting move that unnerved him for reasons he couldn't pin down. It wasn't just nervousness in the presence of a law enforcement agent, and he didn't think he was prone to shyness around attractive women. He'd never been shy around Paula Hendricks and, although she had a few years on Heather Colson, she could hold her own against any younger woman. Unsure of the reason for his discomfort, he put the feeling out of his mind when she started talking.

"I think the place is good. I mentioned this to Rex and Cho, a young Asian guy I work with. They're on board with being in the garage and watching what goes down between you and Brujido Ramos. But I can't guarantee what they will do if it gets really dicey in there. It would have to be a straight bust of two or three guys at the most, in the open. Anything bigger, like a bunch of guys or multiple cars with unknown numbers, and they'll insist on calling backup." When Carlton looked at her inquiringly, she put up her hand as though to fend him off. "Don't hold that against them, Carlton. Rex likes the idea of field work, but I don't think he's cut out for it in real life. And Cho is an analyst, not a field agent. Both of them are ambitious, but in different ways. They have no incentive to get gunned down, because they aren't wild about making a name for themselves as field agents in the Agency."

"I didn't think you were either. In fact, I didn't think you were going to stay with the DEA, not according to what you said in Corpus a few months back."

"Things have changed."

"Since you have a new boss? Stan Ikos is better to work for than Tim Hunnicut, I'm sure."

"Way better."

Carlton smiled. "He's going to be impressed when you bag a major player, especially while you and your buds are just out shopping for panties."

She laughed at that. "I'll tell them about that, they'll like it!"

"Okay. Well, I'll call you asap to tell you if this is the place. If not, it will be a shopping center on Southeast Military Drive called City Base Landing. You know it?"

"The converted Air Force base? I read about it, there was an article in the paper a while back. The city got it for a song back when the Defense Department closed all those bases, right? And now it's a commercial and residential area, very successful from what the paper said."

"Yes, that's the one. But I'm really pushing for this to be the place. I know the area, and that parking garage is a better spot than stepping over disposable diapers in the Walmart parking lot."

Heather took a deep breath and exhaled loudly. "Okay, Mr. Westerfield. Call me as soon as you have the details, so we can get set up."

"Will do, Agent Colson. Oh, and one other thing. When Ramos has his hand on the goods, I'll need about ten seconds to disappear. Make sure your buds have some eyesight problems about that time, and memory problems later."

She looked at him curiously for a few seconds before responding. "Look, we're going to get enough grilling about how we saw this deal going down, established Probable Cause to intervene, and nabbed the buyer. We'll have to claim we recognized Ramos from the pictures passed around during some meeting or another. I don't want to explain why we couldn't get the seller, or even get a good look at him or her. I can get Rex on board with your plan, but Cho might be a different story. He's not much of a maverick. So don't hang around; I can't make any guarantees except one: neither Rex nor Cho scored great in the last handgun tests."

"How about you? How'd you score?"

"Every time I tried. Oh, and I can shoot well, too."

Carlton grinned. "Got it. See you tonight." He watched her drive away and hoped he was doing the right thing by enlisting her help. If not, he might be spending his retirement years behind bars.

Carlton went back in the restaurant and had a cup of coffee. He went to the same table and sat, going over in his mind all the details of the looming transaction. With the DEA agents on hand for help, he needed to make sure they saw what clearly amounted to an illegal action taking place to protect themselves from a clever defense attorney and an internal affairs investigation. He had to watch out for Ramos' backup crew and hope his own backup guys didn't jump the gun. He had to get Brenda to perform perfectly, something he didn't have much faith in, given her previous performance. It might prove to be a difficult night, he thought.

He checked the time. It was just before two, and Tino had said he would check out the covered garage setup soon, so he decided to wait near the restaurant and see if any questions arose. He pulled down to the Target parking lot, shut off the engine and dialed Tino.

"Bueno?"

"Tino, it's Carlton. Are you close to the shopping center?"

"Taking the exit right now. Are you still there?"

"Yes. Why don't you come to the Target parking lot and pick me up. We'll drive through the garage, and you can point out any problem areas, maybe suggest the best spot for the exchange."

"Sounds good. See you in five."

Tino pulled in driving his red F-250 crew cab pickup. Sergio Estrada sat in the passenger seat, with Estéban and Reynaldo in the back. Carlton squeezed in beside them, and Tino entered the south entrance to the garage and drove through slowly. Carlton listened to the others' observations and comments, again noting carefully the layout, the distances between concrete support structures, the access from each good spot to the nearest exit. After two trips, Tino declared the garage a good spot, while Reynaldo declared it off-limits to another pass-through.

"Don't want to make the security guys too curious." He turned to Carlton. "Did you see everything you needed to check out?"

"Yes, I think so. I went through earlier with Agent Colson. I told her how I hoped it would go down, and that I needed a few seconds to get lost while they're cuffing Brujido Ramos."

"So you're sure she'll do it? Let you slip through?"

"I think so. If not, I'll have to rely on her being off-duty and not having Probable Cause from what she's going to see. Also, it's on record that I have acted as a confidential informant, only a few days ago. It was successful, so I don't think they want to burn me just yet. Oh, one other thing in my favor: Cecilia. I told Heather the entire story, so she knows I'm trying to spring a little girl, and the deal must go down smoothly until she gets delivered to Brenda. Now, Heather doesn't know for sure how I'm going to arrange that part—neither do I, not exactly—so she'll be afraid that putting cuffs on me would endanger Cecilia."

"Good, that's a good point! Just be careful and make yourself scarce as soon as Ramos takes delivery."

"I'm going to get there first and go into a store to call Ramos with my exact location in the garage. I'll get somewhere near the middle, away from the security cameras if I can. If not, I'll position the briefcases for as little exposure to them as possible while handing them over. Or I might stand aside and let Ramos and his helper retrieve them from the pickup."

"Do the security cameras really pose a problem?" Sergio asked.

"No, because I don't think they're being manned to watch for specific activity in real time. They're used to identify a shoplifter or car break-in after the fact. But I want to be careful just the same, in case the DEA bust goes sideways and somebody decides to look at the videos."

"I'll have people in two cars," Tino said. "Let me know where you are, we'll park somewhere outside the garage. You driving the little pickup tonight?"

"Yes. It's as good as any for this. I'll head back now, and I'll make the call to Ramos from your office. Everyone can hear exactly what the arrangements will be, and I can get the payoff stuff. Oh, and the Glock."

CHAPTER 25

By four o'clock, Tino's office was full of people. Paula had come with Raul and Caterina Vega, and stood chatting with Reynaldo Gomez. The Estrada brothers, Arturo Matamoros, and David Avila talked quietly among themselves, as did another small group of guys Carlton had seen, but couldn't call by name. Tino sat behind his desk, a harried look on his usually impassive face. When Carlton walked in, everyone turned to look, and most issued a wave or some greeting. Embarrassed, he smiled and gave a wave to everyone, which made him feel even more foolish.

He decided to get the call over with; it was the biggest hurdle toward being successful at getting Cecilia back safely. During the inspection of the parking garage, Tino had declared that, if Ramos refused to play ball, he would immediately head for his territory and start the retaliation which, in his words, "should have already happened." Therefore, it was time to find out how the night would begin—which would dictate how it might end.

Tino rapped on his desk, and the crowd noise fell to a murmur, then to silence. When they looked to the boss, he jerked a thumb toward Carlton, who was already punching in Ramos' number.

"Mr. Ramos, this is Carlton Westerfield. I got in about an hour ago, and—

"That's bullshit! You didn't go nowhere! Tell me what flight you were on."

"Please don't interrupt. I don't have time for your interrogation over something so silly."

"Tell me the goddam flight number!"

"It was flight 3884 from Phoenix, arrived on time at SAT at two-fifty-five. Now shut up and listen if you want the money!" He waited a few seconds to

see if he had Ramos' attention, then continued. *"I'm here with the cash and product. It's in two black briefcases, almost identical. I will—"*

"You better not try any bullshit with me! You better be alone when you come, and—"

"Quit interrupting! I'm tired, I'm pissed, and I don't care if you never get any of this! So if you want me to deliver, listen to what I'm telling you. You will go to the underground parking at Park North shopping center at Blanco Road and Loop 410 at exactly eight o'clock. I will be parked as close to the center of the garage as possible. I will be in an old yellow Mazda pickup with 'Medina Plumbing' signs on the doors. You will park near me, facing my car, and flash your lights. I will flash my lights in return. At that time, you will order the girl's release. You got it so far?"

"Yeah, yeah, I got it. We gonna flash lights, right? Your yellow Mazda pickup, Medina Plumbing truck. I don' give two shits about that. When you gonna' give me my stuff?"

"When I receive the phone call from Brenda Ramos telling me that she has Cecilia with her and no one else is around. She will be headed toward the Terrell Hills Police Department on North New Braunfels, or in their parking lot when she calls. So you need to have someone ready to hand over Cecilia at eight o'clock, at her house. You understand? Because if she doesn't call—"

"What the hell you trying to do? What's this—"

"Shut up and listen, dammit!" Carlton shouted. Everyone in the small office jumped, most of them having never heard the even-tempered Anglo raise his voice and certainly not utter any profanity. *"I'm going to be certain that she and Brenda are safe, then I will step out of my pickup and walk away. You will go over to it immediately and get the briefcases from the front seat. Take them back to your car, count the money, try the product, whatever, but you have one minute to look inside them. Then I'm walking back to my pickup and leaving. If you've found anything unsatisfactory, you can call me, and we will sit in our cars and discuss it by phone. I will not look toward your car, and you don't look at me. Got it?"*

"Yeah, sure. Now where is this place?"

"Park North Shopping Center at Blanco Road and Loop 410. Inside the loop."

The conversation stalled while he evidently conferred with someone. Then: *"What the hell you tryin' to pull, you gringo asshole? I'm not driving to a place you pick! What if the briefcases aren't right? You think I got to do this shit like you want it? Huh?"*

"Only if you want the cash and product. Otherwise, you don't get anything,

because I'll be with Tino Perez, shooting up your side of town, like I told you. Then I'll be home in bed, because I'm tired from my trip, and I'm tired of you being a crybaby. Now describe the car you'll be driving."

Carlton could hear grumbling and a few loud comments in Spanish, which continued for almost a minute before Ramos spoke again. *"I will be driving a black Mercedes. And I might just come take my money away from you, Gringo, and then I'll take the girl where I want to."*

"Yeah, why don't you do that, Mr. Ramos. Please come over to my vehicle and try to take the money. It will be the best thing that could possibly happen, because I'll blow your sorry ass to hell, along with anybody you bring with you! I've done it before, remember? Eight o'clock. Got it?"

Carlton snapped his phone shut and shook his head, exhaling loudly. "What a jackass!"

The office instantly erupted in murmuring and a few scattered laughs and muted cheers. Tino was smiling broadly. "Don't be so polite, Carlton, just tell him what you think!" The boss' remark served as a seal of approval for more cheers from the crew members.

Raul Vega stepped quietly up to Carlton. "That was good. I think he knows who is the *jefe* now. But you must be very careful. He will have time to think about your demands, and it will make him angry, maybe even too angry to care about the money."

"I know, Mr. Vega. I have to depend on his being desperate for the money and flake, but I appreciate your concern. Reynaldo told me the same thing, and I know both of you are more experienced than I. I don't think we have a choice, though."

Reynaldo had moved beside Raul while he spoke and was nodding in agreement at Carlton's viewpoint. "You looked up flight numbers and times. He tried to trip you up, but it didn't work."

"He may have had somebody at the airport, but I think he was just bluffing; I don't think anybody from his bunch could identify me in a crowd. Like you said, he was just trying to trip me up, rattle my cage a bit."

"I was afraid you'd say something about his using the girl for getting his money, or hiding behind a young girl. That might have pushed him over the edge. I think you played it just right."

"I thought it best to play toward his greed without insulting him. Oh, and reminding him that a gunfight wouldn't end well for him. Last time was a lot of luck, but he doesn't know that. I want him to keep on thinking I'm a gunslinger, but it was embarrassing to do it with everyone listening."

The men laughed at that and stepped aside for Paula. "Thank you, Carlton," she said, giving him a hug.

"Don't thank me yet, we've got a long way to go. I need for you to call Brenda and tell her what's going to happen. She needs to be waiting in the driveway of her house, car door open, and ready to drive straight to the police station. It's on New Braunfels, not too far from her house. She has to do all this quickly and do it right. Timing is crucial on this; I've got to be sure they're safe when I let him get the money. Then I've got to split. I can't hang around if it goes sideways, okay? In fact, I can't hang around, no matter what!"

"Sure, I understand. I'll call her now in case she has any questions I can't answer."

Carlton texted Heather that he had spoken with Ramos and asked that she call him when she could talk. Then he wandered over to where Tino was holding court with several of his top lieutenants and stood by quietly, listening to instructions being issued in English and Spanish. He struggled to pick up the words in Spanish, catching their meaning by mood and context, but he couldn't stay up with the boss' rapid-fire delivery.

After another five minutes of intense discussion, everyone nodded and the groups broke into smaller knots. Tino turned to him "Sorry, I didn't mean to ignore you. Trying to get everyone up to speed on that garage. I sent Arturo over there to get a visual on all the exit points of that shopping center; he'll report to David, Enrique, and the rest of their crew members, so they will be familiar with it. He'll jump in with them, so they don't have to drive through and check it out; they can just pick a spot with a clear view of the center and park. I told them to go inside and shop or something, don't sit there and draw attention from the security guards. They can come back two at a time at eight o'clock. It's almost five now. I want two cars in place by seven, and I'll get there with my group just after seven."

"So I've got three carloads for backup, instead of two?"

"Yes, but Reynaldo, Raul, and I will be outside the garage. We both know Ramos will have backup in place, and some of his crew could recognize me or Raul. No sense poking a stick in his eye, maybe this will just go smoothly. Now, tell me about your meeting with the pretty DEA agent."

"She and two of her co-workers will be in the garage. She knows my vehicle and I'm going to give her Ramos' car description when she calls me.

Her biggest problem will be establishing Probable Cause to search Ramos' car for the bust. I may have something in mind for that."

Tino nodded. "Let me know what that something is, okay?"

"As soon as I finish the call with Brenda and I know Cecilia is safe, I'll call you and leave my phone on speaker function. You'll be able to hear, and I'll give a running narrative while I'm there. But don't come in or send anybody in unless I request it, okay?"

Tino nodded reluctantly. "Okay. Hopefully, the freelancers from DEA will be busting him, and you won't need any assistance."

"Yep. Only if it goes south the minute we meet would I call y'all in. We know he'll have backup, so maybe you can spot them. If so, let me know, and I'll try to give that info to Heather."

Paula waved to him and walked toward them. "Okay, I told Brenda to be ready just before eight o'clock, that everything had to go right, starting with her call to you. She knows to call you the second Cecilia is safely in her car and they're on their way to the police station."

"Perfect! Thanks for handling that. I don't think Brenda gets a big kick out of talking with me. But she's got to be on her toes tonight. This operation has a lot of moving parts."

Tino thought about it for a minute. "That's an understatement. This plan is really complicated, Carlton. Everything and everybody has to fall into line, do what they're supposed to. And that's a stretch for Brujido Ramos, on his nicest day."

"I know. But what's Plan B?" Carlton asked. Tino shook his head, knowing the answer. At that instant, Carlton's phone rang, and he flipped it open and answered without checking the caller ID; only one person had that number.

"Carlton?"

"Hi. We're on for eight o'clock, in the Park North underground garage. Ramos will be driving a black four-door Mercedes, the big sedan. I'll be in that little yellow pickup with 'Medina Plumbing' on the doors. What will you be driving?"

"Oh, my new car. A dark blue Honda Accord, with paper license plates. You need the number?"

"Nope. Lucky you! Nice car, I can find the one with dealer tags."

"Thank you. How are you going to hand off the stuff?"

"He and I will flash headlights, his signal to release the little girl. I'll wait for a phone call from Cecilia's mother telling me she's got her in her car and is

heading to the Terrell Hills Police Department. I get out of my pickup and walk away. He walks to it, gets two black briefcases out of the front seat. I'll be watching from a distance; when he's back in his car, I'll give him one minute—exactly sixty seconds—to peek at the goods. Then I'll walk to my vehicle and drive away."

"What if he drives away immediately, before you're back to your pickup?"

Carlton had already considered that possibility; it posed a problem for the renegade DEA agents. *"I guess y'all should tag him while I disappear into the theater or one of the stores. Can you invent P.C. under that scenario?"*

"We've seen pictures of Brujido Ramos, so if we see him picking up briefcases from someone else's car, maybe it will stick. If not, we'll all be looking for a job."

"I certainly hope it doesn't come to that..." his voice trailed off as he thought about alternatives to the free-lance DEA agents ridding Tino of Ramos. Everything else involved bloodshed, no question about that. *"Look, just make the decision that works best for y'all, don't endanger your careers—or your lives. Getting the girl back safely is the main goal here. Ramos can wait for another day, and I'll owe you, big time."*

"I really want to take him down." Her voice confirmed the statement.

"Good, I want him taken down. But however you do it, be careful. This guy's always been dangerous, and now he's nuts, trying to copy the big cartel guys."

"I will." She paused a few seconds before adding, *"You do the same."*

Carlton shut his phone and realized that Paula was standing a few feet away, watching him. Her face said she'd been there throughout the phone call, maybe hearing his end of the conversation. He'd already failed to follow Heather's advice about being careful.

CHAPTER 26

After checking everything for the third or fourth time, Carlton headed toward the north side of the city just before seven o'clock, catching the interstate rather than taking U.S. 281. Even then, evening traffic was still heavy on IH-10, stop-and-go in places. He pulled into the covered parking garage, briefcases by his side and Glock in his trusty cargo pants pocket, at seven fifty-five. As he drove slowly toward the middle section, he scanned the vehicles. He spotted the new Accord gleaming under the lights and saw that the dark tint reflected the garage's lighting in a way that made it impossible to see inside. Good and bad, he thought, but at five minutes until showtime, the drug enforcement agents were surely sitting in the car…not shopping for panties.

He drove slowly to the end and looped around, heading back to the garage's center. He found a center section with only three other cars and pulled in. The stairs and elevators were at the garage's perimeter, so most shoppers parked near them instead of the center, saving a few steps. For once, he was pleased to see lazy American shoppers doing something in his favor. His position left him facing the Honda, but fully fifteen or twenty spaces away, over a hundred feet. He killed the engine and looked around for Ramos' backup, as well as his own, but didn't spot anything right away. With few exceptions, most cars looked pretty much the same in the subdued light, so he scanned the parking places car by car, row by row. He finally saw what appeared to be the Estrada brothers' Impala at the far end of the row where Heather had parked. He didn't know what the second car was, he hadn't asked Tino, because it wasn't critical that he know. He figured Ramos' keepers were in place earlier, just as his own were, but it was almost eight o'clock now and no sign of a black Benz, and not enough time to leave and call Ramos from a store as he had planned. Not important, he thought; he's either going to show or not, and there's no need to look like a random shopper just yet.

By three minutes after eight, he was harboring thoughts of a no-show for the unpredictable drug trafficker and contemplated what to do next. If he got a call demanding that he deliver elsewhere, he could call Heather, then Tino, and give them the update. Right now, his main concern was getting Cecilia released, and he craned around to make sure he hadn't overlooked his contact's vehicle. He needn't have bothered; a black Mercedes four-door swept down the row and passed behind him, going too fast for a parking garage. Tires squealing, it made the U-turn at the end and started back up a couple of rows over, and he felt certain it was Ramos, just running a little late. When it pulled into a space two rows over and facing him he watched intently for headlights, but it was a full minute before that occurred. He returned the flash immediately and checked to see that his phone was on, anxious to get Brenda's call.

The next six minutes dragged by, the longest Carlton could recall. What could take so long about calling and saying phrases of five or six words? He tried to envision the scene at Brenda's house; the phone conversations, the coordination between the parties, the distance up the driveway...when almost seven minutes had passed, his phone rang in his hand, making him jump and nearly drop it.

"This is Carl Weiss."

"This is Brenda Ramos." Her voice sounded thin and strained, as though she hadn't inhaled enough air to make the announcement. *"Myra just let Cecilia out of the car, and she's getting into my car."*

"Okay, get her in and buckled up. Leave your house immediately. Put your phone on speaker and lay it on the console. I'll be listening to what's going on."

"Okay. She's in the car now." Her voice was close to panic, and Carlton could hear her breathing raggedly, as though she suffered from asthma.

He waited, then heard a clatter as she put the phone down, then nothing. He was afraid she'd cut off the call, but seconds later, he heard another voice, and the sound of a door closing. He strained to hear the engine start, but couldn't make it out. A minute passed, then two. He couldn't stand it. *"Brenda, are you on the street, heading to the police station?"*

"Yes—no, not quite. I'm..."

He couldn't make out what she said next, if anything. He was having trouble himself, trying to control his rage at this woman who couldn't back a car out of a driveway in order to save her own life and her daughter's. He waited another sixty seconds to speak. *"BRENDA, ARE YOU ON THE WAY TO THE POLICE STATION?"*

"Yes, yes I'm driving on the street now."

"It should only take you five or six minutes to get there. Is everything okay? No cars around you?"

"No, no, everything is okay." A few seconds later, he heard the phone clattering again as she picked it up and took it off the speaker function. *"Okay, we're going that way, just getting on New Braunfels. We should be there in a couple of minutes."*

"Tell me when you are pulling in, then get both of you out of the car and go inside. Tell the desk officer you want to stay there a few minutes because someone was following you."

"But no one is following me! Why would I do that?"

Carlton's hand gripped the phone so tightly he thought it would shatter. *"Brenda, just SAY that! They won't know; just make up a car description. Tell them you don't feel safe, and you just want to stay there a few minutes. Play along with whatever they say."*

"OH! I understand now."

Thank God, Carlton thought…finally!

Her voice interrupted his silent thanks to a Higher Power. *"Okay, we're pulling into the parking lot now. Oh, wait! This isn't it, this is City Hall."*

"You turned into the wrong driveway, Brenda. It's one more down the street. Turn around in the parking lot and go to the next driveway. <u>That's</u> the Police Station, the building with 'Police Department' on the front."

Another maddening three minutes went by before she spoke again. *"Okay, we are in the Police Department lot."*

Okay, do it like I said. Just make up a car description, say it was following you, two men in the front seats. The police will check into it and keep you there for a while, but they'll let you leave after a while. Meanwhile, just go along with them."

He snapped his phone shut, exasperated from the ordeal, but unable to take a break and cool off. Timing was critical, and it was running late for all parties, giving rise to the chance that someone would grow impatient and do the wrong thing. He got out of the pickup and turned away from Ramos' car, walking toward a stairwell. Behind him, he heard a car door open, faint footsteps on concrete. He kept walking, not varying his pace. When he reached the stairwell, he reached for the handrail and turned left onto the first step. By the third step, he was able to turn his head casually and glance back the way he'd come. A tall, thin man was approaching the little pickup. Carlton slowed his upward trip slightly, waiting for Ramos—was it actually him?—to reach into the Mazda and get the briefcases.

The man briskly opened the passenger door and reached inside. One briefcase came out. He set it on the concrete and reached back in, emerging with the second, larger, briefcase. When it cleared the seat of the pickup, it fell open and several plastic bags spilled onto the concrete. The bags looked exactly like what they were: one-kilogram bags of powdered cocaine. The man muttered a curse and scrambled around the garage floor, scooping up the bags, tossing them back into the briefcase which lay open under the Mazda door. Within seconds, the bags were back in place, and he slammed the lid and tugged on it, testing the latch. It popped open again, so he had to set them atop each other and carry them like firewood. He hefted the awkward load as though judging their weight and headed for the black Mercedes.

Carlton watched the retreating figure from the fifth, sixth, and seventh step, still going up slowly. One or two more steps, and a partition wall would block his view across the garage floor to the black car, a situation that worked both ways: neither could he be seen from the black car. He quickly took three more steps and stopped to listen. Another car drove by, and he was unable to hear the sound of Ramos closing his door. He froze in place, cursing the other patrons of the garage as yet another car drove by, music blaring. After counting slowly to sixty, he turned and headed back down the stairs. When he again reached the seventh step, he paused. Three teenagers brushed by him, talking loudly, laughing at Carlton's timid pace on the stairwell, giving him an opportunity to look toward the black car. It hadn't started, and no interior light shone, but he could see a silhouette in the driver's seat and movement on the passenger side. Clearly, Ramos wasn't alone in the car.

He quickly covered the reasons why Ramos wasn't driving away; none of them were indicative of a peaceful end, and only one made sense: since the briefcase contents *were* correct, he and others in the car were waiting for him to return to his pickup, and not to wave a friendly good-bye. Instead, it was going to be Ramos' time for retaliation over his four dead kidnappers.

Within seconds, Carlton ruled out returning to his pickup as a foolish move; it was time to improvise his escape and leave the drug kingpin to the DEA. He turned and went back up the stairs, intending to disappear into the theater or one of the stores above the garage. As he reached the store level landing, he remembered that he had promised to call Tino and put the phone on speaker as soon as Cecilia was safe. The agonizing ordeal with Brenda and the handoff had caused him to forget the call. He quickly dialed Tino and told him what was happening, then put the device on speaker function and put it back in his pocket. Then he pulled the "Heather phone" and texted her.

Ramos has cases. R u moving on him?

He moved to the side of the stairwell landing and waited a few seconds. Several people passed him in both directions, a surprise, since most people used the elevator. After a long minute with no return text from Heather, he merged with a group of four shoppers and headed back down the stairs keeping them between him and the open part of the garage to his right, the direction of Ramos' car.

Counting down as the group descended the eighteen steps, it happened when he reached number nine. Two quick gunshots rang out, very loud in the cavernous parking garage. Another shot sounded, then nothing for a long three-count. The four people he was using as a cloak stopped, then panicked and tried to turn around on the stairs, succeeding only in stumbling over each other and Carlton.

Then all hell broke loose.

Four more shots sounded and a couple of cars started up. The sound of transmissions being slammed into gear was drowned out by the shrieking of tires spinning on concrete and engines winding up, the vehicles gaining speed as tires took hold. Carlton struggled to get beyond the four bumbling shoppers, three women and a man, and get down the stairwell. By the time he reached the bottom step, he could see the speeding cars slewing around concrete pylons and heading for the exits. Farther away in the garage, multiple gunshots rang out and someone shouted what sounded like a warning, the words unclear.

Incredibly, the black Mercedes wasn't one of the fleeing cars; it was pulling sedately from its parking place, but then lurched to a stop. Wary of this development, Carlton scanned the area and saw movement behind the adjacent car, a Ford Focus with no one inside. Three figures, all armed, rose from a crouch and were boring down on Ramos' car, handguns extended in one hand, badges in the other. The move looked practiced, the three agents moving quickly and efficiently as though they did this every day. *Maybe they do*, Carlton thought, watching their approach.

The sound of a crash stole his attention. At the west end of the garage, a white car had collided with a van, also white. Both cars had shot for the exit at the same time, and it had proven too narrow for the maneuver. From his position at the bottom of the stairwell, he couldn't make out the car, but the color was right for the Estrada brothers' Chevy. His eyes moved to the van, a Ford. Then it hit him: another of Ramos' delivery vans had been used to transport his backup crew to this assignment. One team had made the other, and a gunfight had broken out. Ramos, seeing what was happening, wisely sat still, pleased with the distraction. But he hadn't known about the three DEA agents who were, at this moment, pointing handguns at both front doors of the car, yelling for windows to be lowered and hands to be shown.

Seeing the situation moving in a favorable direction, Carlton reversed his steps once again and started up the stairs. He would lose himself in the big mall and worry about getting home later—*much* later, if necessary. He was halfway back up the stairs when he heard more shots, this time followed by a loud shout and running steps on concrete. The next sound locked him in place: a single gunshot accompanied by a feminine shriek. He turned and hurtled down the stairs, dreading what he would see when he reached the bottom.

Both front doors were open on the Mercedes. A man was squatted in front of the passenger door, looking around the pillar toward the trunk deck. The tall man was striding across the garage, already twenty feet or so away from his car, with a handgun pointed in front of him. Carlton followed the gun barrel's direction and saw his intended target.

Heather Colson had been hit and was frantically crab-walking away from Ramos, but losing the race. Only by keeping the scattered cars between herself and her stalker was she staying alive, but that wouldn't last more than a few seconds. Ramos was quickly gaining on her, pressing his advantage, while his partner was apparently keeping Heather's companions hunkered behind the Benz.

Carlton dashed down the final three steps, reaching into his right pants pocket as he rounded the handrail's end. "RAMOS!" he yelled as loud as he could manage given the recent marathon of stair-climbing.

The tall man turned. Wild-eyed, he had a problem focusing on the source of his shouted name, but he swung the pistol around and pulled off two shots anyway. One whanged off the steel railing where Carlton's hand had gripped it seconds before; the second went wide, and Carlton returned fire with several shots that missed.

Ramos ducked behind the front fender of a Dodge and fired twice more, one of them hitting Carlton's right knee. For a second, he felt only the impact, like being struck with a stick; then it burned like boiling water was being poured on it. He gasped in pain and fell to his left, landing him in plain view of the other gunman, about forty feet from him. His right hand was clenching the Glock, but the bullet had hit a nerve which ran all the way up his thigh and he could do nothing but press with his hand and the gun to ease the shock and pain.

The second man abandoned his view of the trunk and turned toward this new threat. The distance was a long one for a handgun, and despite what Hollywood depicted on-screen, he missed Carlton by several feet with the first two shots. The second pair was closer, zinging off the concrete inches from where he lay on his left side, still stunned by the wound. Through a haze of pain, Carlton saw the man eject a spent magazine and grab for another. The delay might save his life, but he knew he had to do something and do it quickly. He fought to ignore the fire in his leg and pulled his hand away from the wound. The pain increased tenfold, and he felt himself growing faint. If he went into shock, he would die, and so would Heather. He had only seconds to overcome his injury if they were to survive.

The impossibility of ignoring the pain reminded him of an old Army buddy, a lifer on his third tour in Vietnam, who told him he could "channel pain" to his advantage, use its strength to maintain his own. The "old geezer" (probably forty at the time!) had been hit three times in combat and came back to the jungle each time, determined to carry on. The excruciating pain prevented Carlton from conjuring up an image of his face, but his words of—wisdom? fanaticism?—were clear through the agony gripping his body and mind.

He didn't have any idea how to "channel" the pain, but he tried to imagine the pain going away if he could only use his pistol. He raised it and swept his hand to his right, toward Brujido Ramos, squeezing the trigger three times as the barrel's tip intersected with the blurry image now approaching him. Satisfying punches to his palm were accompanied by a strangled cry from his target. Ramos went down, his gun skittering across the floor, but Carlton had already left that target and was swinging the Glock to his left when another round, then another, blasted concrete dust and slivers into his face, ruining his view of the second man.

The last two shots had come very close, and Carlton knew the next one would be corrected—and fatal. The shooter would pull up according to the concrete impacts and hit his target square in the face; twice, if he kept up the one-two shot cadence used by professional shooters.

The realization that the man was more than just a reckless gunslinger passed through Carlton's brain in a nanosecond. He was already swinging the Glock upward and firing continuously through a twenty-degree arc, pulling the trigger as rapidly as he could while the barrel rose. Two more rounds were headed his way, and one grazed his ear. He felt the burning sensation and the wetness of blood before he heard the report, which nearly deafened him. He tried to roll to his right to avoid the next two shots, but he didn't need to bother. The man crumpled in front of the car door, banging his head on the fender well trim as he went down.

The ensuing silence was eerie, almost breathtaking. After the past twenty seconds or so, the transformation was as shocking as the initial sound of gunfire. Carlton couldn't hear anything, but he tried to stand, and was surprised when he managed to get up and hobble beyond the front of the Mercedes to where Ramos had fallen. He carefully swung the Glock toward the interior, thinking he may have been wounded and sought refuge inside, but the drug trafficker/kidnapper was not there. He hated to leave without knowing for sure, but he limped toward the last place he'd seen Heather crawling away from her tormentor.

He stepped carefully around the front of the Ford Focus and saw her leaned against its rear wheel, eyes closed, gun in hand. When he stepped into view, she raised her gun and aimed it at him. "Whoa! Heather! It's me!" he hissed loudly, still unable to hear anything, even his own voice.

She lowered the gun weakly, and Carlton rushed to her side as best he could. At the end of the garage, a new gun battle broke out, and he figured Tino and company had dived onto the wreck scene and were extracting Sergio and Estéban, or so he hoped. There certainly was nothing he could do to help at this moment. He gently pulled Heather's arm from her side and spotted the bright red entry wound to the side of her rib cage. It was impossible to tell the angle of the bullet; it may have angled away in a shallow path, or it may have angled steeply into her chest cavity. Neither was good, but a shot to the chest cavity was bad news.

"Where the hell is your bullet-proof vest?" he said to her, his smile looking more like a freak grimace. The pain in his knee—no longer being "channeled" into useful action—had returned with a vengeance, and he hurt like hell.

"You know I couldn't try on panties while wearing one of those," she replied weakly, but smiling with enough strength to push aside the chest cavity theory.

"I'd call for help, but there will be more than enough here in another minute or so. I've got to get going. Are you okay for a few minutes?"

The question sounded absurd to him; blood was seeping from the front of her blouse, and the exit wound had to be worse. Carlton was reminded of the scene in *Butch Cassidy and the Sundance Kid* where both lay badly wounded, asking each other if they were alright. He was delighted when she replied: "You call that cover? I was getting my ass shot off over here!" He figured she had somehow seen the ancient movie and had caught on to his wry comment. Being able to paraphrase an old movie line gave him hope that she would survive.

Meanwhile, he knew he wouldn't if he didn't get away soon. In the distance, sirens were converging on the scene, and he had to remind himself that all the shooting had taken place in less than a minute; therefore, police response was pretty fast. The main concern now was the mall security force, already on site. Where were they?

He rose shakily, looking at Heather's face as he stood. When he saw her eyes open wide, he thought for a second she was going into shock, but couldn't recall from his military training if that would be the right diagnosis. Then he heard the sound of a shoe scraping on concrete behind him, and he knew he should have continued searching for Ramos before coming to check on her.

With no time left on the clock, he did the only thing he could do. Pivoting and pushing off on his left leg, he dove backward and away from Heather, raising the Glock as he fell and pulling it up through an arc that would carry the barrel face-high on a man less than twenty feet away. Pulling the trigger as he went backward, the gun rocked in his hand once, twice… then nothing. The third and fourth squeeze to the trigger did nothing because the slide was open due to the empty clip, and he wondered where the gunfire to his right was coming from.

When he hit the concrete, the air went out of him, but he wasn't hurt badly. He'd managed to get his arms back and the impact occurred to the back of his upper arms, then his shoulder blades as the weight overcame the scant cushion of his triceps and elbows. He'd kept his head up and avoided smacking the back of his skull, so he turned toward Heather in time to see her own Glock still rocking in her hand as she pumped rounds in Ramos' direction for several more shots. Then silence.

She had emptied her weapon; the slide was open. His eyes moved from the pistol to her face and hers to his, and for about five seconds, neither spoke. Heather broke the silence, her voice sounding strained and hoarse. "You'd better get out of here. Can you make it to your pickup?"

"Yeah, I think so. I'll ask again: you okay for a few more minutes?"

"Guess I've got to be. Don't contact me at all; I'll contact you when I can."

He nodded and struggled to his feet. The pain in his leg was bad; instead of the sharp, debilitating kind, an overwhelming ache now thundered through the entire right side of his body. He figured there had to be some extreme nerve damage to inflict such torture. He stumbled to his vehicle, but pulled up short when he saw movement behind the Mercedes. He tensed and swung the Glock in that direction, then panicked when he remembered the empty clip. Leaning against the Mazda, he reached into the left pocket and found the spare magazine. Within a few seconds, he had ejected the empty and slammed the full mag home, then thumbed the slide release. The sound of the slide picking up the first round of the fresh clip was the best thing he'd heard in a while.

He supported his weight on the bed of the pickup and moved slowly toward the black car. The gunman's body lay slumped into the wheel well, his head propped against the tire. The sight struck Carlton as odd; it looked as though he were a pit crew member at a race track, trying to get the tire changed, and he nearly laughed. The scuffling noise behind the car came again, and Carlton locked the sights on the rear bumper, awaiting the first glimpse of whoever was hiding there.

Rex Baxter stuck his head around the bumper and peered in Carlton's direction. Their eyes met, and Carlton lowered his pistol. "Rex! You okay?"

"Not so good, I'm afraid. Where is Heather?"

"Over there." He gestured roughly in the direction he'd come from. "She's hit, but she'll make it."

"Aren't you supposed to be leaving? You want to get arrested for handing over cash and drugs to a major trafficker?"

"I was just leaving, Agent Baxter. You going to be okay for a few minutes?"

"Don't have much choice, do I? Hurts like hell, but yeah, sounds like the cavalry is on the way."

Carlton nodded and clawed his way back toward his pickup. Getting in was pure agony, but he made it and started the engine, pulling it into gear and driving away slowly toward the exit to the east. In his mirror, he saw a swarm of police cars just outside the west exit, looking tiny at this distance.

Cops were out, guns drawn and pointed at the two cars that had collided just inside the exit opening.

As he headed toward the exit, forcing himself to drive slowly, he saw three bodies sprawled on the concrete at the doorway of the north elevator. They appeared to be security guards, and from the layout of the grizzly scene, they had all used the same elevator to respond to the first series of gunshots. Unfortunately, when the door opened, shooters from one backup crew or another had gunned them down, accounting for the absence of mall cops.

The scarcity of law enforcement was quickly changing, though. In addition to the crowd of officers behind him, he now saw a patrol car speeding into the garage from the east, through the opening he was trying to reach. Emergency lights were flashing, and the sirens assaulting everyone's ears in the confined space wailed to a stop as the officers realized the futility behind bursting their own eardrums along with every other occupant of the garage. Carlton eased to the right, hoping he could slide by in his non-descript little pickup. After all, it wasn't the type of vehicle normally associated with a big drug-bust shootout between DEA agents and narcotics traffickers.

However, his hopes crashed as the black-and-white slewed to a stop sideways in front of him. Two officers jumped out, weapons drawn. "Freeze! Get out of the car! GET OUT OF THE CAR!" The officers were splitting up, wisely diverging and approaching both sides of his pickup, weapons pointed directly at his face. "LET ME SEE YOUR HANDS!" the one on the driver's side screamed.

Carlton's mind raced for a way out, but nothing presented itself. He slowly took his hands from the wheel and eased them toward the window until both hands extended beyond the opening. He sat stock still, waiting for the next order, but the cops seemed content to continue training their weapons on him, as though waiting to see what came next.

What came next was a miracle—for Carlton, that is.

Another police car came barreling in from a side entrance to the south, the drive perpendicular to the main strip through the center of the garage where Carlton's pickup sat, trapped by the now-unoccupied black-and-white. Whether going too fast, unable to see beyond the slight downward slope of the entrance drive, the change in lighting between outside and underground—or some combination—the speeding cruiser smashed into the front of the stopped one, caromed off and headed straight for the officer on the passenger side of his pickup. The cop jumped sideways, and the car slid right in front of Carlton's, nearly taking out the other officer.

Carlton watched in disbelief, then shook his head to clear his thinking. Before the rampaging cruiser came to a complete stop, Carlton was steering around the smashed one and headed toward the open exit ramp. He gave a turn signal, turned right toward the Target store, and left onto Blanco Road while the cops screamed at each other and tried to sort out the mess. Looking in his mirror, all he could see were flashing lights, still pouring onto the scene from the Blanco Road entrances behind him. As he drove sedately down Blanco and approached Jackson Keller, two more cruisers, maybe Castle Hills P.D., shot by him toward the shopping center, now a mile behind him.

Carlton drove toward the south side of the city, trying desperately to ignore the pain in his leg. He tried different positions, to the extent he could manage in the little pickup, but no matter how he shifted around, the burning sensation screamed up the entire right side of his body. Twice he nearly passed out, but each time, he shook his head violently, trying to regain the "pain channeling" trick of his old Army companion. It didn't seem to channel the pain, but it subdued it for a few seconds, during which he concentrated on the road until the extreme pain subsided into the regular agony. Finally, he found a position that enabled him to press the accelerator at a constant pressure while the pain dulled to a throbbing ache, still like nothing he'd ever experienced.

After what seemed like an inordinate amount of time, he found himself pulling into the flea market and wondering how he had made it. Trying to recall the half-hour journey, he realized that large parts of the trip were a complete blank, and he hoped he hadn't caused any accidents. He negotiated the turns around the line of stalls and pulled in front of Tino's office, then killed the engine, thankful to be done with the trip, thankful to be alive, and wondering how to contact Dr. Morales.

And for the first time in several hours Carlton Westerfield was, in spite of his pain, able to relax.

CHAPTER 27

Three o'clock in the morning is not usually a time associated with social gatherings, except for after-hours bars and all-night diners filled with drunks. A medical clinic seldom qualifies, although emergency rooms tend toward a lot of after-hours customers, sans socializing.

In Carlton's case, his current venue was becoming a familiar one. Dr. Morales was standing over him again, this time peering at his shattered knee, while his assistant—a name tag identified her as *Cassie Canales, R.N.*—took his blood pressure for the third time and checked the sticky electrodes on his chest and ribs for yet another EKG. The social gathering consisted of Tino, Paula, Reynaldo, and Raul Vega, all of whom the doctor kept shooing back in two languages.

Carlton's worried bed-side entourage would not be dissuaded. Paula kept gripping his right hand, skewing his blood pressure reading, hence the poor nurse's third try. Tino bombarded the doctor with questions, while Reynaldo and Raul carried on their own conversation in Spanish about the events of the evening. But despite the concerns of the bedside visitors, one emotion outweighed all, even the obvious seriousness of Carlton's condition: *relief*.

Cecilia Ramos was safe, the threat removed permanently, and everyone who had a part in the handoff and extortion exchange was alive for the moment and likely to survive. It was a far cry from the last confrontation on the interstate which had left four young men dead and devastated Faustino Perez's extensive community.

For the third time, Tino eased around Dr. Morales and smiled down at the patient. "I can't believe you would want to leave a life like this; '*check out*,' as you call it. Where else could you get all this attention, Shifty?"

"Well, you have a point there, Lefty," Carlton answered through gritted teeth. He winced again as Dr. Morales completed winding the bandage around his knee, then looked up to Tino's grinning face. "I'm just glad everyone made it back. I couldn't think clearly enough to get to Dr. Morales' clinic, and my phone battery died from leaving it on the whole time. Besides, I didn't know his number. I could barely find your place."

"You wouldn't put the number in your phone, anyway. What about your other phone, the one you call the DEA lady with?"

"I took the battery out of it. Heath—Agent Colson is in the hospital I'm sure, and anyone snooping around her phone might try to contact the last call completed on it and figure out my location."

"A good precaution," Reynaldo observed. "For somebody who is so careful, tonight must have been an absolute nightmare," he added, stepping forward to stand by Tino, further irritating Dr. Morales.

"Yep, pretty much. You and Raul were right, of course. It was way too complicated, and it showed. I was concentrating on making sure Cecilia was safe, but the handoff to Brenda was a fiasco. She was nervous and had trouble getting to the police department. After that, everything else went screwy. The timing was off, I didn't play it like I wanted to, everybody got antsy, shots were fired… it's a miracle no one on our side was killed, because there was a lot of gunfire exchanged. The only one I don't know about for sure is another member of the DEA team, a younger guy named Cho."

"I'll see what I can find out," Tino offered. "Cho, you said? I have some people in the ambulance business who can check."

"And all the others got away?" Carlton asked. "And y'all were able to get the weapons out of the Estradas' car?"

"Yes, fortunately," Reynaldo replied, taking over the narrative again. "Arturo was driving the other backup crew. When it all went down without getting called to help you, he started pulling out of the garage, but didn't make it. He drove right by Ramos' other backup car, and his crew recognized somebody in our car and opened fire. They exchanged several shots, and Arturo thinks we got two of theirs, with nobody hit in our car. Meanwhile, some security guards stepped off an elevator, and Ramos' guys shot them down. David knew that would bring down major heat, so he got our guys out of there immediately.

"I drove Tino and Raul up to the crash scene, and they grabbed Sergio's and Estéban's guns, put them in our car. Then we started helping out like concerned citizens, applying shirts to bleeding cuts, that kind of thing. When the police arrived, they took everyone in the van, plus Estéban and Sergio. They've got nothing on them, though, because the van rammed the Chevy. Also, the van was full of guns, so they'll be taking a long vacation inside."

"What about the little Mazda pickup?" Carlton asked. "It's going to show up on the video at the garage. Oh, and I think I put the Glock under the seat, but I was pretty dizzy when I got out at Tino's office. I don't even remember how I got here."

Reynaldo started to answer, but Tino cut in and waved away his concerns. "Don't worry, the pickup is well-hidden and the gun has been wiped down and tossed. Besides, that pickup is still titled in Manny Medina's name, and he's been dead for several years. If it ever shows up, there's no way to trace it to any of us."

"Good. I was worried about those two things, but couldn't do much about them."

"That's what a backup team is for, remember?"

"Yep, I remember. And tell everyone I appreciate it."

"The DEA ought to be pretty pleased with you right now," Tino said. "You give them Ramos' vans and a load of blow, then you hand them another van and his crew, plus Ramos two days later. Oh, do you think your agent friends will come out of the internal investigation okay?"

"I hope so. Remember, I told you I was going to try and help with their Probable Cause problem?"

"Yes, but you kept it a secret, as usual."

"It wasn't a secret, Tino, I just didn't know how I was going to do it. Anyway, I'm telling you now. I jacked with the latches on the larger briefcase, the one with the snow. When Ramos picked it up, several bags fell out in the garage floor. He had to scramble around and pick up his shipment. I'm sure they can testify to seeing that happen. They're DEA agents; they know what bags of cocaine look like. Besides, there's no one left to dispute the story."

Raul Vega had been listening intently, being his usual quiet self, but now he spoke. "The three agents will maybe get a...how you call it? *Promoción?* It will look like they overcame a big trafficker and his bodyguard without any help at all. And while they were shopping, or going to a movie, not even on duty!"

"And your complicated plan worked after all," Reynaldo concluded, a big smile on his face.

Judging by his demeanor for the last half hour, he seemed the most pleased of all by the night's outcome. Carlton was certain he knew why, but he wondered if this was the time or place to bring it up. He felt woozy from the pain medication and it was working, maybe too well. Like having a third beer, inhibitions over uncomfortable subjects were fading away in his mind. Might as well find out now, he thought. *Or should I?*

Reynaldo took the decision away from him. "We have a lot to talk about, Carlton, you and I. You carried on without knowing all the facts, and I appreciate that. But you deserve to know everything," he added, glancing over at Paula and Tino.

An uncomfortable silence settled over the room, broken by Dr. Morales issuing his verdict and the sentence. "Your ear will need some cosmetic surgery, but the wound is not serious. However, you suffered a bad wound to that knee, Mr. Westerfield. The bullet passed through, doing quite a lot of damage. It will require surgery, maybe more than one, to make it heal properly. Afterward, there will be physical therapy to make it work well, but don't expect miracles. You may have a limp for the rest of your life.

"I will set up the surgery with an associate of mine, Dr. Abdelazeem. He is an excellent surgeon who works out of the Methodist Ambulatory Surgery Hospital, over on Huebner. We can trust him to remain silent over the cause of your injury. I will give Faustino all the information tomorrow.

"The biggest concern now is infection. I have given you all the antibiotics I can for the present, and here is a prescription for more, plus pain medication. Be sure and take all of the antibiotics, just as scheduled. You must stay here tonight, and I will come by tomorrow to check on you. This back room is seldom used and is quite private." He smiled and added. "I would order you to get plenty of rest, but I can see that is going to be difficult. Get some sleep as soon as you can get all these people out of here. Oh, and if you need anything, or wake up with pain, just press the call button on your left. Either I or Ms. Canales will be here in a few minutes. We both live very near here."

"Dr. Morales, I can't begin to thank you. This is the second time you've come to save me after hours. I'm sorry to be such a problem patient."

"It is not a problem, none at all. You are very…*helpful* to all of us, and that is how you suffer these injuries." He paused for a moment as though unsure whether to continue. "You see, I am a doctor, but my old friend Faustino discusses many things with me besides medical matters." He seemed embarrassed by admitting his knowledge of the seamy side of life and changed subjects. "But you can best repay me by taking care of yourself."

"I will do that, I promise. Thank you again, Doctor. And you too, Ms. Canales."

Raul Vega spoke up, informing them that he would leave too, if Dr. Morales would give him a lift. The doctor readily agreed, and the three left the room together, chatting like the old friends they probably were. It reminded Carlton of how little he knew of this close-knit community he had been thrust into by past misdeeds, but had come to accept, even like. For a loner like me, that was something, he thought.

The back door closed a few minutes later, and the remaining group heard two cars start up and leave. Apparently, the doctor's "old friend Faustino," was entrusted to lock up the clinic, but that didn't appear to be happening soon. Instead, chairs were gathered from the waiting area, and Carlton's guests seated themselves around his bed. Tino was right, he thought. *Where else could I get all this attention?*

Paula pulled her chair closer and retook his hand. "Carlton, thank you for getting Cecilia back. I appreciate it more than I can say, because I felt so… helpless. I couldn't do anything to help my own daughter, and once again, you've come to my rescue."

"I know she's important to you, despite the circumstances of your agreement with Brenda and Julian. I'm glad I was able to get her away from her uncle, because nothing good was going to come from that, even if he hadn't been power-crazy. Have you spoken with Brenda?"

"Yes, she texted me that she and Julian were taking off for a few weeks. They're going to Mexico City to be with Cecilia for the first part of her school year."

"Has she heard about her brother-in-law?"

Paula shook her head. "She didn't say, but I don't think so. She was so happy to have Cecilia back, and she and Julian have already planned to get away from here, at least for a while. I didn't think I should be the one to tell her that Brujido won't be coming around anymore. And I don't know how Cecilia will take it when she learns her uncle was killed in a gun battle."

Carlton nodded. "Nope, not our place to give them the bad news. He was Julian's brother, after all, so it may impact the family pretty hard. I'm sure they saw it on the news, or Myra has let them know."

Tino cleared his throat. "They know about the firefight and Ramos. I've already heard from several sources, the news is all over the place. I'll see if anyone can find out how Cecilia is reacting."

Another voice spoke up, this time Reynaldo Gomez. "It's been a tragedy, this entire mess caused by one maniac who wanted to be more than what he was. And a further tragedy that his death will affect innocent people, but it was the only way it was going to turn out."

"True enough," Carlton agreed. "Brujido Ramos was not going to die peacefully in his sleep. Whatever changed in him ended any chance of that. Those cartel guys must have really made an impression on him."

"That doesn't speak very well for this industry, does it?" Reynaldo asked, the question directed at everyone. "That violence is a code to live by, something to be copied, and a man's death is necessary for everything to turn out right."

"The illegal narcotics trade isn't the only industry with that reputation," Carlton retorted. "That's why I'm hoping to find another way to utilize my time and skills. I was serious about getting away from this lifestyle, even if it sounds absurd for someone my age to be looking for a new beginning."

Reynaldo shook his head. "Not at all. But this time, your ability to do the job saved a little girl's life. And we won't ever forget that, Carlton. You have no idea how much it means."

Carlton was quiet for a moment, wondering if the time was right. He decided it was. "I think I do, Reynaldo," he said simply, looking at him, not Paula. "It took a while to figure out, but I did. Cecilia is your daughter."

The stunned silence in the room seemed like thick, heavy air before a thunderstorm. It was so quiet they could all hear the big industrial-sized wall clock ticking seconds away. For almost a minute, no one spoke.

"How did you know?" It was Paula asking.

"Several things, but the clincher happened when I asked Brenda to show me a picture, and she did. Any girl would love to look like her mother if she looked like you, Paula. But Cecilia is doubly gifted; she got the best genetics of both of you. I saw instantly that she looked like Reynaldo, and I started putting the pieces together. All the mystery started to dissolve, including why you were kidnapped first, why Tino agreed to pay the ransom so readily, and why Reynaldo Gomez was first on the list to help Tino with his problem competitor. Oh, and an offhand question from Tino asking me what I was going to do about you—right after we met with Reynaldo."

"I apologize that we had to keep you in the dark," Reynaldo said. "We—I thought it was the best way to handle it."

Carlton wasn't through. "Handle it by not trusting me? Look, an emergency occurs, a possible tragedy in the making. I'm brought on board to help resolve it, which is fine, that's what I get paid to do. But no one gave me any background information, so I had to go it alone, which didn't help matters any, by the way.

"I suspected earlier, but when I saw the picture of Cecilia, I knew you were her father. That led to the truth about why you were brought in to help with handling Ramos. When I asked Tino who might be able to help us put together a big deal to take Ramos down, he said 'Reynaldo Gomez' almost immediately; too quickly, in fact. I didn't catch that right away, but after a few other things occurred, I realized you weren't chosen randomly. But no one was forthcoming with that information, I had to figure it out on my own." He turned to Paula and continued. "Then, there was your wardrobe change while you were being held. You explained it later, and it began to make sense why Ramos interviewed you.

"Another major clue was your reaction when I mentioned Reynaldo being in Hondo to meet with us. I could tell by your reaction that he was someone... well, someone important to you." His voice trailed off, further explanation unnecessary.

Paula ducked her head. "Now I'm embarrassed! Did I really act like a teenager?"

Carlton managed a feeble laugh. "I'm sorry. I didn't mean to embarrass anyone," he said, turning his head to include Reynaldo with his statement. "But some things confused me, and still do. For one, a major player would have access to some serious muscle and hired guns. But you continued to let Tino call all the shots, and he relied on me, an over-the-hill mechanic who can't speak much Spanish. Why wouldn't you use your contacts and get some of your help to take Ramos off the board?"

Reynaldo was shaking his head before Carlton finished. "Two reasons. The first is very selfish and was intended only to protect me. I am married, for over twenty years, and my wife is not a forgiving type of woman. I'm not very proud of that reasoning, but it is a fact that I could not let this come to light.

"Second, and more importantly, I needed it to be handled very carefully, without anyone perceiving Ramos to be important enough to draw my attention. In particular, I couldn't let his cartel associates learn that Reynaldo Gomez is leaning on Brujido Ramos over kidnapping a girl, or they would wonder why I was doing it, who this girl was, and why she meant anything to me. It was essential that it be handled as a local problem, no input from me or my people.

"You see, I had dealings with Brujido Ramos in the past, and his cartel friends, too. They know me, know a lot about my business, but they don't know I have a young daughter. But it was possible that it would leak out as time went by, especially if my involvement regarding Tino's dispute with Ramos were discovered. It was bad enough if Ramos bragged to his heroes about grabbing Faustino Perez's sister. That's the reason for the decision to pay the ransom quickly, without much resistance from Tino."

Tino cut in at that point. "You were suspicious about that, Carlton. You saw that as weakness on my part, or that it was too 'choreographed' to be real. Well, you were almost right. The kidnapping was real, but I hoped you could deliver the money, get Paula back, and Reynaldo and I would have some time to plan how best to deal with Ramos. The ransom exchange didn't quite work out that way, and I was afraid it would make Ramos up the ante, and he did. Started killing my crew members and then kidnapped Cecilia."

Carlton nodded, now understanding Tino's mixed reaction to killing the four kidnappers. He turned back to Reynaldo. "Did Ramos know that you're Cecilia's father?"

"I don't think so, but I couldn't take the chance that he would figure it out. After all, you did. Maybe Ramos looks at her one day and thinks *'she looks just like someone I've seen...of course! Reynaldo Gomez! I wonder...'* and he starts putting it together, along with how he could benefit from it. Maybe a long shot, but I couldn't risk putting her in a great deal of danger."

"Yeah, that sounds like how his mind worked, trying to be like the big boys. And getting more power-hungry every day."

"If the Mexico City cartel guys had ever gotten that information, put it together that Ramos' so-called niece is actually my daughter, this local kidnapping business would be nothing compared to what they would do. They controlled Ramos, and he would get a big pat on the back for delivering Reynaldo Gomez' daughter to them, just the kind of thing Ramos would love."

"I take it their violence doesn't stop just because an eleven-year-old girl gets caught up in the mess, then?"

Gomez shook his head emphatically. "Besides the obvious drug-related violence with guns, knives, and torture that gets all the media attention, there is a much darker side to the cartel players."

Not sure he even wanted to hear about it, Carlton raised his eyebrows in inquiry. But Reynaldo didn't answer right away; suddenly he seemed to be overcome with emotion, making it difficult for him to speak. Instead, it was Tino who spoke the distasteful words. "Sex slave trading. They grab young girls—and boys—and sell them, mainly in Mexico and Colombia, but also in Europe and even Asia."

Carlton shook his head in disbelief. "You hear about that stuff on TV documentaries, but I got the impression it was mostly in Europe, Africa, and Asia. And I thought the victims were sixteen, seventeen years old. I had no idea anyone is sick enough to trade for eleven-year-old children. It doesn't really surprise me, though; I just wasn't aware of it."

"Besides bringing in millions of dollars, it's become a status thing among some of the cartel bosses and a terrorism tool to use against competitors. That's why Reynaldo had to lie low, keep anyone from discovering Cecilia was his daughter."

"And that's why Paula was kidnapped first, Ramos wanted her to give him the father's identity. He may have suspected already, then?"

"Maybe so," Tino answered. "We'll never know."

"So what about Brenda and Julian going to Mexico City, putting her in a school there? Isn't that a huge risk?"

Tino didn't reply; he and Carlton looked to Reynaldo for the answer. "There is always the possibility, of course, that someone could find out. But Brenda and Julian are her documented parents, and being away from me, Paula, and San Antonio actually lessens the risk. Also, I have two people, a couple, in Mexico City who work for me on a contract basis. I have already made arrangements for them to monitor everything, see if anything arises that would indicate Cecilia's in danger. And the school she attends is well aware of these types of occurrences. They have a professional bodyguard service that operates on the school property, then accompanies the students to their place of residence."

"Sounds like you're doing everything you can, but I'm sure you'll worry just the same."

"Of course. But no more than any parents worrying about their children. Even with middle-class families with no connection to cartels, there's a risk for drug usage, car accidents, cyber-bullying, monstrous teachers, coaches, priests, cult leaders...the list goes on. Cecilia's circumstances shield her from those ordinary things, anyway."

"It's no wonder that I never had children," Carlton said darkly. "I can only take care of myself, and I sometimes fail at that." He pointed to his heavily bandaged knee to illustrate his point, getting an awkward bedside hug from Paula.

The hug elicited an eye-roll from Tino. "See? I knew you liked all this attention. Hell, you should work for free, Shifty!"

Reynaldo spoke up. "No, Carlton, my friend Faustino is wrong about that. You will be compensated handsomely for tonight's—*last* night's—work. It will help make up for being kept in the dark about everything. Tino and I have already discussed it."

Carlton shook his head and laughed. "That's most considerate, but better wait and see what the medical bills are going to be. I'll bet Dr. Abdullah doesn't work cheap. Need to pay him first."

Tino laughed at his mangling of the orthopedic surgeon's name. "Don't worry about that. We'll take care of Dr. Abdelazeem too. And the therapy. *And* the cosmetic surgery on your ugly ear. Maybe they can fix your face while they're at it."

Carlton grinned weakly at the jab, his strength ebbing as the night headed toward dawn and the painkillers soothed his body. "Okay, Lefty. I'm too sleepy to come up with a clever response right now. Maybe tomorrow, when I'm up and running around."

"Okay, my friend. We'll leave and let you rest. See you tomorrow—today, that is."

"Oh, before you leave, and before I doze off, I do have two other questions. First, why did you steer me toward being the bagman when they grabbed Paula?"

Tino shifted his weight to the other foot, a sign Carlton had come to recognize as a stalling tactic. But tonight was the time for full disclosure, and he didn't stall long. "All the things I told you that night. You're older, less likely to fly off the handle, I trusted you with a lot of money, you don't speak enough Spanish to be insulted by some hot-headed punks…but there was another big reason: all the stuff we just talked about. If they had been able to grab you and squeeze you for information, you had absolutely none to give, no matter what they did to you. The rest of my crew is Latino, and Ramos knows—knew—that they have been with me a long time and were more likely to have inside information on me, Paula, and Reynaldo."

"Okay, I get it. He could have tortured me until the end of time and still get nothing, because I didn't even know she had a daughter. But if you sent one of your crew, he might have tortured him to death, thinking he *had* to know something."

Unable or unwilling to explain further the harsh reality for putting

Carlton at even greater risk than he'd thought, Tino simply nodded in confirmation.

"The second one may be harder. You said Ramos insisted that I be the bagman on the second go-round. I thought it was to get a chance to kill me for his four guys I took out, but it didn't really seem that way, now that I think about what happened in the garage. Why did he insist that I deliver the stuff?"

Tino glanced at the floor, uncharacteristically nervous for a few seconds. Then he took responsibility and looked him in the eye. "He didn't, Carlton."

Carlton thought about that for a minute, then sighed and nodded his acceptance of being set up—twice.

Confessions over, Reynaldo and Tino stepped nearer the bed to shake his hand and headed toward the door, where Tino turned to give a lazy wave. "Get some sleep, Shifty."

Reynaldo grinned at the nickname and said, "Thank you again, Carlton," then followed Tino into the hallway.

Paula lingered until they were out of earshot. "I can't ever repay you for doing that, Carlton. Tino and Reynaldo will take care of you financially, but I don't—"

"You don't have to repay me, Paula," he interrupted. "I wanted to do it, to get Cecilia away from danger. I know how important she is to you. And Reynaldo, too; even Tino. Y'all are the closest thing I've had to friends since I was in the Army, and that was a long time ago. That's what friends do, right? Even ones who fudge on reality to get the job done—the end justifies the means, as the saying goes."

"Are we *just* friends? You and I?"

He hesitated a half-second too long. "Paula, I honestly don't know. I was hoping you could tell me. As much time as we've spent together, the experiences we've had, what we went through together...it's been quite a ride. You'd think I would know all there is to know about Paula Hendricks by now, and either accept it or run away from you. But every time I think I have you figured out, another facet of your life pops up, reminding me that I don't know you at all. As I said earlier, I have to figure out everything on my own."

"And, as usual, you did. You had to know the truth, didn't you? Well, sometimes the truth hurts too much to talk about, and you just shove it under the bed, out of sight. With Cecilia, I guess that's what I've done, but it couldn't be hidden when she got into trouble.

"We all have a past, Carlton. Sometimes we don't want to re-visit the past. And I never thought it was important to tell you about her, or about Reynaldo, mostly because of the circumstances. I was on the ropes emotionally and didn't make good decisions."

"I understand that, and it's none of my business what you did or why you did it. That was years ago. And who says it was a bad decision? It just happened, that's all. But for me, it's a reminder that I don't know you very well and a wake-up call telling me I never will."

"Don't you see? I *want* it to be your business to know about me. And don't say you never will. If it will help, I'll tell you my entire life story, tell you the truth about everything."

"Wasn't that why we spent all that time in Rio?" he asked, smiling to take the edge off the question, the same one he'd asked himself a dozen times.

"Yes, that was the idea," she admitted, looking down to avoid his gaze. "But I've always regretted the agreement to stay out of Cecilia's life entirely, so I left that part out of my story. Anyway, Rio was still fun, wasn't it?" she said, raising her eyes to his and smiling at the memory.

"Indeed it was. And I understand your leaving that part out. I guess I've got a lot to learn about you."

"I hope you stick around to do it."

"Better make it fast, while I'm laid up and can't run away," he replied, smiling again to lessen the impact of his admonition.

For a brief instant, he saw The Hurt Look flicker in her eyes, but she recovered quickly and replaced it with The Smile, knowing the effect it would have on Carlton, drugged to the gills or not. She leaned over the bed, squeezed his hand and kissed him before walking out the door, turning off the light as she went.

Carlton closed his eyes and fell asleep instantly. He dreamed again of the beach in Brazil, the palm frond-covered cabana, and him and Paula on the beach. This time, the dream wasn't interrupted by protestations about not being able to run in a sundress, or the cabana changing to a grimy little shack in a near-ghetto. Instead, when he turned to wait on her for the beach run, Paula had been replaced by Cecilia, the exact Cecilia in the picture he had been shown, down to the Manu Ginobili jersey and beautiful smile.

As he stared at the pre-teen girl in disbelief, she produced a gun, the same revolver he had left in a briefcase for Paula to find—but only after filing down the firing pin. And just as Paula had done on that heart-stopping day months before, Cecilia pointed it at him and pulled the trigger.

EPILOGUE

The evening sun was low on the horizon, slightly obscured behind a thin string of purple clouds that appeared to be hovering over the ocean. The day had been very warm, and even this late in the day the air still held the sun's heat. The man sprawled in the lounge chair was enjoying the warm breeze wafting over him; it felt good to be away from the dreary, rainy cold he'd left…when? Yesterday?

Yesterday had been Christmas Eve, and braving the weather and the airport's holiday crowd had been a challenge, especially on his weakened leg. Now, Christmas Day in Acapulco, he relaxed from the trip and the previous weeks of surgery and painful rehabilitation sessions. The limp was still there, and it might never be gone completely, the doctors had informed him. It was a sobering message, and accepting the fact that he would never be quite as nimble as before was difficult. However, it did clarify a decision he'd wanted to make for over a year, and that almost offset his diminished physical ability. *Almost.*

He glanced over his shoulder at the woman approaching him from the hotel's pool area and watched admiringly as she negotiated through a maze of look-alike chairs, her hips swaying at each turn as she trod through the pristine sand. He saw that her hair was down, the breeze billowing it around her face. When she raised her hand to brush the blowing strands from her eyes, she caught him looking and smiled. Not The Smile, but a pleasant smile nevertheless; provocative, just short of suggestive. It caused an odd feeling inside him, a near-physical quiver in his stomach, but not unpleasant at all.

He rose to pull a chair close to his. Before she sat down, she scooted it even closer, then spread a towel over it before sitting and brushing the sand from her feet. Without touching the sand again, she swung one foot, then the other, onto the chair. "I hate sand beneath my legs," she said. "I'd just as soon lie down in the sand if I'm going to have sand in my chair." She leaned back and pulled her sunglasses down against the sun, which had emerged from the scant clouds as it slid toward the Pacific.

"Well, no point in being uncomfortable. We could have the beach staff come out here and vacuum any stray grains off your chair."

"You're such a perfectionist, you probably would, but I'm fine with my method. Oh, I'm sorry! Did I brush sand onto you?"

Carlton laughed. "No, but you're not sorry. You're just disappointed that you didn't. Anyway, I'm glad you could make it. Was the airport still crowded this morning?"

"Not too bad. Guess everyone got where they were going for Christmas, because today wasn't any worse than a regular weekday. How are you feeling? Your knee give you any trouble on the trip?"

"A little last night, after a full day of travel yesterday. Remember, I had a layover in Mexico City, so it took all day to get here. I've only been here on the beach a couple of hours."

"Well, the next few days will be a good opportunity to rest it. Maybe you can recover completely while we're here."

"I'm supposed to continue the rehab exercises every day. I didn't today, it was just too tender after stumbling through airports. But tomorrow, I'm back on it, because I don't want to end up walking with a limp for the rest of my days."

"No, limp won't do." The remark was made with a mischievous grin.

"I heard there was a special rehab program to eliminate limp. I'm going to look into it."

Agent Heather Colson of the Drug Enforcement Agency laughed. "*That* rehab program might entail different exercises."

"How about you? Looks like they did a great job on the entry wound; I couldn't see it at all when you raised your hand to brush your hair back."

"Yeah, that one came out pretty good. I'm not sure about the back, though. Even with a mirror, I can't see it very well. Wanna see?" Without waiting for his answer, she rolled to her left, exposing the right side of her rib cage.

Carlton raised his sunglasses and looked. The scar was white, a thin crease about two inches long, extending along the anterior side of her torso about level with the third or fourth rib. As he had speculated (and hoped) minutes after the shooting, the bullet had entered at a shallow angle and exited well above anything critical to life function. He touched it gently and smiled at her.

She rolled back, the question in her eyes as she spoke "Well? Am I maimed beyond redemption? No centerfold pictures for this girl?"

"Heather, I've had bigger scars on my eyeballs! That will probably disappear in the next two months."

"You liar! But thank you. It's going to be a while before I do much that requires any core strength. It's pretty painful when I raise my right arm too quickly. And sit-ups are out of the question right now. Anyway, I've got six months' leave with full pay. If I can't pass the physical then, I'll have to accept straight office duty or leave the Agency."

"No more shoot-outs with drug lords for you? What about Rex and Cho?"

"Rex is recovering nicely, but he'll be off for six months, too. Cho was hit in the upper arm, but he's already back at work. He told me his arm aches like crazy, but he's an analyst, so he can avoid taking the physical for a while."

A waiter from the pool area wandered over to the two late beach-goers and offered lemonade, which both readily accepted. He left, and the pair fell into a comfortable silence. Almost ten minutes had passed when Heather spoke again. "I suppose we should both consider ourselves lucky, getting shot up three months ago, and now being able to recover here in luxury."

"It could have gone a lot worse," Carlton agreed. "I really worried about you when I saw the wound, because I knew how badly I was hurting after being shot with the same weapon. And mine was just an appendage, not through my side."

"I worried about you too, until I saw you dive backward and shoot out the clip. Pretty good move for a guy your age—no, I take that back. *Any* age. You're a helluva shooter, Carlton. Ramos was down for good before I got off my first round."

"Thanks, but it was luck. Anyway, I was able to find out your condition and keep tabs on every change, but I nearly went crazy waiting to hear from you."

"Really? How did you find out where I was taken? And how did you get updates?"

Carlton shrugged. "Paula's brother has a lot of hospital contacts through his ambulance service. No reason not to take advantage of that."

At the mention of the woman's name, Heather got quiet for another minute or so. When she spoke, it was blunt and to the point, just as Carlton had observed her to be on other occasions, different subjects. "Where does your relationship with Paula stand?"

Having given that exact question a lot of thought during the past three months, he didn't hesitate. "It's as unsure as the day I met her, and that bothers me. I won't try to blow any smoke about this, Heather; she has qualities that attract men like flies. Obviously, she's pretty. That's the part everyone sees, men and women alike. But she's also smart, intriguing, mysterious...and the most evasive human being I've ever known."

"Evasive is a good thing where women are concerned?"

"Not for me, it's not. Every time I thought I knew her pretty well, something else comes up and shows a different side to her that I couldn't have imagined. We've had a couple of getaway sessions that were supposed to be tell-all meetings of the hearts, no matter what. But she has a problem producing the entire truth during those sessions."

"Well, sometimes the truth hurts. Maybe too much to tell it, no matter how much full disclosure was intended or promised."

Carlton was struck by the statement. Paula had uttered almost identical words the night of the shooting as she sat by his hospital bed. Now, another woman, vastly different from Paula, but equally attractive, smart, and desirable was saying the same thing. Plus, Heather's words raised a defense for the other woman; surprising, since he knew she did not care for Paula and the hold she exercised over men—in short, jealousy. His disturbing thoughts were interrupted again by another bold question.

"What are you going to do about her?"

"I'd love to tell you I'm dropping her like a hot rock, but you'd point out that I said that before. So I'll put it this way: I need to be disconnected from anyone I can't fully trust, no matter how good everything else is."

"Maybe you've finally learned your lesson."

"You mean I'll start thinking with the big head instead of the little one?"

"You're not *that* smart yet. No man is," she added with a laugh that took the abrasiveness off the observation, if not the veracity.

Unable to think of a valid reply, Carlton smiled at her and changed the subject. "And how about you? What's the latest on the internal investigation? You told me last week they were still hanging around asking questions."

"The I.T. people were able to enhance the security films a lot. They showed the briefcases being pulled from the pickup and something falling out, but no amount of enhancement could bring up the individual packets of coke. Of course, the same briefcases were later seized in Ramos' Mercedes, broken latches, cash, cocaine, and all."

"So the video evidence links the briefcase with the dope to the one pulled from the pickup with the jacked-up latches. There shouldn't be a problem then, right?"

She shook her head. "I don't think so, but not absolutely sure yet. The big question for me, Rex, and Cho is how did we know it was bags of cocaine that fell from the briefcase, and not bags of flour or something? It all has to do with Probable Cause, which the Agency wants to nail down even though there won't be any backlash from a defense lawyer."

"I guess not, with no one left alive to defend."

"Right. No live perps, so no defense lawyers, and no case for the district attorney to prosecute. This has to do with Internal Affairs' investigation. Even though it was found to be the real thing later, how did we know it was when we rousted him?"

"Oh, for cryin' out loud! That's absurd! Don't the investigators think y'all know what a drug deal looks like? And bags of white powder in a briefcase usually don't turn out to be flour?"

"Of course. That's just the system we work under. Internal Affairs has already ruled the shootings of Ramos and his sidekick as justified, so we won't be facing murder or manslaughter charges. Not even a reprimand or additional training required. They didn't even say anything about different bullets being found in Ramos, ones not fired by my weapon. Still, the investigators are curious as to how we happened to be there, how did we *know* it was a drug transaction, blah, blah. Follow-up work, they call it."

"How much longer will they keep at it?"

"Not much longer. Ikos went to bat for us. Our personnel files indicate clean action records, no past problems with being trigger-happy. Plus, having Cho with us helped. He's an analyst—a good one—and clearly not the cowboy type. Also, the others were caught and charged with shooting the security guards. Another bunch of Ramos' guys wrecked a van just like the one we nabbed at the checkpoint, and the occupants were carrying guns. Clearly, it was a drug deal gone bad for them, good for the DEA. So I think we'll slide."

"Good. I was concerned about that. I thought the busted latches would spill the stuff and give y'all a clear look at an obvious drug buy. And a free pass on the P. C. problem."

"That was good work on your part, by the way, perfect setup. The first one was okay, the one with the money. He plopped it down on the concrete and thought nothing about jerking the other one out. We saw it clearly, but the camera didn't pick it up, even though it was closer than we were. Just bad luck or crappy cameras. I'm not worried, so let's forget it while we're here, okay?"

"Done. Are you hungry?" he asked.

"Oh, no, not at all! I had a bag of peanuts and a coke on the plane."

He turned to look at her. Seeing the grin on her face, he leaned back. "Good. I'm starving too. We'll go into town and eat at the most outrageously expensive place the cab driver can find."

"Sounds great." She paused a few seconds, then turned to look at him. "What happens later, Carlton?"

He turned to meet her eyes, suspecting a trick question had just been thrown at him, but this time her face conveyed nothing. "Um, that's entirely up to you," he answered cautiously, wishing he had uttered something more clever, if not as chivalrous.

She leaned over toward his chair, moving her arm to support herself on her left elbow. The move caused her to wince slightly.

"No sit-ups, remember?" He reached to steady her arm and smiled.

"It's okay, I just have to move slowly," she said, returning the smile and placing her hand on his.

Propped up now, she brushed some strands of hair away from her eyes, the same gesture he'd noted earlier, and it caused the same reaction; a little flip-flop sensation in his stomach. This time he likened the feeling to the one he always experienced while peeking over the edge of a high cliff, but much more pleasant. He shifted forward slightly and looked into her eyes, hoping she would close the remaining distance between them—and knowing how awkward it would be for both of them to retreat from this position if she didn't.

After three long seconds she tilted her head and parted her lips slightly, then leaned toward him while matching his gaze. He felt her warm breath and sensed the need to increase his own respiration rate, though he dared not breathe and break the spell. When her blue eyes came too close to focus on his, she closed them. Carlton followed suit and felt his pulse quicken as their lips touched, parted for an instant of uncertainty, then joined again in that unmatched exhilaration that is every first kiss.

And just as Carlton had thought, it was worth the wait.

Printed in the United States
By Bookmasters